Kingdoms of Elfin

Also published by Handheld Press

Kingdoms of Elfin

by Sylvia Townsend Warner

Foreword by Greer Gilman
with an Introduction by Ingrid Hotz-Davies

Handheld Classic 5

First published in the UK in 1977 by Chatto and Windus.
This edition published in 2018 by Handheld Press Ltd.
72 Warminster Road, Bath BA2 6RU, United Kingdom
www.handheldpress.co.uk

ISBN 978-1-9999448-1-0

3 4 5 6 7 8 9

Series design by Nadja Guggi and typeset in Adobe Caslon Pro
and Open Sans.

Printed and bound in Great Britain by Short Run Press, Exeter.

Acknowledgements to the first edition
Except for 'The Climate of Exile' and 'The Late Sir Glamie',
these stories first appeared in *The New Yorker.*

Acknowledgements to the 2018 edition
The text of the stories reproduced here was taken from the 1978
Penguin paperback edition. The punctuation has been restyled,
and some proof-reading errors have been silently corrected.

Contents

Greer Gilman is the author of *Moonwise* and *Cloud & Ashes*, and two critically-acclaimed novellas about the poet Ben Jonson, as well as poetry and criticism. Her fantasy fiction, rooted in British myth and ritual, has won the Tiptree, World Fantasy, and Shirley Jackson Awards. Her essay 'The Languages of the Fantastic' appears in *The Cambridge Companion to Fantasy Literature*.

Foreword

Sylvia Townsend Warner. She saw herself as 'Frau Noah leaning out of a window with a coffee cup in her hand admiring last night's flood'; I can see her as a clear-eyed river goddess, or the numen of a spring. Wise-hearted and well-tempered, she began as a scholar of early music, and her prose is formally Baroque. 'Her heart was with the hunted always', said her friend William Maxwell. Yet at eighty, when her mortal love had died and she was 'tired of the human heart', she wrote on the unkindliness of faerie. *Kingdoms of Elfin* is a last book as ruthlessly exquisite as a silver frost.

Her first is autumnal: *Lolly Willowes* (1926) is on the fierce joy of unleaving. Laura escapes the prison of a useful spinsterhood — life as an occasional table — to become a witch. She does no great magic — turns milk, stirs a wasps' nest — only dares to set herself outside her family and society: to walk the woods at her will, to travel wind-borne, as a leaf does, and to sleep where she settles, in contentment at the roots of things.

Over and again in her writing, Warner would return to fugue. Her stories of Elfin, brilliantly witty and disquieting, are of captivity and flight. The cages here are courts, Gormenghastly in their etiquette; but glittering. There are no marvels here, save wings, which Elfins share explicitly with lower creatures, and so disdain. Yet rarely, they take flight. Here's Tiphaine, the Queen of Elfhame, with her Thomas:

> Once, they came to a wide rattling burn, with a green lawn on the further bank. He leaped across, and held out his hand for her to catch hold of. It was too wide a leap for her and she took to her wings. It was the first time in her life she had flown, and the sensation delighted her. She rose in another flight, curling and twirling for the pleasure and mastery of it, as a fiddler plays a cadenza. She soared

higher and higher, looking down on the figure at the burnside, small as a beetle and the centre of the wide world. He beckoned her down; she dropped like a hawk and they rolled together on the grass. (23)

They are not us; unless they are — at times — the wrong side of our weaving: turn the figured silk and we can trace the bloodknots of cruelty, the blind entanglements of custom. At times, they meet us with aplomb, as at the funeral of the gipsies' Queen Jocasta: 'As a mark of respect, visibility would be worn' (191). They are not fey: not mysterious, uncanny, twilit, but 'straightforward as the scent of a rose, as a wasp sting'. A 'race of pragmatists' (257), they see their glamour through our borrowed eyes, and break us in their curiosity: 'when the brown bed-hangings from the Librarian's bed-chamber are hung on the line and the dust beaten out of them, they are discovered to be cloth-of-gold and fall to pieces' (199).

Winged creatures are ephemeral. The Elfins, not immeasurably long-lived, are spooked and fascinated by these shadow-selves, their analogs, which Warner studies with the silver-eyed dispassion of a Leeuwenhoek. 'No one fancies the thought of being cut in two like a wasp in the marmalade' (242). Moths, bats, dragonflies are portents; five black swans will come for Tiphaine, who will be the sixth. Gulls are nemesis itself: 'Blood ran through their breast feathers, their beaks were red with blood ... The ship moved silent as a ghost under her crown of beating wings and incessant furious voices' (159).

Unspoken, save in one prophetic vision, and most dreadful, is their fear that mortals — butcher's meat — will triumph over old creation. Transient, uncouth, our human kind will conquer by outbreeding, by infernal engines. One such terrible device — a bicycle — comes crashing into Castle Ash Grove with its riding harbinger: a drunken midwife who uncorks apocalypse, a disinfectant with a fearful smell. But let Dame Bronwen speak:

'When I fainted it was because of what was shown me. I saw trees blighted and grass burned brown and birds falling out of the sky. I saw the end of our world, Morgan — the end of Elfin. I saw the last fairy dying like a scorched insect.' She was mad. But she spoke with such intensity it was impossible not to believe her. (119)

Take heart. It is not yet; it is not fate. Futurity means nothing to the Elfins. No clock will strike for them; the horses of their endless dusk run free. Those mortal lovers who can meet them in their endless *now here nowhere* are fortunate: they know a brief but absolute felicity. Here is Thomas of Ercildoune at play with Tiphaine:

Love was in the present: in the sharp taste of the rowanberries he plucked for her, in the winter night when a gale got up and whipped them to the shelter of a farm where he kindled a fire and roasted turnips on a stick, in their midnight mushroomings, in the long summer evenings when they lay on their backs too happy to move or speak, in their March-hare curvettings and cuffings. For love-gifts, he gave her acorns, birds' eggs, a rosegall because it is called the fairies' pincushion, a yellow snail shell. (23)

The mortal of the pair is wiser than the Queen of Elfhame; he refuses 'to make trial of the elixir of longevity', to stall and harness time, and put it, jaded, to the plough:

He flung away from her, saying she must love him now, instantly, before the lightning broke cover. A time would come when he would grow old and she would abhor him: he could tell her that without any exercise of prophecy. The storm broke and pinned them in the present. When it moved away they built a cairn of hailstones and watched it melt in the sunshine. (24)

Tiphaine is rare among Elfins. Most are fleetingly diverted by such pretty things as Thomas, gathered with the dew on them, at their perfection, and discarded as they wither. Otherwise, Elfins much prefer still life. They see no moral in a memento mori, only the beauty of the thing itself.

In Bourrasque, the mortal servant Gobelet gives Lady Fidès an exquisite token: a 'crow's skeleton, wrapped in a burdock leaf. Every minutest bone was in place'. It is carrion, transfigured by its burial. 'In her rapture she forgot to thank him, and he went away thinking she was displeased' (140).

Gobelet had been a gift himself, at seven, when 'Fidès' husband … took a fancy to his roly-poly charm, and had him stolen, giving him to Fidès for St Valentine's Day. Gobelet grew up short-legged and stocky, and inexpugnably mortal' (140). Fidès finds him repulsive: he is not her kind. Yet she repudiates her own chance-got child because Grive is 'just another Elfin: he had never been, he could never become, a bird' (141). Only 'Gobelet pitied the pretty child who had suddenly fallen out of favour' (142).

He becomes Grive's inseparable playfellow. As much for himself as for the Elfin child, he gives him toys of transience:

> He cut him a shepherd's pipe of elder wood, taught him to plait rushes; carved him a ship which floated in a footbath. By whisking up the water he raised a stormy ocean; the ship tossed and heeled, and its crew of silver buttons fell off and were drowned. On moonlight nights he threw fox and rabbit shadows on the wall … When these diversions were outgrown, they invented an interminable saga in which they were the two last people left alive in a world of giants, dragons, and talking animals. (142)

That romance is unfinished: like all mortals past their prime, Gobelet is too unsightly to be kept. Fidès discards him. Grive thinks of his old servant dead in a ditch 'with the crows standing round like mourners' (143), but the peasant will live by his wits.

Grown old, he halts his way across a devastated world, through pestilence and famine, to renounce his fairy overlords: 'to look … and turn away' (149). But all the court has fled — all but Grive, who is dying, and so must be saved. Gobelet has walked into their old fantasy of endless rescue and escape. He picks it up again, as easily as a cat's cradle, turn and overturn between their hands:

With Grive 'high overhead, circling while Gobelet walked, sailing on the wind' (150), they go east and south, disputing where the swallows winter. Grive 'was master. It was part of Gobelet's happiness that this was so' (151). He lives at first by 'pell-mell pleasures: a doubled rainbow, roasting a hedgehog' (150). But imperceptibly, their picaresque and pastoral is changing genre, quickening toward the sea, the ship, the fury of the gulls: Grive's terrible apotheosis.

Other mortals fall in love, not with a fey, but with faerie: the idea of it, the unobtainable. Take James Sutherland, MA of Aberdeen— 'spoken of behind his back as Fairy Sutherland' (245). As a scholar, he has channeled his desire into research. 'Ever since he could remember, they had fascinated him. His nurse sang him to sleep with ballads about them; he pursued the hinds and shepherds on his father's estate for stories … read everything he could find on their subject' (244). He 'was not above examining Pictish remains, in case they afforded a small footprint' (245). Taken sleeping on Foxcastle, he wakes in captivity, a specimen for study:

> The fingernail explored the convolutions of his ear, left it, traced the lines on his cheek. Other hands were fingering him, lightly, delicately, adroitly. His shoes were taken off, his toes parted, the soles of his feet prodded. His coat was unbuttoned, his shirt opened. Fingers tweaked the hair in his armpits. The watch was pulled from his fob pocket. He knew they would not stop at that. (247)

It is as if he had been buried in an ant-hill, like Gobelet's crow: an object for their cabinet of curiosities, much handled.

It was impersonal, the traffic of water flowing over a stone. And one day, when they were finished with him, he felt a pat on his shoulder. It intended him no harm, no good — and it almost destroyed him. It was as if he were falling apart with happiness. For the first time, a fairy hand had rested on him with the wastefulness of a caress. He froze, he burned; he was immortally awake, he was overwhelmingly sleepy; he experienced all the vicissitudes of love simultaneously. (251)

But 'it was impossible to love them: they were too inconsistent to be loved. It was unavoidable not to be drawn to them' (257). If he could only connect. Let to wander at last in their society, he finds himself eluded. For this man of the Enlightenment, 'accustomed to a methodical social order where time is respected and persons occupy the portion of space where you expect to find them', Elfin vagaries exemplify the Rabelaisian principle of *Fay ce que vouldras*: Do what thou wilt.

Some devoted themselves to astronomy. Others practised the French horn. Others educated squirrels. Some, he presumed, made measurements. [He has, appallingly, been measured.] ... Whisking from one pursuit to the next, they never collided. The best comparison he could draw from the outer world was the swarm of mayflies, indivisibly borne aloft, lowering, shifting, veering, like a shaken impermeable gauze veil over the face of a stream. (254)

Elfins are unknowable, a cloud of bright particularities. Or particles, perhaps, with charm and strangeness — Huons? Their otherness is sharp, if only you could pin it down; they are unshadowy as lightning, as elusive.

Abandoning time — his watch, 'sole ally of his rational man' (248), stopped long ago — Sutherland 'lived a tranquil truant, dissociated from himself as though by a slight agreeable fever — such a fever as one might catch by smelling a flower' (255).

The fever cannot last. He is cast off, quite literally, by the knitting Queen: "'And one purl. And break off'" (259). He fell asleep in a wig and small clothes; and emerges, then and there, into an alien future:

> The speaker ... carried a most peculiar hat in a gloved hand. He had spoken to a group of ladies, who were even more oddly dressed than he, wearing white shifts down to the ground. Their waists were under their arms, the shifts fluttered in the wind and showed the shape of their legs. A couple of young men made up the party; they, too, had waists under their arms, and a general resemblance to clothes pegs. But all these were mortals. (260)

Clear-eyed, dispassionate, impartial — ah, but never cold, not unkind — Warner casts him off. She finishes the pattern that she had in mind, 'everything exactly as it is', the folly of both kinds intermingled, purl and plain. Like Elfindom itself, she means him no harm, no good. You could weep for him, standing on that cold hill's side. You could weep — not for the faerie that he found and lost, but for the faerie that eludes us, that is always elsewhere. Take heart: you have this book.

Greer Gilman
Cambridge, Massachusetts

Ingrid Hotz-Davies is Chair of English Literature and Gender Studies at the University of Tübingen. Her most recent research publications have been about gender performativity and modern women's writing.

Introduction

BY INGRID HOTZ-DAVIES

She started with the short story 'Something Entirely Different' in the early 1970s, and from then on wrote in an astonishing rush, producing more and more stories set in the world of fairies. In this way, after the devastating loss of her beloved partner Valentine Ackland, and towards the end of her own life, Sylvia Townsend Warner entered new territory: Elfindom. She was keenly conscious that she was embarking on a new journey, a challenge and an adventure. As she remarked in an interview, 'I suddenly looked round on my career and thought, "Good God, I've been understanding the human heart for all these decades. Bother the human heart, I'm tired of the human heart. I'm tired of the human race. I want to write about something entirely different"'.[1] To William Maxwell, her friend, fellow writer, and long-time editor from *The New Yorker*, she wrote that she was pleased that *The New Yorker* would print 'Something Entirely Different' (renamed 'The One and the Other' in *Kingdoms of Elfin*): 'I admire the story myself, and feel justified by it: justified, I mean, in supposing that *something entirely different* is still possible for me, that I can still pull an unexpected ace out of my sleeve'.[2]

The sixteen stories that were for the most part first published in *The New Yorker* would come together in *Kingdoms of Elfin* (1977), the last of her books that Warner would see published in her lifetime. They are indeed different, though her willingness to be intrigued by the fairy world dates back to the 1920s, anticipating much of what was to concern her in the 1960s and 1970s.[3] Warner was prodigiously productive and versatile, as well as a consistently stubborn writer. Her works include seven novels, roughly 150 short stories, many essays and lecture scripts, a biography, and the moving collection of the letters exchanged over a lifetime between herself and Valentine Ackland, which she prepared for publication after Ackland's death.

Kingdoms of Elfin displays Warner's characteristic command of meticulous narrative technique, but it breaks a fundamental rule for fiction. Warner insisted that these stories were skeletal writing: 'there is practically no flesh on it at all, and no breath of human kindness. But it seems to me that the bones live'.[4] *Kingdoms of Elfin* is an experiment in reduction: the excision of all empathy from the narrative. The stories do feature creatures endowed with a variety of emotions, and empathy may well reside in the heart of the reader, but at no point must there be any 'breath of human kindness' in the narrative itself. 'The One and the Other' gives us a good sense of what lies ahead in its opening paragraph:

> When the baby was lifted from the cradle, he began to whimper. When he felt the rain on his face, he began to bellow. 'Nothing wrong with his lungs,' said the footman to the nurse. They spread their wings, they rose in the air. They carried the baby over a birchwood, over an oakwood, over a firwood. Beyond the firwood was a heath, on the heath was a grassy green hill. 'Elfhame at last,' said the nurse. They folded their wings and alighted. A door opened in the hillside and they carried the baby in. It stared at the candles and the silver tapestries, left off bellowing, and sneezed. (1)

Within a few lines, we come to understand that what appears comfortably familiar and even dated — a baby, a footman, a nurse — is no such thing, as this baby is being taken away by creatures who take to their wings as easily as you or I would walk down a road. The baby, at first a 'he', very subtly mutates into an 'it', and a little further on we learn that the first procedures to be visited on this baby are invasive and denaturing ('denaturing', that is, from a human perspective), designed to 'abate the human smell' (1) and finally render 'it' 'sufficiently inhumanized to be given its new name' (2).

Within a few sentences, ordinary points of orientation come loose, and this disorientation is pursued systematically to the story's end as we follow the changeling human in Elfhame as well as the changeling fairy among the humans. The story is a hall of mirrors in which the different sides reflect each other disconcertingly:[5] we see humans from fairy perspectives and fairies through human eyes, and the environments of both changelings are defamiliarised and challenged by their very presence.

When Adam, the fairy child left in place of the baby, is told that the cat that suckled him as a baby has died, his first response is to dissect it in order to understand mortality, a very reasonable obsession for someone half remembering the near-immortality of his species. The family's servant Ailie is dismayed, but how sentimental should one's attachment be to a suckling cat, even if one weren't an elf? Throughout these stories, casual cruelties abound in both worlds — famines, wars, exploitation among the humans, and the cruelties of aristocratic boredom among the fairies. These arise sometimes from veritable inhumanity (though what can '(in)human' mean in these stories?), and sometimes out of the necessities of life. In 'The One and the Other', for example, the baby's mother fails to notice the theft of her baby because 'she was busy making sausage meat and pork pies that day; and this was not her first child, to be studied like a nonpareil. Indeed, it was her ninth, though not all of them had lived' (2). The fairy baby left behind in the cradle needs to be de-elfinised for the transition as much as the changeling needs to be inhumanised, in his case by having his wings 'extirpated' and his blood 'dosed with an elixir of mortality, compounded from tears and excrement of changelings', and finally we come to understand one of the mysteries of spiritualism: 'The transfers die, but tardily and with extreme difficulty, and some have been known to hover briefly in the air — a phenomenon called levitation and usually ascribed to saintliness' (6).

All of this is described with profound detachment. We are made observers through the eyes of a narrator who may slip in and out of the characters' minds, or choose to stay outside them altogether, but who at no point gives us the luxury of *feeling with* these characters. We may envy some of them for some of the time, find others disgusting, sigh at human or elfin folly, but at no point are we invited to 'identify', that staple of so much fiction, with any of them. So detached is this narrative voice that at least one reader has wondered whether the narrator might, at least part of the time, actually be a fairy. [6] In their contents, too, the stories exhibit a marked degree of narrative coldness in that they eschew poetic justice, providence, or morally centred vision. Moral judgment is already prevented by the narrative voice remaining an observer, sometimes an amused one, but never one that judges, an activity of which Warner herself was severely critical. She thought that the injunction 'Don't point!' was 'sound advice and should be given more often and to all ages'.[7]

In 'The Blameless Triangle', for example, we follow a group of fairies who have little value in their German home kingdom of Wirre Gedanken, as they leave to wander among humans. In this they are not unlike the Grimm Brothers' tale of the Musicians of Bremen, four downtrodden creatures, a donkey, a rooster, a cat and a dog, who win for themselves a home through solidarity, courage and guile. In contrast, Warner's 'discards' — Ludo, Moor, Tinkel, Nimmerlein and Banian — search for a place where they might engage in the 'Socratic scrabbling' (44) which they have come to enjoy after their abandonment by their court, a place where they might follow the 'wish to meditate' which 'took hold of them' (45). They find a 'disused chapel on a lonely hillside' which is 'dirty and cluttered with Christian odds and ends' (46–47), but which would do. In the Grimms' template of the story, finding this refuge would be the ending, the rejects having found a home, but Warner makes this their new beginning. We see the Brotherhood of the Blameless Triangle learn to meet their daily material needs, squabble Socratically, inadvertently cause the death of a priest who comes to exorcise their occupation of the church, and travel through south-eastern Europe where they observe human activities. 'Once, alighting in a park, they found a burned-out mansion and a row of impaled cadavers tottering on a fence'. But lest we think that this is a principled indictment, a little further on 'they saw the country-side grow calm, well tilled, prosperous, coloured by the blue-green of poppy fields' (53). Their new host, the local governor Mustafa Ibrahim Bey, is proud of acquiring some fairies for his needs, and 'he had thought of having their wings torn out. Common sense prevailed; none of them showed the slightest inclination to fly away, so why go to extremes?' (62). However, such stereotypical cruelties of the East are here as unreliable as anything else in this fickle world, for Ludo cannot bear to leave this place where '"for the first time in my life I have lived in comfort without fearing and scheming"' (63). In turn, the Governor longs for a friend, '"a disinterested European friend, the real article"', and is delighted by Ludo's decision, and the story ends in a way that no reader could have foreseen at the beginning. It is also one in which the ethics of the solution are kept coolly out of the picture.

Warner's technique can be described as ethnographic: a rich description of the local customs of Elfin and human worlds from the perspective of an observer who has access to people's minds, but who tries to be dispassionate and, above all, neutral about what is being observed. In 'The Revolt at Brocéliande', for example, we witness the habits and rituals of a fairy court in Brittany where Queen Melior hits on a new fashion for the court that will emulate the supposed customs of the ancestral Fairy Courts in Persia: 'no one had thought of eunuchs' (66). What ensues is a thick description of this court, castrations included, and the life experiences, by no means merely horrific, of the two changelings chosen to become eunuchs. 'The Late Sir Glamie' explores the theological implications of that impossible thing, a fairy ghost (fairies have no souls and hence no afterlife), and the relative impact of short and long life-spans on human and fairy psychology and social custom. 'Castor and Pollux' features the fairy Hamlet, a 'mental libertine' (207) who adores all things human and their absurdities, among them the theatre. His eager but uncomprehending elfin wife becomes pregnant by a human actor, and dies inevitably in childbirth, twin humans proving fatal for the fairy birth canal. The twin boys pursue ecclesiastical careers and their father Hamlet founds a theological college for them in which they can indulge their (and his) fascination with theological questions strictly prohibited in fairyland: 'Hamlet could not believe his luck. They were more innocent than the puppets, more wholeheartedly ludicrous than the players. Whatever the cost, he must keep them' (221). 'The Occupation' shows us, in a series of dazzling reversals, the occupation of a parish church and Presbyterian rectory by a group of fairies, who embark on an Elfin ethnography of the parish priest and his life, driving him insane in the process (so much for the non-invasiveness of the ethnographic impulse).

For a de-centred ethnographic exploration of social structures and habits of action and feeling, fairies are an excellent vehicle. Fairies have a long history of being conceived of as alien to humans, mischievous, cruel, 'an invention that almost wholly lacks moral engagement',[8] or, in Warner's words, inventions grounded in 'the calm negation on which all Elfindom reposes' (199). While they mirror us, for example in their social stratifications, they are very different from humans, in their longevity, atheism, and general amorality. As John Simons has noted, in *Kingdoms of Elfin* Warner draws on a wide range of historical sources, and 'appears to spend as much time on the loving reconstruction of the fine detail of fairy ritual and material culture as she does on the pursuit of the twists and turns of her narrative'.[9] Warner found this work of 'reconstruction' exhilarating, commenting on a story having 'a great deal of information about Elfhame unknown till now as I have just invented it. Oh, how I long to give it learned footnotes, and references. There is such heartless happiness in scholarship'.[10] *Kingdoms of Elfin* is thus an exuberant ethnography of two communities that share human concerns (love, power, freedom, faith, social custom) while one of these also has a dimension of alien characteristics: inhuman longevity, extreme atheism, freedom from shame, and an indifference to human suffering.

Kingdoms of Elfin is certainly unusual in the rigour with which the manipulation of empathy is pursued. But Warner's approach to storytelling also links these stories strongly with her oeuvre as a whole. *Kingdoms of Elfin* can be seen not so much as a new departure than as the continuation of an ongoing project: how to tell without 'pointing a finger'. Warner's novels *Lolly Willowes* (1926), *Mr Fortune's Maggot* (1927), *Summer Will Show* (1936), and *The Flint Anchor* (1954), as well as many of her short stories, set out again and again to explore the life-worlds of dispassionately observed individuals. This seems to be the hallmark of her art. Critics have variously described her approach as 'impersonal', 'eccentric', and 'indifferent', favouring an investigation of cognition over a psychology of self, or practicing *besideness* rather than a central perspective.[11] Perhaps *Kingdoms of Elfin* is most closely connected to *The Corner that Held Them* (1948), a novel that pursues, scrupulously and minutely, but with barely any of the 'breath of human kindness', the history of a community of medieval nuns as things happen, good, bad, terrible or simply indifferent, in which the potential for emotional drama from individual lives is levelled out by the perspective of time.

This ethnographic approach also differentiates Warner's use of fantasy from that of the mainstream. In her first foray into the fantastic, in *Lolly Willowes*, the heroine becomes a witch. Kate Macdonald, following Farah Mendelsohn's taxonomy, classifies *Lolly Willowes* as an 'estranged fantasy', a 'subdivision of the immersive fantasy', in that it 'immerses the reader into a realist world in which witches happen to live, and the reader finds this quite natural'.[12] This would also be a good description of *Kingdoms of Elfin*. After *Lolly Willowes*, Warner repeatedly resorted to fantasy elements in her writing and seems to have come full circle in *Kingdoms of Elfin*. As with witchcraft in *Lolly Willowes*, which draws on contemporary witchcraft scholarship,[13] *Kingdoms of Elfin* builds on older elfin lore, for example the delightful late seventeenth-century *The Secret Commonwealth: An Essay on the Nature and Actions of the Subterranean (and for the Most Part) Invisible People, Heretofore Going Under the Name of Elves, Fauns, and Fairies* by the Reverend Robert Kirk, from which Warner quotes extensively. *Kingdoms of Elfin* is also a forerunner to the explosion of fantasy stories in the present day that revolve around fairy courts; genre writing that finds its place alongside vampire, werewolf, or magician stories and their seductions and gratifications.[14] Today's fairy fantasies, too, tend to foreground the alienness and potential cruelty of fairy worlds, for instance in Charles de Lint's *The Wild Wood* (1994), Neil Gaiman's *Stardust* (1999), Susanna Clarke's *Jonathan Strange and Mr Norrell* (2004), and Holly Black's fairy trilogy beginning with *Tithe* (2002). However, they often follow models that are centred on and told from a specific perspective, often built on a hero's quest motif. Almost inevitably, they give us a character to identify with, human or fairy, either in first-person narratives or in third-person narratives offering a strongly foregrounded point of view for the reader to enter.[15] This is precisely what Warner's stories seem to be designed to actively prevent, and in her 'The Power of Cookery', which favours the art of good cooking over Romance questing, this scepticism becomes explicit. Love and desire are still at the heart of many of her stories, but these do not function as the narrative fulfilment, unlike the essentially identity-centred recognition structures created by later fairy fantasists.

Continuing to explore the theme of love in Warner's writing, it is clear that her stories dwell on a question that has recurred throughout her oeuvre (particularly in *Mr Fortune's Maggot*): what exactly is the connection, adverse or causal, between love and freedom? 'Elphenor and Weasel' relates how a wandering fairy couple's enjoyment of the human world depends precisely on those things that result from the shortness of human life-spans. This is explicitly linked to the recklessness of their love which ends with an ordeal where 'death by lightning would have been easier'

(42) as the price to pay for the ecstatic freedom that comes with love. 'Winged Creatures' follows other doomed but exhilarating loves and longings. Lady Fidès, for example, fails to become a bird, but invests birds with all of her love, above even the love of her child: 'Love was what she felt for birds — a free gift, unrequired, unrequited, invulnerable' (141). Gobelet the changeling in turn enjoys a short spell of bliss with Lady Fidès's fairy son Grive — the French name for a thrush, but also only one letter less than *grieve* — who for a time provides the greatest attachment and at the same time the greatest freedom of his life.

> With that morning Gobelet began the happiest epoch of his life. As nearly as possible, he became a fairy. He lost all sense of virtue and responsibility and lived by pleasures —pell-mell pleasures: a doubled rainbow, roasting a hedgehog. (150)

This story provides a marvellously complex opening of the imagination on matters of desire, need, freedom and constraint, where nothing is ever tied down. 'Foxcastle', the story that closes the collection, resonates forcefully with Warner's life-long concern in her fictions, and arguably also in her life, with the question: how to be, become, and make one another free. The story centres on a human who is captured and studied by fairies. Ultimately indifferent to him and what knowledge he can give them, the fairies quickly lose interest, and the protagonist remains in Elfindom, until his visible ageing makes him noticeably undesirable, and he is returned as an old man to the human world again. For him, the experience is a revelation of freedom that results, quite in contrast to 'Elphenor and Weasel', not from the reckless bliss of love but rather from the promise of detachment.

> For by the simple act of discarding his fetters and walking up a winding stair he had attained the wish of his heart. Watching these happy beings for whom weeping was

impossible, he had become incapable of grief; watching their inconsistencies, he had become incapable of knowing right from wrong; disregarded by them he had become incapable of disappointment [...] he lived in a perpetual present. (258–59)

When he is returns to his own kind, he totters towards some passers-by 'making noises' which they fail to understand, for he 'had lived so long with the fairies he had forgotten his native speech'. Our last sighting is of someone giving him some alms with the instruction that returns us abruptly to how humans do things: 'Take it, take it,' said the gentleman, 'Go away, and be grateful' (261).

What we see in *Kingdoms of Elfin* and what characterises Warner's oeuvre as a whole, is a remarkable degree of artistic independence that has consistently led to the somewhat bemused recognition with which so many appreciations of her work start, a 'commonplace of criticism',[16] that she has been inexplicably neglected. In Claire Harman's words, not unlike the fairy creatures she created who remain for the most part unseen to human eyes, Warner seems like 'a ghostly figure in twentieth-century letters'.[17] This independence can also be seen in her life as she seems to have weathered challenges and changes without fuss, and without losing sight of what was important to her. Luckily for readers of her fiction, much of her life can be found in Warner's correspondence, her diaries, and Harman's luminous account of her life.

Sylvia Townsend Warner was born in 1893 into a family both privileged and intellectually stimulating. Her father, George Townsend Warner, was, by all accounts, an exceptionally gifted teacher of history at Harrow School.[18] Warner herself was first educated by her mother Eleanor Mary Townsend Warner, née Hudleston, who seems to have had little interest in her daughter once she began to grow up because, as Warner thought, she was not a son.[19] Warner seems to have been very close to her father. Claire Harman's biography includes a haunting photograph of a teenage

Sylvia skating with her father, a beautiful image of mutual grace and consideration, poised together in a spin, holding onto each other but also pursuing their own trajectories. The task of educating their only child moved from Warner's mother to her father. As a result, she had access to her father's considerable library as well as his expertise as a historian and as a teacher, and as a meticulous stylist in both writing and speech. This meant that she received an excellent education: 'By the age of seventeen or so, Sylvia's erudition was both phenomenal and perfectly natural. In the opinion of some, she was "the cleverest fellow we had", to others she was known — somewhat disparagingly — as the best boy at Harrow'.[20] It also meant that Warner completely escaped *formal* educational disciplines, schools, curricula, and the influence of the state in determining what young people should learn and read.

Warner maintained a close allegiance to historiography throughout her writing life: *Kingdoms of Elfin* is, among other things, an exploration of historical, regional and national environments.[21] 'History' here means an especial commitment to historical materialism, the belief that the material lives of people, where their food comes from, how their money is earned, what their clothing is made of, as well as the general habits of a specific class or group, are instrumental in influencing what can be thought, felt, and communicated, and how. Warner returned repeatedly to different forms of the historical novel, for example her exploration of the February 1848 revolution in France in *Summer Will Show* (1936), medieval England in *The Corner that Held Them* (1948), and the world of the nineteenth century in *The Flint Anchor* (1954). At the same time, however, she would retain the autodidact's freedom to bypass prescribed ideas of the canon. In her lecture on the historical novel Warner claimed that 'when I was young, I read everything in the house',[22] and this seems to have set her free to seek and find inspiration where she felt she would find it.

In her lecture 'Women as Writers' (1959), Warner set out to demonstrate not so much that women wrote, still less who the 'great' women writers were, if any existed, but rather *how* they wrote, claiming that they were 'remarkably adept at vanishing out of their writing so that the quality of immediacy replaces them'.[23] She gleefully demonstrates this 'immediacy' — a quality which she associates with the egoless artistry of women writers, and values highly — with quotations from women's voices in non-canonical sources: a cookery book, Florence Nightingale's reports from the front, a fifteenth-century letter, Julian of Norwich's description of her perception of God. This virtue of 'immediacy' is very much a virtue of style, of a non-fussy, 'immediate' use of language, and Warner would have been her own best example. In a complicated irony she sees immediacy as the special domain of the marginalised woman writer, writers who eschew the pointing finger and dispense with trying to be 'literary' altogether, since this is tacitly reserved for male writers: 'But I have sometimes wondered if women are literary at all. It is not a thing which is strenuously required of them, and perhaps, finding something not required of them, they thank God and do no more about it. They write. They dive into writing like ducks into water. One would almost think it came naturally to them — at any rate as naturally as plain sewing'.[24]

Her first intellectual love, however, was directed more towards music than writing. In 1917 she was appointed to the editorial committee of the Tudor Church Music Project, on which she worked for twelve years. As late as 1975, at the end of a long writing career, she would describe herself as 'that odd thing, a musicologist'.[25] She moved to London and, alongside the Tudor church music, began a life of writing in earnest. In 1925 she published her first collection of poems, *The Espalier*, and her first novel in 1926, *Lolly Willowes*, which became a Book of the Month in the US. She continued to publish poetry alongside novels and short stories (many published in the *New Yorker* from 1936 on). Later in life, she also translated from the French: *A Place of Shipwreck*, a translation of Jean-René Huguenin's *La Côte Sauvage* (1962), and *By Way of Sainte-Beuve* (translation of Marcel Proust's *Contre Sainte*-Beuve, 1967). In 1967 she published a commissioned biography of the acclaimed and troubled English writer T H White. While her status as a literary figure may have been on the margins rather than at the centre, she maintained a distinguished career, and her long collaboration with *The New Yorker* ensured some financial stability. For *The New Yorker*, she was a regular contributor of stories, while being free to pursue her art without considering too much what her market was willing to accept. This makes the assignment of her work to one 'school' or another difficult, and may have hindered her scholarly reception, which is notoriously category-dependent. Yet Warner's works have always had faithful readers, and this republication of *Kingdoms of Elfin* by Handheld Press gives new readers the opportunity to encounter her original, engaging and challenging writing.

In 1930, at the age of 37, Warner moved in with and became the lover of the poet Valentine Ackland, the woman who would become the love of her life. At this point, Warner's only long-term relationship had been with the musician Percy Carter Buck, with whom she had begun a secret affair when she was nineteen. He was married, twenty-two years older than her, and had five children, and he had been her music-teacher since she was sixteen.[26] Falling in love with a woman should have been a momentous shift of direction in terms of Warner's sense of identity — she was, after all, now the lover of a woman thirteen years her junior, who was a rather dashing cross-dresser as well. They lived together in Dorset for the rest of their lives. The story 'A Love Match' (1966), from her collection *A Stranger with a Bag*, which displaces the sexual transgression from lesbianism to incest, provides the wry assertion that one did not have to move to Paris's left bank if one wanted to pursue an unorthodox relationship; one could stay right where one was and count on the general inertia of one's neighbours.

Their relationship began at a time when far greater dangers than lesbianism were looming on the horizon. The two women, like many anti-fascists of the period, joined the Communist Party of Great Britain in 1935. During the Spanish Civil War they joined a Red

Cross unit and were active in the 1937 International Association of Writers for the Defence of Culture.[27] Warner's political commitment found its expression for a while in an active involvement in Communist activities and in general anti-fascist work.[28] We can also see the effect of her unfailing adherence to her father's passion for history, in her case with an unwavering commitment to historical materialism[29] as she explores, with an unfailing precision of vision, how we come to be who we are through the forces of society, class, and history. At the same time, her stories often revolve around the question of how a person might *escape* from these constraints rather than be defined by them.

In general, there is a free-spiritedness and independent-mindedness in Warner's life choices that seem in tune with the cool matter-of-factness of the ethnographic gaze in her fictions. Her narrative voice rarely registers outrage or surprise at even the most unusual behaviours exhibited by her fictional creatures. 'She had the knack of melting across barriers, rather than defining herself against them'.[30] Her relationship with Valentine was troubled by Valentine's tumultuous affair with the American scholar Elizabeth Wade White, as well as Valentine's addiction to alcohol.[31] But their relationship was Warner's life's project: exploring how freedom could be reconciled with love. While she felt that many of their letters could not be published as long as people mentioned in them were still alive, after Valentine's death in 1969 Warner spent much time sorting and arranging their lives' correspondence, constructing an autobiographical framework for their story and preserving the history of their love. The edited letters that would eventually be published posthumously as *I'll Stand by You* (1998) are a moving and lucid account of a relationship, and an important contribution to the archive of lesbian history of which there is so much need and in which there are so few entries.[32]

Warner's two parallel literary occupations at the end of her life seem diametrically opposed: the painstaking and grief-driven autobiographical reconstruction of their lives in letters, and the composition of the stories that would make up *Kingdoms of Elfin*. These stories are so alien to human concerns that it has been surmised that Warner may have 'wanted a change even from warm-bloodedness'.[33]

Indeed, the collection is profoundly disturbing because the centre of perception, value, and vision is not human, but has been replaced with a complex set of mutual observations, amusements, cruelties, and simple incomprehensions.[34] The empathy Warner withdrew from her storytelling may be supplied by her human readers, who may feel that the stories, after all, *critique* cruelty and do side with human suffering.[35] Jennifer Poulos Nesbitt, for example, produces the following reading of the ending of 'Elphenor and Weasel', the first paragraph quoted here:

> No one could account for them, or for the curious weightless fragments of a substance rather like sheet gelatine which the wind had scattered over the floor. They were buried in the same grave. Because of their small stature and light bones they were entered in the Register of Burials as *Two Stranger Children.*

> The verb *account* [...] marks failures of imagination and sympathy for those outside the community. No curiosity is voiced about the excess matter, and their bodies are classified erroneously in an effort to dismiss their incongruity.[36]

Failures of imagination and sympathy for those outside the community, effort to dismiss: the passage (and those preceding it) censures the characters in the story for their active indifference. But the narration Warner offers simply states what happened: that one species' suffering may be another species' matter of indifference, and not only among fairies. At the same time, the humans in the story, in contrast to the readers, are not privy to the extraordinary flowering of love between Elphenor and Weasel so that this ending also ensures that the secrets of the fairies are guarded from intrusive sympathy from creatures who are of next to no account to them. Positing the non-dominance, even the irrelevance of humans, is Warner's startling anticipation of the 'post-human' moment: the realisation, which we are arriving at only now through an awareness of our Anthropocene age, that human beings are not the centre of the universe, and that they need to explore and accommodate themselves to this fact. 'Bother the human heart' becomes a parting instruction as well as an indictment. This last phase of her writing was indeed 'Something Entirely Different'.

Works Cited:

Bingham, Frances, 'The practice of the presence of Valentine: Ackland in Warner's work', *Critical Essays on Sylvia Townsend Warner, English Novelist 1893-1978*, (eds) Gill Davies, David Malcolm, and John Simons (Lewiston: Edwin Mellen, 2006), 29-44.

Datlow, Ellen and Terri Windling, eds, *The Faery Reel: Tales from the Twilight Realm* (New York, 2006).

Ewins, Kristin, 'The question of Socialist writing and Sylvia Townsend Warner in the Thirties', *Literature Compass* 5 (2008), 657-667.

Hahn, Rebecca, 'Encounters between elves and humans in Sylvia Townsend Warner's *Kingdoms of Elfin*', *Journal of the Sylvia Townsend Warner Society* (2010), 53-68.

—, *Sidestepping Normativity: The Short Stories of Sylvia Townsend Warner*. Dissertation University of Tübingen, 2017.

Harker, James, '"Laura was not thinking": Cognitive minimalism in Sylvia Townsend Warner's *Lolly Willowes*', *Studies in the Novel* 46 (2014), 44-62.

Harman, Claire, 'Introduction', in Sylvia Townsend Warner, *New Collected Poems*, (Manchester: Carcanet, 2008), 1-11.

—, *Sylvia Townsend Warner: A Biography* (1989; London: Penguin, 2015).

James, David, 'Realism, late modernist abstraction, and Sylvia Townsend Warner's fictions of impersonality', *Modernism / Modernity* 12 (2005), 111–131.

Joannou, Maroula, '"Our Time": Sylvia Townsend Warner, Virginia Woolf and the 1940s', *Literature Compass* 11 (2014), 732–744.

Judd, Peter Haring, *The Akeing Heart: Letters between Sylvia Townsend Warner, Valentine Ackland and Elizabeth Wade White* (Reading: Handheld Press, 2018).

Macdonald, Kate, 'Witchcraft and non-conformity in Sylvia Townsend Warner's *Lolly Willowes* (1926) and John Buchan's *Witch Wood* (1927)', *Journal of the Fantastic in the Arts* 23 (2012), 215–238.

Mars-Jones, Adam, 'Introduction', in Sylvia Townsend Warner, *Mr Fortune's Maggot* and *The Salutation* (New York: New York Review of Books, 2001), vii–xiii.

Micir, Melanie, 'Not of national importance: Sylvia Townsend Warner, women's work, and the mid-century historical novel', in *Around 1945: Literature, Citizenship, Rights*, (ed.) Allan Hepburn (Montreal and Kingston: McGill-Queen's University Press, 2016), 66–83.

—, '"Living in two tenses": The intimate archives of Sylvia Townsend Warner', *Journal of Modern Literature* 36 (2012), 119–131.

Montefiore, Janet, 'Sylvia Townsend Warner Scholarship 1978–2013', *Literature Compass* 11/12 (2014), 7886–811.

Nesbitt, Jennifer Poulos, *Narrative Settlements: Geographies of British Women's Fiction between the Wars* (Toronto: University of Toronto Press, 2005).

Plock, Vike Martina, 'A note on Sylvia Townsend Warner's "The Kingdom of Elfin" (1927)', *Journal of the Sylvia Townsend Warner Society* (2015), 6–8.

Powers, Elizabeth, 'On situating Sylvia Townsend Warner: How (not) to become a "classic" writer', *The Yale Review* 104 (2016), 88–100.

Priest, Hannah, 'The unnaturalness of a society: Class divisions and conflict in Sylvia Townsend Warner's *Kingdoms of Elfin*', *Journal of the Sylvia Townsend Warner Society* (2010), 1–16.

Purkiss, Diane, *At the Bottom of the Garden: A Dark History of Fairies, Hobgoblins, and Other Troublesome Things* (New York: New York University Press, 2000).

Rattenbury, Arnold, 'Literature, lying and sober truth: Attitudes to the work of Patrick Hamilton and Sylvia Townsend Warner', *Writing and Radicalism* (ed.) John Lucas (London and New York: Longman, 1996), 201–244.

Silver, Carole G, *Strange and Secret Peoples: Fairies and Victorian Consciousness* (Oxford: Oxford University Press, 1999).

Simons, John, 'On the compositional genetics of the *Kingdom of Elfin* together with a note on tortoises', *Critical Essays on Sylvia Townsend Warner, English Novelist 1893-1978* (eds.) Gill Davies, David Malcolm, and John Simons (Lewiston: Edwin Mellen, 2006), 45–60.

Steinman, Michael (ed.) *The Element of Lavishness: Letters of Sylvia Townsend Warner and William Maxwell, 1938-1978* (New York: Counterpoint 2004).

Sutherland, Helen, 'From Elphame to otherwhere: Sylvia Townsend Warner's *Kingdoms of Elfin*,' *Journal of the Sylvia Townsend Warner Society* (2005): 21–32.

Sykes, Rosemary, 'This was a lesson in history': Sylvia Townsend Warner, George Townsend Warner and the matter of history', *Critical Essays on Sylvia Townsend Warner, English Novelist 1893-1978* (eds) Gill Davies, David Malcolm, and John Simons (Lewiston: Edwin Mellen, 2006), 103–115.

Wallraven, Miriam, *Women Writers and the Occult in Literature and Culture: Female Lucifers, Priestesses, and Witches* (New York: Routledge, 2015).

Warner, Sylvia Townsend, 'The Historical Novel' (1940), in *With the Hunted: Selected Writings*, (ed.) Peter Tolhurst (Norwich: Black Dog Books, 2012), 268–270.

—, 'Women as Writers' (1959), in *With the Hunted: Selected Writings* (ed.) Peter Tolhurst (Norwich: Black Dog Books, 2012), 231–240.

—, 'In conversation with Val Warner and Michael Schmidt in 1975' (1981), in *With the Hunted: Selected Writings*, (ed.) Peter Tolhurst (Norwich: Black Dog Books, 2012), 399–406.

—, *I'll Stand By You: Letters of Sylvia Townsend Warner and Valentine Ackland,* (ed.) Susanna Pinney (London: Random House, 1998).

List of Publications:

For the establishment of this list, I am indebted to Claire Harman's (2008) very detailed chronology and to Janet Montefiore's bibliography (2014). Place of publication for Chatto and Windus is always London.

1925: *The Espalier* (poems, Chatto and Windus)

1926: *Lolly Willowes* (novel, Chatto and Windus)

1927: *Mr Fortune's Maggot* (novel, Chatto and Windus)

1928: *Time Importuned* (poems, Chatto and Windus)

1929: *The True Heart* (novel, Chatto and Windus)

1931: *Opus 7* (poem, Chatto and Windus)

1931: *A Moral Ending and Other Stories* (short stories, London: Furnival Books)

1932: *The Salutation and Other Stories* (short stories, Chatto and Windus)

1933: *Whether a Dove or Seagull* (poems, with Valentine Ackland, New York: Viking Press)

1934: *Whether a Dove or Seagull* (poems, with Valentine Ackland, Chatto and Windus)

1936: *More Joy in Heaven* (short stories, London: Cresset Press)

1936: *Summer Will Show* (novel, Chatto and Windus)

1938: *After the Death of Don Juan* (novel, Chatto and Windus)

1940: *The Cat's Cradle Book* (short stories, Chatto and Windus)

1943: *A Garland of Straw* (short stories, Chatto and Windus)

1947: *The Museum of Cheats* (short stories, Chatto and Windus)

1948: *The Corner that Held Them* (novel, Chatto and Windus)

1949: *Somerset* (non-fiction, London: Paul Elek)

1951: *Jane Austen* (criticism, London: The British Council)

1954: *The Flint Anchor* (novel, Chatto and Windus)

1955: *Winter in the Air* (short stories, Chatto and Windus)

1957: *Boxwood*, first edition (poems, Monotype Corporation)

1958: *By Way of Sainte-Beuve* (trans. of Marcel Proust, *Contre Sainte-Beuve*, Chatto and Windus)

1960: *Boxwood*, second enlarged edition (poems, Chatto and Windus)

1962: *A Place of Shipwreck* (trans. of Jean-René Huguenin, *La Côte Sauvage*, Chatto and Windus)

1962: *A Spirit Rises* (short stories, Chatto and Windus)

1966: *A Stranger With a Bag* (short stories, Chatto and Windus)

1967: *T. H White* (biography, Jonathan Cape)

1968: *King Duffus and Other Poems* (poems, privately printed)

1971: *The Innocent and the Guilty* (short stories, Chatto and Windus)

1977: *Kingdoms of Elfin* (short stories, Chatto and Windus)

Posthumous publications (excluding reprints):

1978: *Azrael*, intr. Peter Pears (poem, New Bury: Libanus Books)

1980: *Twelve Poems*, pref. Peter Pears (Chatto and Windus)

1981: *Scenes of Childhood and Other Stories* (short stories, Chatto and Windus)

1982: *Collected Poems*, ed. Claire Harman (Manchester: Carcanet)

1984: *One Thing Leading to Another*, ed. Susanna Pinney (short stories, London: Women's Press)

1985: *Selected Poems,* ed. Claire Harman (Manchester: Carcanet)

1988: *Selected Short Stories*, ed. Susanna Pinney and William Maxwell (Chatto and Windus)

2001: *The Music at Long Verney: Twenty Stories*, ed. Michael Steinmann (Washington, DC: Counterpoint Press)

2006: *Dorset Stories*, ed. Peter Tolhurst (Norwich: Black Dog Books)

2008: *New Collected Poems*, ed. Claire Harman (Manchester: Carcanet)

2008: *Journey from Winter: Selected Poems of Valentine Ackland*, ed. Frances Bingham (Manchester: Carcanet). Contains full text of *Whether a Dove or a Seagull* (1934)

Stories from *Kingdoms of Elfin* published in *The New Yorker*:

Jan 22, 1972: "Something Entirely Different", 28–33. In *Kingdoms of Elfin*: "The One and the Other".

June 23, 1973: "The Five Black Swans", 36–39.

Sept 10, 1973: "The Revolt at Brocéliande", 38–42.

Oct 1, 1973: "Visitors to the Castle", 36–40.

Feb 18, 1974: "The Mortal Milk", 32–38.

Apr 29, 1974: "Beliard", 32–37.

Aug 19, 1974: "Winged Creatures", 32–41.

May 20, 1974: "The Blameless Triangle", 37–45.

Dec 16, 1974: "Elphenor and Weasel", 39–45.

Aug 4, 1975: "The Political Exile", 28–34. In *Kingdoms of Elfin*: "The Power of Cookery"

Sept 15, 1975: "Castor and Pollux", 33–40.

Sept 29, 1975: "The Search for an Ancestress", 33–36.

Nov 10, 1975: "The Occupation", 45–51.

Dec 15, 1975: "Foxcastle", 38–44.

Elfin story not included in *Kingdoms of Elfin*:

Sept 20, 1976: "The Duke of Orkney's Island", 38–44

Endnotes

1 'In conversation with Val Warner and Michael Schmidt in 1975' (1981), in *With the Hunted: Selected Writings*, (ed.) Peter Tolhurst (Norwich: Black Dog Books, 2012), 399–406, 402–3.

2 Steinman, Michael (ed.) *The Element of Lavishness: Letters of Sylvia Townsend Warner and William Maxwell, 1938–1978* (New York: Counterpoint 2004), 216.

3 Plock, Vike Martina, 'A note on Sylvia Townsend Warner's "The Kingdom of Elfin" (1927)', *Journal of the Sylvia Townsend Warner Society* (2015), 6–8.

4 Warner's letter to William Maxwell, in Steinman 2004, 215.

5 Sutherland, Helen, 'From Elphame to otherwhere: Sylvia Townsend Warner's *Kingdoms of Elfin*,' *Journal of the Sylvia Townsend Warner Society* (2005): 21–32, 26.

6 Rebecca Hahn, *Sidestepping Normativity: The Short Stories of Sylvia Townsend Warner*. Dissertation University of Tübingen, 2017, 173.

7 quoted in Melanie Micir, '"Living in two tenses": The intimate archives of Sylvia Townsend Warner', *Journal of Modern Literature* 36 (2012), 119–131, 126.

8 Purkiss, Diane, *At the Bottom of the Garden: A Dark History of Fairies, Hobgoblins, and Other Troublesome Things* (New York: New York University Press, 2000), 8; Silver, Carole G, *Strange and Secret Peoples: Fairies and Victorian Consciousness* (Oxford: Oxford University Press, 1999), 149–184 on Victorian fairy cruelties.

9 Simons, John, 'On the compositional genetics of the *Kingdom of Elfin* together with a note on tortoises', *Critical Essays on Sylvia Townsend Warner, English Novelist 1893–1978* (eds.) Gill Davies, David Malcolm, and John Simons (Lewiston: Edwin Mellen, 2006), 45–60, 47.

10 quoted in Simons 2006, 47.

11 For example, David James, 'Realism, late modernist abstraction, and Sylvia Townsend Warner's fictions of impersonality', *Modernism / Modernity* 12 (2005), 111–131; James Harker, '"Laura was not thinking": Cognitive minimalism in Sylvia Townsend Warner's *Lolly Willowes*', *Studies in the Novel* 46 (2014), 44–62; Hahn 2017.

12 Macdonald, Kate, 'Witchcraft and non-conformity in Sylvia Townsend Warner's *Lolly Willowes* (1926) and John Buchan's *Witch Wood* (1927)', *Journal of the Fantastic in the Arts* 23 (2012), 215–238, 224.

13 Wallraven, Miriam, *Women Writers and the Occult in Literature and Culture: Female Lucifers, Priestesses, and Witches* (New York: Routledge, 2015).

14 on the continuity today between fairy and vampire worlds, see Purkiss 321–2.

15 see for example Datlow, Ellen and Terri Windling, eds, *The Faery Reel: Tales from the Twilight Realm* (New York, 2006).

16 Powers, Elizabeth, 'On situating Sylvia Townsend Warner: How (not) to become a "classic" writer', *The Yale Review* 104 (2016), 88–100, 88.

17 Harman, Claire, 'Introduction', in Sylvia Townsend Warner, *New Collected Poems*, (Manchester: Carcanet, 2008), 1–11, 1.

18 Claire Harman, *Sylvia Townsend Warner: A Biography* (1989; London: Penguin, 2015), 20; Sykes, Rosemary, 'This was a lesson in history': Sylvia Townsend Warner, George Townsend Warner and the matter of history', *Critical Essays on Sylvia Townsend Warner, English Novelist 1893-1978* (eds) Gill Davies, David Malcolm, and John Simons (Lewiston: Edwin Mellen, 2006), 103–115.

19 Harman 1989, 13.

20 Harman 1989, 20.

21 Sutherland 2005.

22 Warner, Sylvia Townsend, 'The Historical Novel' (1940), in Tolhurst 2012, 268–270, 268.

23 Sylvia Townsend Warner, 'Women as Writers' (1959), in Tolhurst 2012, 231–240, 236.

24 Warner 1959, 234.

25 Warner 1975, 399.

26 Harman 1989, 24.

27 Rattenbury, Arnold, 'Literature, lying and sober truth: Attitudes to the work of Patrick Hamilton and Sylvia Townsend Warner', *Writing and Radicalism* (ed.) John Lucas (London and New York: Longman, 1996), 201–244, 220–222.

28 Ewins, Kristin, 'The question of Socialist writing and Sylvia Townsend Warner in the Thirties', *Literature Compass* 5 (2008), 657–667; Joannou, Maroula, '"Our Time": Sylvia Townsend Warner, Virginia Woolf and the 1940s', *Literature Compass* 11 (2014), 732–744.

29 Sykes 2006; Joannou 2014, Micir 2016.

30 Mars-Jones, Adam, 'Introduction', in Sylvia Townsend Warner, *Mr Fortune's Maggot* and *The Salutation* (New York: New York Review of Books, 2001), vii–xiii, ix.

31 See Peter Haring Judd, *The Akeing Heart: Letters between Sylvia Townsend Warner, Valentine Ackland and Elizabeth Wade White* (Reading: Handheld Press, 2018).

32 Micir 2018.

33 Mars Jones 2001, xiii.

34 Hahn, Rebecca, 'Encounters between elves and humans in Sylvia Townsend Warner's *Kingdoms of Elfin*', *Journal of the Sylvia Townsend Warner Society* (2010), 53–68.

35 Priest, Hannah, 'The unnaturalness of a society: Class divisions and conflict in Sylvia Townsend Warner's *Kingdoms of Elfin*', *Journal of the Sylvia Townsend Warner Society* (2010), 1–16.

36 Nesbitt 107–8.

The Rev. Dr Opimian: You are determined to connect the immaterial with the material world, as far as you can.

Mr Falconer: I like the material world. I like to live among thoughts and images of the past and the possible, and even of the impossible, now and then.

— Thomas Love Peacock, *Gryll Grange*

1 The One and the Other

When the baby was lifted from the cradle, he began to whimper. When he felt the rain on his face, he began to bellow. 'Nothing wrong with his lungs,' said the footman to the nurse. They spread their wings, they rose in the air. They carried the baby over a birchwood, over an oakwood, over a firwood. Beyond the firwood was a heath, on the heath was a grassy green hill. 'Elfhame at last,' said the nurse. They folded their wings and alighted. A door opened in the hillside and they carried the baby in. It stared at the candles and the silver tapestries, left off bellowing, and sneezed.

'It's not taken a chill, I hope,' said the footman.

'No, no,' said the nurse. 'But Elfhame strikes cold at first.' She took off the swaddling clothes, wrapped the baby in gossamer, shook pollen powder over it to abate the human smell, and carried it to Queen Tiphaine, who sat in her bower. The Queen examined the baby carefully, and said he was just what she wanted: a fine lusty baby with a red face and large ears.

'Such a pity they grow up,' she said. She was in her seven hundred and twentieth year, so naturally she had exhausted a good many human babies.

'And what is he to be called, Madam?' asked the nurse.

Tiphaine considered. 'It's quite six decades since we had a Tiffany,' she said. 'Let him be named Tiffany. And see to the seven weasels.'

Elfhame is in Heathendom. It has no christenings. But when a human child is brought into it there is a week of ceremonies. Every day a fasting weasel bites the child's neck and drinks its blood for three minutes. The amount of blood drunk by each successive weasel (who is weighed before and after the drinking) is replaced by the same weight of a distillation of dew, soot, and aconite. Though the blood-to-ichor transfer does not cancel human nature (the distillation is only approximate: elfin blood contains several unanalyzable components, one of which is believed to be magnetic air), it gives considerable longevity; up to a hundred and fifty years is the usual span. During the seven days, the child may suffer some sharpish colics, but few die. On the eighth day it is judged sufficiently inhumanized to be given its new name.

'Dear little thing,' said Tiphaine. 'I hope he won't age prematurely.' For when grey hairs appear on the head of a changeling he is put out of the hill to make the rest of his way through the human world; which is why we see so many grey-haired beggars on the roads.

Mrs Tod, the baker's wife, did not notice the difference between her baby which had been stolen away and the elf-baby left in its stead. She was busy making sausage meat and pork pies that day; and this was not her first child, to be studied like a nonpareil. Indeed, it was her ninth, though not all of them had lived. It was Ailie, the servant, who noticed that the baby had lost flesh all of a sudden.

'Well, if you won't, you won't,' said Mrs Tod, putting it from her breast. 'I can't wait all day for you. There's the paste to raise and the master's supper to get. Here, Ailie! Give it the milk rag.'

Ailie washed out the rag, dipped it in milk, and offered it to the baby. It would not take it, and looked at her with staring green eyes. This put it into her head to lay it among the cat's kittens. The baby sucked the cat, who purred and laid her paw over it. So it went on for three days, the baby refusing Mrs Tod's breast and Ailie pretending it took the milk rag— for she did not care to speak of the cat. On the fourth day Mrs Tod said to her husband, 'We'll lose this Adam like we did the other. It must be christened before it slips away.'

The Minister named the child and poured water on it. It lay in his arms, neither stirring nor uttering. He looked grave, and poured on more water. Still the child neither stirred nor uttered. 'God forgive me,' said the Minister, 'but I think I have baptized a changeling!'

Taking the parents aside, he explained to them that as the child had made no remonstrance at the water, there could have been no sin to be driven out of it; therefore, it must be an elfin, a soulless being between Heaven and Hell and of no interest to either. So the best thing to hope for was that the changeling, already sickly and peevish, should die.

But it did not. Between Ailie and the cat, it strengthened, took broth and spoon meat, cut its teeth, learned to speak plain. It was the Minister who died. The thought that he had baptized a changeling so preyed on his mind that he took to walking in his sleep, stumbled into a beehive, and was stung to death. Lacking his sad looks to remind them, the Tods thought less of their misfortune in having a changeling child. Adam was doing well enough. The Minister might have been mistaken. No other person knew of it. Within a handful of years they had no doubt but that the boy was their own child and likely to be a credit to them.

In Elfhame everyone agreed that Tiffany was the prince among all the other stolen children. His cheeks were polished every morning like prize apples. His motions were examined by the court physician. He had a new suit once a month, gold boots, a Shetland pony to ride, and a drum to beat on. He was everybody's pet and pleasure and his every wish was indulged—save one. From the day when he saw the undernursemaid spread her wings and fly off to fetch a pillowcase, he was wild to be given a pair of wings. His tutor explained to him that wings cannot be fastened to a human back, and told him the story of Icarus. His governess assured him that flying is a horrible sensation and would certainly make him sick. Both these persons had wings but kept them neatly folded away. Servants, grooms, stable lads, people who went on errands flew because it was their lot in life; they were brought up to it and it did not make them sick. But in court circles no one dreamed of using his wings unless in an extreme emergency. In all her seven hundred and twenty years Tiphaine had never been known to leave the ground.

In spite of these examples and admonishments, Tiffany thought there could be nothing so glorious, so marvellous, as the act of flying. The ease of the performance convinced him that, wings or no wings, if he gave his mind to it he could go flying himself, as he already did in his dreams; and to study how it was done, he took to frequenting flying company, slinking off to the stables or the kitchen quarters whenever he got the chance. This was reported to Tiphaine. Unannounced and terrible, she came into the servants' hall. 'Tiffany,' she said. 'Come away. I wish to speak to you.'

Half the servants fell on their knees. The other half flew up into the rafters, where they felt pretty sure their angry Queen would not follow them. Glancing neither upward nor downward, Tiphaine went silently along many passages and up several flights of stairs to her bower; and Tiffany followed her with his heart in his boots.

'Shut the door,' said she. 'I do not wish anyone to hear you rebuked.' She looked so beautiful that he trembled. 'I did not have you fetched to Elfhame,' said she, 'to gape after wings and keep company with people who, however useful and necessary they may be, are no better than sparrows. You must put all thought of flying out of your head. If you do not, you will be sent away and never see me again.'

His face, his neck, his hands turned scarlet. His ears stood out like flags in a gale.

'Promise me, Tiffany.'

He promised with all his heart. She laid her hand on his hot cheek. 'There's my good Tiffany! It would have made me sad to send you away. Tomorrow, you shall have your first billiard lesson. And when you put on your next new suit of clothes we will have a banquet.'

It was a splendid banquet. New clothes were issued to all. People in corridors murmured to each other, 'I shouldn't be surprised if—' and, 'I've thought so for a long while.' All agreed that Tiffany had every qualification for the Green Ribbon—though some of the court ladies did so rather wistfully. For the Green Ribbon tied about a boy's waist denotes that when he is old enough he will be the Queen's love and that in the meantime no woman may lay a finger on him.

Duly, at the banquet, the Green Ribbon was tied round Tiffany's waist by the Lord Chamberlain and the Ambassador from Thule.

After the old Minister died, a new one came. He was called Guthrie. His wife was sickly and hadn't enough strength in her arms to knead dough, so he bought bread from Tod's bakery. One day he noticed Adam, who was drawing 'A's and 'B's on the floor with a wet finger. 'Your boy's young to know his alphabet,' he said.

'I wouldn't say that he knows his alphabet,' answered Mr Tod, 'but he copies the letters off the advertisements. I wish he were as forward in walking. His legs are rickety, that's the truth of it.'

Adam could not fly. Elfindom is an aristocratic society, and jealous of its privileges. Before an elf-baby is sent into the human world its wings are extirpated and it is dosed with an elixir of mortality, compounded from the tears and excrement of changelings. Neither process is wholly satisfactory. The transfers die, but tardily and with extreme difficulty, and some have been known to hover briefly in the air—a phenomenon called levitation and usually ascribed to saintliness.

Mr Guthrie said that when the boy was old enough to walk so far he would take him into the school. Next day, Adam had crawled to the doorstep. Though he was the youngest child in the class, he was soon at the head of it. In his fifth year he was learning the Hebrew alphabet, and so set on scholarship that in the great snowfall of that winter he cajoled his eldest brother into making him a pair of stilts, and got to school that way. After the snow came a long hard frost. Ice formed on the river. The boys went sliding and played ice hockey. One afternoon when they were tussling together and whacking at each other's shins, the ice cracked and parted beneath them. It was a shallow reach of the river, and they got off with nothing worse than a wetting, except Jimmie Guthrie, who had measles coming out on him. His mother had forbidden him to go out, and he was afraid to go home and be whipped for disobedience, so he hung about waiting for his clothes to dry. By the time they dried, he was in a fever, and soon after then he was dead.

His schoolmates went to the funeral, Adam among them. Adam's attention wandered. He was counting the lozenge panes in the window when he heard his name spoken by the Minister. 'For as in Adam all die' were the words. He was not the only Adam in the village, but he felt sure that the words had been spoken of him. It was as if he had heard an important secret. Thinking it over, he decided he must be the Angel of Death. He had often heard his mother and Ailie say he was not like the others. As they had as often told him not to boast or think himself remarkable, he kept the important secret to himself.

Since he was so quick at his books and so undersized, it seemed meant that he should go into the Ministry. Mr Guthrie began to teach him theology. They soon got to the

Fall of Man, and the true sense of the text in First Corinthians. Adam was glad he had kept his fancy about the Angel of Death to himself. If he had told of it, he would have been laughed at. But the word 'Death' had somehow taken root in his mind—as if he might have a special vocation or talent for the subject. As a step in the right direction, he studied epitaphs and watched pig killings. In his heart he thought he would rather be a surgeon than a minister; but it was by his excellence in theology that he won a bursary and was admitted (for all he was under age) to the Dollar Academy.

When he came home for the half-year holiday, the first person he met was Ailie. She was weeping. 'You should have got here an hour earlier,' she said. 'She waited on for you, poor old Pussy! But you're too late. She's gone. Pussy Bawdron's gone.'

She took him into the woodshed, and there, beneath a cloth, was the dead cat.

'Under God, you wouldn't be here if it hadn't been for her,' said Ailie with another outbreak of weeping.

He looked at the body. He felt in his pocket. There was the knife; and there, where the teats protruded from the shabby fur, was the place where he would make the first incision.

'I must have her,' he said. 'Fetch me a bowl of water and some rags.' And he turned back his sleeves.

When Ailie came back, he had already laid the body on the chopping block and cut open the belly. Ailie said no word. She had two things in the world to love: one was the boy, the other the old cat. In an hour, she had lost them both.

It was the custom of Elfhame that when the Queen tired of a lover she sent him a willow leaf. The Willow Leaf was conveyed privily by her confidential woman, and within an hour everyone at court knew about it. Tiffany's tenure of the Queen's love lasted so long that people gave up speculating when the Willow Leaf would be delivered. A year, two years, four years, seven years: even in a timeless society such a span of love causes remark. The aspiring Green Ribbon wearers began to grow impatient at their protracted virginity and to despair of ever getting into any bed. The livelier court ladies felt their Queen's fidelity (one would not, of course, call it infatuation) slightly scandalous. The nurse who had purloined him from the bakery said she had foreseen it from the moment Tiphaine set eyes on him and exclaimed that he was just what she wanted. Even the malcontents admitted that Tiffany was fit to set before a Queen. His black eyes glanced and danced in his ruddy face like black cherries bobbing in claret cup. He was large of limb, light of foot, sweet-breathed. He had a baritone voice, and his large red fingers were light as butterflies on the strings of a lute. He was also a brilliant mimic and could make Tiphaine laugh. He was perfectly good-natured and just stupid enough to be delightful. His demeanour, his unaffected enjoyment of a rewarded sensuality, made him as popular as a song.

For thirteen years, Tiffany was the Queen's love.

Shortly before the Willow Leaf dismissed him, a girl baby was born to one of the handsomest ladies at court. Fertility is rare among the Elfin aristocracy, though common enough among working fairies. Some speculative thinkers put this down to the fact that working fairies use their wings, pointing out that wrens, tits, sparrows, etc, are notoriously fertile, whereas the pedestrian dodo is extinct. Be this as it may, aristocratic fairies are passionately fond of children and a birth in court circles is an occasion for much rejoicing. Titania (so this baby was named) was on show daily from two to four. At her naming ceremony she was attended by ninetynine sponsors, headed by Tiphaine and Tiffany hand in hand. Her parents were given a pension and the Order of the Pomegranate, Tiphaine made her a cowslip ball and the working fairies, who were quite as much excited about her as if they had no babies of their own, clubbed together and presented a Noah's ark, imported at great expense from the outer world.

Tiffany, who was rather at a loose end after receiving the Willow Leaf, spent many an empty hour playing with Titania, sitting on the floor for her dolls' drinking bouts, playing carpet bowls, pretending to be a bear who would hug her to death, and pulling hideous faces to amuse her. She was a courageous, tyrannical child. The bear could never growl loud enough nor hug fiercely enough to satisfy her, the faces had to be intimidating before she would be amused by them, Tiffany frowned till his brows ached while she sat smirking like a snowdrop. Her governess complained that he over-excited the child, who was hoyden enough already. But he flattered the governess and kept his entry to Titania's nursery, and to her schoolroom. Even when she was going through her awkward age and people were finding her a nuisance and being disappointed in her, he still kept her as a pet; fished her out of scrapes, and shot snipe for her dinner.

Of course, she was not his only interest. The Willow Leaf had dispensed him from his vassalage to Tiphaine. He had enjoyed several bachelor friendships and several love affairs as well as improving his average at golf. The latest of his ladies was a stickler for traditions. Now it was the thirteenth of February and he still had not completed the valentine he ought to send her. He was sitting in the North Gallery, where he hoped to be undisturbed, and considering rhymes to 'azure' when he saw Titania steal in at the farther end of the gallery and come toward him. He signalled to her to be quiet. For once, she was in a biddable mood. She sat down and busied herself with her embroidery. He had decided on 'embrasure' and was modelling a sentiment to include it when there was a sudden Crack! and a whirr, as though a fan had been flirted open. He looked up. Titania was overhead. Five times she flew down the whole length of the gallery and back again. She folded her wings and alighted beside him, as dexterously as though she had spent her whole life flying on errands. 'Titania!' he exclaimed. 'What ever will you do next? You know you mustn't fly.'

'Don't tell on me,' she said.

He could no more resist her than he could fly himself. For when he looked up and saw her swallow flight up and down the gallery, his old fascinating rapture at the act of flying exploded like a rocket. Crack! Whirr! He was in love with Titania.

From that hour, he was her delighting, miserable slave. All his other loves, the affairs since the Willow Leaf, his thirteen years with Tiphaine, seemed no more than music lessons or practices on the putting green, preliminaries merely to equip him for the reality of love. In fact, these lessons were of little use, except for the patience and tact he had learned with Tiphaine. He had every need of these. Titania was as wilful as a kitten, tart as a green fruit. She established a bond of mutual guilt between them: her reckless indecorum of flying, his disloyalty of consenting to it. There could not have been a worse moment for such behaviour. Under the influence of her latest love (the eighth since Tiffany's day) Tiphaine had set about reforming the court. Regulations were tightened up, etiquette insisted on. If it were known that Titania flew, her reputation would be lost. She knew this as well as he did. She placed a high value on her reputation, since her future pleasures must depend on it. But future pleasures were not so interesting to her as the present pleasure of tossing Tiffany between agonies of anxiety lest she should take to the air and agonies of rapture when she did. She grew so brazen about showing her wings that she even flew in public rooms, hovering overhead during state functions and harp competitions. Sometimes he dreamed of some blessed turn of events by which Titania would be expelled from Elfhame and he would follow her: they would wander over the heath, living on mushrooms and cloudberries, and perhaps take up with the gypsies. More often, he wished himself dead.

It was she, viewing him from above, who saw he was going grey. She had the grace to be embarrassed, and did not tell him. He was left to find out for himself, dully growing aware that his friends were not so friendly as they had been, appeared to shun his company, turned their backs on him when he spoke; that ladies whispered in groups, eyeing him through the sticks of their fans; that servants were impertinent. But as all he thought of was Titania, he supposed he was in disgrace because she had been caught flying and he was suspected of having seduced her into it.

One evening, during a pause in the music, the Lord Chamberlain came up to Tiffany, holding a tray covered with a black cloth. The cloth was lifted. On the tray was a lock of grizzled wool, a large pair of spectacles, and a miniature pair of crutches. Every face was averted as Tiffany was led to the door in the hillside and put out, to make the rest of his way through the mortal world.

Ailie outlived Mr Tod and his wife. By then she wasn't good for much. She helped herself to a ring off Mrs Tod's finger and bought a lottery ticket. It was the winning number, so she finished the rest of her days better than she ever expected to.

While she was still at the bakery she saw Adam three times. Each time he gave her a guinea. She took the guineas but felt no gratitude. The cat lay between them.

Adam could ill afford the guineas. He gave them out of pride, to show that he did not come home as a Prodigal Son. For all that, both his parents considered him such. If he had kept to the path laid down and swept for him, he would have been in the Ministry by now, with a manse, and printed books of sermons to his credit. Since they would only sigh at him, he went to brag of his travels to Mr Guthrie. One time it was Montpellier, in France; the next, Ratisbon; the next again, far Finland to see the aurora borealis. Mr Guthrie enjoyed the traveller's tales; they were as good as a coal fire in the grate. After Adam had gone, he knelt down and prayed that Adam might not be led into becoming a Papist.

Travelling costs money. Adam hired himself out as a travelling tutor to sons of good families and showed the testimonials he had got from the Dollar University, all praising his learning and steady character. For a time, Adam and the boy would travel very sociably; then Adam would grow tired of this, and load the boy with lessons, keep him in, and allow him to eat nothing till he could ask for it in Latin, wake him before sunrise to study mathematics; and then, when he judged the moment ripe, send him out to buy a hat. The boy would see his chance and run away. Then Adam wrote a sorrowing letter to the parents and went off on his own devices.

Mostly he walked. He was as strong as a flea, and had an engaging manner with strangers. In his knapsack he carried a magnifying glass, his testimonials, and the skull of a marmoset. If he had been asked what he was in search of, he would have been hard put to it to say. He used his intellect as he used his legs: to carry him somewhere else. He studied astrology, astronomy, botany, chemistry, numerology, fortification, divination, organ building, metallurgy, medicine, perspective, the kabbala, toxicology, philosophy, and jurisprudence. He kept his interest in anatomy and did a dissection whenever he could get hold of a body. He learned Arabic, Catalan, Polish, Icelandic, Basque, Hungarian, Romany, and demotic Greek. He had no religious feeling, didn't drink, was an early riser, and cared only for very large women. Every time he crossed over a bridge the rumbling echo seemed to admonish him.

But it was an inarticulate admonition, and as what he valued was exact knowledge, he disregarded it.

It was in Cracow that he heard a Rosicrucian speak of the transcendental elements—among them, of magnetic air, which runs in the veins of sylphs, and gives them their buoyancy and immortality. Adam listened as though the echo under the bridges had suddenly become articulate, reiterating the sentence which had struck him during Jimmie Guthrie's funeral: 'For as in Adam all die'. He had been too hasty in putting by his first interpretation of those words. In a deeper sense, it was true: all his journeys and learnings and languages and dodges, his nights under the stars and with very large women, had accumulated and died in him. He was a compendium of deaths. Death, then, must be his proper study. To understand death, he must approach it through its opposite: the incapacity to die. He must catch a fairy, draw blood from it, identify that special element of magnetic air.

Having bought a fleam and practiced phlebotomy, he spent the next thirty years haunting dells, fountains, forests, fairy rings on lawns and in pastures, caves, tumuli—every place where fairies were said to resort. Yearly, as Midsummer Eve drew on, he was in a fever of anticipation. Nothing came of it, except that he was forty years more travelled and forty years uglier. Otherwise, he felt no older. He was active and limber as ever he had been, and, for all the nights he had spent in dells and damp pastures, without a trace of rheumatism: it was almost as though magnetic air ran in his own veins. He decided to lower his ambition and pursue Brownies; they, too, were of the fairy kind, though vulgarized and more like Lars. Brownies were common in Scotland, so to Scotland he went, and lodged in a wayside inn near Dumfries. A noisy brook ran beside it. Wakened during his first night by shouts and mutterings, he thought he was hearing a Kelpie. Kelpies are fierce immortals; Brownies would be easier to deal with; yet a Kelpie within a stone's throw ought not to be neglected. While he was debating this, he came to distinguish between the noise outside the house, which was the brook contesting with its rocky bed, and the noise within it, the voice of someone raving in a high fever, so near at hand that he could hear the bedstead creak as the sick man tossed and turned. In the morning he complained of this disturbance to the woman of the inn.

'I don't suppose you'll be troubled with him much longer,' said she. 'But if you like, I'll move him to the out-house. I only took him in for pity's sake. One doesn't want the scandal of a tramp dying on one's doorstep. He's a big man, though, and his fever makes him as awkward as a ram. Perhaps you'd lend a hand with him?'

'Willingly,' said Adam.

It was the remains of a handsome man that lay on the bed, and of a man who before age and beggardom had broken him must have belonged to the gentry. When they began to pull away the blanket, he came out of his stupor, sat up, and said arrogantly, 'What now?'

'We're just moving you,' said the woman.

'Leave me alone, please,' said the sick man. 'Kindly leave me alone, so that I may get back my strength. For I'm on my way to Elfhame, I must be there before nightfall. Leave me alone, woman—and you, whoever you may be. Leave me alone, I tell you. Aren't I in torment enough?' His fever came back, he began to cry and boo-hoo, and clutched the blanket to his breast.

'Elfhame,' said Adam. 'Where may that be? Is it far from here?'

'It's no place for a respectable man to go to,' said the woman, tweaking away the blanket. 'That's all I care to know of it. But he's forever raving about how he's on his way back there.'

'Let him be for a day longer,' said Adam. 'Mercy never comes amiss.'

He could scarcely believe his luck.

He put some money in the woman's hand. When she had gone, he sat down to listen. Presently the man began to rave again.

'Titania! Titania! What have they done to your wings? Why don't you fly to me? Why don't you come, you cruel child? Oh, they've caught her! They've tied her! O Titania, my little love, what have they done to you? My bird's in a cage, and the cage has a black cloth over it. The Chamberlain of Elfhame put it there. Wait till I get at him! Don't flutter so, my bird. Sit patiently till I come. I'm on my way. I'll be home before nightfall. I'll knock on the hill—it's all brambles now—the door will open. There they'll all be, singing and dancing like bees in a hive. Elfhive. Elfhame. They'll make me welcome. But I won't speak to one of them, no, not to Tiphaine herself, till I've pulled off the black cloth and kissed your wings. Titania! Titania! O my darling!' He hugged the bolster to him, so hard that the feathers burst out of it. Adam sat and pondered.

Fairies can take any shape they will; so much is agreed by the best authorities. Yet if this derelict greybeard were indeed a fairy, why did he lie bemoaning on a dirty bed instead of resuming himself and flying to that Titania he called on? If he were a fairy, threescore years and ten would be nothing to him—so there was no need to be precipitate. But again, if he were a fairy, in a flash he might cast off his disguise of mortality and fly to Elfhame, taking the secret of his unexplored blood with him. And if he were not, it would be waste of time to hang about waiting for a dying man to declare his mortality by dying.

This last consideration settled it. That night, when all were asleep, Adam took his fleam and his vials and his test tubes and a basin and a candle and went to the bedside. There lay the man, talking gently to the bolster. The fleam pierced the vein, the blood spurted out. Adam carried the basin to a corner of the room and set to work. It was poor blood, even for such an old, undernourished man; indeed, it was more than half water. It contained an unaccountable deposit of carbon. It tasted slightly bitter. It was totally unmagnetic. Adam repeated his analysis several times. Either Master Hieronymus of the Rosy Cross was wrong about the transcendental element of magnetic air or the man on the bed was no fairy. Adam now glanced toward the subject of his experiment. He had not plugged the vein sufficiently after the phlebotomy. The bed was soaked in blood. A lagging trickle still flowed from the wound. Ceased. Began again. Ceased. With the last impetus of the heart, a few gouts of blood emerged, till the last of them sealed the wound. So the poor wretch was not a fairy; and the bedding would have to be paid for. But if the body could be got to the anatomists in Edinburgh, thought Adam, taking heart again, I shall break about even. He straightened it, put his things together, and went to bed.

2 The Five Black Swans

Portents accompany the death of monarchs. A white horse trots slowly along the avenue, a woman in streaming wet garments is seen to enter the throne room, vanishes, and leaves wet footmarks; red mice are caught in the palace mousetraps. For several weeks five black swans had circled incessantly above the castle of Elfhame. It was ninety decades since their last appearance; then there were four of them, waiting for Maharit, Queen Tiphaine's predecessor. Now they were five, and waited for Tiphaine. Mute as a shell cast up on the beach, she lay in her chamber watching the antics of her pet monkey.

The mysterious tribe of fairies are erroneously supposed to be immortal and very small. In fact, they are of smallish human stature and of ordinary human contrivance. They are born, and eventually die; but their longevity and their habit of remaining good-looking, slender and unimpaired till the hour of death has led to the Kingdom of Elfin being called the Land of the Ever-Young. Again, it is an error to say 'the Kingdom of Elfin': the Kingdoms of Elfin are as numerous as kingdoms were in the Europe of the nineteenth century, and as diverse.

Tiphaine's Kingdom lay on the Scottish border, not far from the romantic and lonely Eskdalemuir Observatory (erected in 1908). Her castle of Elfhame—a steep-sided grassy hill, round as a pudding basin—had great purity of style. A small lake on its summit—still known as the Fairy Loch; and local babies with croup are still dipped in its icy, weedless water—had a crystal floor, which served as a skylight. A door in the hillside, operated by legerdemain, opened into a complex of branching corridors, one of which, broadening into a set of anterooms, led to the Throne Room, which was wainscotted in silver and lit by candles in crystal sconces. It was a circular room, and round it, like the ambulatory of a cathedral—and like the ambulatory of a cathedral fenced off by pillars and a light latticing—ran a wide gallery where the courtiers strolled, conversed, and amused themselves with dice, *boutsrimés*, news from other Kingdoms and the outer world, needlework, flirtations, conjectural scandal and tarot. The hum of conversation was like the hum of bees. But at the time of which I write, no one mentioned the five black swans, and the word 'death' was not spoken, though it lay, compact as a pebble, in every heart.

Dying is not an aristocratic activity like fencing, yachting, patronizing the arts: it is enforced—a willy-nilly affair. Though no one at Elfhame was so superstitious as to suppose Tiphaine would live forever, they were too well-mannered to admit openly that she would come to her end by dying. In the same way, though everyone knew that she had wings, it would have been *lèse-majesté* to think she might use them. Flying was a servile activity: cooks, grooms, laundresses flew about their work, and to be strong on the wing was a merit in a footman. But however speedily he flew to the banqueting room with a soup tureen, at the threshold he folded his wings and entered at a walk.

In these flying circles of Elfhame, Tiphaine's dying was discussed as openly and with as much animation as if the swans were outriders of a circus. A kitchen boy, flying out with a bucket of swill for the palace pigs, had been the first to see them. On his report, there was a swirl of servants, streaming like a flock of starlings from the back door to see for themselves. The head gardener, a venerable fairy, swore he could distinguish Queen Maharit in the swan with the long bridling neck: Maharit had just such a neck. Tiphaine's servants were on easier terms with death than her courtiers were. They had plucked geese, drawn grouse and blackcock, skinned eels. They had more contact with the outer world where they picked up ballads and folk stories, flew over battlefields, and observed pestilences. The mortals among them, stolen from their cradles to be court pets and playthings, and who, failing in this, had drifted into kitchen society, seldom lived into their second century, even though on their importation they were injected with an elixir of longevity, as tom kittens are gelded for domestication. Thus death was at once more real to them and less imposing. Every day their loyalty grew more fervent. They said there would never again be such a queen as Tiphaine, and had a sweepstake as to which lady (Elfindom inverts Salic law) would be the next.

In Elfindom the succession is determined by the dying ruler naming who is to come after her. If, by some misadventure, the declaration is not made, resort is had to divination. At sunrise half a dozen flying fairies are sent up to net larks—as many larks as there are eligible ladies, with a few over in case of accidents. During the morning the larks, one to each lady, are caged, ringed, and have leaden weights wired to their feet. On the stroke of noon the court officeholders—Chancellor, Astrologer, Keeper of the Records, Chamberlain, and so forth—wearing black hoods and accompanied by pages and cage bearers, go in torchlight procession to the Knowing Room, a stone cellar deep in the castle's foundations, where there is a well, said to be bottomless. One by one, the larks are taken from the cages, held above the well while the name of their lady is pronounced, and then dropped in. The weights are delicately adjusted to allow the larks a brief struggle before they drown. Its duration is noted with a stopwatch by the Court Horologer and when one by one the larks have drowned, the lark which struggled longest has won the Queenship for the lady it was dedicated to. The officials throw off their mourning hoods and go back to the Throne Room, where they kiss the hand of the new Queen and drink her health from a steaming loving-cup of spiced and honeyed wine which recovers them from the cramping chill of their ordeal in the Knowing Room.

At Elfhame, however, all this was hearsay: Tiphaine and the two Queens before her had been named. Lark patties and the loving-cup were all anyone expected.

Early in the new year the weather changed. Rain pock-marked the snow that lay in rigid shrouds over the black moorland; the swans were hidden in a web of low-lying cloud. Suddenly they reappeared; the wind had shifted into the north and there it would stay, said the head gardener who remembered Queen Maharit, through the three long months ahead—the starving months, when shrew mice feasted underground, and deer and cattle wandered slowly in search of food, eating frozen heather, rushes, dead bracken, anything that would stay the craving to munch and swallow.

It was warm in the castle, where the walls of solid earth muffled the noise of the wind. Chess tables were laid out in the gallery: matches lasted for days on end, protracted by skilful evasions, long considerings before the capture of a pawn. From the musicians' room came intermittent twangings and cockcrowings, flourishes of melody broken off, begun again, broken off again, as the court band of harps and trumpets rehearsed the funeral and coronation marches which would soon be needed. In Tiphaine's chamber the Head Archivist sat by her bed, waiting to take down her dying command about her successor. Every morning he was brought a new quill pen. Every night he was replaced by the Sub-Archivist, who had a peculiar aversion to monkeys, unfortunate but also convenient, since it kept him reliably awake.

The monkey's life depended on Tiphaine's. Royal favourites are seldom popular in court circles. The monkey had amusing tricks but dirty habits; few would put in a good word for it when Tiphaine's death plunged the court in sorrow. Nothing at all could be pled for Morel and Amanita, Tiphaine's latest importees from the mortal world. Strictly speaking, they were not changelings, for they had been bought with good fairy gold. This in itself was against them; but, however got, they would have been detested. They were twins, and orphans; their parents had been burned as heretics during the Easter festivities in Madrid, and the Brocéliande ambassador, on his way back from the Kingdom of the Gaudarramas, had stolen them from the convent of penitents to which they had been assigned. Tiphaine had bought them from him. For a while she was devoted to them—as devoted as she had been to the still remembered changeling Tiffany, who for thirteen years she had kept as her lover. Tiffany, in his mortal way, was tolerable. Morel and Amanita were intolerable from the start. They thieved, destroyed, laid booby traps, mimicked, fought each other like wildcats, infuriated the servants and tore out the Chief Harpist's hair. (Custom dictated that it be worn long and flowing as in olden days.)

For as in the kitchen loyalty grew daily more ardent and more undiscriminating, in the gallery it developed a sense of historical perspective. There had been some regrettable incidents in the past—blown up by scandal, of course; but there is no smoke without fire. Tiphaine was indiscreet in her choice of Favourites—the fault of a generous character, no doubt, but she was often sadly deluded. Admittedly, she was headstrong—but to live under the rule of a vacillating Queen would be far more exhausting. Beauty like hers could atone, for everything—or almost everything. Perhaps her complexion had been a shade, just a shade, too florid? 'You would not think that if you saw her now,' retorted the Dame of Honour.

'I suppose so, I suppose so.' The words sounded slightly perfunctory. The speaker was looking at the chessboard, where Morel and Amanita had rearranged the pieces.

By now, it was the end of March and cold as ever.

The Sub-Archivist had entered the bedchamber, seated himself, wrapped a foxskin rug over his knees, taken the virgin parchment, the day's quill pen. The monkey sat hunched before the fire. Dwindled, mute, a dirty white like old snow, Tiphaine lay among her snow-white pillows, and did not notice the replacement. She was remembering Thomas of Ercildoune.

It was May Day morning, and she rode at the head of her court to greet the established spring. Doves were cooing in the woods, larks sang overhead, her harness bells rang in tune with them. She pulled off her gloves to feel the warm air on her hands. The route took them past a hawthorn brake and there, lolling on the new-grown grass, was a handsome man—so handsome that she checked her horse's pace to have a completer look at him. She had looked at him and summed him up when suddenly she realized that he had seen her and was staring at her with intensity. *Mortals do not see fairies.*

She spurred her horse and rode fast on from the strange encounter.

That night she couldn't sleep, feeling the weight of her castle stopping her breath. An hour before sunrise she was in the stables, scolding a sleepy stableboy, had a horse saddled, and rode at a gallop to the hawthorn brake. And he was not there and he did not come. She rode on over the moor. The sun was up before she saw him walking toward her. She reined in her horse, watching him approach. Keeping her pride, she looked down on him when he stopped beside her. 'You're out early, Queen of Elfhame,' he said. She couldn't think of anything to say. He put his arms round her and lifted her from the saddle, and she toppled into his embrace like a sheaf of corn. The dew was heavy on the grass, and when they got up from their lovemaking they were wringing wet and their teeth chattered.

From then on it was as though she lived to music. To music she followed him barefoot, climbed a sycamore tree to look into a magpie's nest, made love in the rain. Once, they came to a wide rattling burn, with a green lawn on the further bank. He leaped across, and held out his hand for her to catch hold of. It was too wide a leap for her and she took to her wings. It was the first time in her life she had flown, and the sensation delighted her. She rose in another flight, curling and twirling for the pleasure and mastery of it, as a fiddler plays a cadenza. She soared higher and higher, looking down on the figure at the burnside, small as a beetle and the centre of the wide world. He beckoned her down; she dropped like a hawk and they rolled together on the grass. He made little of her flying, even less of her queenship, nothing at all of her immense seniority. Love was in the present: in the sharp taste of the rowanberries he plucked for her, in the winter night when a gale got up and whipped them to the shelter of a farm where he kindled a fire and roasted turnips on a stick, in their midnight mushroomings, in the long summer evenings when they lay on their backs too happy to move or speak, in their March-hare curvettings and cuffings. For love-gifts, he gave her acorns, birds' eggs, a rosegall because it is called the fairies' pincushion, a yellow snail shell.

It was on the day of the shell, a day in August with thunder in the air, that she asked him how it was he saw her, he who had only mortal eyes. He told how on his seventeenth birthday it had come to him that one day he would see the Queen of Elfhame, and from then on he had looked at every woman and seen through her, till Tiphaine rode past the hawthorn brake. In the same way, he said, he could see things which had not happened yet but surely would happen, and had made rhymes of them to fix them in his memory. She would live long after him and might see some of them come true.

With one ear she was listening for the first growl of thunder, with the other to Thomas' heartbeats. Suddenly they began to quarrel, she railing at him for his selfish mortality, his refusal to make trial of the elixir of longevity. He flung away from her, saying she must love him now, instantly, before the lightning broke cover. A time would come when he would grow old and she would abhor him: he could tell her that without any exercise of prophecy. The storm broke and pinned them in the present. When it moved away they built a cairn of hailstones and watched it melt in the sunshine.

The Sub-Archivist woke with a start. The Queen was stirring in her bed. She sat up and said fiercely, 'Why is no one here? It is May Day morning. I must be dressed.'

The Sub-Archivist rushed to the door and shouted, 'The Queen has spoken! She wants to be dressed.'

Courtiers and women servants crowded in, huddling on their clothes. There was a cry of 'Keep those two out,' but Morel and Amanita were already in the room. They saw their hearts' desire—the monkey. The monkey saw them. It screamed and sprang onto Tiphaine's bed, where it tried to hide under the coverlet. The Court Physician hauled it out by the tail and threw it on the floor. While the court ladies crowded round the bed, chafed the Queen's hands, held smelling salts to her nose, urged her not to excite herself, and apologized for their state of undress, Morel and Amanita seized the monkey. At first they caressed it; then they began to dispute as to which of them loved it best, whose monkey it should be. Their quarrel flared into fury and they tore it in half.

The smell of blood and entrails still hung about the room when the Sub-Archivist took up his evening watch. Everything had been restored to order: the bed straightened, the floor washed and polished, a fresh coverlet supplied.

Tiphaine had been given a composing draught, and was asleep. That deplorable business with the monkey had made no impression on her, so the Court Physician assured him. She might even be the better for it. Morel and Amanita had been strangled and their bodies thrown on the moor as a charity to crows. With every symptom so benign, they could hope she would return to her senses and name her successor.

As the virgin parchment had been crumpled during the scuffle, the Sub-Archivist was given a new one, and left to himself.

The room was so still that he could hear the sands draining through the hourglass. He had reversed it for the third time when Tiphaine opened her eyes and turned a little toward him. Trembling, he dipped his quill in ink.

'Thomas—O Thomas my love.'

He wrote this down and waited for her to say more. She grunted once or twice. The room was so still he could hear the swans circling lower and lower, and the castle beginning to resound with exclamations and protesting voices. The swans rose in a bevy, and the chant of their beating wings was high overhead, was far away, was gone.

No one at court had a name remotely resembling Thomas, so preparations for the ceremony of divination were put in hand.

3 Elphenor and Weasel

The ship had sailed barely three leagues from IJmuiden when the wind backed into the east and rose to gale force. If the captain had been an older man he would have returned to port. But he had a mistress in Lowestoft and was impatient to get to her; the following wind, the waves thwacking the stern of the boat as though it were the rump of a donkey and tearing on ahead, abetted his desires. By nightfall, the ship was wallowing broken-backed at the mercy of the storm. Her decks were awash and cluttered with shifting debris. As she lurched lower, Elphenor thrust the confidential letter inside his shirt, the wallet of mortal money deeper in his pocket, and gave his mind to keeping his wings undamaged by blows from ripped sails and the clutches of his fellow-passengers. Judging his moment, he took off just before the ship went down, and was alone with the wind.

His wings were insignificant: he flew by the force of the gale. If for a moment it slackened he dropped within earshot of the hissing waves, then was scooped up and hurled onward. In one of these descents he felt the letter, heavy with seals, fall out of his breast. It would be forever private now, and the world of Elfin unchanged by its contents. On a later descent, the wallet followed it. His clothes were torn to shreds, he was benumbed with cold, he was wet to the skin. If the wind had let him drown he would have drowned willingly, folded his useless wings and heard the waves hiss over his head. The force of the gale enclosed him, he could hardly draw breath. There was no effort of flight; the effort lay in being powerlessly and violently and almost senselessly conveyed—a fragment of existence in the drive of the storm. Once or twice he was asleep till a slackening of the wind jolted him awake with the salt smell of the sea beneath him. Wakened more forcibly, he saw a vague glimmer on the face of the water and supposed it might be the light of dawn; but he could not turn his head. He saw the staggering flight of a gull, and thought there must be land not far off.

The growing light showed a tumult of breakers ahead, close on each other's heels, devouring each other's bulk. They roared, and a pebble beach screamed back at them but the wind carried him over, and on over a dusky flat landscape that might be anywhere. So far, he had not been afraid. But when a billow of darkness reared up in front of him, and the noise of tossing trees swooped on his hearing, he was suddenly in panic, and clung to a bough like a drowning man. He had landed in a thick grove of ilex trees, planted as a windbreak. He squirmed into the shelter of their midst, and heard the wind go on without him.

Somehow, he must have fallen out of the tree without noticing. When he woke, a man with mustachios was looking down on him.

'I know what you are. You're a fairy. There were fairies all round my father's place in Suffolk. Thieving pests, they were, bad as gypsies. But I half liked them. They were company for me, being an only child. How did you get here?'

Elphenor realized that he was still wearing the visibility he had put on during the voyage as a measure against being jostled. It was too late to discard it—though the shift between visible and invisible is a press-button affair. He repressed his indignation at being classed with gypsies and explained how the ship from IJmuiden had sunk and the wind carried him on.

'From IJmuiden, you say? What happened to the rest of them?'

'They were drowned.'

'Drowned? And my new assistant was on that ship! It's one calamity after another. Sim's hanged, and Jacob Kats gets drowned. Seems as though my stars meant me to have you.'

It seemed as though Elphenor's stars were of the same mind. To tease public opinion he had studied English as his second language; he was penniless, purposeless, breakfastless, and the wind had blown his shoes off. 'If I could get you out of any difficulties—' he said.

'But I can't take you to Walsham Borealis looking like that. We'll go to old Bella, and she'll fit you out.'

Dressed in secondhand clothes too large for him and filled with pork pie, Elphenor entered Walsham Borealis riding pillion behind Master Elisha Blackbone. By then he knew he was to be assistant to a quack in several arts, including medicine, necromancy, divination, and procuring.

Hitherto, Elphenor, nephew to the Master of Ceremonies at the Elfin Court of Zuy, had spent his days in making himself polite and, as far as in his tailor lay, ornamental. Now he had to make himself useful. After the cautious pleasures of Zuy everything in this new life, from observing the planets to analyzing specimens of urine, entertained him. It was all so agreeably terminal: one finished one thing and went on to another. When Master Blackbone's clients overlapped, Elphenor placated those kept waiting by building card houses, playing the mandora, and sympathetic conversation—in which he learned a great deal that was valuable to Master Blackbone in casting horoscopes.

For his part, Master Blackbone was delighted with an assistant who was so quick to learn, so free from prejudice, and, above all, a fairy. To employ a fairy was a step up in the world. In London practice every reputable necromancer kept a spiritual appurtenance—fairy, familiar, talking toad, airy consultant. When he had accumulated the money, he would set up in London, where there is always room for another marvel. For the present, he did not mention his assistant's origin, merely stating that he was the seventh son of a seventh son, on whom any gratuities would be well bestowed. Elphenor was on the footing of an apprentice; his keep and training were sufficient wages. A less generous master would have demanded the gratuities, but Master Blackbone had his eye on a golden future, and did not care to imperil it by more than a modest scriptural tithe.

With a fairy as an assistant, he branched out into larger developments of necromancy and took to raising the Devil as a favour. The midnight hour was essential and holy ground desirable—especially disused holy ground: ruined churches, disinhabited religious foundations. The necromancer and the favoured clients would ride under cover of night to Bromholm or St Benet's in the marshes. Elphenor, flying invisibly and dressed for the part, accompanied them. At the Word of Power he became visible, pranced, menaced, and lashed his tail till the necromancer ordered him back to the pit. This was for moonlight nights. When there was no moon, he hovered invisibly, whispering blasphemies and guilty secrets. His blasphemies lacked unction; being a fairy, he did not believe in God. But the guilty secrets curdled many a good man's blood. A conscience-stricken clothier from a neighbouring parish spread such scandals about the iniquities done in Walsham Borealis that Master Blackbone thought it wisest to make off before he and Elphenor were thrown into jail.

They packed his equipment—alembics, chart of the heavens, book of spells, skull, etc—and were off before the first calm light of an April morning. As they travelled southward Elphenor counted windmills and church towers and found windmills slightly predominating. Church towers were more profitable, observed Master Blackbone. Millers were rogues and cheats, but wherever there was a church you could be sure of fools; if Elphenor were not a fairy and ignorant of Holy Writ he would know that fools are the portion appointed for the wise. But for the present they would lie a little low, shun the Devil, and keep to love philtres and salves for the itch, for which there is always a demand in spring. He talked on about the herbs they would need, and the henbane that grew round Needham in Suffolk, where he was born and played with fairies, and whither they were bound. 'What were they like?' Elphenor asked. He did not suppose Master Blackbone's fairies were anything resplendent. Master Blackbone replied that they came out of a hill and were green. Searching his memory, he added that they smelled like elderflowers. At Zuy, elderflowers were used to flavour gooseberry jam—an inelegant conserve.

At Zuy, by now, the gardeners would be bringing the tubs of myrtle out of the conservatories, his uncle would be conducting ladies along the sanded walks to admire the hyacinths, and he would be forgotten; for in good society failures are smoothly forgotten, and as nothing had resulted from the confidential letter it would be assumed he had failed to deliver it. He would never be able to go back. He did not want to. There was better entertainment in the mortal world. Mortals packed more variety into their brief lives—perhaps because they knew them to be brief. There was always something going on and being taken seriously: love, hate, ambition, plotting, fear, and all the rest of it. He had more power as a quack's assistant than ever he would have attained to in Zuy. To have a great deal of power and no concern was the life for him.

Hog's grease was a regrettable interpolation in his career. Master Blackbone based his salves and ointments on hog's grease, which he bought in a crude state from pork butchers. It was Elphenor's task to clarify it before it was tinctured with juices expressed from herbs. Wash as he might, his hands remained greasy and the smell of grease hung in his nostrils. Even the rankest-smelling herbs were a welcome change, and a bundle of water peppermint threw him into a rapture. As

Master Blackbone disliked stooping, most of the gathering fell to him.

It is a fallacy that henbane must be gathered at midnight. Sunlight raises its virtues (notably efficacious against toothache, insomnia, and lice), and to be at its best it should be gathered in the afternoon of a hot day. Elphenor was gathering it in a sloping meadow that faced south. He was working invisibly—Master Blackbone did not wish every Tom, Dick, and Harry to know what went into his preparations. Consequently, a lamb at play collided with him and knocked the basket out of his hand. As it stood astonished at this sudden shower of henbane, Elphenor seized it by the ear and cuffed it. Hearing her lamb bleat so piteously, its mother came charging to the rescue. She also collided with Elphenor and, being heavy with her winter fleece, sent him sprawling. He was still flat on his back when a girl appeared from nowhere, stooped over him, and slapped his face, hard and accurately. To assert his manly dignity he pulled her down on top of him—and saw that she was green.

She was a very pretty shade of green—a pure delicate tint, such as might have been cast on a white eggshell by the sun shining through the young foliage of a beech tree. Her hair, brows, and lashes were a darker shade; her lashes lay on her green cheek like a miniature fern frond. Her teeth were perfectly white. Her skin was so nearly transparent that the blue veins on her wrists and breasts showed through like some exquisitely marbled cheese.

As they lay in an interval of repose, she stroked the bruise beginning to show on his cheek with triumphant moans of compassion. Love did not heighten or diminish her colour. She remained precisely the same shade of green. The smell, of course, was that smell of elderflowers. It was strange to think that exactly like this she may have been one of the fairies who played with Elisha Blackbone in his bragged-of boyhood, forty, fifty years back. He pushed the speculation away, and began kissing her behind the ear, and behind the other ear, to make sure which was the more sensitive. But from that hour love struck root in him.

Eventually he asked her name. She told him it was Weasel. 'I shall call you Mustela,' he said, complying with the lover's imperative to rename the loved one; but in the main he called her Weasel. They sat up, and saw that time had gone on as usual, that dusk had fallen and the henbane begun to wilt.

When they parted, the sheep were circling gravely to the top of the hill, the small grassy hill of her tribe. He flew leisurely back, swinging the unfilled basket. The meagre show of henbane would be a pretext for going off on the morrow to a place where it grew more abundantly; he would have found such a place, but by then it was growing too dark for picking, and looking one way while flying another he had bruised his cheek against a low-growing bough. At Zuy this artless tale would not have supported a moment's scrutiny; but it would pass with a mortal, though it might be wise to substantiate it with a request for the woundwort salve. For a mortal, Master Blackbone was capable of unexpected intuitions.

The intuitions had not extended to the reverence for age and learning which induced Elphenor to sleep on a pallet to the windward. Toward morning, he dreamed that he was at the foot of the ilex; but it was Weasel who was looking down at him, and if he did not move she would slap his face. He moved, and woke. Weasel lay asleep beside him. But at the same time they were under the ilex, for the waves crashed on the screaming pebble beach and were Master Blackbone's snores.

At Zuy the English Elfindom was spoken of with admiring reprehension: its magnificence, wastefulness, and misrule, its bravado and eccentricity. The eccentricity of being green and living under a hill was not included. A hill, yes. Antiquarians talked of hill dwellings, and found evidence of them in potsherds and beads. But never, at any time, green. The beauties of Zuy, all of them white as bolsters, would have swooned at the hypothesis. Repudiating the memory of past bolsters, he looked at Weasel, curled against him like a caterpillar in a rose leaf; green as spring, fresh as spring, and completely contemporary.

She stirred, opened her eyes, and laughed.

'Shush!'

Though invisible, she might not be inaudible, and her voice was ringing and assertive as a wren's. She had come so trustingly it would be the act of an ingrate to send her away. Not being an ingrate he went with her, leaving Master Blackbone to make what he would of an early-rising assistant. They breakfasted on wild strawberries and a hunk of bread he had had the presence of mind to take from the bread crock. It was not enough for Weasel, and when they came to a brook she twitched up a handful of minnows and ate them raw. Love is a hungry emotion, and by midday he wished he had not been so conventional about the minnows. As a tactful approach, he began questioning her about life in the hill, its amenities, its daily routine. She suddenly became evasive: he would not like it; it was dull, old-fashioned, unsociable.

'All the same, I should like to visit it. I have never been inside a hill.'

'No! You can't come. It's impossible. They'd set on you, you'd be driven out. *You're not green.*'

Etiquette.

'Don't you understand?'

'I was wondering what they would do to you if they found out where you woke this morning.'

'Oh, that! They'd have to put up with it. Green folk don't draw green blood. But they'd tear *you* in pieces.'

'It's the same where I come from. If I took you to Zuy, they might be rather politer, but they'd never forgive you for being green. But I won't take you, Weasel. We'll stay in Suffolk. And if it rains and rains and rains—"

'I don't mind rain—'

'We'll find a warm, dry badger sett.'

They escaped into childishness and were happy again, with a sharpened happiness because for a moment they had so nearly touched despair.

As summer became midsummer, and the elder blossom outlasted the wild roses and faded in its turn till the only true elderflower scent came from her, and the next full moon had a broader face and shone on cocks of hay in silvery fields, they settled into an unhurried love and strolled from day to day as through a familiar landscape. By now they were seldom hungry, for there was a large crop of mushrooms, and Elphenor put more system into his attendances on Master Blackbone, breakfasting soundly and visibly while conveying mouthfuls to the invisible Weasel (it was for the breakfasts that they slept there). Being young and perfectly happy and pledged to love each other till the remote end of their days, they naturally talked of death and discussed how to contrive that neither should survive the other. Elphenor favoured being struck by lightning as they lay in each other's arms, but Weasel was terrified by thunder—she winced and covered her ears at the slightest distant rumble—and though he talked soothingly of the electric fluid and told her of recent experiments with amber and a couple of silk stockings, one black, one white, she refused to die by lightning stroke.

And Master Blackbone, scarcely able to believe his ears, madly casting horoscopes and invoking the goddess Fortuna, increasingly tolerant of Elphenor's inattention, patiently compounding his salves unassisted, smiling on the disappearances from his larder, was day after day, night after night, more sure of his surmise—till convinced of his amazing good fortune he fell into the melancholy of not knowing what best to do about it, whether to grasp fame single-handed or call in the help of an expert and self-effacingly retire on the profits. He wrote a letter to an old friend. Elphenor was not entrusted with this letter, but he knew it had been written and was directed to London. Weasel was sure Master Blackbone was up to no good—she had detested him at first sight. They decided to keep a watch on him. But their watch was desultory, and the stranger was already sitting in Master Blackbone's lodging and conversing with him when they flew in and perched on a beam.

The stranger was a stout man with a careworn expression. Master Blackbone was talking in his best procuring voice.

'It's a Golconda, an absolute Golconda! A pair of them, young, in perfect condition. Any manager would snap at them. But I have kept it dark till now. I wanted you to have the first option.'

'Thanks, I'm sure,' said the stranger. 'But it's taking a considerable chance.'

'Oh no, it isn't. People would flock to see them. You could double the charges—in fact you should, for it's something unique—and there wouldn't be an empty seat in the house. Besides, it's a scientific rarity. You'd have all the illuminati. Nobs from the colleges. Ladies of fashion. Royal patronage.'

The stranger said he didn't like buying pigs in pokes.

'But I give you my word. A brace of fairies—lovely, young, amorous fairies. Your fortune would be made.'

'How much do you want?'

'Two-thirds of the takings. You can't say that's exorbitant. Not two-thirds of the profits, mind. Two-thirds of the takings and a written agreement.'

The stranger repeated that he didn't like buying pigs in pokes, the more so when he had no warrant the pigs were within.

'Wait till tonight! They come every night and cuddle on that pallet there. They trust me like a father. Wait till they're asleep and throw a net over them, and they're yours.'

'But when I've got them to London, suppose they are awkward, and won't perform? People aren't going to pay for what they can't see. How can I be sure they'll be visible?'

Master Blackbone said there were ways and means, as with performing animals.

'Come, Weasel. We'll be off.'

The voice was right overhead, loud and clear. Some cobwebs drifted down.

Elphenor and Weasel were too pleased with themselves to think beyond the moment. They had turned habitually toward their usual haunts and were dabbling their feet in the brook before it occurred to Elphenor that they had no reason to stay in the neighbourhood and good reason to go elsewhere. Weasel's relations would murder him because he was not green, Master Blackbone designed to sell them because they were fairies. Master Blackbone might have further designs: he was a necromancer, though a poor one; it would be prudent to get beyond his magic circle. Elphenor had congratulated himself on leaving prudence behind at Zuy. Now it reasserted itself and had its charm. Prudence had no charm whatsoever for Weasel; it was only by representing the move as reckless that he persuaded her to make it.

With the world before them, he flew up for a survey and caught sight of the sea, looking as if ships would not melt in its mouth—which rather weakened the effect of his previous narrative of the journey from IJmuiden to the ilexes. Following the coastline they came to Great Yarmouth, where they spent several weeks. It was ideal for their vagrant purposes, full of vigorous, cheerful people, with food to be had for the taking—hot pies and winkles in the marketplace, herring on the quayside where the fishing boats unloaded.

The air was rough and cold, and he stole a pair of shipboy's trousers and a knitted muffler for Weasel from a marine store near the Custom House. He was sorry to leave this kind place. But Weasel showed such a strong inclination to go to sea, and found it so amusing to flaunt her trousers on the quayside and startle her admirers with her green face, that she was becoming notorious, and he was afraid that Master Blackbone might hear of her. From Yarmouth they flew inland, steering their course by church towers. Where there is a church tower you can be sure of fools, Master Blackbone had said. True enough; but Elphenor tired of thieving— though it called for more skill in villages—and he thought he would try turning an honest penny for a change. By now he was so coarsened and brown-handed that he could pass as a labouring man. In one place he sacked potatoes, in another baled reeds for thatching. At a village called Scottow, where the sexton had rheumatism, he dug a grave. Honest-pennying was no pleasure to Weasel who had to hang about invisibly, passing the time with shrivelled blackberries. In these rustic places which had never seen a circus or an Indian peddler, her lovely green face would have brought stones rattling on their heels.

Winter came late that year and stealthily, but the nights were cold. Nights were never cold in Suffolk, she said. He knew this was due to the steady temperature under the hill, but hoping all the same she might be right he turned southward. He had earned more than enough to pay for a night at an inn. At Bury St Edmunds he bought her a cloak with a deep hood, and telling her to pull the hood well forward and keep close to his heels he went at dusk to a respectable inn and hired the best bedroom they had. All went well, except that they seemed to look at him doubtfully. In his anxiety to control the situation he had reverted to his upper-class manner, which his clothes did not match with. The four-poster bed was so comfortable that he hired the room for a second night, telling the chambermaid his wife had a headache and must not be disturbed. It was certainly an elopement, she reported; even before she had left the room, the little gentleman had parted the bed curtains and climbed in beside the lady. After the second night there was no more money.

They left on foot, and continued to walk, for there was a shifting, drizzling fog which made it difficult to keep each other in sight if they flew. Once again they stole a dinner, but it was so inadequate that Elphenor decided to try begging. He was rehearsing a beggar's whine when they saw a ruddy glow through the fog and heard a hammer ring on an anvil. Weasel as usual clapped her hands to her ears; but when they came to a wayside forge the warmth persuaded her to follow Elphenor, who went in shivering ostentatiously and asked if he and his wife could stand near the blaze: they would not get in the way, they would not stay long. The blacksmith was shaping horseshoes. He nodded, and went on with his work. Elphenor was preparing another whine when the blacksmith remarked it was no day to be out, and encouraged Weasel, who stood in the doorway, to come nearer the fire.

'Poor soul, she could do with a little kindness,' said Elphenor. 'And we haven't met with much of it today. We passed an inn, farther back' —it was there they had stolen the heel of a Suffolk cheese—'but they said they had no room for us.'

Weasel interrupted. 'What's that black thing ahead, that keeps on showing and going?'

The blacksmith pulled his forelock. 'Madam. That's the church.'

They thanked him and went away, Elphenor thinking he must learn to beg more feelingly. The blacksmith stood looking after them. At this very time of year, too. He wished he had not let slip the opportunity of a Hail Mary not likely to come his way again.

The brief December day was closing when they came to the church. The south porch, large as a room, was sheltered from the wind, and they sat there, huddled in Weasel's cloak. 'We can't sleep here,' Elphenor said. For all that, he got up and tried the church door. It was locked. He immediately determined to get in by a window. They flew round the church, fingering the cold panes of glass, and had almost completed their round and seen the great bulk of the tower threatening down on them, when Weasel heard a clatter overhead. It came from one of the clerestory windows, where a missing pane had been replaced by a shutter. They wrenched the shutter open, and flew in, and circled downward through darkness, and stood on a flagstone pavement. Outlined against a window was a tall structure with a peak. Fingering it, they found it was wood, carved, and swelling out of a stem like a goblet. A railed flight of steps half encircled the stem. They mounted the steps and found themselves in the goblet. It was like an octagonal cupboard, minus a top but carpeted. By curling round each other, there would be room to lie down. The smell of wood gave them a sense of security, and they spent the night in the pulpit.

He woke to the sound of Weasel laughing. Daylight was streaming in, and Weasel was flitting about the roof, laughing at the wooden figures that supported the crossbeams—carved imitations of fairies, twelve foot high, with outstretched turkey wings and gaunt faces, each uglier than the last. 'So that's what they think we're like,' she said. 'And look at *her!*' She pointed to the fairy above the pulpit, struggling with a trumpet.

Exploring at floor level, Elphenor read the Ten Commandments, and found half a bottle of wine and some lozenges. It would pass for a breakfast; later, he would stroll into the village and see what could be got from there. While he was being raised as the Devil at Walsham Borealis, he had learned some facts about the Church of England, one of them that the reigning monarch, symbolically represented as a lion and a unicorn, is worshipped noisily on one day of the week and that for the rest of the week churches are unmolested. There was much to be said for spending the winter here. The building was windproof and weatherproof, Weasel was delighted with it, and, for himself, he found its loftiness and spaciousness congenial, as though he were back in Zuy—a Zuy improved by a total removal of its inhabitants. He had opened a little door and discovered a winding stone stairway behind it when his confidence in Church of England weekdays was shaken by the entrance of two women with brooms and buckets. He beckoned to Weasel, snatched her cloak from the pulpit, and preceded her up the winding stairs, holding the bottle and the lozenges. The steps were worn; there was a dead crow on one of them. They groped their way up into darkness, then into light; a window showed a landing and a door open on a small room where some ropes dangled from the ceiling. Weasel seized a rope and gave it a tug, and would have tugged at it more energetically if Elphenor had not intervened, promising that when the women had gone away she could tug to her heart's content. Looking out of the cobwebbed window, he saw the churchyard far below and realized they must be a long way up the tower. But the steps wound on into another darkness and a dimmer lightness, and to another landing and another door open on another room. This room had louvred windows high up in the wall, and most of its floor space was taken up by a frame supporting eight bells, four of them upside down with their clappers lolling in their iron mouths. This was the bell chamber, he explained. The ropes went from the bells into the room below, which was the ringing chamber. There was a similar tower near Zuy; mortals thought highly of it, and his tutor had taken him to see it.

Weasel began to stroke one of the bells. As though she were caressing some savage sleeping animal, it presently responded with a noise between a soft growl and a purr. Elphenor stroked another. It answered at a different pitch, deeper and harsher, as though it were a more savage animal. But they were hungry. The bells could wait. The light from the louvred windows flickered between bright and sombre as the wind tossed the clouds. It was blowing up for a storm.

They would be out of the wind tonight and for many nights to come. January is a dying season, there would be graves to dig, and with luck and management, thought Elphenor, he might earn a livelihood and be a friend to sextons here and around. Weasel would spare crumbs from the bread he earned, scatter them for birds, catch the birds, pluck and eat them: she still preferred raw food, with the life still lively in it. On Sundays, she said, they would get their week's provisions; with everybody making a noise in church, stealing would be child's play. The pulpit would be the better for a pillow, and she could soon collect enough feathers for a pillow, for a feather mattress even: one can always twitch a pillowcase from the washing line. The wine had gone to their heads; they outbid each other with grand plans of how they would live in the church, and laughed them down, and imagined more. They would polish the wooden fairies' noses till they shone like drunkard's noses; they would grow water-cresses in the font; Elphenor would tell the complete story of his life before they met. Let him begin now! Was he born with a hook nose and red hair? He began, obediently and prosily. Weasel clamped her eyes open, and suppressed yawns. He lost the thread of his narrative. Drowsy with wine, they fell asleep.

He woke to two appalling sounds. Weasel screaming with terror, a clash of metal. The bell ringers had come to practise their Christmas peal, and prefaced it by sounding all the bells at once. The echo was heavy on the air as they began to ring a set of changes, first the scale descending evenly to the whack of the tenor bell, then in patterned steps to the same battle-axe blow. The pattern altered; the tenor bell sounded midway, jolting an arbitrary finality into the regular measure of eight. With each change of position the tenor bell accumulated a more threatening insistency, and the other bells shifted round it like a baaing flock of sheep.

Weasel cowered in Elphenor's arms. She had no strength left to scream with; she could only tremble before the impact of the next flailing blow. He felt his senses coming adrift. The booming echo was a darkness on his sight through which he saw the bells in their frame heaving and evading, evading and heaving, under a dark sky. The implacable assault of the changing changes pursued him as the waves had pursued at the boat from IJmuiden. But here there was no escape, for it was he who wallowed broken-backed at the mercy of the storm. Weasel lay in his arms like something at a distance. He felt his protectiveness, his compassion, ebbing away; he watched her with a bloodless, skeleton love. She still trembled, but in a disjointed way, as though she were falling to pieces.

He saw the lovely green fade out of her face. 'My darling,' he said, 'death by lightning would have been easier.' He could not hear himself speak.

The frost lasted on into mid-March. No one went to the bell chamber till the carpenter came to mend the louvres in April. The two bodies, one bowed over the other, had fallen into decay. No one could account for them, or for curious weightless fragments of a substance rather like sheet gelatine which the wind had scattered over the floor. They were buried in the same grave. Because of their small stature and light bones they were entered in the Register of Burials as *Two Stranger Children*.

4 The Blameless Triangle

Wirre Gedanken was a small Elfin Kingdom, never of any importance and now extinct. In the Austrian section of the Countess Morphy's 'Recipes of all Nations', *Wirre Gedanken* (translated 'Troubled Thoughts') designates a kind of fried bun; but there does not seem to be any historical connection. The Castle of Wirre Gedanken was situated in a gloomy crevice of the Harz Mountains. As it lay beneath one of the main routes to the Walpurgisnacht Festival on the Brocken, the excited screamings and hallooings of witches and warlocks flying overhead was a recurrent nuisance and a recurrent subject of conversation. There was also the plight of the marmots to be deplored. The great bonfires burned so hotly that the snow melted and seeped into the marmot burrows, prematurely wakening the harmless little animals to die of hunger and pneumonia. So Queen Balsamine declared. Compassion for marmots was the soft spot in a character otherwise so irritable and arbitrary that Balsamine survives in English folklore of the nineteenth century as the Red Queen. The castle resounded with the weeping of maid-servants, the moaning of bower-women, the howls of pages under the lash. The Headsman was always at the ready—though in fact few executions took place, as Balsamine's attention was constantly diverted to a new offender and the Headsman went in fear of being blamed for striking off the wrong head. He drew a large salary and liked his comforts.

One day in early spring the Queen was bitten by a mouse.

The result was totally unforeseen. Exhausted by the cares of sovereignty, Balsamine decided to go for a rest cure to Bad Nixenbach, the fashionable Elfin health resort. The greater part of the court went with her, for she did not wish to travel like a nobody. Those she discarded remained at Wirre Gedanken, with a small staff and on the equivalent of board wages.

The discards were named Ludo, Moor, Tinkel, Nimmerlein, and Banian. Ludo was her Consort. Moor, Tinkel, and Nimmerlein had been at various times Royal Favourites. All had proved disappointments and were now middle-aged. Banian was young and slender, and had been chosen to make one of her party till at the last moment he became a disappointment by coming out in an anxiety rash.

For the first days after Balsamine's departure the unwonted quiet kept them awake all night. But by degrees they gained confidence and began to converse. Banian, being young, was the first to speak. His anxiety rash had disappeared, and he remarked on the beauty of the spring. 'The boy chirps,' commented Moor to Nimmerlein. Nimmerlein replied that Banian's mind needed stimulating. The next day he asked him if he thought marmots were happy. If so, why? If not, why not? In either case, what reasons had he for thinking so? Etc. Stimulated by this Socratic scrabbling, Banian objected that he was not a marmot. At this, the others joined in. Would he like to be a marmot? How was he so sure he was not a marmot? What is it in Elfins which distinguishes them from marmots? Banian was half out with the marmot's capacity to sleep throughout the winter when they all fell on him with the capacities of reason and speculation. By nightfall Banian had learned a quantity of new words and longed to use them.

One of the words was 'prolegomena'. Another was 'symposium'. 'Shall we have another little symposium?' Ludo would ask—tenderly, as though offering daisies to a lamb. It was delightful to be able to talk so freely, at such leisure, without fear of rebuke or contradiction or decapitation. They all felt this, but Ludo felt it most, for he was the longest sufferer among them.

'I wish we could make a regular thing of it,' he said. 'Nothing formal. Just to meet and exchange ideas.'

Moor said such meetings might be taken for plotting.

'Well, just to meet and meditate together.'

'What about?' asked Nimmerlein.

Anticipating Goethe, Ludo replied, 'Goodness, and truth, and the beautiful.'

'Then we shall soon be at each other's throats,' said Tinkel, who in his youth had invisibly attended a conclave of bishops.

Banian said that if they just meditated, in time they might hit on something to meditate about.

The wish to meditate took hold of them. In the mortal world there were whole religious communities who devoted their lives to meditation. But even in monasteries, the travelled Tinkel objected, there is dissension, and far too much singing. They wanted something quieter. Discussing what it was they wanted, they found that what they essentially and unanimously wanted was to get away from Wirre Gedanken. Where to, and what to meditate on, would resolve itself later. Not to know where they were going, Moor pointed out, was a positive advantage. One cannot be fetched back from the indeterminate. The chance of being found by accident would be at least a hundred to one, increasing according to the square of the distance they travelled. To insure the indeterminate, they must leave as unobtrusively as possible. Before dawn, said Banian. With only a valet apiece, added Ludo. And leave packing till the night before, said Nimmerlein.

As one strips an artichoke, they simplified their departure till they reduced it to the anonymity of leaving by air, sans valets, and each carrying the barest necessities in a small portmanteau. Tinkel was the only one of them who had any experience of flying. Fairies in the Almanach are strictly brought up not to use their wings, which is servile and *infra dig*. Tinkel, however, though as well imbedded in the Almanach, as the rest of them, had resorted to flying during his *Wanderjahr*, sacrificing dignity to the pursuit of experience. He assured them that it was really quite easy and that they would find themselves doing it by nature, once they had made the leap. It was just a question of unfolding one's wings—a brief effort but not more than dragonflies accomplish when they begin their dragonfly life. He led them to a secluded meadow to make experimental flights. It took them much longer to decide what they would carry in their portmanteaux, but at last this was settled, and on a May morning they took off from the tallest tower of the castle and headed southeast, Tinkel in the lead.

A fairy's wings are small but constructed for a very high velocity. During the experimental flights across the meadow only about thirty per cent of full velocity had been attained. As the Wirre Gedanken party gathered speed, they began to feel dizzy and rather sick. They saw the landscape reel and tumble beneath them, and felt it would be impossible to alight on it. This was followed by a feeling that it would be impossible to fly on much longer. When Tinkel guided them down onto an upland pasture, they alighted clumsily but painlessly, and sat staring about them like children awakening in a strange bed. They ate some sausage, and fell asleep. Waking several hours later, they felt too stiff and exhausted to fly further, and spent the night in a haystack.

To Banian, opening his morning eyes on Nimmerlein sparkling with dew, the haystack seemed the very place they wanted, and he prepared himself for days and days of meditation. But his elders meant to fly on. Not till the afternoon of the third day did they find a shelter which fitted their requirements. It was a disused chapel on a lonely hillside with a brook near by. It had a sound tiled roof and narrow windows, many of them still glazed. It was dirty and cluttered with Christian odds and ends, but among the litter were some moth-eaten altar and pulpit cushions, a pitcher, and a useful font. A furry bell rope hung from a single bell. Tidied up, and cleared of its cobwebs, the chapel would make a very adequate place to meditate in.

They had unpacked their portmanteaux and were allotting cushions when they heard voices and the twang of zithers. A band of gipsy musicians was coming up the track in a very accustomed manner. In a very accustomed manner they crowded into the chapel, propped their instruments against the wall, gave the bell rope a friendly tweak, collected the cushions, and settled themselves on and around the altar. The men lit up their pipes. Some of the women unpacked baskets and brought out loaves of bread, cooked chickens, salami, and flasks of wine, while others laid and kindled a wood fire. As the fire gathered heart, an iron pot was placed on it.

The fairies watched all this in impotent despair. Court life at Wirre Gedanken had unfitted them for self-assertion. At Wirre Gedanken their tribulations had been blunted by large and regular meals. Now they were extremely hungry, for the last remains of their sausage had been honourably shared among them at breakfast. The lid was lifted from the iron pot and its contents stirred. An invigorating smell arose. Before the lid had been replaced, Banian snatched out a carrot and flew off, licking his scorched fingers. Meanwhile the loaves had been sliced, the cold chickens dismembered. Hovering invisible above the altar, Ludo, Moor, Tinkel, Nimmerlein, and Banian shared the gipsies' meal. Under the circumstances, the ordinary conventions of polite table manners were hard to keep up. At first, they helped themselves to undistributed bits—fragments which would not be missed. Before long, they were filching from the very hands of their hosts. A small irate gipsy turned on his neighbour, accusing him of snatching a drumstick from between his jaws. Anything in a fairy's possession partakes of his invisibility, so while the two men wrangled, Nimmerlein smiled down on them with his mouth full, gently waving the drumstick. When it was stripped, he placed it behind the accused man's ear, where its coquettish appearance was seen as an insult by the accuser. Knives were drawn, a general quarrel seemed imminent till the lid was lifted from the iron pot, the pot lifted from the fire. Here the gipsies had less to contend with, for their fingers were thicker-skinned. The fairies withdrew to finish up the salami and the wine. Seeing their hosts guzzling so complacently, they began to pinch them—at first playfully, then with intention and a plan of campaign. Pinched here, nipped there, attacked on all sides, the gipsies snatched up their belongings and made off, followed by Moor, who hurled himself on the percussion player and stole his triangle.

'What's that for?' asked Banian, who was daily growing less respectful. 'Are you going to play on it?'

Moor replied that tomorrow they would begin to meditate on it.

Ludo's mother had been pietistic, and there was a sort of Christian proverb he remembered her quoting, to the effect that one must pass through many tribulations to enter the Kingdom of Heaven. They had certainly been through tribulations—hunger and thirst, going unshaved, sleeping in a haystack, evicting gipsies (a rather vulgar affair, he had not altogether enjoyed it). But now they would enter the realm of meditation.

Moor attached the triangle to a bough of a wild cherry tree. It glittered in the morning sun. He said, 'Observe it,' and they did so. After a pause, Moor continued, 'You will have observed that it has three sides, and that each side is of equal length. In other words, it is an equilateral triangle. What ideas spring to our minds? Equality. Therefore, serenity. Indifference to time and place. Again, serenity. Total reversibility. Whichever way up, it is always the same. Again, serenity. Indisputability. It cannot be confuted. Serenity, again. Positive abstraction. It is passionless, purposeless, involuntary, inexpressive. No blame can be attached to it. It exists by being itself; or, in philosophic terms, it is the *Ding an sich*. In a word, serenity.' To illustrate his words, Moor moved the triangle one point round, and stepped back, saying, 'You see? Serenity.'

Tinkel had been showing dissatisfaction. Now he remarked, 'That's all very well, my good Moor. But why pick on a triangle? A square will do as well. With all this three-sidedness, we shall be meditating on the Trinity before we know what's what. And where's your serenity then?'

A rather acrimonious discussion followed, during which Nimmerlein was vehemently partisan about the circle. It was allayed by Ludo saying that of all Christian views of the Godhead, which in any case did not concern them, the Trinity was surely the least offensive; and that as Moor had so cleverly got the triangle they had best stick to it.

The Brotherhood of the Blameless Triangle, as they decided to call themselves, fell into a regular pattern of life. In the morning, Moor expounded, going deeper and deeper into the inexhaustible charms of equilaterality, listing other triangular possibilities only to reject them, and promising that later on he would delight his companions with the twelfth root of two. After their midday meal, they meditated. At sundown, an *Abendmusik* on the triangle and the bell was performed by Banian and Nimmerlein. For sustenance they depended on the bosom of Nature, except for bread, which Nature does not naturally supply, and wine, cheese, and butter, where Nature has to be processed. They discovered there was a village shop within easy flying distance. Approaching it, Nimmerlein put on visibility and entered with a friendly 'Good day.' The first purchases were paid for in mortal currency. Every Elfin Kingdom keeps a gold reserve. The coffers of Wirre Gedanken were exceptionally well filled, and Tinkel had sensibly brought away a quantity of specie in his portmanteau. Fairy gold, as everybody knows, is only operative in Elfin; received by mortals, it turns into withered leaves by the morrow. Having established creditability by his first payment, Nimmerlein bought on account. For the rest, the bosom of Nature supplied watercress, wild garlic, thyme, and quantities of hares and rabbits. As Banian was the nimblest flier among them, he was huntsman. He also skinned and paunched. Once or twice they found a lost lamb. Nimmerlein cooked. The font made an admirable wine cooler. As none of them had ever had to shave himself, they let their beards grow, and looked increasingly unworldly—except for Banian, whose beard, being new, unthwarted, and silky, looked pastoral.

After that little set-to about the Trinity, Moor was anxious to avoid touching on any extra-geometrical aspect of geometry. The square had passed without remark; he managed to throw a veil over the rhomboid. The hexagon followed. By now, it was past midsummer, the stork's nest on the chapel roof had brisk young birds in it, and the Brotherhood sat in the chapel for coolness' sake. Moor was deducing the hexagon from the triangle when Ludo, hitherto his most silent and enlightened listener, interrupted with beehives. Moor assented in parenthesis (he hoped it was in parenthesis) that bees are a model community. But the breach had been made. In rushed materialism, saying, What about wasps? Moor disliked wasps and had never studied their architecture. Searching his memory, all he could recall was a gooseberry bush with a shapeless object, rather like an old grey sock, hanging in it. Living in non-geometrical surroundings, he said, wasps were necessarily disorganized and inharmonious. He was hoping to get back to the symmetry of the hexagon when Nimmerlein exclaimed, 'There's a man coming up the hill.

He's dressed in black and he's got a boy with him.'

Ludo said that if the man came into the chapel to shelter from the heat it would be uncivil to molest him.

The man in black toiling toward them was a priest, the boy was his acolyte. The gipsies' account of how they had been driven out of the chapel had spread through the countryside. Disused chapels are often taken over by demons. The good man was coming to exorcize them.

He entered the chapel. The boy staggered in after him. The bag, holding the appropriate accessories, was heavy.

The priest wiped the sweat from his tonsure, took a piece of chalk from the pocket of his soutane and drew a pentagram on the floor. Standing within it, he began to command and conjure Satan and his demons to go away.

For a man so out of breath he spoke loudly and well. Where his memory failed him (exorcism is a long ritual) the acolyte, holding the service book, prompted him, as well as speaking the responses. The fairies watched the performance with mild amusement, even a certain tenderness. The poor old man had come a long way, in great heat, to recite an interminable deal of Latin, all with good intentions and to no purpose. Ludo whispered to Moor, 'Do you think we ought to tip him?'

The exorcist paused. His expression was that of a workman who has made a good job of it and is about to put on the finishing touches. He turned to the acolyte, who produced a large bottle, uncorked it, and poured water into a bowl. He then handed the exorcist a sizable whisk. The exorcist dipped the whisk in the water and sprinkled the acolyte, who murmured a few words of thanks; he then proceeded to sprinkle everything in sight. His gestures grew larger and more commanding, he charged the whisk ever more amply, he was plainly enjoying himself. Though it was only holy water, the fairies tried to keep out of its way. Banian sneezed. Hearing the sneeze, the exorcist whisked vehemently in its direction. Banian dodged, but Tinkel received a full charge of salt and water in the eye. He seized the exorcist and began to shake him. The exorcist gasped out something to the effect that Satan had no power, and Tinkel went on shaking him. The exorcist turned blue in the face, his eyes protruded, his tongue hung out, he went limp as a rag doll. When Tinkel let go of him, he slumped to the floor, hiccupped convulsively, and died. The acolyte fled, screaming.

It was felt that Tinkel had gone rather too far, even for a convinced rationalist.

As a corpse, the priest seemed much larger. It was a problem how to dispose of him. The hillside was smooth as an apple, not a pit or gully in it. They had a scruple about dumping him in the brook, where his corruption would poison the water. Cremation was out of the question; it was hard enough to find sufficient fuel to cook on. So they must dig a grave. Spades would be needed, and could be bought in the village; but if the acolyte were gossiping, buying spades might look suspicious. Five pairs of willing hands, said Moor, should be enough to scrape a hole. He was too sanguine. They rose at dawn to scrape. By midday their nails were worn to the quick and the hole was negligible. They looked at their chapel, so calm till this mortal incursion. It would always be dear to their hearts, but they must leave it. A quick farewell is best. They packed and by dusk they were gone.

They flew by the stars, which during their stay had disconcertingly shifted position. In any case, they were uncertain where to go. Nimmerlein wanted a respite from cooking; they all felt the need for a spell of civilized comfort: to be visible guests in a reputable inn would have suited them nicely, if it had not been for the currency question. Apart from the first down payment at the village shop their mortal capital was intact. They could not hope to keep up such economy at an inn. There was an Elfin Kingdom in Styria which Tinkel favoured. Its Queen, so he had heard, was high-flown and romantic, the very person to welcome an anonymous band of brothers—for as such, Ludo insisted, they must travel. Their shabbiness and shagginess could be accounted for by explaining they were carrying out a geological survey, a survey so confidential that their incognito did not allow them attendants. A fortnight at Dreiviertelstein, soft beds, mountain air, manicure, would benefit them all. They had repudiated court life but not its amenities. Ludo refused to be benefited. Sooner or later, he said, the cat would be out of the bag. There would be a reference to Wirre Gedanken; one or the other of them would inadvertently address him as Your Royal Highness. Balsaminc had cousins in every court. They would be traced; he would be done for. Like all meek characters, Ludo had a will of iron. They gave in.

From Vienna, where they stayed at a cheap inn in the suburbs, they followed the course of the Danube, alighting whenever the landscape below looked promising. Sometimes the landscape was obliterated by smoke and they heard cannon fire. Once, alighting in a park, they found a burned-out mansion and a row of impaled cadavers tottering on a fence. Still following the Danube, they flew on and saw the country-side grow calm, well tilled, prosperous, coloured by the blue-green of poppy fields. To the south, they saw a mountain range. Among the foothills at its base was a small white building, too tall for a farm, too plain and unencumbered to be a church or castle. Descending, they saw it had pillars and a pediment. In place of their disused chapel they had found a forsaken temple. As they mounted the steps, a large snake reared its head and looked at them with a flat glittering eye, but did not move away. 'A temple to Aesculapius!' said Tinkel. Even Tinkel's clever voice was awed.

They sat down and began rubbing their legs to restore circulation, impaired by so many days of flying. Before them stretched a vast undulating landscape of tillage, punctuated by lines of cypresses. The air was clear as crystal; every detail was distinct and in perfect perspective: it was as though they were looking at an enormous chessboard. Bands of women were at work in the fields. They moved slowly and sang in mournful voices. Here and there plumes of bluish smoke rose from heaps of smouldering trash or low-roofed dwellings. In the middle distance the roofs gathered together into a little town. Water was led through the fields in chessboard channels, with willows and mulberries growing alongside. The clank of a wind pump came at long intervals. Here was the serenity, the benign serenity, Moor had promised them in his first talk on the triangle, a serenity which had evaded them till now. The sun touched the horizon and a distant yelling broke the silence. The air was so clear that they could see the minute shape of a man gesticulating from the top of a slender tower. A prisoner, they supposed, calling for help. The women working in the fields paid no attention and presently he gave up. Dusk gathered, the noises of dusk arose: croaking frogs, cicadas, nightingales, then an owl. It was too dark to unpack. They pillowed their heads on their portmanteaux and fell asleep. Sunrise woke them. The prisoner on the tower was renewing his yells, poor creature! When they had heard him yelling for several days, always at the same pitch and always at the rise and set of sun, they concluded he was clockwork.

They breakfasted on figs and goat's milk. They found the milk in a bowl on the steps, and drank it gratefully, without much considering whether the snake had a prior claim to it. Old Sofia, coming for her bowl, noticed it had been licked clean. The next morning she brought a larger bowl; and when that, too, had been licked clean, she brought her largest bowl, with so much milk in it that they could leave some for the snake. She came so furtively that all they knew of her was the milk. Many years before, her daughter had lain dying of marsh fever. In desperation, Sofia remembered a proscribed belief, and went to the temple to implore the holy serpent. He listened, and she had been grateful ever since—though privily; for the local church was oppressed and therefore without mercy for backsliders. One morning, having heard the God in his empty temple playing a wind instrument, she bought a loaf of rye bread and two eggs.

The loaf was very welcome to the Brotherhood of the Blameless Triangle, who till now had depended on what they could glean out of the stubble. Eggs were easier, for hens lay astray. They found provisioning harder in this bounteous landscape than on the bare hillside, though that, said Moor, was because they had not got into the way of it. For himself, he was looking forward to cheroots: a tobacco crop was being harvested; he had joined the harvesters and had leaves drying on the temple floor. Other crops were rye, maize, poppies, tomatoes, and pumpkins. Workers were busy in the fields, with overseers among them, and at night the overseers kept watch, sitting in raised seats, each with a dog beside him. Invisibility could make light of such obstacles; but since that misadventure with the exorcist they had lost their innocence and stole halfheartedly, hampered by recollection of public opinion. Nimmerlein flew back from the town saying it was no pleasure to shop there. The shopkeepers were a glum lot, and insisted on being paid on the nail, though other customers, with knives in their waistcloths and chewing sweetmeats, took the best of everything and swaggered away with never a word of payment. They were gendarmes, he supposed; for he had seen them marching ahead of a fat yellow person in a chariot, who wore a jewelled turban and joggled a boy on his knee. It was all a sad contrast to the village shop, so friendly and obliging, and he saw no hope of establishing an account.

But they were too happy to dwell on these hardships. It was a dreamy, complacent happiness, as if they breathed it in from the warm poppy fields. The triangle hung from a beam, Banian played a flute he had nicked from an overseer, Moor rustled his dry leaves, and in the mornings there was the milk.

It was still rich autumn when the cranes came flying from the north. They flew in vast flocks, one flock following another, clamouring as if they were riding on broomsticks to a Walpurgisnacht. A few days later, it began to rain.

It rained for a week—a steady, drenching rain that washed the colour from the fields. When it left off, the sky was a different blue and the mountains seemed to have closed in on the plain. And there was no more milk. The snake had died, weakened by malnutrition, and Sofia had come on the body, which Tinkel had thrown into some bushes. Hearing her wailing, they hoped it wasn't wolves. They missed the milk badly, the more so since the weather had grown bitterly cold. Men came into the fields with teams of oxen, ploughing in the remains of the summer's crops. They wore sheepskin coats and cloth leggings. Nimmerlein was sent to the town to buy winter outfits. He went against his will, and returned saying that five sheepskin coats would be more than he could carry and that the shopman refused to believe that five coats were wanted by one man, though he had held up five fingers. They must go in a body.

At the entrance to the town they put on visibility. It made them no warmer, and impaired their self-esteem. They had grown accustomed to looking like tramps, but not to being looked at as such. Their shoes were down at heel, their knuckles dirty, their noses red. They walked on dejectedly till a familiar sound put heart into them. It was the note of a triangle, briskly dominating a band of drums and bagpipes. Round the corner came the band, and after the band a mounted escort and a chariot. The habit of court life mastered them, they drew themselves up and stood in a row, bowing to the fat yellow man who lounged in the chariot. He still had the boy on his knee but held him inattentively. Seeing them, he sat up and stared sharply. They effaced themselves in the crowd and went on to the outfitters. When they learned the price of the sheepskin coats they were appalled. If they had not already put them on, they might have refused to buy. But the warmth, and even the smell of mutton fat, was so restorative that they paid down the money and left the shop, looking much like everyone else in the street. Outside the gates, they put their coats on back to front, so as to free their wings, and flew back to the temple.

No milk, no resources, no leggings (leggings were too expensive—but they were beginning to feel the lack of them for the temple was drafty), no spiders (to supply the example of perseverance when all seems lost), a handful of horse beans, and a frost-bitten pumpkin: it was a stern moment. Nimmerlein emptied the purse. There was even less in it than they supposed, for the outfitter had passed them a bad coin. The four seniors exchanged glances. Moor looked at Ludo. Ludo nodded. With a heavy sigh, Moor said, 'Let us reconsider the triangle. So far we have considered it in passivity, and found it serene. Let us now consider it as an active principle, possessing Will and Notion. Let us suppose, for instance, that such a triangle wished, for reasons we need not go into, to lodge itself in a square. Which part of itself would it direct to that end? A side, or one of its equilateral angles? Surely, it would be the latter?'

There was a hum of assent. Moor continued, 'Let us further suppose that one of these angles, departing from equilaterality, was slightly prominent, slenderer and therefore more insinuating. Have we any reason to doubt but that this would be the angle our hypothetical triangle would choose for its purpose—and rightly so?'

They agreed that there could be no possible doubt of this. Ludo quoted another of his mother's pious proverbs, this one in the form of a distich:

The Littling do not disallow,
A pebble laid Goliath low.

Banian saw them looking at him and realized that something was expected of him. He said, hesitatingly, 'Like a gimlet?'

'Exactly!' they said with enthusiasm, and Tinkel got up and patted him on the back.

'Going back to Moor's original triangle,' said Nimmerlein, 'The passive, serene one. If I remember rightly, it was perfect whichever way up it was. You couldn't accuse it of inversion.'

'No blame could be attached to it,' said Moor.

Tinkel remarked he had seen a lot of it in England. After a pause he exclaimed, 'Strike while the iron is hot!'

All this time, Banian had been reconsidering the triangle. He was now slightly hypnotized, and the warmth of his sheepskin enveloped him like his featherbed at Wirre Gedanken. He woke to learn it was more or less settled that he should prostitute himself to the fat yellow man.

'That I won't!' he cried. 'I'd die, rather. And why should I?'

'For the general good,' said Ludo.

'To improve our living conditions,' said Tinkel.

'To make yourself useful, for once,' said Nimmerlein.

This stung Banian. 'Make myself useful? And when haven't I made myself useful? Who was huntsman? And water carrier? Who swept the floors and paunched the rabbits and polished the triangle?'

'No more paunching rabbits,' said Nimmerlein artfully.

'Listen to reason, Banian,' said Moor. 'The facts are irrefutable. We have no money to speak of and nothing to eat but horse beans, for the pumpkin is already decayed. We, too, are decayed. We have lost our youthful charms. We exemplify the Law of Diminishing Returns. You, on the other hand, are in the flower of your youth. You are desirable and have only to make yourself desired—for he is obviously tired of that boy. And numerically we are four to one.'

'Do not think us harsh,' added Ludo. 'We are all very fond of you; we have your best interests at heart. It proves how carefully we have preserved your innocence that you should be making all this fuss. Submit, dear Banian, submit! We all have to submit at some time or other. You will find it a great deal easier to submit to a man than to a woman, I can assure you.'

'But to that revolting old suet pudding—'

'He may have beauties of the mind. My mother used to say—'

'And I don't know a word of his beastly language—'

'The language of love is international.'

As Ludo spoke, a man wearing splendid boots came up the steps. With the instinct of a well-trained servant he instantly recognised Ludo as the head of the party, bowed deeply, and handed him a letter on pink paper, gilt-edged. The letter was written in Turkish, Sclavonian, and bad French—the language of diplomacy. It ran:

Messieurs,

Our holy religion enjoins us to show hospitality to strangers. Yielding with pleasure to the Heavenly requirements, I do myself the gratification to invite you all to spend the winter under my roof.

A conveyance awaits. Peace!

Mustafa Ibrahim Bey
Provincial Governor

Dusk was falling as they mounted the steps of the Residence. After a clatter of drawing bolts, unhooking chains, and turning keys, the door was opened. The Provincial Governor stood just inside. His expression was coyly expectant, he wore white kid gloves and held a bunch of red roses. As he gave each of them a rose the door was rebolted, rechained, and relocked. 'Please don't think you have come to a jail,' he said. 'But there are nasty people about, and how sad I would be if our first night were disturbed. Tranquillity! Don't you love tranquillity? I pursue it of all things.'

They agreed that they pursued tranquillity; they also agreed it was hard to attain. Agreement followed agreement. He so quickly put them at their ease that after supper (which except for lacking wine was delicious) Tinkel asked him how he knew where to find them. 'A little bird told me,' he replied. Coffee was served. Iced water accompanied it. Conversation continued, but less briskly. Banian fidgeted and looked constrained; so, too, did the Provincial Governor. A silence fell, broken by the Provincial Governor saying, 'I am about to make a strange request. I hope you won't think me too forward.' Ludo, Moor, Tinkel and Nimmerlein implied that they couldn't dream of thinking it, and looked tutorially at Banian. 'I am a poet,' continued the Provincial Governor. 'I expand myself in poetry. What a seraglio is to some, my poems are to me. But like a seraglio they are secluded. No one listens to them. May I read you one of my poems?' Without waiting for assent, he clapped his hands. A servant brought in a large basket filled with scrolls. 'Naturally, I compose them in Turkish.' He picked a scroll, and began to read aloud. His voice was rich and commanding. He read slowly, waving his hand to mark the stresses, and pausing at frequent intervals, as though to inhale some particular beauty. 'Now I will read it in French.'

The reading in French took even longer, as he had to break off and complain of the inadequacy of the French language. The poem seemed to be mainly about camels eating green sprouts in a wilderness and finding spiritual assurance by chewing the cud. As an expression of his intentions toward Banian it was too recondite to hit its mark. Banian gazed at the ceiling and twiddled his thumbs.

'Do read it again,' said Ludo.

The request was complied with, in both languages. More poems were read, with more disquisitions. Moor sat bolt upright in a condition of fixed wakefulness; the others listened with their limbs relaxed and their eyes closed. At midnight the Provincial Governor explained that he must tear himself away in order to sign some mandates, and they were shown to their bedrooms. In the morning, new suits were laid out for them. Later in the day, the shoemaker came to measure them for slippers. Their sheepskin coats were removed without comment and replaced by sables.

Though to the eye of the flesh Mustafa Ibrahim was a repulsively ugly little man, and in the eyes of History a tyrant, he was an excellent host. During the day he only appeared at mealtimes. After supper there were poetry readings. These began with Mustafa politely asking his guests if they had written any poetry during the day. As they had not, he read his own.

Ludo had been blooded to poetry at his mother's knee. Though the manner of Mustafa's poetry was unlike that of his mother's favourite authors, he recognized a similarity of mood. Mustafa, expressing his desire to penetrate the ineffable, was bolder in metaphor than they; but the gist was much the same: they were alike lovesick for an *au-delà*. As the winter advanced, there was rioting; Mustafa would break off, not to inhale a beauty or point out a technical nicety but to listen to a volley of shooting in the streets. He listened with critical attention, and when the insurgents had been taught their lesson he returned to his poems like a dove returning to her nest. Ludo could not avoid remembering Balsamine's tenderness for marmots. It did not alter his feelings about Balsamine, but it oddly increased his affection for Mustafa.

Twice a week Mustafa drove in an open carriage through the streets. He now held an Armenian acrobat on his knee. Watching such a departure, Tinkel remarked that an assassination would be awkward for them. 'I'd be thankful!' exclaimed Banian. 'No more poetry!' He deeply resented the Armenian.

One of Mustafa's little birds had told him all he wished to know about his guests—where they came from, who they were, what they were. At the height of his rapture at having secured an audience, he had thought of having their wings torn out. Common sense prevailed; none of them showed the slightest inclination to fly away, so why go to extremes? Perhaps they would feel a migratory instinct later on. Meanwhile his little birds kept him up to date with the latest news. One day he came out of his office with a grave face and told Ludo that Queen Balsamine was dead. He feared this meant he must lose his dear, his sympathetic hearers. Arrangements for their return to Wirre Gedanken were already in train, their mourning outfits getting ready—to ease their departure was the least he could do. 'If you start at sunrise tomorrow, you will be in excellent time for the obsequies. Now I will leave you to your grief.'

Ludo lay awake all night, listening to the heartless excitement of the others as they ran from room to room, seeing that nothing had been overlooked by the packers, and chattering about their dear Homeland.

At sunrise, Mustafa stood at the head of the steps, amidst mountains of luggage. Speeches were made, hopes of a later meeting expressed. He looked even uglier in the light of sunrise, and increasingly fat as the luggage was gradually removed. 'Pillage'... 'Booty'... the words dinned in Ludo's mind. He turned from his travelling companions and ran back up the steps.

'Provincial Governor, Your Excellency, I will never forget your hospitality. Thanks to you, for the first time in my life I have lived in comfort without fearing or scheming. I can scarcely tear myself away.'

'Then how foolish to tear,' said Mustafa. 'Delight me by staying. My life is monotonous. I divide it between being a slave to duty and a slave to pleasure. What I need is a friend, a disinterested European friend, the real article. Stay and be that friend.'

'Drive on!' he cried to the cavalcade. As it drove off, taking Ludo's luggage with it, Ludo and the Provincial Governor waved, then went in, arm in arm. Ludo gave up flying, forgot his past, and learned Turkish. They lived together till Mustafa's death, after which Ludo moved to Venice, where he wrote Mustafa's biography, now considered to lack prejudice.

5 The Revolt at Brocéliande

Wace, a Norman poet of the mid-twelfth century, had heard so much about the fairy Kingdom of Brocéliande, in Brittany, that he went to see its wonders for himself; and found nothing, except that he had gone on a fool's errand:

> Là allai je merveilles querre,
> Vit la forest et vit la terre,
> Merveilles quis, mais ne trovait:
> Fol m'en revins, fol y allai,
> Fol y allai, fol m'en revins:
> Folie quis, por fol me tins.

His intention defeated his purpose. His mind was full of preconceived ideas of what he was in search of, so his eyes saw nothing.

Mortals do not see fairies—the generalization is as nearly a rule as anything in this turning world can be. It is certain that they cannot be seen by those who are looking for them. If a fairy of Brocéliande were seen, it was by some peasant whose mind was taken up with his own concerns—hunger, a leaky roof, a lost cow. He saw it out of the tail of his eye, and wished he hadn't, since to see a fairy is unlucky. It was on a day in mid-winter, with the north wind thundering in the forest and hail spiking the air, that the turf-cutter's son who had been sent out to find enough wood to warm a Sunday dinner saw his fairies: two fat men, dressed in scarlet, who sat under a live oak, holding hands and weeping. He ran home in terror, hitting his frostbitten feet against tufts of frozen grass, and told his parents. Before the end of the week he was dead of fever—which proved again that it is unlucky to see a fairy.

But this was long before Wace's expedition. Seeing nothing, he suffered no more than a passing mortification, and lived to versify the story of King Arthur and the Round Table.

Brocéliande was the foremost Elfin Court in all Western Europe, the proudest and most elegant. It claimed that it had preserved the pure tradition of ancient Persia, where the elfin race originated. Its queens wore a pink turban instead of the usual crown; the royal wand was of cedarwood from the banks of the Euphrates, so massively encrusted with jewels that it took a team of courtiers to wave it; its ladies-in-waiting distilled an exquisite rosewater; it kept a particular breed of long-furred cats and an astrologer. It was peculiar in having preserved a belief in a supernatural world, peopled by spirits of incalculable power, called Afrits. The obligation to worship these Afrits, while at the same time averting their intervention, was carried out by quarterly ceremonies of propitiation. These ceremonies were preceded by a round of pious cockfights, after which the victor cock was sacrificed.

Apart from the element of piety, court life at Brocéliande was much the same as in other Kingdoms. There were fashions of the moment—collecting butterflies, determining the pitch of birdsongs, table-turning, cat races, purifying the language, building card castles. There were expeditions to the coast to watch shipwrecks, summer picnics in the forest, deer hunts with the Royal Pack of Werewolves.

Ambassadors from other courts complained that the palace, situated in the depth of that immense forest, was sombre and damp; even so, they admitted that everything was carried on in the best of taste, and that its peculiar mixture of piety and fickleness was enchanting. It was, of course, an expensive embassy. There was not a corner of the palace where a wager was not in progress: which of two hailstones would be the first to melt, the span of a cat's whiskers, which way it would jump. And every debt was a debt of honour.

There was a regular programme of racing events—the Scullery Cup, the Laundry Half-Mile, the Staff Handicap. Lineaged fairies, who would rather be seen dead than seen flying, felt a practical admiration for the speed of those who flew on errands or obeyed the summons of a silver whistle. Servants who excelled in pace or endurance were transferred to the specialized seclusion of race horses and exercised morning and evening; a famous valet who had the misfortune to break a wing was kept at stud and sired several winners.

It was a custom that each new queen should introduce a fresh Persian tradition. When Queen Melior assumed the pink turban she was at a loss for Persian traditions till, gazing at her eyebrows in a looking glass, she realized, with the amazement with which one contemplates the dullness of one's predecessors, that no one had thought of eunuchs. She called an assembly and announced, her wand being waved before her, that she proposed to add eunuchs to her retinue. For the present, two would be enough.

There were loud murmurs of approval, low murmurs of doubt. Who was she going to pick on? Obviously some working person; yet here, too, there were difficulties. The calm balance of society depended on people remaining in their proper stations.

The wand was waved again. Queen Melior continued. From each, she said, according to his disposability. The eunuchs should be drawn from the ranks of the changelings, whose abundance could always supply another pair if anything went wrong with the first experiment.

Fairies are constructed for longevity, not fertility. Many of the aristocracy do not breed at all; those who do, at long intervals. But this does not prevent them from delighting in small children. Couriers are sent prospecting, and where they see a baby left unguarded make off with it. Strong ruddy babies are most in request; their unlikeliness to the fairy race makes them engaging. They grow up as court playthings, fondled, indulged, and kept much cleaner than they would be in human homes. Some penurious Kingdoms, like Elfhame in Scotland, injected them with a drug which prolonged their natural span. This was never done at Brocéliande, where the freshness of youth was the prime desideratum.

All when smoothly. Two handsome well-matched boys in their early teens were chosen. The castration was performed by a skilled surgeon who flew from Constantinople. A special uniform was designed; they were given a course in etiquette and deportment, learning to walk with measured steps and stand still without fidgeting, and a new rank was invented for them, between the Directors of Piety and the Ladies of Honour. Their names were Ib and Rollo.

They were not altogether happy in their advancement. Their feet swelled and their backs ached from so much standing about in their attendance of the Queen. Other changelings laughed at them. Some of the Ladies of Honour were offended that mere mortals should take precedence of them, and affected to shudder at the proximity of anything so unnatural as a eunuch; others, less squeamish, were sorry for the poor creatures and questioned them maternally. Their outstanding friend at court was the Royal Favourite. Male companionship, however imperfect, was a support to him. He was handsome and silly, and when Melior was cross they repaired his selfesteem. By the time he was replaced and the new Favourite, who was handsome and intensely musical, had set the whole court to singing in four-part harmony, Ib and Rollo had ceased to be novelties. Their traditional significance—which was in fact as meaningless as a vestigial button on a suit—was forgotten. However, they were for the time being useful, as soprano voices in the part-singing.

Persons deprived of their sex are deprived of their intuition: there is no leap of the heart, toward or against. They cannot even make mistakes. Existing in the equable winter of reason, the best they can do is to see clearly and arrive at a correct judgement. Sometimes in dreams both Ib and Rollo returned to the pell-mell spontaneity of their young selves and were delighted, infuriated, embarrassed before they could say why. But time went on—a clock that never lost a minute, never ran down. The dreams came less often, the waking was less lacerating. Eventually, it was not lacerating at all. They woke remembering that there was something further to be observed, an unaccountable smile, gesture, tilt of the voice to be considered and fitted into the correct judgment of a character or a situation. It is this imperturbable power of judging and assessing which makes eunuchs so powerful in court intrigues and palace revolutions. But that is in mortal courts. At Brocéliande, there was a perfect loyalty to things as they were.

The boredom of court life closed in on them —the boredom in which one stares, day after day, at the same face in a tapestry hanging. Their function kept them together, idling about till some occasion called them to stand on either side of the throne. They did not talk much: there was nothing much to talk about; they exchanged comments, and agreed with each other. They were figures in the tapestry—rather portly figures by now, for their mortal origin made them large eaters. One evening Rollo remarked, 'We have not seen the Astrologer since the new moon. I wonder what he does, sitting alone in his tower. He can't watch the stars by day.' After a pause for thought, Ib said, 'I suppose he sleeps.' This degree of speculation was so unusual that it pricked them into an impulse. Melior had taken a new Favourite and gone early to bed. Their absence from the tapestry would not be noticed. They climbed the long stairway to Master Tarantula's apartment at the top of the tower, and knocked on his door. It swung open, and closed behind them. In the middle of the room was a table spread with a meal for two. Master Tarantula was playing solitaire. 'Sit down,' he said. 'I was expecting you.' It was not so surprising that they had been expected: he was a Magian, cast horoscopes, read future events in the stars. What took them aback was to find themselves welcomed and drawn into conversation. They began to talk, found they had things to say, found themselves listened to. The moon shone in through the open uncurtained window. Clouds sailed across it, moving smoothly and rapidly on a steady wind. Suddenly Master Tarantula got up, threw off his cloak, and unfurled a pair of large wings. With one powerful stroke, he was out of the window, breasting the air like a strong swimmer. They watched him soar upward, vanish in a cloud, emerge from it, a black speck against the moonlight blue of the sky, vanish.

They were still speechless when he returned, neatly diving into the room with his wings packed to his sides, and finished the wine in his glass. Breathlessly (Master Tarantula was not in the least out of breath) Ib asked, 'How do you find your way back?' 'I call that a very sensible question,' said Master Tarantula. 'I will explain when we next meet. But now I must send you away. It is already daybreak in Bohemia.'

Next week the great Winter Candle was lit and everyone went into furs. After the festivities had died down, Master Tarantula sent a message to the Queen asking for a private audience. Leaning on a stick and looking very old, he made his bow and explained his purpose. The stars had warned him that it would be a very unpropitious winter, with a number of Afrits about. He was an old man, his powers were failing. The last Afrit had almost got the better of him, slipping between his spells. He had managed to divert its malignancy to a village west of the forest, now in ashes, but he could not hope to keep off the next assault single-handed. Would Her Majesty grant him a couple of assistants? They need not be experts in Art Magic: he could supply all that himself; all he asked was that they should be strong and obedient. And virgin. The least flaw in virginity would provoke the Afrits to fury. And here lay the difficulty. Young people are careless of their virginity; one day they may have it and the next not. What was needed was a trustworthy, an inexpugnable virginity. Would Her Majesty lend him her eunuchs? It had been well drummed into Melior in her girlhood how Afrits feel about virginity. She handed over Ib and Rollo without demur.

For many years they lived happily in Master Tarantula's tower, playing three-handed whist, learning a few tricks of magic, listening to his conversation, keeping off the Afrits, and becoming almost as agnostic as he. Because he respected nothing, they began to respect each other, finding each other likable instead of merely habitual. At the propitiatory ceremonies they attended him as formerly they had attended the Queen. Sometimes he feigned weakness and leaned on them. In fact he was uncommonly strong and limber which he put down to the fresh air and exercise of his nocturnal flights. One night, he failed in his usual neat entry and made several blundering essays before he got through the window. His teeth chattered, his clothes were wet through. When he recovered his breath, he asked for brandy. With his teeth knocking on the glass, he told them he had been badly mauled in a thunderstorm. They got him to bed and heaped blankets on him. He was no sooner asleep than he began to leap like a fish in a net. Toward morning, he opened his eyes and did not recognize them. Death was hearsay to them, and seeing him fall into a quiet sleep they supposed he was recovering, till the old bedmaker came with her broom and bucket and told them he was dying and would be gone by nightfall. She had been his servant since his college days and thought the world of him. At dusk she came again. He seemed to be dying easily and contentedly. 'There. He's gone,' she said, and held a mirror to his lips. His wings started out; he looked like a dead crow. But such deathbed erections are not unusual, she said. The wings are folded back, and nothing said of it.

The new Astrologer wanted no assistants. Ib and Rollo resumed their former service. They had been absent from court life for so long that they felt out of date. New niceties of etiquette had been introduced and these, familiar to everyone else, left them at a loss. With Master Tarantula they had got into a way of talking quite freely, questioning, contradicting, saying whatever came into their heads. It was difficult to discard this; they talked too much, and laughed, and were thought impertinent, or they could find nothing to say and were thought stockish. It was held against them, too, that they were inseparable.

The ladies who had taken offence when these mortal beings were thrust into court society had not forgotten their grudge (the Elfin memory is proportioned to Elfin longevity}, and petitioned the Queen that Ib and Rollo should be included in the next batch of elderly changelings to be deposited on the Island of Repose—a reef off the Pointe du Raz, covered in seaweed, lashed with spray from Atlantic cross-currents, a place of no return. Bretons knew it as the Isle of the Dead, and fishermen reported hearing the howls of souls in Purgatory there. Melior objected. Ib and Rollo were part of Brocéliande's precious heritage of Persian traditions: old and smelly they might be, but they were still her eunuchs, and she could not possibly appear on state occasions without them; but she would give them new suits.

The next state occasion was the Snuffing of the Winter Candle, when everybody put off furs and began to carry fans. The weather was appalling. Gales raged round the castle, the forest clanged with the ice frozen on to trees, the servants could only venture out on foot. In the midst of all this an

Afrit eluded the new Astrologer, changed its shape into a starving weasel, got into the palace mews and killed all the fighting cocks.

During the following tumult of rage, consternation, suggestions, objections, counter-suggestions, the Chancellor's daughter said to her bosom friend (she was at the age of bosom friends), 'Why don't they have a eunuch fight?' She had not meant to be overheard, but a low voice catches every ear. Her remark was considered the height of absurdity or else marvellously witty, but within a few days the idea of a eunuch fight was being seriously discussed. It would be something to bet on and something to laugh at.

Living with Master Tarantula, Ib and Rollo had lost the knack of observing and forming correct judgments. When Aquilon, Master of the Werewolves, affably appealed to them to lighten the gloom of life without cocking by a small set-to between themselves, they were flattered, saw a chance to win their way back into favour, said that if they were younger, almost agreed. They were nailed to agreement by Aquilon's friends assuring them that a great deal of money had been staked.

The fight took place in a ring of cheering spectators. As they could not be expected to fight to the death, a referee was appointed, who would ring his bell after a round of five minutes (no one expected them to last out longer). They had, of course, witnessed a great many ceremonial cockfights, and noticed that fighting cocks aim at the eye. They flinched at this, but buffeted each other's face. When Rollo drew blood from Ib's nose, there was great applause. It swelled to a storm when the flustered Ib miscalculated his aim and hit Rollo's eye. The eye swelled and closed. The referee rang his bell, declared the fight over and Ib the victor. Congratulating spectators swarmed into the ring and supervised the combatants' being revived with hot towels and vinegar.

There is always a charm about amateur efforts: they are at once so silly and so sincere. Ib's nose, Rollo's black eye, the bruises that came out on their soft skins, roused an almost genuine solicitude in their backers. They were given a punch-ball, bottles of liniment, tonic pills; each was privately urged not to clench his teeth in the next fight. For somehow—they did not quite know how—there was going to be another fight.

It was not such a success. In their anxiety not to hurt each other's face they repeatedly hit below the belt. There was laughter and some booing. The referee declared the match a draw.

This peaceable decision angered them. For the first time in their lives, they quarrelled—quarrelled to the quick, because they had been humiliated. In a desolate reconciliation they vowed they would never fight again, never betray the friendship which was all, in a society of flippant, arbitrary, alien beings, they could rely on. And a couple of days later each had betrayed it, for each had been separately approached and told that the other had agreed to a third fight—a fight to settle all, since by then the new cocks would be arriving from Morocco. Furious with each other for having been tricked, they consented with indifference to the proposal that for this last fight they should be spurred—symbolically, of course: the spurs would be blunted.

Embarrassed by these toy-sized weapons fastened to their heels, they walked stiffly into the ring, bowed to the spectators, bowed to each other. Every male in the palace— courtiers, servants, changelings—had been ordered to attend, and it was known, though not mentioned, that Melior and her ladies were in the screened gallery above, pressed together like hens on a perch. The referee stepped out of the ring and struck his bell. They turned on each other and began to fight.

They fought with the frenzy of the betrayed; they fought and would not leave off. They tore out each other's hair, wrenched at each other's ears, set their teeth in each other's flesh and worried it, kicked at each other's shins. The spurs had not been blunted. They discovered how to use them, and blood spurted out. The applause was incessant. Suddenly it was dominated by a frightful caterwauling as the two eunuchs began to scream at each other. Maddened by the sound, the spectators fell to fighting among themselves, Rollo's backers shouting defiance at Ib's, Ib's trying to get at Rollo's. So many old scores were being wiped out, so much dissembled loathing gratified, that for some time nobody noticed that the caterwauling had ceased. But when the spectators left off fighting and glanced toward the centre of the ring, they saw a man who grovelled and a man who stood over him, and thought, though they could not be sure, that the standing man was Rollo and the grovelling man Ib, hamstrung by Rollo's battering spur.

Fortunately, the Moroccan cocks arrived next day. They were splendid birds. Their proud strut, their eyes glittering like sequins, ennobled everyone's spirits and redeemed Brocéliande from an inelegant memory. A black eye here or there was ignored; scratched faces were restored with very becoming strips of black court plaster. The principal Director of Piety explained that whatever had happened—he himself had seen a certain indecorum—was undoubtedly the work of the same Afrit who had come among them in the disguise of a weasel. The Chancellor's daughter, who had started it all, was questioned before Melior by a panel of Ladies of Honour, but exonerated, as she had only meant to be helpful. When she had left the room, the Ladies of Honour turned to the Queen and begged to renew their former petition, which earlier she had graciously refused. They did not dispute the traditional importance of her eunuchs, but she really could not be attended by a cripple and a stammering idiot. Surely the time had come when they should be retired to the Island of Repose. Melior assented. The Ladies of Honour spread the news.

Apparently, the Afrit had not finished his work. Aquilon, using such words as 'shabby' and 'iniquitous', declared that Ib and Rollo had suffered enough, and threatened to resign his Mastership of the Werewolves if they were now deported to the Island of Repose. His friends supported him; the changelings banded themselves under his leadership, saying that they had been downtrodden for too long and were stolen property anyway. The Ladies of Honour urged Melior to be firm, the Directors of Piety begged her to be prudent, the Favourite took mandragora. When the Queen called an assembly, several of the team of Wand Wavers, bowing, put their hands behind them. The revolt spread to the servants, who refused to fly and went about their duties at a leisurely walking pace. This was the last straw. The Ambassador from Blokula—a formalist from a petty northern Kingdom who would be delighted to report that Brocéliande was in a state of insurrection—was hourly expected. Melior gave in. A disused hermitage was reroofed and simply furnished, and Ib and Rollo installed, with a reliable groom of Aquilon's to see to their needs. There, not long after, they ended their days, Ib surviving Rollo by less than a year.

6 The Mortal Milk

It is commonly supposed that fairies, or elfins, are trifling little beings, always on the wing and incapable of dying. This misapprehension has come about because they prefer to live in invisibility—though they can be visible at will, by means of an automatic mechanism, which works rather like the *una corda* pedal or a gearshift. In fact, they are about four-fifths of ordinary human stature, fly or don't fly according to their station in life, and after a life span of centuries die like other people—except that as they do not believe in immortality they die unperturbed. Their life span is portioned into a brief childhood of forty years, an extended plateau of being grown up, a suave decline into old age. As longevity is the common lot, it is taken for granted. The working fairies at the Court of Brocéliande, who flew about their duties, did not find time heavy on their hands; indeed, they sometimes complained that they never had a moment to themselves. The nobility, who marked their social standing by scorning to use their wings, had not much time to call their own, either.

Of all the Elfin Courts in Western Europe, Brocéliande most piqued itself on its adherence to a seasonal calendar of pleasures and ceremonies. On the First of May the Queen was publicly attired in her new pink turban, and an extensive picnic was held during which the Court Functionaries reposed under separate trees, drinking sherbet and eating cake; at Midsummer hay was tossed to the accompaniment of pastoral wind instruments; a bear was baited to drums and trumpets on the First of November; the Egyptian Days were observed by abstaining from love and broad beans (broad beans, a peasant food, were in fact never eaten, but on the Egyptian Days they were served at table and ceremonially refused); etc, etc.

One year it so happened that the beginning of March brought a spell of hot weather. As this was six weeks before the Spring Ceremony, when Brocéliande acknowledged the season by changing from furs and velvets into silks and gossamer lawn, the courtiers sweltered on in winter clothes and kept up their courage by boasting about their inheritance of the laws of the Medes and Persians. The heat continued, a note of merit sharpened the boasting, general conversation became listless. Aquilon, on a pretext of his obligations as Master of the Royal Pack of Werewolves, excused himself from attendance and went for a stroll in the forest. When he was safely out of view, he took off his furred mantle, hat, and gauntlet gloves, and blew his whistle. His valet came flying at the call, and was told to carry them and follow at a distance. Bareheaded and bare-handed, Aquilon walked on the edge of the forest and looked out on the brilliant gaunt landscape, where two peasants were breaking the clods and proclaiming in loud, uncouthly cheerful voices that a peck of March dust was worth a king's ransom. As he stood watching them with a naturalist's unimpassioned interest in some familiar variety of the lesser creation, he heard a rapid wingbeat, and Puck, the whipper-in of the Royal Pack, alighted beside him.

'I've been looking for Your Lordship everywhere,' Puck said in the complaining tone of an old servant. 'Please to come and look at them. The responsibility is getting too much for me.'

Hopping impatiently while Aquilon strolled, he poured out his story. The werewolves had gone off their feed—which he had put down to the untimely hot weather till he noticed that first one, then another had come out in a rash. The sickness had spread through the pack, and now they were scratching themselves raw and vomiting, with matter streaming from their eyes and noses. Even if they recovered, which he didn't expect, it would not be possible to hunt them for weeks; they would be too feeble to pull down a calf.

'Such a fine pack they were,' he lamented. 'I can't account for it.' And went on to account for it by a thought which had often crossed his mind: that their lives were unnatural and that sooner or later Nature would get the upper hand, since werewolves, when all was said and done, were men, and when they ravened for themselves they attacked women and children, women and children were their natural meat; and lacking it the poor creatures' blood had grown impoverished. If he could have his way, he'd let them loose for a while.

'If we did, they'd never come back,' said Aquilon. He spoke feelingly.

As they neared the kennels, the stink of mortal sickness bloomed on the air. The sun beat down on the enclosure, where the werewolves staggered about, colliding with each other, snapping and snarling, too dispirited to fight, and tripping over their dying fellows. Puck chirruped to them through the bars, calling their names. They turned for a moment at the sound of his voice and stared with bleared eyes. It was plain that they despaired of themselves. One of them was calling for a priest.

Aquilon felt a hand on his shoulder. It was his cousin Beliard, who came to remind him of the afternoon's entertainment of roast chestnuts.

'If you don't want to offend the Queen, dress yourself properly and hurry back. What's wrong with your werewolves? Moulting?'

'Dying.'

'That won't do you any good. I daresay they won't all die. I'm sure Duke Billy won't. Bet you a hundred Duke Bill won't die.'

'Done.'

Not to accept the bet would have been ill-mannered, but

Aquilon was perfectly indifferent to the upshot—tolerably indifferent, too, about the *lèse-majesté* of being late and improperly dressed for roasting chestnuts.

When he was younger, Aquilon took a gamester's pleasure in seeing how far he could go without incurring sentence of exile. Some of his excursions were considerable, as on the First of May when he flew naked round and round the tower, saluting the Royal Standard. No word was said of exile; his pleasure waned. He had enjoyed hunting, charmed by his well-fitting boots and the poetry of those hunts through the forest by moonlight, the stag crashing ahead, the brassy yelling of a pack of werewolves in full cry. But with his Mastership it became an affectation and a bore. He would dice by the hour, enthralled by the careless rattle and the silent incontrovertible throw; but for preference he played alone, right hand matched against left.

Queen Melior was regal enough to enjoy disconcerting public opinion. She countenanced the loyal flight around the tower, remarking that it was only what might be expected from someone whose very infancy was scandalous. Aquilon's mother had no milk. Accredited fairy wet nurses were summoned, but the child refused breast after breast till a mortal was abducted, who wept for her own child while he sucked her and throve. This, according to his Aunt Pervenche, Beliard's mother, accounted for everything: she had foreseen it from the start. Freely admitting her nephew's faults—fickleness, cold-heartedness, sulky temper, misuse of his opportunities, ingratitude, large hands, she blamed them on a tainted constitution.

People who live for centuries are bound to repeat themselves. For the twentieth time Lady Pervenche had confided to the Queen that the milk, etc. Melior listened graciously, laughed in her sleeve, and reflected that however many Aquilon's offences, at least he wasn't a bore. But her attention having again been drawn to his hands, she had to admit to herself that they were large. What else had Pervenche said? A sallow complexion? It hadn't been mentioned, but it was true. What else? Ingratitude. Ingratitude! It darted upon her like a hail of arrows how often she had given him cause to be grateful, how often she had condoned, overlooked, ignored, made allowances for, laughed away, forgiven—forgotten, almost. And in return for all this?—to see her mercies taken for granted. She'd show him! Public opinion should see her showing him. Public opinion saw, and marked, and felt it was high time. It also saw Aquilon responding with such egregious civility and meekness that he might have been playing opposite his Queen in a charade of The Henpecked Husband. Melior broke off the performance. Righteous wrath improves with keeping. She would bide her time—time was never lacking at Brocéliande—till she had a faultless occasion to show the ingrate she was not a queen to be trifled with. Public opinion calmed down. The November bear-baiting restored a sense of ordered harmony. That year's bear was a particularly fine bear. It defended itself with fury and disembowelled several dogs. When it sagged from the stake and lay dying, spectators in the front row saw real tears fall from its eyes.

Melior did not have long to wait. The murrain among the werewolves supplied the ideal pretext for disgracing Aquilon with impartiality. The werewolves were one of Brocéliande's distinguishing glories; the murrain was a calamity: all deplored it and no one could suspect her of a personal spite. Nevertheless, at that evening's Assembly, she opened the subject in the voice of a grieving mermaid, condoling with Aquilon, whose devotion had been frustrated by the negligence of an underling: Puck was to blame. Beliard saw what she was after, and made imploring eyes at his cousin— but in vain. Aquilon declared that Puck was an admirable servant. If any remnant of the pack were saved, it would be entirely Puck's doing. And having made an eloquent eulogy of his whipper-in, he cut the ground from under Melior's feet by resigning his Mastership before she could deprive him of it.

The ground presently gave way under his own feet, too, for more than half the werewolves recovered. He was left in the mortifying position of having made a grand gesture about nothing crucial. Melior noted this, and remembered that the third time is lucky.

She waited till after the Spring Ceremony to call a Council. Even when it was assembled, she delayed a little longer, announcing trifling changes, seasonal adjustments, before she delivered her blow: Aquilon, freed from his obligation to the werewolves, was to go as Ambassador to the Court of Blokula.

If she had appointed him Groom of the Scullery, she could hardly have appointed him to greater ignominy. Embassies to Blokula were not even punitive; they were insignificant sinecures bestowed on persons of no significance. Everyone present admired the composure with which he thanked her. He would have admired it himself, but he was engaged in trying to account for his start of pleasure. Blokula was a petty Kingdom in Sweden. Its courtiers were referred to as the Trolls. Their only interests were eating, drinking, horseplay, and pedigrees. They drank spirits, sang interminable ballads, were bearded. Their banquets were so rowdy that the very name of Blokula was synonymous with gross revels held by mortals. Their Queen was a dwarfish child. Such were the reports brought back by Brocéliande's returning ambassadors—those who returned: some were finished off by the climate or lost at sea. What other charming details could he recall? They ate goat's-milk cheese and were surrounded by wolves and bears. Yet he had felt unmistakable pleasure, and apparently had shown it.

Why was he taking it so calmly, asked Beliard when they were alone. What had become of his self-respect? Tact was all very well, but it was carrying tact too far to look positively pleased.

'She seemed rather disconcerted. I am never lucky with my tact.'

'You never mean to be.'

'Perhaps I shall be luckier at Blokula. I might be quite a success at Blokula.'

'Cooped up with Trolls.'

'Travel will improve my mind. I might go on with my study of mortals—I have a notion they vary from place to place. If they don't vary, I'll study Trolls. A spell of coarse feeding might be just what I need. That foster mother of mine, you know. My first tug at a mortal breast ruined me for polite society.'

There was a pause. His face fell, and he said—for once speaking without affectation—'The worst of it is that for the journey I shall have to be visible. And among all those hulking mariners of Penker's. I hate being made to feel small.'

Ivo Penker, Master of the sailing ship Amicable, was a Channel Islander, who boasted he had never fumbled a harbour entrance or paid a customs duty. Brocéliande relied on him for smuggled goods and sea transport. The Amicable was a high-built ship, and could pack away an embassy as easily as the ship's cat's kittens.

Though Blokula was such a hole-and-corner little Kingdom, Melior saw to it that Aquilon should do her credit. His wardrobe, his cellar, the flasks of rose water and Eau de Brocéliande, his outfit of table silver, his silver chamber pot were of the finest, marked by the final ostentation of modesty. His retinue, selected for their mediocrity, were well dressed as waxworks. His chariot was drawn by four perfectly matched bays. All this took time. It was August before he embarked.

Ivo Penker was accustomed to the measurements of Elfin; his only concern over the discrepancy between his stature and Aquilon's was that he had to bow that much deeper—an effort for a man of his girth. Aquilon felt the contrast acutely, and spent the voyage sulking in his stateroom. At Göteborg he disencumbered himself of his waxworks, ordering all but his body servants, coachman, grooms and two secretaries to return to Brocéliande with dispatches to Queen Melior— dispatches, he said, of urgent importance. At the last moment he reprieved the Court Geographer, who had battled his way into the party because he wanted to see a snow mountain. The senior secretary, who had fair-copied observations on English cooking and cockroaches, supposed Aquilon was not quite so much in disgrace as was rumoured, since he corresponded with the Queen in code.

From Göteborg to Uppsala the route was well enough. The remnants of the rye harvest were being carted into red-painted barns, women and hens gleaned in the stubble fields, and the air was somnolent with the sweetness of warm grain. The senior secretary travelled with him, saying at intervals that Uppsala was a historic city. Blokula was far to the north of Uppsala and they had not got to Uppsala yet. At Uppsala the horses were rested and reshod.

They continued northward, groping their way through a cold sea fog. It was on the third day after leaving Uppsala that Aquilon had a curious adventure.

They had put up at an inn used by previous embassies, and after supper he went to the stables to see if the horses' legs had been washed and if they were properly rugged. All was well. He said good night to the grooms, who were sleeping with the horses, and was turning back to the inn when he heard a voice in the fog say, 'To Blokula!' and a second voice repeat, 'To Blokula!' Fog distorts sound, and it seemed to him the speakers were standing on a roof. They were loud mortal voices—such speakers could not be going to an elfin court. When another voice went past him saying more urgently, 'To Blokula!' he remembered the word's chawbacon associations, determined to witness a Blokula, and set out to follow the voices. The fog swirled round him, he was splashing through cat-iced puddles, he had lost sense of direction, knew he was being a fool and should give up the chase; but for the sake of foolery he shouted out, 'To Blokula!' A halloo of voices answered him. He went on and was in a changed world.

The fog had cleared. The rising moon cast his shadow on the turf. He stood on the edge of an enormous meadow with a large barn at the farther end of it. The barn doors were open, figures were passing and repassing, dark against its candlelit interior. 'Where they'll feast,' he thought. He had no time to think further, for suddenly they all turned and came swooping down on him, crying, 'Antecessor!' As they neared him, the enthusiasm died from their voices. They stopped short, shaking their heads, and backed away. A moment later they swept off like a flock of starlings, and began a wild follow-my-leader dance over the meadow. Somehow he had joined them, his shadow prancing with theirs, and when they shouted again, 'Antecessor, Antecessor!' he shouted with them and joined in the rush toward what he saw as a tall man standing on a hillock, and then saw as a hoary standing stone. It was certainly a stone; for when he kissed it, as they did, it was rough and cold to his lips. But to them it must have seemed a man, for they kissed it devoutly and spoke to it, and danced round it in a worshipping circle; and women who had children with them lifted the children high in the air as children are lifted above the level of a crowd to see a procession go by. A tooting horn sounded from the barn. They crowded in and sat down at a long table, eating and drinking and all talking at once. He did not understand their language, but he laughed with them and made pleased noises.

By now, the children were yawning. The sight made him yawn in sympathy, and he was glad when he was shown into a room with a curtained bed in it. In the bed was a naked girl. She was clean and plump and willing, and he thought, 'Now I am going to possess a mortal.' He had done so—very little artistry was needed—and she was contentedly grunting herself to sleep, when the bed curtains were parted and a tall grey-eyed woman looked down on them. There was no stir of expression on her face. He watched her draw the curtains together again, and fell asleep.

When he woke, he felt the bed melting from under him, the girl and the bed curtains gone. He looked round for his boots. They were on his feet, he was lying on the ground, the first light of day was hovering over a blackened waste of moor. He had fallen asleep out-of-doors. But where was he, and why was he here? He had gone out to look at the horses. He could remember every detail of the stables, the speckled light from the lantern, how he had talked to the grooms; after that, vaguely, someone standing on a roof; after that, nothing.

Beliard, that easy believer, would have said he was bewitched. He was arguing with Beliard in his mind when he heard a cock crow, and a second cock answering it. Guided by the two cocks, he walked over the moor till he saw the roofs of a village, and entering the village, came to the inn. He remembered his retinue, and asked himself whether they were snoring or faithfully searching and inquiring for him and would greet him with a history of all they had suffered. The innkeeper told him they were still asleep. It struck him that the man was looking at him curiously. 'Wake them; tell them I shall start in half an hour's time. And get me my breakfast. And tell my barber to come to me.' After his night out-of-doors the inn smelled intolerably fusty.

In an hour's time, they were off. He had berated them so efficiently for oversleeping that no one ventured to ask him if he had slept well. As he got into the chariot he saw a strange man on the box. The innkeeper explained that this was the ostler, whose duty it was to guide visitors through the rest of the journey to the castle. The route was difficult; even with the ostler to direct them, it would be six days before they got to Blokula.

The thought of six more days enclosed with the senior secretary was so appalling that Aquilon invited the Court Geographer to travel with them, and then remembered the junior secretary and invited him, too. The junior secretary was so extremely junior that this act of condescension made the senior secretary silent with rage. The Court Geographer was a man of no conversation. Though the rearrangement made the chariot incommodiously crowded, it secured a whole day's silence. The chariot lumbered on through freezing fog. Sometimes a stony clatter told him of a waterfall he could not see. Once he heard an owl. Once, when they had paused to let the baggage wagon catch up with them, he heard the twang of a guitar, which the barber was playing to divert his fellow-passengers, On the second day the senior secretary began to conjecture that they must be nearing Lapland, and if it were not for the fog they would see the northern lights. He was now on speaking terms with the junior secretary, and the junior secretary expanded and was informative. After the third night, there were no more inns; the ostler took them to farmhouses, which were hospitable and charged them a great deal for accommodation they shared with sheep, pigs, and cattle. On the fourth day the fog cleared and was replaced by swarms of midges. The horses made better going, were moving at a trot, when there was a violent jolt. The chariot reeled and stopped. The nearside leader had fallen, the three other bays were plunging and kicking. Aquilon and the ostler went to their heads, the grooms ran up and disentangled the fallen horse. It had broken both knees. There was nothing to be done but knock it on the head and leave it for the wolves. When they got going again, Aquilon said he would walk. He was in such a fury against Melior for sending this beautiful creature to die in the wilderness that he dared not trust himself in company. Its screams were still in his ears when he returned to the chariot, where the junior secretary was telling the Geographer about the barbarities of the northern latitudes. 'They strip themselves naked and dance round him till they foam at the mouth. And then he feasts them on entrails and toad broth and dead children. Every year they are bound to give him thirteen children for his own use. I assure you, it's true. I read it in a treatise.' The senior secretary said that much the same thing obtained among Christians, whose bishops—He sank his voice for the bishops. The junior secretary shuddered, but maintained his case. 'And the Lappish witches—'

A pity I don't have the pair of them knocked on the head and left for the wolves, thought Aquilon. If he travelled with anybody on the return journey, it should be with the barber.

On the seventh morning the ostler told them the rest of the way was straightforward, and asked to be paid off. Early in the darkening afternoon they came to the Castle of Blokula. It stood in a pass between mountains—squat, massive, rectangular. It was larger than he expected. He sent the secretaries to announce his arrival and sat in the chariot, wishing he had not arrived; or rather, that he had not been sent. He sat for a long time. Then he heard an extraordinary braying sound which echoed back and forth between the mountains. The castle door had opened, a procession of welcome approached, speeches were made, he was conducted into the castle. As he went in, the trumpeters sounded another solemn bray.

The castle was built round a courtyard open to the sky. A number of motionless tall men stood about in it, taller even than those who escorted him—and most of these were taller than he. They were wooden men, badly carved and exactly lifelike. One by one, the court officeholders introduced themselves. They spoke Court Elfin, so correctly that at first he found it hard to understand them. Their civilities took a long time; so did supper. But when he climbed into his gigantic bed, the linen was so fine, the pillows so soft and plump, that he felt a surge of esteem for these simple good-hearted Trolls. On the morrow he would be received by Queen Serafica.

It took him all the morning to be washed and shaved and dressed and combed and polished to his satisfaction. He watched the process with deepening gloom. However much his own appearance might do him credit, he would be disgraced by his deplorable tail. Young girls are quick to see the ridiculous. What would Queen Serafica think when she saw him advance, followed by the senior and junior secretary, the Court Geographer, and a page? Why hadn't he thought of this before dismissing the politer part of his retinue? In the end, he decided to break with all protocol and go into the throne room unattended. Later on, he would mention that a coachload of his followers had fallen over a precipice.

The token of Queen Melior's esteem which he was to present had been on exhibition at Brocéliande, and everyone had admired its suitability for a child sovereign. It was a fan with ivory sticks; the spread, painted on chicken skin, showed a group of grotesque musicians in a pastoral landscape; the reverse was scattered with exquisitely painted daisies; it was enclosed in a box of white shagreen, scented with musk, and wrapped in daisy-painted paper with white bows.

At noon precisely he entered the throne room. He noticed a stir among the officials and some glances at the door when no one else came in, but he carried it off. At the end of the long gallery a cluster of court ladies stood on either side of the throne. He had no eyes for them; he had been hard put to it not to blink; he had not expected the child queen would wear spectacles. Whoever had brought her up, she had been very well trained. She sat upright and motionless, with the dignity of some well-set jewel. She was so small that when he knelt before her his forehead was on a level with hers. Like a white radish, he thought: the wide brow, the spacious setting of the eyes, the contraction into a long narrow chin. At odds with the radish comparison was a large hooked nose, an ancestral nose, too large for her face. Though so small, she was no dwarf but well proportioned. The hand she put out to be kissed was firm and well knit. Queen Melior's letter was delivered and read, then came the turn of the fan. The last bow was untied, the last layer of wrapping paper unfolded by one of her ladies, who handed the shagreen box back to him to give to the Queen. She took out the fan, unfurled it, examined it, closed it—and snapped it in two. Shrew, he noted; for there was nothing of childish naughtiness about the act, and though 'shrew' was not the right word, he could not immediately think of a better. He could not immediately think what to do next, either. She saved him the trouble by asking about his journey. Revealed as a shrew, she became of more interest, and though she said nothing remarkable, the narrative of the journey lasted much longer than the time allotted for the *baisemain*. He forgot to mention the coach falling over the precipice.

As he retired, walking backward—a thing he did rather well—a cat ran between his legs. To save his balance, he leaped in the air. The cat trotted on; Aquilon continued his respectful withdrawal. There was a faint hum of admiration. Afterward he was congratulated on his agility and aplomb. He praised the cat for knowing its own mind. The chancellor said it was a good thing he didn't object to cats; he would be meeting a good many of them. Her Majesty's cats, Aquilon asked. No, they were Dame Habonde's cats. No doubt he would meet Dame Habonde, too. She was the Queen's governess. No, she was not present this morning; she did not attend state functions. She was an admirable person, her late Majesty had entrusted the infant Serafica to her care, she was most admirable ... He paused. The Treasurer went on for him: 'But she is not quite one of us.' They were all so discreet that Aquilon was forced to conclude that Dame Habonde was a mortal. No one referred to the fan.

In due course Dame Habonde's pupil would charge him with her compliments to Queen Melior and a *quid pro quo* for the fan. He would return to Brocéliande. Meanwhile, his encounter with the cat had endeared him to the Trolls. They consulted his opinion about dogs and heraldic bearings, told him anecdotes, and slapped him on the back. Several swore an eternal friendship. He was entertained with ceremonial fireworks, bonfires on the mountains, excursions by sleigh. He sat beside the Queen at banquets, rode in the same sleigh with her. Learning that he had never seen an eagle owl, she took him to her aviary. The owl came strutting out of its grotto at her call. Its eyes were red as a furnace, its feet were covered with a close-fitting plumage of nutmeg-brown feathers, as though it wore spats. She fed it through the bars with gobbets of raw meat. It snatched them, and would have snatched her hand as greedily. It was difficult not to think of her as a child. 'Take care!' he exclaimed. But the shrew who had snapped the fan (so suitable with its daisies for a child sovereign) reappeared and froze him.

Other entertainments were laid on by Nature. The Geographer could not be torn from watching the northern lights.

But still Dame Habonde did not appear, and still he was not summoned for his *congé*; and the Chancellor, breaking off from an account of the network of third cousins five times removed which connected his wife with Harold Blue Tooth to call for more logs and another bottle, remarked that winter was fairly upon them and that for the next three months the road to Uppsala would be impassable. 'We were thinking of a bear hunt tomorrow,' he continued. 'Killed many bears?'

It was not that he wanted to go back to Brocéliande; but three months of being warmheartedly bored at Blokula was an extreme alternative. And he was beginning to grow fat.

The bear hunt was postponed. He was summoned for a private interview in the Queen's study. 'I have written a letter to Queen Melior,' she said. 'I wish you to read it.'

Perhaps there was still time to get away.

The letter was written in a large clear hand:

> Queen and Good Sister,
>
> I have much pleasure in acquainting Your Majesty that I have decided to appoint Your Ambassador, Lord Aquilon, to the post of Royal Favourite in My Court of Blokula.
>
> Your Majesty's loving Sister,
> Serafica R

He asked leave to sit down.

At various times women had thrown themselves at his head, and he had come to disapprove of it. But he didn't want to bruise her dignity, her dauntless self-will. At the back of his mind he heard Melior's laughter, the titters and repartees enlivening the Court of Brocéliande. Fortunately, there was a civil way out.

'You do me a very great honour'—he saw her fingers tighten as they had tightened on the fan. 'But, Madam, you have overlooked a formality. Before a Royal Favourite can be appointed, he must be preceded by a Consort. I think, Madam, you are still unmarried.'

'Not at all. I am the bride of Antecessor.' Her voice was brilliant as a wren's. 'So tomorrow I shall call a Council and make the announcement. You must be there, of course.'

He seemed to have heard the name before. 'Madam, who is Antecessor?'

'It was so long ago I can't exactly remember. But Dame Habonde will tell you. She knows all about it. She's in the anteroom. Go and ask her.'

He got up obediently and was halfway to the door when he heard her foot tap on the floor. She sat rigidly composed, the image of anxiety. Even when he was standing beside her, she did not move. He stooped down, pulled off her spectacles, and kissed her eyes.

In the anteroom was the tall woman who had drawn aside the bed curtains. The moment he recognized her he remembered that forgotten night: the hoisted children, the shouts of 'Antecessor', the leaping and prancing, the mortal rowdiness and noise and fervour in which he had consented.

'Who is this Antecessor?' he asked roughly.

'My master,' said she.

'And you are a witch, I suppose?'

'I am a witch of Lapland. We rank high among witches.'

'And among bawds! Such a high-flying, enterprising bawd that you foist yourself into Elfindom to procure that child for your Antecessor, to—'

'Listen. I had good reason.'

She explained that by power of second sight she had foreseen her death, and Serafica left uncounselled in a ring of sottish suitors, of whom she would infallibly choose the worst—as her mother had done; that as a measure of precaution she had taken the child to a Sabbath, telling her to look well at the tall man called Antecessor, who one day would make her his bride; that Serafica, remembering little else but fastening on this idea of a precontract, which she would certainly observe, since she had a very faithful disposition ...

He interrupted, infuriated by this mortal speciousness. 'You and your good reasons! You and your good offices! And no doubt it was you who put that girl in the bed.'

'And the cat between your legs.'

The door flew open. Serafica rushed in, her eyes bolting from her head. 'Aquilon, Aquilon! What are you shouting about'? Why are you so angry?'

'He's angry because he's jealous. It's a new experience, and he doesn't like it.'

Dame Habonde put an arm round her pupil and they went out together.

On the way back to his apartment Aquilon had to cross the inner courtyard where the tall wooden men had seemed so portentous on the day of his arrival. A drizzle of snow was falling. It was the moment between daylight and dusk, the northern lights were wandering, faint presences, across the sky. He leant against a wooden man and tried to collect his thoughts. There was the Geographer, and his valet, and the barber. The rest he would send back to Brocéliande when the road was open again, accompanying the bearers of Serafica's letter to Melior. The drizzle of snow closed soberingly round his rage, round his consternation. The dice fall; one does not dispute them. In six months' time the snow would have melted, he would have seen spring come to a strange country—though by then it would not be a strange country; he would know the names of the mountains, the voice of the frozen river, every step in Lady Witta's consanguinity with Harold Blue Tooth. The favour of Blokula, the contempt of Brocéliande, the Geographer's delight—he could be sure of these and discount them, discount them because he was sure of them. But how was he to be sure of himself? It was as though he had been introduced to a total stranger, a stranger of an hour's acquaintance who was out of his mind.

He moved to another wooden man. The stranger was there before him, occupying wooden men by right, for he was the Royal Favourite. As such his behaviour had been uncivil, calling the Queen's governess a bawd. Yet some allowance must be made for him, for it is a disturbing recognition of love to be catapulted into it by jealousy. Tomorrow Serafica would announce his appointment, and, as she had said, he must of course be there. He ought to be wearing a new suit; but the only unexhibited suit in his wardrobe was a black one, in case of a funeral. He must discredit her in brown and silver. The stranger of an hour's acquaintance thought these considerations trivial, but Aquilon could not entirely agree. It was the original Aquilon, the Ambassador from Brocéliande, she had chosen. The catapulted stranger she had not met.

7 Beliard

There was a time when the spring called Barenton was the most renowned thing in the Kingdom of Brocéliande—more renowned than the court, than any of its queens, than Vivien who imprisoned Merlin in her spells; more renowned and better thought of. Its water was cold, even in the sweltering days of late summer, the spring jetted in a quiet twirl of silver from the sandy bottom of the pool, filled it always to the same level, and flowed away unseen through a bed of reeds. It was as though it had a life of its own, apart from the rest of the world. There was nothing striking about it, except itself. The peasant women who resorted to it sometimes found a lady there, bathing or sitting thoughtfully beside it. She was tall, stately as a queen, and always very pleasant, talking to them in the patois. It was as if she too had a life of her own, apart from the world of Faery; for she was visible to any mortal, familiar as a neighbour, and helpful in their mortal misfortunes. But as time went on and religion spread through the district, they came to mistrust her and be of two minds about her character; when they resorted to the spring, they did so secretly, and if she happened to be there they crossed themselves and drew back. And so by degrees it became a sin to go to the spring, and also a waste of time, since one had only to go to the new church to find Our Lady of Brocéliande and the stoup of holy water, with no sin about them and always available.

Dando the Cosmographer, the Court Archivist, who wrote the standard work on Elfindom, maintained that Barenton was coeval with the stones of Carnac, and that the Kingdom of Brocéliande was formed around it, probably about the time when the forest, overthrown by the Great Gale, had put up enough second growth to afford shelter to the vagrant tribe of

Fairies, or Peris, driven out of Persia by the magicians Aaron and Moses. He held that the first settlement consisted of simple reed huts round about the spring, and that it was not till much later that the court was established in another part of the forest, over two miles away. Be this as it may (Dando's conclusions were questioned by some later scholars), the court of Brocéliande paid a respectful lip service to Barenton—such as the Dean and Chapter of Salisbury might pay to Stonehenge. It figured in sonnets (ladies as pure, and even colder). Its water was an ingredient in the famous Eau de Brocéliande. A ceremonial picnic took place beside it every twenty-five years, and if a visitor happened to be of the party Queen Melior would tell the legend of the beautiful lady who bathed there at midnight on Midsummer's Eve—to which an ambassador from the Scottish Kingdom of Elfhame had replied by telling her of a kraken in Loch Ness. Apart from these polite acknowledgements, Barenton fell into disesteem. It was in an uncouth part of the forest, all midges and brambles, and had regrettable associations with poaching mortals, who soused their scabby children in it and threw in farthings for luck. True, it was a very long time since any poaching had gone on; only peasants desperate for firewood or acorns ventured so deep into the forest. But its reputation was dubious—not to speak of that bathing person, whoever she was. Dando had no doubt who she was: one of those indigenous fairies of Brittany, contemporary with the Nine Maidens of miraculous power mentioned by Pomponius Mela, whom common speech referred to as 'the Old Lot'. Dando, invisibly frequenting alehouses and the company of midwives, learned that the indigenous fairies were still remembered by mortals. It was from two old women scalding a pig that he heard about the fairy who pulled a drowning boy from the pool of Barenton and took such pity on him that she followed him into the mortal world to be his nurse.

It was from Dando, grown very old and ramshackle, that Beliard heard the same story in his childhood, and was immediately seized by a passionate longing to be nursed by a fairy. His nurse and nursemaids were fairies; his mother, Lady Pervenche, was a fairy of unblemished lineage; he was born into the most distinguished of Elfin courts; he had never seen anything but fairies—and he longed with childish violence to be nursed by a fairy. Now he was grown up, unassuming and short-sighted but for all that a credit to his upbringing. He had an intermittent ambition to play the flageolet, and used to steal off to the pool of Barenton, where he could practise undisturbed.

He was working at the open-pipe octave, where a hoot at the bottom and a squeak at the top are equally hard to avoid, when he heard approaching wings and saw Puck, the old whipper-in of the Royal Pack of Werewolves, with four stout kennel lads carrying buckets, alight by the pool.

'Sorry to disturb Your Lordship, I'm sure,' said Puck righteously. 'And if it had been tomorrow, we wouldn't have. But today's their last chance, poor creatures! Tomorrow it'll be worms.'

'Do you mean that the pack is to be killed?'

'No. He wouldn't do that. It would be hurting their feelings. And he's all for feelings, is My Lord Melilot. But he thinks it's hard on the lads to be fetching water from here, so the drinking troughs are to be filled from the rainwater tank. You can't drink rainwater without getting worms, that's a known fact. But it's no part of my place to know better. Time will prove, that's all.'

They flew off. The ripples slapped against the bank, slowed, died into silence.

It was the end of September. The reeds were changing colour, and they whispered more harshly, as though admonishing him. He had meant, this time, to work at his flageolet seriously, to practise every day, to master the chromatic scale, soar into the upper octave, play gavottes and airs with graces instead of the melancholy little tunes within the compass of a fifth, which had been all he could manage before. But the reeds were turning colour, it would soon be too cold to practise by the pool, and he had not done half as well as he had intended.

As he was a bachelor, he still shared his mother's apartment. This made indoor practising difficult. When he had gone up the scale without a hoot or a squeak, she would interrupt him with a 'Don't go on, dear. You'll strain your heart,' or ask why he didn't play those nice little tunes he used to play. Lying (practice had made him nearly perfect at that), he would explain that he had promised to attend a cockfight or play a match with So-and-So, and leave. Picking his way down back stairs, skirting the tennis courts, he would walk demurely till it was safe to run, run like a hunted stag till he came to the pool, recover his breath, take the flageolet out of its velvet sleeve, and begin his preliminary exercises. *Do, re, mi, fa, sol, la, si, DO. Do, mi, la, DO, la, mi, do.* And so on, a degree higher; for by now he could practise agility most of the way up the scale. The silver twirl rose through the stilly water, the unchanging level of the pool flowed away through the reeds and sank beneath a small swamp. And Lady Pervenche would glide along the gallery which the younger members of the court called 'the Hen's Parade', to visit her friend Lady Renoncule (they belonged to the epoch when it was fashionable to be called after field flowers), to declare that Renoncule's Persis grew prettier every day, to drink a cup of chocolate, and to conceal her sorrows; for as she hoped to make a match between Persis and Beliard it would not have done to admit how much it distressed her to see Beliard always passed over when there was a court appointment going.

'Have you heard about poor old Dando? I must admit I had almost forgotten he was still alive.'

Dando the Cosmographer was dying. He had been brought down from his garret and laid in the State Death Bed, amid black curtains and under a black tester. His mind was decayed, but he was conscious and complained that the mattress was lumpy. His feet were rubbed, his beard combed, he was given strengthening soups, and for a time he rallied, and talked in a wandering way about things long past and forgotten. Once, he called for a secretary, as he wished to have an annotation set down. But he was far away from the cares of this world, for when the Queen's Procurator arrived with two underlings and suggested he might like to make his will, he replied there wasn't enough to trouble about. A couple of days before his end, he was heard to chuckle and sigh and repeat snatches of ballads learned in his alehouse days. A coughing fit nearly finished him, but he got the better of it and began to clamour about a boy: he wanted to see the boy. He became so insistent that they eventually asked him which boy. The boy who wanted to be nursed by a fairy, he said. It was plain he had some mortal boy in mind, and this made it even more impossible to oblige him. 'Be-li-ard!' he shouted. It was like the angry bellow of a ram. Beliard was fetched to the bedside. Dando's glance wandered up him from a boy's height to a man's. 'Did you get her?' he asked. Beliard shook his head. 'None left, none left,' said Dando, and an attendant, thinking he spoke of his empty bowl, came up with more soup.

The funeral was superb. Music, specially composed in the antique style, was performed, and several panegyrics were spoken. Of these, the most eloquent came from the Archivist of a Kingdom in Wales, so small and unimportant that it had not been notified; but he had somehow heard the news and travelled to Brocéliande to praise Dando, above all for his compelling hypothesis of the Great Gale.

By the time all this was over, it had grown too cold to practise by the pool of Barenton. Beliard put away his flageolet and settled down to the customary gaieties. It was an implacably hard winter. There were skating parties on the ornamental moat, with braziers set at intervals along it. Lady Pervenche's ankles did not allow her to skate, but as she was young at heart she sat in an ice sleigh and was pushed by Beliard. Persis, she thought, could not fail to observe how strong he was, and how kindhearted: such a husband is a treasure for centuries. Observing Beliard's kindheartedness, Melilot skated up to them to suggest he should have the pleasure of pushing the sleigh for a few rounds. Beliard, who was more out of breath than any scale passage could have left him, was ready to accept, but Lady Pervenche cried out, 'No, thank you, no, thank you! You really are too kind. But you have *other* duties, you know.' She had known Melilot to be a scheming interloper ever since his appointment to the Mastership of the Werewolves, a post she had designed for Beliard.

Melilot smiled, bowed, hoped for another time, and skated away.

At the assembly that evening, Beliard detached himself from watching the cardplayers to make some atonement. Melilot bore no malice. His wish to please everybody extended into a belief that everybody was pleasing. When Beliard asked how the pack were doing, he said how grateful they were for an issue of blankets. 'Splendid fellows! You should have seen how they snatched at them.' Blankets were not his only innovation. He had begun to add vegetables to their diet. After a spell of carrots they looked much glossier—or so it seemed to him. If Beliard could spare time to look in at a morning feed …

Beliard woke the next morning with the agreeable thought of having something to do. As he neared the kennels he heard hammerings: they were breaking the ice on the rainwater tank. He remembered Dando's statement that the pool of Barenton never froze. Dando had some scientific explanation of why this was so, which Beliard could not remember; he had not read the Cosmography very attentively. He decided that after doing the polite at the kennels he would walk on and see for himself.

The snow was speckled with dead birds. They were so weightless with starvation that they lay on its surface like decorations on a pudding. The sky was lead-coloured; the dull dazzle of snow wrenched at his shortsighted eyes. A shinier patch of snow, trodden down into ice, and a few trampled wisps of hay, showed where fodder had been put out for the deer.

The pool lay before him, black and alarming. He felt his heart jolt. An old woman was crouched beside it. The hood of her peasant's cloak had fallen aside; he could see her grizzled hair, and the cadaverous face she bent over the water. It was because she was so unexpected that he had been frightened. But this fright kept him motionless, staring at the blotch of darkness she made. After a while she scrambled to her feet and made off through the reeds and was gone. In his fright he had almost forgotten his reason for being there. He went forward to the pool, and saw that the water was unfrozen, the spring twirling up as usual. Thus looked down into, the pool did not seem dark and alarming at all; the sandy bottom gave it an appearance of being sunlit. And the old woman was nothing to be alarmed by. The frost was everywhere, a stranglehold on mortals, on cattle licking snow with parched tongues. She had known in her old woman's memory that the pool of Barenton never froze, and had come with her pitcher, defying regulations, chancing the poacher's death on the gallows, to fetch water.

All the same, she had given him a fright.

He returned to the palace to be told what he had missed: the Queen had been reading aloud from the Cosmography.

The expense of the funeral had not been in vain. Dando was rediscovered as a classic. His accounts of other Kingdoms were most entertaining, his theories ingenious, his solemn language a delight. Books Three and Four, 'Of Brocéliande' and 'Of Customs', were indisputably Dando at his best. Who could have believed that the quiet old man, so retiring in his habits, so shabby in his apparel, was—here opinions diverged, some saying, 'Such a man of the world', others, 'Such a master of the occult'. The readings continued. There was talk of an abridged Cosmography—with some of the scandals, some of the Druidical bits left out—for children. Only the Directors of Piety disagreed; Dando should certainly not be abridged for children: his sources were dubious, his opinions those of an atheist. Nowhere in Book Three was there a word about Afrits, tutelary spirits peculiar to the Brocéliande dynasty, whose patronage could only be secured by the intervention of the Directors of Piety.

During all this, Beliard said nothing of his familiarity with the pool of Barenton; he wanted to keep it for his flageolet. The snow was still lying, the kennel lads hammering, when he visited it again. He had half an idea the old crone might still be drawing water from it. She was not there. It was natural to suppose that she was dead. He had taken his flageolet with him, and with freezing fingers he played a little tune, just to hear what it sounded like in that icy, dying world.

A week before the Spring Ceremony, there was a sudden thaw. He went to the pool two days running, and each time she was there. He had not the courage to approach her. He did not know what to think. Dando would have known. But he was glad that Dando was spared from knowing. It would have grieved him to know that the benign, stately lady who bathed there, sat musing on the bank, talked like a neighbour to the peasant women, had shrunk into this pitiable old crone.

The Spring Ceremony took place in a violent hailstorm. The day after, it was warm as summer and the Directors of Piety emerged like tortoises and bashed in justification. The Afrits had struck—Melilot had been killed by the werewolves. He had gone into their enclosure to distribute some tidbits, and stumbled over a bone. In an instant they rushed on him, pulled him down, and tore him to pieces. The court went into mourning, the Directors of Piety imposed a general fast, the opening of the hunting season was postponed, the Cosmography was put on the Index, Puck was sacked. In the storm of controversy over the future of the werewolves, various arguments were put forward: they were a traditional glory; they were quite out of date; no one wanted them; they were the envy of every other court. Melior seemed to incline to the traditionalists; then, for she prided herself on her spontaneity, passed the death sentence. They were hanged.

With history being made at such a rate, it was easy for Beliard to slink off to the pool. As an excuse to himself, and an insurance against the disappointment he would feel if the old woman were not there, he took his flageolet. Once, when he was practising, she passed behind him and sat down in her usual place. He wanted to speak to her—some noncommittal remark about the beauty of the morning—but he was afraid to. For all he knew, he was invisible to her: her survival (he was convinced by now she was a survival) hung on so delicate a thread that the smallest shock might blow her away. And that would be a cruel deed: if she were so faithful to the pool, she must love it a great deal. He looked at her as little as possible: a direct glance might fall on her like a blow. In the light of spring, her age was more apparent, and her ugliness. It was not a solemn ugliness: it was grotesque, a clay likeness of a frog.

When she was not there he felt a dull bereavement, like a bruise.

It was ironical that at this time he should hear so many evocations of her at court. With the Cosmography on the Index, not to admire Dando was to be in mothballs. Barenton again figured in sonnets, but now—for fashions change— as the water of youth where the poet's mistress had been immersed, where immersion would be superfluous. Book Four, 'Of Customs', governed taste. Round dances ousted cotillions, monoliths were a passion. Melior was importuned to revive the custom of bathing in Barenton, and the Court Architect designed a light tent. Beliard did not feel his tenancy menaced. He knew that the more a project is talked of the less likely it is to take place. Meanwhile he had found a new way to practise undisturbed, by hiding in the laurels and serenading Persis. His heart was cold, his feelings engaged elsewhere, and he probably played the better for this. One night it occurred to him to leave his hiding place and to play by the pool. Persis had opened her casement and said something about nightingales—but he stole away and followed the path, which was now so familiar and in its hoarfrost of moonlight curiously strange, and peopled by mysterious shadows.

She was there—a darker blotch of darkness in the moonlight than ever by day. The impersonality of moonlight made him bold. He walked up to her, stopped beside her. She was staring down at what he took to be the reflection of the moon in the water. But it was not the moon. It was her own reflected face she was staring at: a smooth, calm, youthful face, with faintly smiling lips.

He felt no astonishment, no awe. He felt at ease and profoundly contented, as though he had come to the end of a journey and was looking down into the valley which was his birthplace. The dawn wind brushed the reed bed, he heard her breathe a slow, contented sigh; she got up, gave herself a little shake, and moved away. The sun had risen, the dragonflies were hawking over the pool, the midges swarming round him, before he walked back through the awakened forest.

It was as though he had won some transcendental bet—a bet against all odds. She was one of the Old Lot, persistent as the little twirl of the spring, indigenously young. Her disguise of old age was as trifling as a cobweb. He was so sure he had seen her that he was sure he would see her again, her true likeness, herself smiling at herself in the pool. How would it be by daylight? Did she, did he, need the moon? By now copies of the forbidden Book Three and Book Four were passing from hand to hand, vanishing up cuffs or into bodices. He borrowed a copy of Book Three and read it attentively. There was no particular mention of moonlight. Moonlight came in later, with the Druids. And why should moonlight be needed? If she had only bathed by moonlight, Dando would have said so. He went early to bed that night, and fell asleep in a trance of trust.

A dream stabbed him awake. In the dream, the Court Architect exhibited a small straw hat, saying it was the Queen's bathing tent. He woke in a panic. If that bathing scheme came to anything, she might be driven away, affronted by the invasion of her solitude. He would never see her again.

It was late; he had overslept. The Hens were rushing up and down their Parade, calling for daisy chains. In the Morning Saloon, the programme for the day was being read out. The Queen with her ladies, pastorally dressed, would be carried to Barenton in litters. The bathing tent would be set up near the pool. The litter bearers and tent peggers would wait at a distance. Her Majesty, assisted by her ladies, would disrobe and enter the pool at noon precisely, wearing a gossamer shift and protected by a Chinese parasol. She would bathe in the pool for five minutes. Bath towels, warmed, would be in readiness. After she had reposed, there would be a light collation and the party would start back, reaching the palace at 3 pm. The programme had been decided on overnight, at the last moment, but it was hoped that all would go smoothly.

'You'll be eaten alive by midges!' he shouted. Melior turned and beckoned him toward her. 'Are they awful?' she asked. 'Swarms of them,' said he. 'And frogs? Are there many frogs? I'm terrified of frogs.' If he had kept his wits about him, he could have made as many frogs as midges and the bathing party might have been cancelled. It was a fatal omission.

Melior was so amazed that anyone at court could consider her welfare before his own that she kept him in conversation for some while after; and when she had thanked and dismissed him, and ordered that every member of the party should be sprayed with oil of verbena and the Court Physician be in attendance, and made a mental note to find some post for her honest man, Beliard was so buttonholed, questioned, and congratulated that he despaired of getting away in time.

But he was in time—she was there. And moonlight was not essential; the pool reflected her daytime face, which was slightly more rounded and mature. She seemed to listen to him as he poured out the news of the bathing party, the invasion of her privacy, his inability to protect her. But how could he tell if she really were listening? That momentary pucker on her brow might just as well have been a tremor on the surface of the pool. It would only be for a few hours, he assured her. By the evening all would be as it had been.

'Beliard, dear! What are you thinking of? You mustn't be here. The Queen will arrive at any moment.'

He heard the violins strike up, a clatter of voices, his mother's skirts catching on the grass as she hurried to take her place with the rest. He cast himself down headlong to kiss the face in the water. It vanished under his lips. The ripples darted up the bank, his mouth was full of grit, he felt the water evading him, deserting him. The reeds heeled over in the vehement current as the pool of Barenton drained away.

When the pages unrolled the carpet from the bathing tent to the rim of the pool, they saw Beliard lying face down on the wet sand, his hand clutching the last trickle of water from the spring.

The carpet was rolled up, the tent dismantled, the litters filled higgledy-piggledy, no precedence observed. Melior sat behind closed curtains, her gloves half buttoned, her mind in bitter disarray. Only that morning had she found an honest, disinterested courtier. He was not dead; the Court Physician had revived him and diagnosed his malady. But he could never be given a post of confidence. Brocéliande would not accept a Minister with epilepsy.

8 Visitors to a Castle

Mynnedd Prescelly is the westernmost mountain in Wales. It is of only moderate height but its sweeping contours, rising from a gentle countryside, dominate the skyline. Sometimes it is there, sometimes not. Giraldus Cambrensis, who wrote the 'ltinerarium Kambriae', must often have looked inquiringly toward it from his birthplace, Manorbier Castle. In the 'Itinerary', however, all he has to say of Prescelly is that a man dwelling on its northern slope dreamed that if he put his hand into a certain spring he would find a rock and beneath it a golden torque; and being covetous, did so, was bitten by a viper, and died. It may be that Giraldus wrote more fully about Prescelly in a lost chapter of the 'Itinerary'; otherwise, this is another instance of his credulity distracting him from more serious matters.

Since time out of mind, there has been a small Elfin Kingdom of Castle Ash Grove, which lies in a valley of Mynnydd Prescelly. Its name harks back to a time when its inhabitants did not care to build and had not developed a social hierarchy of flying servants, strolling gentry. At nightfall, regardless of class distinctions, they flew up into the boughs of an ash grove and slept there.

They were still sleeping in trees when a mortal came among them, a civil old man in a single garment, very coarse and verminous, who had voyaged from Ireland into St Brides Bay on a slab of granite. This he told them, while they hospitably combed the lice from his single garment. True hospitality includes receiving travellers' tales, and they asked him how he had made the granite slab seaworthy. He replied, 'By Faith.' The word was new to them. He preached them a sermon on the nature of Faith, and how its apartness from knowledge, its irreconcilability with all human experience, proved that it was a spark of the heavenly mind. 'Faith can remove mountains!' he exclaimed. But Faith was not for them. Being Elfins, they had no souls. Without souls, they could not enjoy the advantages of Faith, not so much as to say to a pebble, 'Be thou removed.'

Till now, they had listened politely. But at this last statement their Welsh pride put up its hackle. They did not contradict him to his face, but when he had limped on to convert the heathen in Carmarthenshire they exploded with resentment and set themselves to disprove it, each and all saying to his chosen pebble, 'Be thou removed!' Not a pebble stirred. They decided that pebbles were too small to be worth removing anyway, and that it would be simpler to work on Mynnydd Prescelly. Prescelly did not comply; their Welsh pride would not yield. Matters were at a deadlock when the Court Poet's nephew said that if they seriously wished to remove Mynnydd Prescelly they must sing. There is nothing so powerful as singing. Everyone who sings knows this with an inward certainty.

He was a stout young fairy with a light tenor voice. Previously, no one had paid much attention to him. Now he assumed command. When they proposed to sing immediately, he quelled their impatience: they must give their voices, hoarse and ravelled from shouting at pebbles, a chance to recover. Not a note till sundown tomorrow; meanwhile, a light supper and early to bed after a gargle of blackberry juice and honey. For his part, he would compose a special Removal Song to be sung without accompaniment, and of narrow compass so that all could join in.

At sundown precisely, they met to sing. Not a cough was heard among them. The Poet's nephew mounted a stool and took them through the Removal Song till they had it by heart. The tune, as he had promised, was one they all could join in. It was in a three-beat measure and within the compass of a sixth. The words 'Mynnydd Prescelly, Be thou removed' they knew already, and after a few niceties had been attended to he signalled them to a pause and said, 'Now, all together. One, two, three!'

They began with their gathered breaths. At first, they sang in unison. Then they sang in thirds. As the power of song took hold of them, they threw in spontaneous descants. When they realized that the song could be sung in canon, like Three Blind Mice and Tallis's Evening Hymn, their joy knew no bounds. They sang. They sang. The Poet's nephew, singing himself and conducting with both hands, led them from an ample *forte* to a rich *fortissimo* and tapered them down to a *pianissimo espressivo* and roused them again and again calmed them. Each sang, putting his whole heart into it as though everything depended on him, and at the same time felt the anonymous ardour of those singing with him. They sang so intently that they did not hear the ash trees rustle as though a solemn gale blew over them. When the Poet's nephew had brought them back to a unison and slowed them to a close, they looked round on each other as though on well-met strangers. Glorified and exhausted by a total experience, they ate an enormous supper, climbed into their ash trees, and slept till well past sunrise.

It was as though they had woken in a new country. Rubbing their eyes, they stared at an unfamiliar aspect of day. The mountain was gone. When they flew up to see what had happened to it, they saw the distant coastline and the mysterious pallor of the sea.

A dandelion clock could not have vanished more peacefully. There was no sign of uprooting; the hare tracks printed their established pattern but on level ground, the brook ran in its same bed, but unhurrying. Wherever the mountain had gone to, it had gone without ill will.

Three nights later it came back, unobserved, and was settled in its old place before day.

Its return was more sobering than its departure had been. It had gone because they had willed it to do so. It came back of its own will. The Court Poet in his Welcoming Ode compared it to bees, cats, pigeons, and other animals with homing instincts, but it was felt that he was using too much poetic licence. There were stories from the Kingdom of Thule of individualistic underground springs which burst into towering activity and deluged everybody with hot water and cinders. Though nothing of that sort had ever happened in Wales, neither had a disappearing and reappearing mountain. But Mynnydd Prescelly embraced its inhabitants as quietly as ever, and sheltered them as reliably from the north wind, and bumblebees hummed up and down its slopes, and harebells grew where they always did. Presently the more light-minded and scientific fairies began to experiment in removal by Faith—not the mountain, of course, but rocks and stones which nobody needed—and when there was a small landslide, nothing would content them but another singing assembly. Again the mountain disappeared—this time in a heavy sea fog; and again it came back, looking, as one might say, unmoved. Before five centuries had passed, moving the mountain had become a regular ceremonial, carried out because the mountain would expect it. By then, research had established what happened. Mynnydd Prescelly rose up in the shape of a cloud, and travelled to Plynlimon for the inside of a week, the cloudy Mynnydd Prescelly would travel back, fall as rain, solidify as mountain. And human beings who had noticed its absence from the skyline would say, 'There's Mynnydd Prescelly again, so we'll start harvesting.'

Whether one sleeps in an ashtree cradle or under the thatch of a modest castle, a moist mountainy air is a better soporific than any good conscience. The Elfins of Castle Ash Grove prided themselves on being good sleepers, and had remarkably inoffensive consciences. Music was their preoccupation. They brewed an incomparable mead. They also prided themselves on being good neighbours: if a peasant's cow strayed into their park, they allowed it to graze; if a peasant's horde of children wandered into their valley, they sat in trees and watched them with benevolence. This did not happen very often, however; it was a poor countryside and thinly populated. As the martyred Irishman's teaching spread among the descendants of his hearers, being an Elfin good neighbour became less easy: women pestered them with offerings, tied dirty rags on their trees, and dipped scrofulous babies in their brook; men threw stones at them, aiming in the direction of their voices. But the music and the mead continued, and the link with Plynlimon, and the satisfaction of knowing that they were instrumental in swelling the baby Severn into a real river. For though it rains copiously on Plynlimon, the contributions of their own Mynnydd Prescelly must surely count for something: if they had not all sung so powerfully to confute the Irishman and for the honour of Wales, the mountain— extraordinary thought!—might never have removed.

Perhaps it aided time to slip away so peacefully that all their queens were called Morgan. There was the notorious Morgan le Fay. There was Morgan Philosophy, whose long scholarly amour with Taliesin taught him to be a salmon and acquainted him with Alexander the Great. There was Morgan Breastknot of Music, whose page, grown old, wept on his death bed because all living memory of her singing would perish with him. The reign of her successor, Morgan Spider (so titled because of her exquisite fine spinning), saw a new manifestation of Castle Ash Grove's devotion to music. Ignoring the traditional Elfin aloofness from mankind, a party of music lovers democratically disguised themselves as mortals and went to Worcester Cathedral, masked and in riding mantles, to hear Thomas Tomkins play on the organ; and later, wearing bonnets and top hats, attended a performance of the Messiah at the Three Choirs' Festival.

By now we are within sight of the twentieth century.

It was a fine autumn evening in 1893. The mountain had just come back from Plynlimon. Morgan Spider and some of her court were strolling in the park, saying how pleasant it was to feel sheltered from the outer world again, when they heard an astonishing assortment of noises—a frantic ting-a-ling, a metallic crash, loud mortal bewailings and cries for help. They moved cautiously toward the cries. Where their valley curved under the slope of a steep hillside they saw a massive young woman in a dark-blue uniform sprawled on the grass, weeping convulsively and draped in what seemed to be a tattered metal cage—and was, in fact, a bicycle.

In order not to alarm her, they made themselves visible, as they had made themselves visible at Worcester and the Three Choirs' Festival in order not to be sat on.

'I'm afraid you're in some trouble,' said Morgan Spider.

'I should think I am in some trouble,' replied the young woman. 'My brake wouldn't hold and my bike's smashed and my knee's cut to the bone. And I'd like to know what's been going on here,' she continued, glaring at them. 'It wasn't like this last week.'

Consulting among themselves, they agreed that this was not the moment in which to explain about the mountain.

The young woman launched into a resentful narrative of a road which went on going uphill, so she knew it must be the wrong one, of the track she had turned into which led to a bog, of the tracks leading nowhere, of exhaustion, desolation, bulls, gnats, distant cottages which turned out to be sheepfolds, birds that got up behind her with a noise like a gun, vipers that threatened her with their stings, and never

a sign of life and always uphill. 'And if that wasn't enough—'
She broke off and exclaimed, 'Where's my bag?'

A large black bag lay nearby. Morgan Spider's page picked
it up and handed it to her.

When she opened it, they all started in horror at the
appalling smell that came out. She pulled up her skirts,
rolled down a black stocking, and displayed a bloodied
knee. She unstoppered a small bottle. The appalling smell
was redoubled. Dame Bronwen fainted. The mortal poured
a well-known disinfectant on a wad of cotton wool, laid the
wad (with howls) on her knee, and tied on a white bandage
very deftly. Looking up, she saw them ministering to Dame
Bronwen. 'One of those who can't stand the sight of blood,'
she remarked. 'My job wouldn't suit her.'

A mortal who delighted in the sight of blood was not the
guest they would have chosen. But hospitality is a sacred
duty among Elfins. Trying not to inhale her, they supported
the young woman to the castle, sat her down in the parlour,
and gave her a glass of mead. There was a rather long silence.
Morgan Spider looked out of the window and saw Dame
Bronwen approaching, and the page doing his best with the
bicycle and the bicycle retaliating. And she looked at the
tranquil darkening sky, and then at the massive, reddening
young woman, who was twirling her glass.

But hospitality requires more than refilling a glass. Morgan
Spider mentioned that the mead was homemade, and the
young woman commented that they were quite old-fashioned,
weren't they.

'And where do you come from? Is it far away?'

'Nottingum.'

A beautified simper spread across the young woman's face,
and she dwelt upon the word as though it were a jujube.
'Nottingum,' she repeated, and held her glass out dreamily.
'Born there. Educated there. And look at me now. All my

qualifications, and they've sent me to this back-of-beyond district. And that Mrs Jones I saw last week sends a message to say she's taken unexpected and would I come soon as I could. And if I lose her, I suppose they'll blame me. Slave driving, I call it.'

'Where does this Mrs. Jones live?' demanded Morgan Spider. The young woman started. She groped in her pocket and handed over a screw of paper. 'It's in Welsh. Even if I could say it, it wouldn't get me there. It's my poor bike I'm worrying about.'

While she wept, Morgan Spider told the page to fetch her muff—for it would be a cold night to fly in.

'Madam, Madam! Your Majesty's surely not going to fly?'

'The woman's in labour. Do you expect me to go in a procession?' She snatched the muff and ran out. They saw her flicker down the valley like a bat. The uppermost thought in every heart was envy.

When Morgan Spider returned, rosy with triumph and night air, she heard singing. As she entered, it broke off. Her whole court was assembled round the District Nurse, who lay on the floor dead drunk, with her right hand clenched on a pair of scissors.

After her departure, they explained, the mortal talked about lockjaw and said she must renew the dressing on her knee. The bandage was peeled off and rerolled with exactitude. The bottle was unstoppered, the wad soaked and reapplied. As before, she howled, but now a great deal louder. Brandishing a pair of scissors, she staggered round the room trying to get at the page in order to cut the grin off his face, tripped over the Keeper of the Archives—a slow mover—and subsided on the floor. There she had lain ever since. All felt she should be removed. None was willing to approach her, in case she might come to. The Keeper of the Archives, with a quotation from Vergil, said that in special difficulties one should turn to tradition. For a great many centuries the mountain had been removing itself unprompted, but he supposed the Removal Song would be as effective as ever. After a few false starts, they remembered the tune. Altering the words so that there should be no misunderstanding, they began singing, and had been singing for an hour and three-quarters:

'Nottingum, Nottingum,
Be thou removed.'

Morgan Spider said they must put more life into it. It was a fine old tune, and would stand up to a little impiety. Joined by their Queen, the singers did better; some almost believed they saw the dark-blue mass rise a few inches from the floor.

Morgan Spider clapped her hands. 'Stop! I see what's wrong. We're barking up the wrong tree. "Nottingum, Nottingum, Be thou removed" means nothing to her.'

They objected that the mortal had said 'Nottingum'.

'She said she was born there. Wherever it is, it's just a place.'

One of the younger ladies said, with a giggle, 'Suppose it's working there?'

'That's no affair of ours. It isn't working here. But if we cannot remove her, we can remove ourselves. So we'll have a quick supper and then fly to Plynlimon.'

She spoke to be obeyed. On the morrow, glittering in the rays of the newly risen sun, they descended like a swarm of fireflies on the vast, green, featherbed expanse of Plynlimon.

When they had recovered from the fatigue of the journey, they found themselves delighted to be there. Even Elfins are susceptible to the Zeitgeist. The Zeitgeist of the day was to resort to the Simple Life—nature, nuts, sleeping out-of-doors, an escape from convention and formality. Plynlimon afforded exactly that. Doing nothing, they were never at a loss for something to do. They snared rabbits and roasted them over a wood fire they had rekindled from the ashes of a fire abandoned by travelling gipsies. Collecting enough fuel to keep the fire going was a labour of love, eating rabbit with their fingers was a feat. When the Keeper of the Archives found a thrown-away iron cauldron in a ditch, they cooked gipsy stews, flavouring the rabbit with chanterelle mushrooms and wild garlic, and supping the broth from snail shells. All these things called for much time and invention and were achievements—unless they went wrong, when they were things to laugh about. The more active went for immense walks. Others picked watercress and wild strawberries or sat talking on large subjects. At night, they admired the stars. Their feet were usually wet and they were all in perfect health.

Morgan Spider, but for whom they would not have come to Plynlimon, disclaimed any particular hand in it. It was a mass rising, she said; she had chanced to speak first, but the thought was in every mind. The voice of Nature had said, 'Be thou removed,' as it spoke to swallows and cuckoos and ice-cream vendors and nightingales; and the happy migrants obeyed. When the voice of Nature directed, they would fly back to Castle Ash Grove, and settle down for a comfortable winter, telling stories and brewing more mead. Every trace of the visitor would have been broomed and aired out of the castle. It had been left in the care of reliable changelings, who had detested Nottingum as only blood relations can.

One thing only slightly troubled her—Dame Bronwen's incapacity to delight in what everyone else found so delightful. At the announcement that they would remove to Plynlimon, Bronwen had welcomed the idea, so impatiently that she wanted to start at once. On their first day there, she was the earliest to be up and about, as excited as a child by the change of air, the change of scene, the prospect of an entirely new way of life. By midday, the bright morning clouded over. Politely admiring, politely enjoying, she remained aloof. Though Morgan Spider had for the time shaken off the responsibilities of a queen, she still felt the obligations of a hostess. It occurred to her that Bronwen was sulking because she felt in some way slighted.

A little favouritism might put this right. Noticing the tufts of wool which brambles and thistles had plucked off passing sheep, she had idly planned to take home the best of them to card and spin during the winter. She invited Dame Bronwen to come wool gathering. Sometimes they wandered together, sometimes apart. The air was perfectly still. There were a great many flies about, which they beat off with bracken whisks. Morgan Spider fell behind to pull some particularly fine tufts from a thorn brake. Beyond the thorn brake, she came on Dame Bronwen, who was standing motionless in a cloud of flies. She whisked her bracken frond. Dame Bronwen started violently; it was as if she had been found out in some atrocious fault.

'A penny for your thoughts, Bronwen.'

It was the wrong thing to say. Dame Bronwen locked up her face, and after a pause remarked on the flies, saying that they were the only drawback to Plynlimon; adding politely that they were only a nuisance on windless days.

They walked on together, Morgan Spider making experimental conversation and getting nothing but a Yes or No for her pains. There was a crooked sloe bush ahead of them, and she said to herself, 'Before we reach the sloe bush I'll get it out of her.' But they were level with the bush before she said, 'Bronwen, what ails you?'

Bronwen said, 'A bad smell.' She pressed a branch of the sloe to her bosom as though its thorns would help her to speak. 'Do you remember the smell that came out of the bottle?'

'And it was so appalling that it made you faint? Of course I remember it. But by the time we go back, Castle Ash Grove will have been cleaned and aired. I shall send the page ahead of us to make certain; we won't start till he tells us the smell is gone.'

'It will never be gone.'

Dame Bronwen pressed the branch so hard to her bosom that a sloe burst and its juice spurted out.

'When I fainted it was because of what was shown me. I saw trees blighted and grass burned brown and birds falling out of the sky. I saw the end of our world, Morgan—the end of Elfin. I saw the last fairy dying like a scorched insect.'

She was mad. But she spoke with such intensity it was impossible not to believe her.

9 The Power of Cookery

The servants' hall at Schloss Dreiviertelstein—an Elfin court in Styria—was a Gothic apartment with an oriel window overlooking the poultry yard. At the head of the long table was a discarded throne, and there sat Ludla, the cook. In order of hierarchy, the throne should have been the house-keeper's, but Ludla's pre-eminence was indisputable, so the housekeeper sat at the other end of the table in a handsome chair of Spanish workmanship. At Ludla's right hand sat Ernolf, the butler; at her left, the cellarer, Gunf. The housekeeper was supported by the chief lady's maid and the head huntsman. Valets, footmen, grooms, housemaids, kitchen maids, laundresses, etc, sat in ordered ranks on either side.

All these were working fairies and their sleeping accommodation was poky. It was compensated for by their victuals. Their food was identical with the food served at the Queen's table—only hotter. Count Horn, the Royal Favourite, sometimes paused at the stairhead and sniffed wistfully. When Horn was young he was the soul of poetry and often forgot to eat. Many years had passed over him since. He retained his post (Queen Aigle was a traditionalist), but the poetry had waned to regretfulness and greed.

Ludla's cooking was renowned throughout Elfindom. Dreiviertelstein was an unimportant Kingdom, but to go on an embassy to Dreiviertelstein was something to be contested for, boasted of, and ardently remembered. Nowhere else was stuffed goose such a fulfilling experience, eel soup so exhilarating, haunches of venison of such a texture, substantial yet yielding, game pies so autumnally fragrant, dumplings in such variety of modest perfection, apple strudel so beguiling;

though whether Ludla's brandied plums in marzipan jackets did or did not surpass her apple strudel was a pious debate.

Ambassadors timed their visits to coincide with Royal Birthdays, which were solemnized by Ludla's crawfish soufflé. The preparation for this fleeting delicacy began at dawn, when the crawfish were netted from the brook by teams of hardy scullions. They were plunged into precisely boiling water, and as they boiled, the Schloss cats set up an impassioned, visionary mewing. The flesh, freed from every fragment of shell, was gently, methodically pounded in marble mortars to a smooth paste by kitchen maids; cream skimmed from the wide bowls of overnight milk was added, while other kitchen maids whipped the whites of countless eggs. When all this was done to Ludla's satisfaction, and the ovens stoked to a steady heat, she did the flavouring. The flavouring was her secret. While she was at it, everyone was banished from the kitchen, and a holy silence settled on court life. It was of crawfish soufflé that Count Luxus committed his only metaphor. 'It is like eating a cloud,' he said. His cousin Count Brock, who had a more searching mind, replied, 'But, unlike a cloud, it nourishes.'

The only person at Dreiviertelstein unmoved by Ludla's cooking was Queen Aigle. For her, meals recurred like sunrise and sunset. If a sauce had been curdled, a dumpling petrified, she would have acknowledged its cometlike apparition without feeling personally involved.

Aigle was a High Romantic. She saw life as an occasion for achieving the improbable, for aiming at the unseen, and enforced this frame of mind on others. For the enforcing, she relied on quests. She could not go questing herself, being a Queen, or send her ladies on them, questing being unsuitable for ladies; and the working fairies already had their duties to carry out. But for the male half of her court she invented one quest after another. The quests necessarily complied with the seasons: in the winter months they were domesticated, their objects ranging from a lost thimble or the Absolute to a B flat in *alt*. With the spring, they soared. There was the Quest for the White Gentian, when the mountain slopes were speckled with stooping questers. There was the Quest for the Toad in a Stone, when the mountain peaks rang with the tap-tap of geological hammers and the curses of those whose hammers fell awry. There was the quest for the Purple Carp, the Chamois Shod in Silver, the Ring Hung on the Topmost Bough, the Crested Hazel Hen. For several summers there had been a Quest of the Dragon, but this was abandoned, not so much because dragons were out-of-date as on account of so many questers being lost in caverns, some never to be found again. When Aigle's invention faltered, there was always the Quest of the Four-Leafed Clover to fall back on. There was also the twice-yearly competition for the First and Last Rose of Summer.

In the servants' hall opinions differed about the quests. The valets disapproved of them because of the clothes to be brushed and the boots polished, the housemaids because of the dirt tracked indoors. The kitchen fairies were sympathetic, and laid bets. Ludla invented a recipe for the Purple Carp, whose colouring she proposed to reinforce with beetroot. Meanwhile she put up picnic lunches.

The only valet who had no grounds for complaint was Prince Ingobaldo's. Ingobaldo was the Royal Consort, and felt it his duty to stay indoors to protect Aigle if the castle were struck by lightning. (Privately he wished it might be; he came from a Cisalpine Kingdom, and preferred a calmer style of architecture.) Marriage had brought him a severe disappointment. Pacing the distances and then measuring them with a wheel, he found that Dreiviertelstein was situated at five-eighths of the ascent from the valley to the mountain summit. Anxious not to condemn too hastily, he sought for a stone at the three-quarters mark. There wasn't one. But he had Ludla's cooking, perfection in an imperfect world; he had a quest of his own, an indoor quest for a sublime hour when his collection of striking clocks (five of them musical) would strike the hour simultaneously and the favourite melodies of Thuringia, Bohemia, the Veneto, Switzerland, and Capri mingle as one; and he enjoyed naming cats. There was no child of the marriage.

During the long summer hours when the questers were out, the elder court ladies slept, played cards, or wrote their memoirs; the young ones gathered sprigs of rosemary and bay, shook the insects out of them, and wove the daily garland with which Queen Aigle might crown whoever had achieved the current quest. The garland was seldom awarded. Every now and then, someone would find a four-leafed clover; the First and the Last Rose were reliable events. But though the White Gentian had been found and the garland bestowed, a cloud hung over the proceedings. The gentian was pallid, rather than white, and lacked the usual gentian stamina. There was a suspicion, though no one voiced it publicly, that its finder had blanched it artificially under an inverted flowerpot. The rosemaries and the bay trees grew in tubs along the South Terrace, and by the time they were brought in to winter in the conservatory, they looked impoverished, as they were also requisitioned by Ludla—the rosemary for roast pork, the bay leaves for game pies and custards. Like her Queen, Ludla was a traditionalist. A boar's head would have had no breath of the wild for her without a lemon between its jaws and celery whiskers.

Another summer was closing, the last of its Last Roses had been found, the last garland of the season given, and Aigle was inscribing this event in the Chronicle of Dreiviertelstein. The quality of the ink varied from time to time, but otherwise there was not much variation in the entries. A death, the first snowfall, a birth, an avalanche, an embassy ... these were things expected. Everything in nature submits to becoming something to be expected. The hopes fastened on a new quest submit to the law of averages and fade. A stranger appears in an embassy, a travelling clockmaker stumbles through the snow and is sheltered for the night; they come again, and are no longer strangers. Schloss Dreiviertelstein was out of the way of interesting arrivals. The day of Wandering Minstrels, Tired Pilgrims, was over. In any case, these would probably be mortals, and as such irrelevant to a factual Elfin chronicle.

Even so, at that moment an interesting arrival, a seedy-looking young fairy, was circling over the castle and snuffing the air attentively.

His luck never failed him: it was a Michaelmas goose! He flew to a distance, alighted, closed his wings, and began to walk genteelly up the track. The plan of campaign formed in his mind. He would be mysterious, even a trifle standoffish. He would not fall in love, or scratch himself, or talk with his mouth full. If the hospitality lived up to the promise of that smell, he would presently disclose that he had long known of the quests (which they had laughed about at the inn). He would hardly dare to ask if he, too ... By the time he reached the castle, the plan was irreproachable. By the time he was within it, it was tossed away. Plans are an encumbrance. One does much better when prompted by truth and the moment.

That night Queen Aigle reopened the Chronicle and wrote the date, and beneath it: *Tamarind, Political Exile from the Kingdom of Tishk in the Ural Mountains.*

What charmed everyone was his frankness.

Exile is a discreditable term. Aigle had never imagined herself welcoming an exile; a political exile would presumably be someone even more skulking and hangdog than the ordinary kind. Candour irradiated Tamarind's account of the situation at Tishk: the young Queen's power usurped by a militaristic uncle, the rising savagely put down, its leaders executed, their supporters exiled to beyond the Volga. No doubt such political rowdiness was typical of a Kingdom in the Urals. It was a greater effort of the imagination—few made it—to conceive the remoteness of Tishk. How long had the journey taken? How long had he travelled? For a moment, he hesitated. 'Necessity knows no law. I must admit it. From time to time, I flew.' And he described how he had flown over the Volga, so wide a river that he could not see its farther bank. There, on the farther bank, he lay exhausted, kissing the ground where every step would bring him nearer to Western civilization; and immediately had been set on by ignorant monks, who denounced him as a demon and handed him over to the police, who proposed to hang him as a spy. But one of them was venal and humane, and let him escape. 'One has only to be in adversity,' Tamarind exclaimed, gazing round on the table with his bright, rather bulging eyes, 'to learn the good-heartedness of the poor and oppressed.'

Aigle listened with her hands clenched in her lap and her mouth open. The clocks and the favourite airs had told midnight before anyone thought of going to bed.

Tamarind's frankness not only charmed his listeners; it infected them. They felt a compulsion to unbosom themselves to this unguaranteed exile from a Kingdom no one had heard of. They pursued him into corners and told him of doubts suppressed, smothered dissatisfactions, hopes strangled at birth, the true story—in time, several true stories—of the White Gentian; other true stories of machinations, favouritism, and neglected sunstroke; of law-suits, armorial bearings, and little adjustments that would make the whole difference. The elder ladies read him their memoirs. Count Horn resurrected his juvenilia and recited them. Ingobaldo consulted him about the clocks.

When Tamarind could be persuaded to leave off talking himself, he was a sympathetic listener and an adept questioner. At the end of a week he was in an unsurpassed position to make mischief. But he had higher aims. Aigle, with her quests taken out of some worm-eaten tapestry, Aigle, stiff as her stays, a dedicated offering to old age, who listened, biting her lip like a virgin, Aigle, that withered child, had not unbosomed herself of a shred of confidence. His talent for understanding, for fellow-feeling, for reciprocation was wasted on her. It was mortifying. He could not make it out. Meanwhile, he played with real children—for there were children at Dreiviertelstein, though they seemed out of place there. They fastened on him as though he were food for the starving—they shouted, buffooned, rolled on the ground. He told them about good bears and bad bears, and of Baba Jaga the witch who was, he said, his aunt. He also led them on a raid into the kitchen, where they stuffed themselves with candied violets and licked caramel off their fingers. Ludla officially disapproved, but if he had come without those distracting children she would have told him any secret he chose to ask, even the secret of the crawfish soufflé.

All this was hard to account for. He was ungainly and pastyfaced, his voice was harsh, he knocked things over, he had thick lips, his ears stuck out like an animal's; when he arrived his clothes were in tatters and he looked like a tramp. Ingobaldo supplied him with new clothes and an accomplished valet, and the result of this kindness was that he looked like a tramp who had pillaged a nobleman. Yet everyone liked him; even the working fairies liked him. He was lively, he was happy, and his happiness diffused like a scented oil. Every day confirmed Tamarind's belief in the good-heartedness of the poor and oppressed—for such he judged the courtiers of Dreiviertelstein to be.

And still their Queen eluded him.

She did not avoid him; she did not make even that acknowledgment of his zeal to release her deeper feelings.

It was her morning custom to take a brisk walk in the tilt-yard. As usual, she was walking alone; as usual, he joined her; as usual, she hoped he had had a good night. The turf was lightly crisped with overnight frost. The air was scentless. The season's new-fallen snow glittered on the mountain peak. She stopped and looked at it. 'How wonderful it must be, up there,' she said. 'How remote! How pure!'

Tamarind's luck stood at his elbow.

'Then let us fly there—this very minute.'

'Fly? Fly? But I have never flown.'

Was the poor lady malformed, or merely a slave to convention? He began to persuade. Flying was a delightful sensation, the easiest thing in the world, the most natural. It lifted one into an incomparable sense of freedom. There one is, with the world below one—a new world, seen from above. Today was an ideal day to take wing; the conditions could not be better.

As he spoke, she unclasped her mantle and let it slip to the ground. There were her wings. He had expected them to be puny; they were well developed, dove-coloured, and shone.

'What beautiful wings!' he exclaimed. 'And waiting all these years to be spread.' The question was: Would they spread or had they grown rigid in their folds? She shrugged. They quivered, unfolded smoothly, closed again, not so compactly,

'And so lustrous,' he said.

'My bowerwomen oil them once a week, of course.'

It was her first confidence. This indeed was Western civilization; no one at Tishk oiled his wings. Tamarind felt himself moving in a new world and perfectly at ease in it. He put his arm round Aigle's waist. 'Allow me to support you for the first ascent. Trust yourself to me. Now!'

They rose in the air. She was heavier than he expected —women always are—and passive. He fixed his gaze on the mountain peak, tightened his grasp, and flew vigorously. He felt an erratic counter-rhythm, she wrenched herself free, lurched downward, recovered, and flew with the sudden brilliance of a beginner. He had to fly hard to catch up with her and set her on course again. She had no sense of direction; twice she collided with him. He seized her hand. Unless he could control her it would be impossible to make a safe landing—and the peak was now so near that he could feel its chill on his face. She jerked his hand away, flew vehemently ahead, plunged downward, too late, and much too fast. She'll dash herself to pieces on the rock face, he thought, and shouted to her to slacken speed and veer to one side. Without slackening speed she made a violent turn, lost the rhythm of her flight, tumbled like a shot bird, just missed the rock, and landed head foremost in a lap of snow.

A flurry of snow hid her.

By the time he reached her she had righted herself and was sitting up, with blood dripping from her nose. No fairy likes the sight or smell of blood; life at Tishk had not reconciled Tamarind to its exhibition. He gave her his handkerchief and occupied himself with patting her back and examining her wings. One of them was slightly bent, and she winced as he touched it. He apologized politely and gloomily.

It was a situation where politeness had a shallow ring. Politeness would not quench Aigle's nosebleeding, or ward off the cold which was creeping into him from the snow, or ease the journey back (though it would almost certainly oblige him to carry her) or overcome the awkwardness of their return—for it was bound to be awkward, with a great many questions being asked and no attention paid to the answers. The fault lay in the unnaturalness of a society where the privileged classes debar themselves from their birthright of flying in order to assert a hereditary claim to go on foot, as though they were mortals. Mortals, meanwhile, long, like pigs in the proverb, for wings. It is not enough for them to admit the superiority of the Elfin race; they invent a flying species of mortal, and with exaggeration of ignorance bestow wings in triplicate.

Aigle, earthbound at the summit of her social pyramid, sat beside him bleeding at the nose because she had never flown before, whereas if he had invited one of the working fairies—that fat old cook, for instance, Ludla or some such name—she would have flown like a bird, alighted like a feather. The unnaturalness of society was such a rich theme for meditation that he was startled when Aigle said that her nose had left off bleeding and they should think about getting back. He helped her to her feet, he helped her into the air. From then on, she flew unaided. As they neared the castle she said they must separate. If her absence had been noticed, she would explain she had been looking for her mantle, which had somehow fallen off without her knowing it. He, too, had better have some excuse in readiness. She spoke coldly, and he could not help feeling snubbed. It was unfortunate she had got so over-excited; but he had given her a new experience, and should have received a word of thanks.

Within an hour of their return much of what had happened—and more that had not happened—was known in the servants' quarters, where the working fairies with one accord resumed their right and proper xenophobia. These Russians are all the same, wherever they come from. Tamarind himself had said his aunt was a witch. It was the old story—warm a serpent and he'll sting. Given new clothes, treated like a prince, allowed to wind the clocks even—and all the time casting a spell over Her Majesty. He wasn't a witch's nephew for nothing ... No, no! said others—she was not bewitched! When he grabbed her she fought and struggled for a good half hour; that was when her mantle fell off—torn off, more likely. But all to no purpose, poor lady! Off he flew with her like an eagle with a lamb. And then to land his great fist on Her Majesty's nose—there's gratitude for you! No wonder she had a headache and had to lie down.

Ludla said she wished she could get after him with her rolling pin.

'It's a pity you can't poison him with your pie,' said Ernolf, the butler. 'I'd see to it he got the right helping.'

For the main dish that evening was to be Ludla's Hunters' Pie—a standing pie like a fortress. Already she was stripping the flesh off the bones, breaking the carcasses and putting them in the great stewpan, where they would simmer down to a compounded broth of capercaillie, grouse, pheasant, partridge, woodcock, and hazel hens. The flesh lay on different platters, according to the time required for par-cooking before it was enclosed in the fortress and the fortress went into the oven. A Hunters' Pie was a day's work, and the kitchen maids had been up since dawn, plucking and gutting. Pimentos, chanterelle mushrooms, garlic, juniper berries, segments of orange, anchovy fillets, dried and fresh herbs, salami that holds the mixture together, the grated chocolate that brings it to life were assembled; the flour had been sifted, the shortening flavoured, reduced, and clarified. As the plan of battle lies in the general's brain, when to move the left wing, when to explode the mine, when to bring up the cavalry, so the plan of a Hunters' Pie and the obstacles chance might put in its way—a change in the wind upsetting the oven, an insufficiency of basil, the cat filching the anchovies—had occupied Ludla's mind since daybreak; and when she wished she could get at Tamarind with her rolling pin it was not so much the assault on the Queen she resented as the threat to the concentration demanded by the pie.

However, it was a splendid example of her skill and, preceded by a white soup and grilled trout, it entered the dining room like a conqueror. Only Aigle was unmoved. Her face was plastered with white lead, she wore her diamonds and exuded a strong smell of Four Thieves vinegar. The animation roused by the pie's advent wasn't up to the usual mark; it flickered, and died out. An uneasy glumness settled on the company. Even Tamarind fell silent. He was hungry and the pie was absorbing. Count Horn was heard observing to Ingobaldo that he felt like sending a message of congratulation to the kitchen. 'So do I, so do I,' exclaimed Tamarind. 'Let us send a fraternal greeting, an acknowledgement of our indebtedness. Food is an element in the interdependence of Elfins. Without cooks, we should be reduced to cannib—' His voice strangled in a gasp. He had swallowed too rapidly, something had stuck in his gullet, he had choked. Attention was politely averted. Ernolf came up unobtrusively with a napkin. Tamarind stiffened, glared, flapped his hands; his neighbours thumped his back. There was a piercing scream. Ernolf and the thumpers were thrust aside by Queen Aigle, who seized one of Tamarind's flapping hands, clasped it to her breast, and implored him to speak. 'Say you're not dying. I can't bear it if you die. You're all I have, you're the light of my eyes, I can't exist without you. Tamarind, Tamarind, speak to me!'

Tamarind continued to choke. Tears ran down his cheeks. Aigle's Lady in Waiting, looking sternly in the opposite direction, pushed a bottle of strong smelling salts between them. Tamarind made a violent effort, swallowed convulsively, and said in a weak voice, "I swallowed a bone."

He made a better recovery than Aigle, who fell into hysterics and had to be carried away. The Hunters' Pie was removed. They ate the rest of the meal without knowing what they ate.

An injury to her nose had given the Queen a concussion; her mind was temporarily unhinged. That was the Court Physician's verdict, and everyone was relieved to hear it.

The next morning, a footman was sent to summon the housekeeper to the Queen's chamber. The housekeeper obeyed and was told to fetch the cook.

Aigle was sitting up in a wide bed, propped by a great many pillows. Ludla had only seen her at a distance before. With her first glance, she knew that this was how a Queen in her bed should look.

'Are you the cook?' asked Aigle.

'Yes, Majesty,' said Ludla and curtsied again.

'Last night there was a bone in the pie. I cannot have carelessness. You are dismissed.'

As Ludla did not move, Aigle gestured to the housekeeper to take her away. It was a long way from the bedside to the door. In the doorway Ludla stopped.

'Majesty.'

'Shush,' whispered the housekeeper, who in her heart was sorry for the old servant. 'Shush. You'll only waste your breath.'

'Majesty. I have cooked for you and your Court and your household for more years than I can tell. It will be more years than I can tell before you have another such cook. Dreiviertelstein will be a poor place without me—a poor, dwindled, ill-fed, out-of-the-way castle, with visitors as glad to leave it as fleas leaving a killed rabbit that has grown cold.'

She curtsied again, with her disgraced head held high, and walked out, hauling the housekeeper after her.

In the kitchen a ham was gently boiling, the bread dough was rising under a cloth, a chopping knife lay among the vegetables she had been preparing for a julienne soup. She took off her apron and sat with folded hands while her belongings were packed by the head kitchen maid. With a groom to carry them, she took wing for her birthplace in the forest. Her parents were dead, but her brother still lived on there, a forester and a notorious poacher.

The ham was boiled to rags before anyone remembered to dish it up. The dumplings which accompanied it moved Count Luxus to another of his skyey metaphors: he said they were like thunderbolts. Ernolf the butler whispered to Ingobaldo that Ludla had gone to visit her brother. He had not the courage to admit the truth.

Ingobaldo was not one of those chivalrous persons who strangle their wives and stab their rivals; when he inquired after Tamarind's throat he had no *arrière-pensée* of cutting it. He had sustained another disappointment. For some time, he had thought that Aigle would be the better for a cicisbeo and considered importing one from Italy. When Tamarind arrived—dauntless, romantic, unfortunate through no fault of his own, a high-minded exile from an unknown Kingdom, everything that would appeal to Aigle—Ingobaldo felt that the ideal cicisbeo had been vouchsafed; or rather, the raw material for the ideal cicisbeo, since Tamarind was untutored in a cicisbeo's accomplishments. But he was willing, lofty in his sentiments, anxious to please; all that was necessary was that he should ripen. Unfortunately, the process of ripening had got out of hand. Aigle had ripened too soon. Apparently she was too highly strung to be soothed by a novice cicisbeo. Unsoothed, she would feel slighted, and the consequences could be very painful for Tamarind. For his own sake, he must be got rid of; and he, Ingobaldo, must assert himself and deal the blow. As Royal Consort, it was his duty. He wished it wasn't. Tamarind flew the Volga far too often, and the striking train of the Favourite Air from Thuringia had been out of order ever since he oiled and adjusted it, but he came from an outer world and Ingobaldo would miss him.

He allowed a few meals to elapse before regretting that

Tamarind could no longer be detained from his project of touring Western Europe. After a start of surprise, Tamarind agreed that he could not be detained—and seemed to welcome the thought. His plans were indefinite. He might fly the Channel and visit England. Wherever he went, he could be sure of the good-heartedness of the poor and oppressed.

He departed to a *bon-aller* of cannon, with a great many useful gifts and a newly lined purse, and after embracing everyone in reach. Aigle stood at a turret window, waving a red handkerchief. He took it to refer to the ultimate liberation of Tishk, and was much affected.

A day or two later, meals suddenly improved. Gunf and the head huntsman led a revolt, ousted the kitchen maids, and took over the cooking. Their repertory was limited, they cooked without imagination, they relied too heavily on pimentos and celery seed. But meals were faithful and punctual, and meat eaters found no fault with them. Aigle ate without comment, and ate rather more than usual. She was feeding on grief—a windy diet that demands reinforcing. Ingobaldo had been right after all. What Aigle had needed was a cicisbeo—briefly. Henceforward she cherished an imperishable sorrow and a beautiful unresisting memory. Dead to the world, she had an object in life. She dressed in black, slept like a dormouse, with that sacred handkerchief he had lent her to bleed on under her pillow, dreamed of flying, woke to a breakfast tray and after the breakfast tray an inkpot. Since the entry of '*Tamarind, Political Exile*' she had written nothing more in the Chronicle. But there were a great many inciting blank pages, and she filled them with poems, elegiac or narrative. The elegies, neatly copied by the younger ladies, were given as parting presents to the reluctant embassies that came to Dreiviertelstein—and left very much as Ludla had said they would.

There were no more quests. Her life was too full for quests.

Failing quests, it became the fashion to go for woodland walks. By twos and threes, by sixes and sevens, the woodland walkers, some with walking sticks, some with guns, and equipped with simple luncheons—a ham sandwich, a hard-boiled egg with lettuce—set out soon after breakfast. A couple of hours' walking brought them to Ludla's cottage home with a healthy appetite. There they would sit on the wooden benches outside the door, hearing Ludla pound and chop and stir, breathing up the dear familiar smells escaping when a saucepan lid was raised, an oven door opened. There they would sit, pious as pilgrims, sure of their faith's reward, hearing the forest rustle, and Ludla whisking eggs. And then there would be a clatter of plates and cutlery, and Ludla would come to the door and say, 'You can come in now.' As she had fewer to cook for, she cooked more lavishly. Her charges (which included second helpings) were moderate, and she spent part of her profits on the enhancements and delicacies she had commanded at the Schloss. Her only stipulation was that they should bring their wine.

10 Winged Creatures

When, after many years of blameless widowhood devoted to ornithology, Lady Fidès gave birth to a son, no one in the fairy Kingdom of Bourrasque held it against her. Elfin longevity is counterpoised by Elfin infertility, especially in the upper classes, where any addition to good society is welcomed with delight. Naturally, there was a certain curiosity about the father of Fidès' child, and her intimates begged her to reveal his name so that he, too, could be congratulated on the happy event. With the best will in the world, Fidès could not comply. 'My wretched memory,' she explained. 'Do you know, there was one day last week—of course I can't say which—when I had to rack my brains for three-quarters of an hour before I could remember "chaffinch."'

The baby's features afforded no clue. It resembled other babies in having large eyes, pursed lips, and a quantity of fine fluff on its head. When the fluff fell out, Lady Fidès had it carefully preserved. It was exactly the shade of brown needed for the mantle of a song thrush she was embroidering at the time. As an acknowledgment, she called the baby Grive. Later on, when a growth of smooth black hair replaced the fluff; she tried to establish the child in its proper category by calling it Bouvreuil. But Grive stuck.

In a more stirring court these incidents would have counted for nothing. Even Fidès' lofty project of decorating a pavilion with a complete record of the indigenous birds of France in needlework, featherwork, and wax work would have been taken as something which is always there to be exhibited to visitors on a wet day. Bourrasque preferred small events: not too many of them, and not dilated on. The winds blowing over the high plains of the Massif Central provided all the stir, and more, that anyone in his senses could want.

Indeed, Bourrasque originated in a desire for a quiet life. It was founded by an indignant fairy whose virginity had been attempted by a Cyclops. Just when this happened, and why she should have left the sheltering woodlands of the Margeride for a bare hillside of the Plomb du Cantal, is not known. Apparently, her first intention was to live as a solitary, attended only by a footman and a serving-woman, but this design was frustrated by friends coming to see how she was getting on. Some decided to join her, and a settlement grew up. In course of time, working fairies raised a surrounding wall. A palace accumulated, a kitchen garden was planted, and terraces were set with vines. The vines flourished (it was the epoch of mild European winters); the population grew, and a group of peasants from the northward, disturbed by earthquakes, migrated with their cattle and became feudatories of the Kingdom of Bourrasque. That was its Golden Age. It ended with a total eclipse, which left the sun weak and dispirited, and filled the air with vapours and falling stars, rain and tempests. Late frosts, blight, and mildew attacked the vines. Fog crawled over the harvest before the crops could be gathered, and from within the fog came the roar and rumble of the winds, like the mustering of a hidden army. Bourrasque dwindled into what it afterward remained—a small, tight, provincial court of an unlegendary antiquity, where people talked a great deal about the weather, wore nightcaps, and never went out without first looking at the weather-cock. If it pointed steadfastly to one quarter, they adjusted their errands. If it swung hither and thither like a maniac, they stayed indoors.

It was not really a favourable climate for an ornithologist.

Fairies are celebrated needlewomen, and do a great deal of fancywork. From her youth up, Fidès had filled her tambour frame with a succession of birds in embroidery: birds on twigs, on nests, pecking fruit, searching white satin snow for crumbs. The subjects were conventional, the colouring fanciful, and everybody said how lifelike. On the day of her husband's death (an excellent husband, greatly her senior) Fidès entered the death chamber for a last look at him. The window had been set open, as is customary after a death; a feather had blown in and lay on the pillow. She picked it up. And in an instant her life had a purpose: she must know about birds.

At first she was almost in despair. There were so many different birds, and she could be sure of so few of them. Robin, blackbird, swallow, magpie, dove, cuckoo by note, the little wren, birds of the poultry yard—no others. The season helped her. It was May, the nestlings had hatched, the parent birds were feeding their young. She watched them flying back and forth, back and forth, discovered that hen blackbirds are not black, that robins nest in holes. When no one was looking, she took to her wings like any working fairy and hovered indecorously to count the fledglings and see how the nests were lined. As summer advanced she explored the countryside, and saw a flock of goldfinches take possession of a thistle patch. She picked up every feather she saw, carried it back, compared it with others, sometimes identified it. The feather on her husband's pillow, the first of her collection, was the breast feather of a dove.

An eccentricity made a regular thing of ceases to provoke remark. Public opinion deplored the freckles on Fidès' nose, but accepted them—together with her solitary rambles, her unpunctuality, and her growing inattention to what was going on around her—as a consequence of her widowed state. Her brother-in-law, her only relative at Court, sometimes urged her to wear gloves, but otherwise respected her sorrow, which did her, and his family, great credit.

As time went on, and the freckles reappeared every summer and the feathers accumulated to such an extent that she had to have an attic made over to hold them, he lapsed from respecting her sorrow to admiring her fidelity—which was just as creditable but less acutely so. When she made him an uncle he was slightly taken aback. But it was a nice peaceful baby, and not the first to be born to a bar sinister—which in some Courts, notably Elfhame in Scotland, is a positive advantage. With a little revision Fidès was still creditable: to have remembered with so much attachment the comfort of matrimony through so long and disconsolate a widowhood was undeniably to her credit, and his late brother would have taken it as a compliment.

But as a persuasion to Fidès to stay quietly indoors the baby was totally ineffective. She was no sooner out of childbed than she was out-of-doors, rambling over the countryside with the baby under her arm. 'Look, baby. That's a whinchat. Whinchat. Whinchat.' A little jerk to enforce the information. Or 'Listen, baby. That's a raven. "Noirâtre," he says. "Noirâtre."' The child's vague stare would wander in the direction of her hand. He was a gentle, solemn baby; she was sure he took it all in and that his first word would be a chirp. If her friends questioned her behaviour—Wouldn't the child be over-excited? Wouldn't it be happier with a rattle?—she vehemently asserted that she meant Grive to have his birthright. 'I grew up without a bird in my life, as if there were nothing in the world but fairies and mortals. I wasn't allowed to fly—flying was vulgar—and to this day I fly abominably. Birds were things to stitch, or things to eat. Larks were things in a pie. But birds are our nearest relatives. They are the nearest things to ourselves. And far more beautiful, and far more interesting. Don't you see?'

They saw poor Fidès unhinged by the shock of having a baby that couldn't be accounted for, and turned the subject.

The working fairies, chattering like swifts as they flew about their duties, were more downright. 'Taking the child out in all weathers like any gipsy! Asking Rudel if he'll give it flying lessons! Gentry ought to know their place.'

Only Gobelet spoke up for his mistress, saying that weather never did a child any harm. Gobelet spoke from experience. He was a changeling, and had lived in the mortal world till he was seven, when Fidès' husband saw him sucking a cow, took a fancy to his roly-poly charm, and had him stolen, giving him to Fidès for St Valentine's Day. Gobelet grew up short-legged and stocky, and inexpugnably mortal. No one particularly liked him. To prove satisfactory a changeling must be stolen in infancy. Gobelet's seven years as a labourer's child encrusted him, like dirt in the crevices of an artichoke. He ate with his fingers. When he had finished a boiled egg he drove his spoon through the shell. If he saw a single magpie, he crossed himself; if anyone gave him a penny he spat on it for luck; he killed slow-worms. He was afraid of Fidès, because he knew he was repulsive to her. Yet once he made her a most exquisite present. She had gone off on one of her rambles, and he had been sent after her with a message. He found her on the heath, motionless, and staring at the ground with an expression of dismay. She was staring at the body of a dead crow, already maggoty. Forgetting the message, he picked it up and said it must be buried in an anthill. She had not expected him to show such feeling, and followed him while he searched for an anthill large enough for his purpose. When it was found he scrabbled a hole and sank the crow in it. What the maggots had begun, he said, the ants would finish. Ants were good workmen. Three months later he brought her the crow's skeleton, wrapped in a burdock leaf. Every minutest bone was in place, and she had never seen a bird's skeleton before. In her rapture she forgot to thank him, and he went away thinking she was displeased.

Grive's first coherent memory was of a northeasterly squall; a clap of thunder, darkened air, and hailstones bouncing off the ground. He was in his mother's arms. She was attending to something overhead. There was a rift of brilliant March-blue sky, and small cross-shaped birds were playing there, diving in and out of the cloud, circling round each other, gathering and dispersing and gathering again, and singing in shrill silken voices. The booming wind came between him and the music. But it persisted; whenever the wind hushed, he heard it again, the same dizzying net of sound. He struggled out of his mother's arms, spread his wings, felt the air beneath them, and flew toward the larks. She watched him, breathless with triumph, till a gust of wind caught him and dashed him to the ground. She was so sure he was dead that she did not stir, till she heard him whimper. Hugging him, small and plump, to her breast, she waited for him to die. He stiffened, his face contorted, he drew a sharp breath, and burst into a bellow of fury. She had never heard him cry like that before.

He had come back to her a stranger. Though she still hugged him, the warmth of recognition had gone out of her breast. The angry red-faced stranger buffeting her with small soft fists was just another Elfin: he had never been, he could never become, a bird. She must put the idea out of her head, as when, deceived by candlelight, she stitched a wrong-coloured thread into her embroidery and in the morning had to unpick it.

It had slipped her memory who had fathered him, but she could be sure of the rest. An Elfin called Grive, he would grow up clever and sensible, scorning and indulging her, like her kind parents, her good kind husband, her brother-in-law. He would know she was crazy and make allowances for her; he might even feel a kind of love for her. She could never feel love for him. Love was what she felt for birds—a free gift, unrequired, unrequited, invulnerable.

The angry stranger wriggled out of her arms. She watched him making his way on hands and knees over the wet turf.

Even when he paused to bite a daisy, there was nothing to remind her that she had half-believed he might become a bird. Presently she could say, quite calmly, quite sensibly, 'Come, Grive! It's time I took you back.'

She told no one of this. She wanted to forget it. She had her hair dressed differently and led an indoor life, playing bilboquet and distilling a perfume from gorse blossoms. By the time the cuckoo had changed its interval, she was walking on the heath. But she walked alone, leaving Grive in the care of Gobelet—an uncouth companion, but wingless.

Gobelet pitied the pretty child who had suddenly fallen out of favour. He cut him a shepherd's pipe of elder wood, taught him to plait rushes; carved him a ship which floated in a footbath. By whisking up the water he raised a stormy ocean; the ship tossed and heeled, and its crew of silver buttons fell off and were drowned. On moonlight nights he threw fox and rabbit shadows on the wall. The fox moved stealthily toward the rabbit, snapping its jaws, winking horribly with its narrow gleaming eye; the rabbit ran this way and that, waving its long ears. As the right-hand fox pursued the left-hand rabbit, Grive screamed with the excitement of the chase, and Gobelet said to himself, 'I'll make a man of him yet.'

When these diversions were outgrown, they invented an interminable saga in which they were the two last people left alive in a world of giants, dragons, and talking animals. Day after day they ran new perils, escaped by stratagems only to face worse dangers, survived with just enough strength for the next day's instalment. Sorting and pairing feathers for Fidès for hours on end, they prompted each other to new adventures in their world of fantasy.

But the real world was gaining on them. Gobelet had grown stout. He walked with a limp, and the east wind gave him rheumatism.

The measure of our mortal days is more or less threescore

and ten. The lover cries out for a moment to be eternal, the astronomer would like to see a comet over again, but he knows this is foolish, as the lover knows his mistress will outlive her lustrous eyes and die round about the time he does. Our years, long or short, are told on the same plain-faced dial. But by the discrepancy between Elfin and mortal longevity, the portion of time which made Grive an adolescent made Gobelet an aging man. Of the two, Gobelet was the less concerned. He had kept some shreds of his mortal wits about him and felt that, taking one thing with another, when the time came he would be well rid of himself. Grive lived in a flutter of disbelief, compunction, and apprehension, and plucked out each of Gobelet's white hairs as soon as it appeared. Elfins feel a particular reprobation of demonstrable old age. Many of them go into retirement rather than affront society with the spectacle of their decay. As for changelings, when they grow old they are got rid of. Grive, being measured for a new suit, thought that before he had worn it out Gobelet would be gone, discarded like a cracked pitcher, left to beg his way through the world and die in a ditch with the crows standing round like mourners, waiting to peck out his eyes.

Grive was being measured for a new suit because the time had come when he must attend the Queen as one of her pages. It was his first step up in the world, and having determined he would not enjoy it he found himself enjoying it a great deal. At the end of his first spell of duty he returned to the family apartment, full of what he would tell Gobelet. Gobelet was gone. As furious as a child, Grive accused Fidès of cruelty, treachery, ingratitude. 'He was the only friend I had. I shall find him and bring him back. Which way did he go?'

Fidès put down the blue tit she was feathering. 'Which way did he go? I really can't say. He must have gone somewhere. Perhaps they know in the kitchen, for I said he must have a good meal before he started. As it is, I kept him long after he should have been got rid of, because I knew you had been fond of him. But one can't keep changelings forever. Anyhow, they don't expect to be kept. Be reasonable, dear. And don't shout.' She took up the blue tit and added another feather.

'How it must distress you to think of getting rid of the Queen,' he said suavely. It was as if for the first time in his life he had shot with a loaded gun.

Queen Alionde had felt no call to go into retirement. She brandished her old age and insisted on having it acknowledged. No one knew how old she was. There had been confidential bowerwomen, Chancellors sworn to secrecy who knew, but they were long since dead. Her faculties remained in her like rats in a ruin. She never slept. She spoke the language of a forgotten epoch, mingling extreme salacity with lofty euphemisms and punctilios of grammar. She was long past being comical, and smelled like bad haddock. Some said she was phosphorescent in the dark. She found life highly entertaining.

When the pestilence broke out among the peasantry, she insisted on having the latest news of it: which villages it had reached, how many had died, how long it took them. She kept a tally of deaths, comparing it with the figures of other pestilences, calculating if this one would beat them, and how soon it would reach Bourrasque. Working fairies were sent out to look for any signs of murrain among cattle. They reported a great influx of kites. Her diamonds flashed as she clapped her hands at the news. And rats? she asked. Few rats, if any, they said. The reflection of her earrings flitted about the room like butterflies as she nodded in satisfaction. Rats are wise animals, they know when to move out; they are not immune to mortal diseases as fairies are. If the pestilence came to the very gates of Bourrasque, if the dying, frantic with pain, leaped over the palace wall, if the dead had to be raked into heaps under their noses, no fairy would be a penny the worse. Her court was glad to think this was so but wished there could be a change of subject.

Exact to the day she foretold it, the pestilence reached Bourrasque. Her office-holders had to wrench compliments on her accuracy out of their unenthusiastic bosoms, and a congratulatory banquet was organized, with loyal addresses and the young people dancing jigs and gavottes. Fires blazed on the hearths, there were candles everywhere, and more food than could be eaten. The elder ladies, sitting well away from their Queen's eye, began to knit shawls for the peasantry. By the time the shawls were finished, they were thankful to wrap them round their own shoulders.

Bourrasque, complying with the course of history, had come to depend on its serfs for common necessities. The pestilence did not enter the castle; it laid siege to it. Fewer carcasses were brought to the larderer's wicket, less dairy stuff, no eggs. The great meal chest was not replenished. Fuel dues were not paid. There was no dearth in the land; pigs and cattle, goats and poultry, could be seen scampering over the fields, breaking down fences, trampling the reaped harvest— all of them plump and in prime condition for Martinmas. But the men who herded and slaughtered, the women who milked the cows and thumped in the churns, were too few and too desperate to provide for any but themselves. Others providing for themselves were the working fairies, who made forays beyond the walls, brought back a goose, a brace of rabbits, with luck an eel from under the mud of a cow pond. They cooked and ate in secret, charitably sparing a little goose fat to flavour the cabbage shared among their betters.

On New Year's morning the Queen was served with a stoup of claret and a boiled egg. The egg was bad. She ate it and called a Council. Hearing that they had hoped to spare her the worst, she questioned them with lively interest about their deprivations, and commanded that Bourrasque should be vacated on the morrow. She had not lived so long in order to die of starvation. The whole court must accompany her; she could not descend on her great-great-great-nephew in Berry without a rag of retinue. They would start an hour after sunrise.

Somehow or other, it was managed. There was no planning, no consultation, no bewailing. They worked like plunderers. The first intention had been to take what was precious, like jewellery, or indispensable, like blankets. This was followed by a passion to leave nothing behind. Tusks, antlers, a rhinoceros horn, some rusty swords, two voiceless bugles, a gong, and an effigy of Charlemagne were rescued from the butler's pantry. The east pavilion was stripped of its decorations. They tore down velvet hangings to wrap round old saucepans. Cushions and dirty napkins were rammed into a deed chest, and lidded with astrological charts. By dawn, the wagons stood loaded in the forecourt.

A few flakes of snow were falling.

The courtiers had gathered at the foot of the main staircase. Many of them had put on nightcaps for the journey. Alionde was brought down, baled in furs, and carried to her litter. Behind its closed screens she could be heard talking and giving orders, like a parrot in its cage. A hubbub of last-minute voices broke out—assurances of what had been done, reassurances that nothing had been overlooked. Grive heard his mother's voice among them: 'I don't think I've forgotten anything. Perhaps I'd better have one last look.' She brushed past him, stared up the wide staircase, heard herself being told to hurry, turned back, and was gone with the rest. He stood at the window, watching the cavalcade lumber up the hillside, with the piper going ahead and playing a jaunty farewell. A gust of wind swept the noise out of earshot. Nothing was left except the complaining of the weathercock.

He was too famished to know whether he had been left

behind or had stayed. Like his throstle name-giver, *Turdus philomelos*, he was shy and a dainty feeder; rather than jostle for a bacon-rind or a bit of turnip, he let himself be elbowed away. Now, though he knew that every hole and corner had been ransacked for provision for the journey, he made a desultory tour of inspection. A smell of sour grease hung about the kitchen quarters. He sickened at it, and went into the cold pleasure-garden, where he ate a little snow. He returned to the saloon which had been so crowded with departures, listened to the weathercock, noticed the direction of the snowflakes and lay down to die.

Dying was a new experience. It was part of it that he should be sorting feathers, feathers from long-dead birds, and heavy because of that. A wind along the floor blew him away from the feathers. It was part of dying that a dragon came in and curled up on his feet. It seemed kindly intentioned, but being coldblooded it could not drive away the chill of death. It was also part of dying that Gobelet was rocking him in his arms. Once, he found Gobelet dribbling milk between his jaws. The milk was warm and sent him to sleep. When he woke he could stretch himself and open his eyes. There was Gobelet's hand, tickling his nose with a raisin. So they were both dead.

Even when Grive was on the mend he remained light-headed. Starvation had capsized his wits. If he were left to sleep too long he began to twitch and struggle; wakened, he would stare round him and utter the same cry: 'I had that dreadful dream again. I dreamed we were alive.'

Gobelet was not distressed at being alive; on the contrary, it seemed to him that his survival did him credit. It had been against considerable odds. It was the lot of changelings to be dismissed on growing old. He had seen it happen to others and taken it for granted; he did so when it was his turn to be packed off to find a death in a world that had no place for him. But he had been a poor man's child, and the remembrance of how to steal, cajole, and make himself useful came to his aid. He was too old for cajolery to apply, but he flattered, and by never staying long in one place he stole undetected. He had forgotten the name of his birthplace till he heard it spoken by a stranger at the inn. Then everything flashed back on him: the forked pear tree, the fern growing beside the wellhead, his mother breaking a pitcher, the faggot thrust into the bread oven. Knowing what name to ask for, he soon found his way there. Everyone he had known was dead or gone, but the breed of sheep was the same. Here he hired himself as a farmhand and for a couple of years lived honest, till the sudden childhood memory of a gentleman on a horse who drew rein and asked how old he was so unsettled him that he knew he must have another look at Bourrasque. By then the pestilence had reached the neighbourhood. He hoped to evade it, but it struck him down on the third day of his journey. Shivering and burning, he sweated it out in a dry ditch, listening to the deathowl screeching to the moon. In spite of the owl, he recovered, laid dock-leaf poultices on his sores, and trudged on through the shortening days. He knew he was nearing Bourrasque when he met an old acquaintance, Grimbaud, one of the working fairies, who was setting a snare. From him he heard how the peasants were dying and the palace starving. He inquired after Lady Fidès. Grimbaud tapped his forehead with two fingers. He could say nothing of Grive.

He rose in the air and was gone, lost in the winter dusk.

'Starving, are you?' Gobelet shouted after him. 'No worse than I. And you can whisk off on your wings. No limping on a stiff knee for you.' He felt a sudden consuming hatred for the whole fairy race. He took a couple of steps, caught his foot in the snare, and fell, wrenching his knee. It was his good knee. He crawled away on all fours, and made a bracken hut, where he spent a miserable week nursing his knee, changing and unchanging his mind, and listening to the kites mewing in the fog. In the end he decided to go forward. There was nothing to be got by it, but not to finish his wasteful journey would be worse waste. To look at Bourrasque and turn away would clear the score.

The fog lifted and there it was—larger than he remembered, and darker. The gates stood open. A long procession was winding up the hillside, the piper going ahead. The Queen must be dead at last! It was odd that so many wagons, loaded with so much baggage, should be part of the funeral train. But no doubt, freed from her tyranny, the court would bury her and go on to being better fed elsewhere. He watched the procession out of sight, stared at the smokeless chimneys, and renounced Bourrasque, which he had come such a long journey to renounce. As he was turning away, it occurred to him that he owed himself a keepsake, and that one of Lady Fidès' birds would do. He limped on, and entered the palace by the familiar gully where the waste water flowed away. The east pavilion was stripped bare. He remembered other things he had admired and went in search of them. Some furniture remained in the emptied rooms—gaunt beds with no hangings, cabinets with doors hanging open. Meeting his reflection in a mirror, he started back as if it accused him of trespassing.

He was hurrying away when he saw Grive lying in a corner.

There was time to remember all this during Grive's convalescence, when the excitement of winning him back to life was over and the triumphs of stealing provisions from the homes of the dead had dulled into routine. He compared Grive's lot with his own: no one had tended him in his ditch and never for a moment had he supposed it better to be dead than alive. What succour would a dying Grive have got from a dead Gobelet? The comparison was sharpened because the living Gobelet was afraid. The survivors outside the walls railed against the palace people, who had done nothing for them, feasted while they starved, danced while they were dying, deserted them. If this angry remnant invaded the palace—and certainly it would—Grive and he would be done for.

They got away as smoothly as they did in their serial story. It was a clear frosty night, a following wind helped them uphill, and in the morning they took their last look at Bourrasque, where the villagers, small and busy as ants, were dragging corpses to the plague pit.

With that morning Gobelet began the happiest epoch of his life. As nearly as possible, he became a fairy. He lost all sense of virtue and responsibility and lived by pleasures—pell-mell pleasures: a doubled rainbow, roasting a hedgehog. And, as if he shared the hardiness and resilience of those who live for pleasure, he was immune to cold or fatigue, and felt like a man half his age. Grive had made an instant and unashamed recovery. Most of the time he was high overhead, circling while Gobelet walked, sailing on the wind, flying into clouds and reappearing far above them. From time to time he dived down to report what he had seen. There was a morass ahead, so Gobelet must bear to the left. Another storm was coming up, but if Gobelet hurried he would reach a wood in time to take shelter. He had seen a likely farm where Gobelet could beg a meal. He had seen a celandine.

A day later there were a thousand celandines. The swallows would not be long behind them, remarked Gobelet: swallows resort to celandines to clear their eyesight after spending the winter sunk in ponds; they plunge in, all together, and lie under the mud. All together, they emerge. What proves it is that you never see a swallow till the celandines are in bloom. On the contrary, Grive said, swallows fly south and spend the winter in some warmer climate where they have plenty of flies to prey on. This had been one of Lady Fidès' crazy ideas:

no one at Bourrasque credited it, for why should birds fly to a foreign shore and encounter such dangers and hardships on the way when they could winter comfortably in a pond?

Grive and Gobelet were still disputing this when the swallows came back, twirling the net of their shadows over the grass. By then it was hot enough to enjoy shade. They moved away from the uplands, and lived in wooded country, listening to nightingales. Grive had never heard a nightingale. It was like the celandines—the first single nightingale, so near that he saw its eye reflecting the moonlight, and the next day thousands, chorus rivalling chorus; for they sang in bands and, contrary to the poets, by day as well as by night. Fairies, he said, were far inferior to birds. They have no song; nothing comes out of them but words and a few contrived strains of music from professional singers. Birds surpass them in flight, in song, in plumage. They build nests; they rear large families. No fairy drummer could match a woodpecker, no fairy militia manoeuvre like a flock of lapwings, no fairy comedian mimic like a starling.

He spoke with such ardour that it would not do to contradict him, though privately Gobelet thought that if Grive could not sing like a nightingale he could praise as fluently and with more invention. Grive was as much in love with birds as ever Lady Fidès had been, but without the frenzy which made her throw the lark pie out of the window—which was fortunate, as there were many days when the choice of a meal lay between pignuts and an unwary quail spatchcocked. He left provisioning to Gobelet; whether it was begged, stolen, caught, Grive found everything delicious, and sauced by eating it with his fingers. In other respects he was master. It was part of Gobelet's happiness that this was so.

All this time they were moving eastward. It was in the Haute-Loire that Grive suddenly became aware of bats. As the narrow valley—scarcely wider than the river with its bankside alders—brimmed with dusk, bats were everywhere, flying so fast and so erratically that it was hard to say whether there were innumerable bats or the same bats in a dozen places at once. As birds surpass fairies, he said, bats surpass birds. They were the magicians of flight. With a flick, they could turn at any angle, dart zigzag above the stream, flicker in and out of the trees, be here, be gone, never hesitate, never collide. They were flight itself. Trying to fly among them he was as clumsy as a goose. They did not trouble to scatter before him, they were already gone.

The valley was cold at night, and stones fell out of the hillside. It seemed to Gobelet that wherever he went a fox was watching him. If it had not been for Grive's delight in the bats, he would have been glad to move on. Instead, he set himself to catch a bat. He had seen it done in his childhood; it was not difficult. He took the bat to Grive. Daylight had meekened it. It let itself be examined, its oiled-silk wings drawn out, its hooked claws scrutinized, its minute weight poised in the hand. It was, said Grive, exactly like Queen Alionde—the same crumpled teats, the same pert face. But verminous, said Gobelet loyally. Grive said that if fairies did not wash they would be verminous; he had read in a book that the fairies of Ireland are renowned for the lice in their long hair.

He looked more closely at the bat, then threw it away. It staggered and vanished under a bush. As though a spell had snapped, he said that they must start at once.

He flew ahead, shielding his eyes from the sun to see more clearly. Circling to allow time for Gobelet to catch up, he felt an impatient pity for the old man scrambling up hillsides, gaining a ridge only to see another ridge before him, obstinate as a beetle, and as slow. Gobelet thought he was making fine speed; they had never travelled so fast since the wind blew them uphill on their first morning. It was not till they sat together on the summit of the last ridge that Grive relaxed and became conversational. They sat above a heat haze. Beneath and far away was the glimmer of a wide river. He heard Grive's wings stir as if he were about to launch himself toward it, but instead he rolled over on the turf and said, 'Tonight we will sup on olives.' And he told Gobelet that the river was the Rhône, wide and turbulent, but crossed by a bridge built by pigeons. All they had to do now was to follow it, and then bear eastward. 'Where to?' asked Gobelet. 'To the sea.' All Gobelet's happiness in being mastered (it had been a little jolted by that abrupt departure from the bat valley) flowed back. More than ever before he acknowledged the power and charm of a superior mind.

Later on, when they were walking over the great bridge of Saint-Esprit, he remembered Grive's statement. It seemed to his commonsense thinking that not even eagles, let alone pigeons, could have carried those huge stones and bedded them so firmly in the bellowing currents. He had to bellow himself to express his doubts. Grive repeated that pigeons had done it; they were the architects and overseers, though for the heavier work they might have employed mortals.

For the work of provisioning their journey he still employed Gobelet. They were now among Provençal speakers, but the beggar's tune is the same in all languages, theft is speechless, and bargaining can be conducted by signs and grimaces. Gobelet managed pretty well. One evening he begged from a handsome bona roba (light women were always propitious), who laughed at his gibberish, put money in his hand, ogled Grive, and pointed to an inn. They sat down under an awning, the innkeeper brought bread and olives and poured wine into heavy tumblers. Grive had just begun to drink when he leaped up with a scream, dropped the tumbler, and began frantically defending himself with his hands. A sphinx moth had flown in to his face and was fluttering about him. The innkeeper came up with a napkin, smacked the moth to the ground, and trod on it. On second thought, he made the sign of the cross over Grive.

Gobelet was ashamed at this exhibition of terror. Grive, being a fairy, was not. Trying to better things, Gobelet said it was an alarmingly large moth—as big as a bat. Had Grive thought it was a bat?

'An omen!' gasped Grive, as soon as he could unclench his teeth. 'An omen!'

That night they slept under a pine tree. The moth hunted Gobelet from dream to dream; the stir of the tree in the dawn wind was like the beating of enormous black wings. He sat up and rubbed his eyes. Grive was sleeping like a child, and woke in calm high spirits. After his usual morning flight, when he soared and circled getting his direction, they continued their journey. Of all the regions they had travelled through, this was the pleasantest, because it was the most sweet-smelling. Even in the heat of the day (and it was extremely hot, being late August) they were refreshed by wafts of scent: thyme, wild lavender and marjoram, bay and juniper. There was no need to beg or steal; figs, olives, and walnuts were theirs for the picking. Here and there they saw cities, but they skirted them. Here and there mountains rose sharply from the plain, but there was no need to climb them; they appeared, threatened, and were left behind. The only obstacle they met in these happy days was a fierce torrent, too deep to ford till they came to a pebble reach, where it spread into a dozen channels. It was here that Grive had his adventure with the doves. They were abbatial doves, belonging to a house of monks who lived retired from the world with the noise of the torrent always in their ears. Grive saw the doves sitting demurely on the platforms of their dovecote. He made a quick twirling flight to entertain them, and as he alighted waved his hand toward them. They came tumbling out of their apertures and settled on his raised arm. He stood for a while talking to them, then shook them off. As if they were attached to him by some elastic tether, they flew back and settled again. He cast them off, they returned. He walked on, they rode on him. He flew and they flew after him, and settled on him when he returned to earth. 'Make yourself invisible,' said Gobelet. 'That will fox them.' He did so. The doves stayed where they were, placidly roocooing. Gobelet clapped his hands, Grive pranced and rolled on the ground; nothing dislodged them, till a bell rang and a monk came out shaking grain in a measure. They looked startled, and flew back to be fed.

Grive was pleased but unastonished. It was natural, he said; a matter of affinity. The doves felt his affection flow toward them and had responded. He tried the experiment again, with plovers, with fieldfares. Sometimes it worked, sometimes it did not. Once he fetched down a kestrel from the height of its tower. It landed on him, screaming with excitement, and drew blood with its talons. Flock after flock of birds streamed overhead, flying high up; but he had no power over these, they were migrants bent on their journey. One morning he came down from his prospecting flight, having caught sight of the sea, lying beyond a territory of marsh and glittering waterways. Travelling east of south they skirted another city, another mountain. There was a change in the quality of the light, and large birds, flying with effortless ease and not going anywhere in particular, swooped over the landscape; and were seagulls.

'When we get to the sea, what shall we do then?'

Gobelet hoped the answer would speak of repose, of sitting and looking around them, as they had done in the spring.

'Find a ship going to Africa. And that reminds me, Gobelet, we must have money for the passage.' He snuffed the air. 'That's the sea. Do you smell it? That's the sea.' Gobelet smelled only dust and oleanders and a dead lizard. But he had an uninstructed nose; he had read no books to tell him what the sea smelled like.

Two days later he felt he had never smelled anything but the sea, nor would ever smell anything else, and that the smell of the sea was exactly paralleled by the melancholy squawking cry of the seagulls. He sat on a bollard and rubbed his knee. It pained him as much as it did when he was turned out of Bourrasque. Grive had flown so fast that morning, and paused so impatiently, that he had had to run to keep up with him. The port town was noisy, crowded, and lavish, and ended suddenly in the mournfulness of the quays and the towering array of ship beside ship. In all his inland life Gobelet had never seen anything so intimidating. Their hulls were dark and sodden, their slackened sails hung gawkily, they sidled and shifted with the stir of the water. Black and shabby, they were like a row of dead crows dangling from a farmer's gibbet. At the back of his mind was another comparison: the degraded blackness of the sphinx moth after the innkeeper had smacked it down and trodden on it. In one of these he must be imprisoned and carried to Africa, where there would be black men, and elephants. Yet it depended on him whether they went or no, for he must steal for their passage money. A cold and stealthy sense of power ran through him. And a moment later he saw Grive coming toward him and knew he had no power at all. Grive had found a ship which was sailing to Africa tomorrow at midday. He talked to her captain; everything was arranged. Presently they would take a stroll through the town, prospecting likely places for Gobelet's thieving. But first Gobelet must come and admire the ship. She was a magnificent ship, the swiftest vessel on the Inland Sea, and for that reason she was called the Sea-Swallow.

'The Sea-Swallow, Gobelet. You and your ponds!'

He walked Gobelet along the quays with an arm round his neck. A swirl of gulls flew up from a heap of fish guts; he held out his other arm and they settled on it, contesting for foot-hold. He waved them off and they came back again and settled, as determinedly as the doves had done, but not so peaceably as the doves. They squabbled, edged each other away, fell off and clawed their way back. The Sea-Swallow was at the end of the line. The crew was already making ready for departure, coiling ropes, clearing the decks, experimentally raising the tarred sails. With one arm still around Gobelet and the other stretched out under its load of gulls, Grive stood questioning the captain with the arrogant suavity of one bred to court life. With the expression of someone quelled against his reason, the captain answered him with glum civility, and stared at Gobelet. Asserting himself, he said that anyone happening to die during the voyage must not look for Christian burial. He would be dropped in the sea, for no sailors would tolerate a corpse on board; it was certain to bring ill luck. Of course, said Grive. What could be more trouble-saving?

He shook off the seagulls, and they went for a stroll through the town. It wasn't promising. The wares were mostly cheap and gaudy, sailor's stuff, and the vendors were beady-eyed and alert. Grive continued to say that a gold chain with detachable links would be the most convenient and practical theft. A begging friar stood at a corner, and a well-dressed woman coming out of church paused, opened her purse, and dropped a gold coin into his tray. Grive vanished, and a moment later the coin vanished too. Gobelet felt himself nudged into a side street, where Grive rematerialized.

They had supper at an inn, eating grandly in an upper room, whence they could watch the shipmasts sidling and the gulls floating in the sky. The wine was strong, and Grive became talkative and slightly drunk. Gobelet forgot his fatigue and disillusionment in the pleasure of listening to

Grive's conversation. Much of it was over his head, but he felt he would never forget it, and by thinking it over would understand it later on. The noise of the port died down, voices and footsteps thinned away: the sighing and creaking of the ships took over. They found a garden on the outskirts—garden, or little park, it was too dark to tell—and slept there.

The next morning, all that remained was to acquire the gold chain with detachable links. Grive had displayed such natural talents for theft that Gobelet suggested they should go together. But he was sent off by himself; Grive had a headache and wanted to sit quietly under the trees.

The gold chain was so clear in Gobelet's mind that he felt sure of finding it. It would be in one of the side streets, a shop below street level with steps down into it, the shopkeeper an old man. When he had located the chain, he would walk in and ask to be shown some rings. None would quite do, so the shop-keeper would go off to find others. With the chain in his pocket, he would consider, say he would come again, and be gone—walking slowly, for haste looks suspicious. In one of the side streets there was just such a shop, and looking through the lattice he saw gold buttons that would serve as well or better. But the chain was so impressed on his mind that he wandered on, and when he began to grow anxious and went back for the buttons he could not find the side street. Blinded with anxiety, he hurried up and down, was caught in a street market, collided with buyers and sellers. A marketwoman whose basket of pears he knocked over ran after him demanding to be paid for them. He dived into the crowd, saw a church before him, rushed in, and fell panting on his knees. Looking up, he saw the very chain before him, dangling within reach from the wrist of a statue.

A ceremony was just over, the congregation was leaving, but some still dawdled, and a beadle was going about with a broom, sweeping officiously round Gobelet's heels. There hung the chain, with everything hanging on it. There he knelt, with every minute banging in his heart. When at last he was alone, he found that the chain was fastened to the statue; he had to wrench it off. He burst through the knot of women gossiping round the holy-water stoup, and ran. The usual misfortune of strangers befell him; he was lost. Sweat poured down his face, his breathing sawed his lungs. When he emerged on the quay, it was at the farther end from the SeaSwallow. He had no breath to shout with, no strength to run with. His legs ran, not he.

Grive was standing on the quay. The Sea-Swallow had hoisted anchor and was leaving the port. A rope ladder had been pulled up, the gap of water between her and the quayside was widening. Grive shouted to the captain to wait. The captain spat ceremonially, and the crew guffawed.

Grive leaped into the air. As the sailors scrambled to catch him and pull him on board he spread his wings and vanished. A throng of screaming gulls followed him as he flew up to the crow's nest, and more and more flocked round and settled, and more and more came flying and packed round those who had settled, all screaming, squalling, lamenting, pecking each other, pecking at him. Blood ran through their breast feathers, their beaks were red with blood. The ship was free of the port, her mainsails were hoisted and shook in the wind. The exploding canvas could not be heard, nor the shouts of the sailors, nor the captain's speaking trumpet. The ship moved silent as a ghost under her crown of beating wings and incessant furious voices. She caught the land breeze, staggered under it, heeled over, and recovered herself. The people who stood on the quay watching this unusual departure saw the gulls slip in a mass from the crow's nest and fly down to the water's face. There they gathered as if on a raft. Their raft was sucked into the ship's wake and they dispersed. The onlookers saw the old man who had stood a stranger among them pull something bright from his pocket, drop it into the dirty clucking water, and turn weeping away.

11 The Search for an Ancestress

The Elfin Court of Zuy, in the Low Countries, was wealthy and orderly. No winter gales penetrated its polished windows; if the summer sun shone too vehemently, blinds were pulled down to protect the furnishings. Drinking bouts were long, taciturn, and ended in somnolence. The Queen was celebrated for her pearls.

Wealth, if not a mere flash in the pan, compels the wealthy to become wealthier. Zuy had a profitable stake in the East India trade, importing fine muslins, mazulipatans, spices, and leopard skins for muffs, exporting musical boxes, *marrons glacés*, fowling pieces, starch, suppositories, and religious pictures—the sufferings of the martyrs were always in demand. Reliable working fairies, skilled in accountancy, accompanied the voyages, to keep an eye on the traders and study new lines of export.

This commercialism, though unadmitted, was known and scorned in other Elfin courts. When Sir Eusebius went with an embassy to Brocéliande he was soon made aware that Zuy was little better than a gilded grocery shop. It was not said in so many words, but the implication was enforced by references to Brocéliande's unique cultural heritage, preserved after the original Peri dynasty was lost in the earthquakes and invasions that destroyed its kingdom in Persia. The state and elegance of its Kingdom in Europe reposed on a unique combination of pillage, feudal extortions, money-lending at high interest, insolvency, smuggling, and a fathomless national debt. There was also a steady revenue of profits from the wagers, sweepstakes, gaming-tables, lotteries and sporting events by which the visits of Elfins from other Courts were enlivened. Eusebius, smarting from his losses at cards as he smarted from the midges who sucked his blood during picnics in the forest, felt that despite the honour and glory of Brocéliande it was better to be rich and honest, like Zuy.

It had been a toss-up whether he or his cousin Joost should go with the embassy. Joost was one of those characters who are always considered and always passed over. There was nothing against him; he was well mannered, personable, more obliging than Eusebius, and had better legs; but he was always passed over. Eusebius felt this as a slight on the family. In case Joost should also feel slighted, he was careful, on his return to Zuy, to tell him he had not missed much.

'It rained incessantly. And as if that did not make it wet enough, we had green salads at every meal.'

'And then?' Joost knew what was expected of him, and supplied it.

'The conversation: their incessant brag about those Peris.'

Eusebius spent the next ten minutes deriding the cultural heritage of Brocéliande: the pink turban yearly renewed—when any Indian crossing sweeper would put on a clean one daily; those ineffably peculiar cats—the alley cats of every Asiatic port (did not Master Jacob of the Rosa Mundi keep a dozen in the hold to quell rats?), whose favourite food was fish heads; those laws of the Medes and Persians which dictated when gavottes should be danced and when corantos. He had paused to draw breath for the incompatibility of Afrits with the immutable heavens when he noticed an odd expression on Joost's face, an expression as if he were taking a pleasant walk in his sleep, and asked where he was woolgathering.

'I was wondering if there are any left—a surviving Peri.'

The mischief had been done. Joost was bent on going in search of a Peri. The Peris were a race of beings, formed of fire, according to some authorities, and according to others fallen angels, who inhabited the globe immediately before the creation of man. All Elfindom was descended from them; but it seemed improbable that Joost would succeed in finding one.

From that hour, there were two Joosts—the Joost who had taken leave of his senses and the practical, coolheaded Joost, who said nothing about Peris, whose answers to every objection were so rational that it was the objectors who seemed visionaries. Zuy had never traded with Persia? That was why he proposed the scheme: Zuy's exports would have the appeal of novelty. How would he set about it? He would charter the Rosa Mundi, part-freight her with his own venture, and travel as supercargo. But the expense? He had always lived economically and he had had his lucky moments at the gaming table. And the danger? Persians were notorious for savagery. Had he considered that? He glanced deprecatingly at his shoulders. 'After all, I am not a fairy for nothing. I have wings.'

He embarked on a dusky late afternoon. The ship's lights seemed to grope into the muddy water. The quay and his waving friends glided past him. He was off! Sitting in his state-room he became aware of the noise he would hear for months to come: the tap, creak, rattle of a wooden skeleton with ague. He opened his Persian grammar.

Before the Tropic of Cancer he found himself shaping sentences and holding imaginary conversations. The voyage was perfectly uneventful. It went on and on, like the ocean, measured by the grunts of the men tugging the oars. Not since the Cape Verde islands had he tasted fresh bread. The only other fairy on board was Tomkin, one of the clerks who went on the East Indiamen to keep an eye on Zuy interests. Tomkin was too respectful to be any sort of companion; privately, he surmised that Joost's venture was a cover for something romantically profitable: an unexploited variety of chutney, Alexander's lost money chest. When at long last the Rosa Mundi entered the Persian Gulf, he woke Joost, saying, 'Now for the kill, Your Honour!'

It was still early morning. Joost stood on deck, staring with all his eyes, with all his consciousness, at the enormous bulk of mountain that stretched before him. The tide of rising dawn darkened and outlined it, but showed nothing except that it was enormous, and solemn as if it lay in a deep sleep. The clatter of the boat, the thump of the sea against her sides did not affect his impression of a vast silence. He felt all sound draining out of himself.

He was lost and speechless all day. The wares were unpacked; he heard Tomkin and Master Jacob debating which were likeliest to attract buyers. Daylight perspectived the mountain, broke it into a series of ranges, lit sparkles of snow. He waited for nightfall and the stars: his Persian grammar had included two short poems, one about water, the other about the stars. The silence returned, the stars rose into it. He was afraid to think. Any thought would be out of place, for it would remind him of himself and the fragile ambition of his errand.

He could not maintain this exaltation. He began to be interested, and went ashore in the boat which carried Tomkin and some specimen wares to the small port town, where a market was in progress. He was admiring the shapeliness of the pottery jars heaped round a booth, and trying to understand the vendor's commendations, when Tomkin pulled his sleeve. Behind Tomkin stood a small elderly person with a beard and painted eyebrows. He bowed and bade Joost welcome, speaking in what was recognizably a form of Elfin. From the way he omitted Tomkin from an invitation to drink at a tavern, he was recognizably a fairy of quality. Introducing himself as Farouq, the Court Purveyor, he explained that he had come to buy fish, and was just about to depart when Tomkin halted him with the news that an Elfin from Europe was honouring the market by his presence. 'We can show you better things than this mortal clutter,' the Purveyor said. 'Undoubtedly, we have met by destiny. Can you ride a camel?'

Three camels were waiting. Farouq's two servants and the fish were loaded on the third, Joost was assisted onto the second. Its gait was disconcerting, his height above the ground intimidating, but he managed to stay on. Their route took them by defiles further and further into the mountain, past slopes of scree and under cliff walls of pallid stone that reflected the heat of the sun. Wafts of icy air came from the peaks above. It was dusk when they halted where a trickle of water oozed from the cliff. Farouq produced a small silver cup, watched it fill, and handed it to Joost. The servants licked the water from the cliff face, mumbling a thanks to heaven. They were sent on with the fish, while Farouq and Joost spent the night on the mountain, huddled against their camels for warmth. So they spent the next night, and the night after. During the second day Joost occasionally remembered that this joggle of ascent and descent, snatched views of distant loveliness, unending proximity of rock, was the actuality of that solemn, sleeping bulk he had seen from the Rosa Mundi. By the next day, thirst, the fatigue of riding camel-back, his vision blackening, his ears exploding, his lungs flayed by the alien purity of the air, pinned him to the present. When Farouq told him they were over the head of the pass and that on the morrow it would be easier going, he was incapable of relief. It was only by a change of ache that he realized they were going downhill through cultivated fields and orchards, that above them the wind was blowing a mane of snow off the skyline, that below them was a lake, sunk in a deep valley, with a scatter of villas and cypresses round it.

He was so stiff that when they got to Farouq's house he had

to be carried into it. There he was put into a bath, rubbed and oiled, shampooed and manicured; then laid in bed and given chicken jelly and orgeat. 'I am in the Kingdom of the Peris,' he thought. 'Tomorrow I may meet their Queen.' He licked the spoon and fell asleep.

When he woke, the Purveyor's voice—he was talking to someone about woodcocks—was already familiar. A servant brought in his clothes. They had been cleaned, repaired, and strongly perfumed. After a pause, another servant brought coffee and cinnamon toast. Later, the Purveyor came in and asked if he felt sufficiently restored for a short trip to the island where Queen Pehlevi would receive him. Again he was washed, rubbed, and oiled; he was shaved, his hair was cut, he was incensed with a thurible. There was a long interval, during which he listened to some noisy birds: if they were bulbuls, they were not what his Persian grammar had given him to expect. The Purveyor's voice came and went. At last he reappeared, finely dressed. Coffee was served them in an arbour, where there was a view of the lake and the island. Joost expected a boat, and found they were about to fly. The lake was larger than he expected, the island smaller. It was planted all over with blossoming trees and surrounded by a belt of reeds. The air was windless, yet the Purveyor seemed unable to steer a straight course. At one moment, they were flying toward a group of lilacs; a moment later the lilacs were replaced by a laburnum, the laburnum by a quince. Joost was so perplexed by this—for all the time they seemed to be flying straight-forward—that he commented on it. The Purveyor explained that the island was a rotating island: he was so accustomed to this peculiarity that he had forgotten to mention it. Visitors approaching by boat found it difficult to hit the landing place; often they had to wait through a couple of rotations before they could force their passage through the reeds and jump ashore. The passage by air was easy. Queen

Pehlevi always flew when she wanted to visit the mainland.

A Queen so careless of her dignity that she flew like any working fairy was as surprising to Joost as a rotating island. This Peri Kingdom was indeed a far cry from Zuy.

'But why—'

Farouq was already descending. They alighted on a greensward. The ground beneath them was firm as any other ground, but the thought of the island's rotation made Joost stagger in his first footsteps. An avenue of moss roses led to a modest pavilion. The realization that he was about to meet the Queen of the Peris, the monarch of that fabulous lost race, seized on him with such intensity that he could not believe he had ever contemplated such a possibility. The door of the pavilion stood open. A lady-in-waiting signed to them to enter. They stood in the presence of Queen Pehlevi.

She was sitting on cushions and playing a small oboe. She gave Joost a glance of no expression and continued the slow, wandering melody, that seemed to come to a cadence, hesitate, and turn away. While she played, he looked at her. She was plump, she was white. Her round face was farded with white lead. It was not possible to judge of her countenance, because the oboe pulled down her upper lip. Her eyebrows almost met and were so identically arched that an architect might have drawn them. She wore no ornament except a diamond belly-jewel. It flashed through the diaphanous white robe, that floated over her breasts and thighs and belly as though a veil had been thrown over an exquisite sofa. Her wings had the tranquil colour of moonstones. She was wearing a narrow-brimmed hat with a tall cylindrical crown, made of black gauze stretched over a whalebone frame.

The music ended; her upper lip retracted. She put down the oboe and held out her hand to be kissed—there was a rosy bloom of rouge in the palm. The lady-in-waiting brought forward a hassock. He sat down and waited for Pehlevi to speak.

'Are you fond of music?'

'I am devoted to music.'

'So am I.'

As if everything necessary had been said, there was silence.

'Have you nothing to say?'

'Madam, in my country one waits for a Queen to speak first.'

'That must be very dull.'

'Madam, it is. The climate, too, is dull, and the horizon flat. We have little to admire, except our pleasure gardens.'

'Are you fond of flowers?'

'Passionately.'

'So am I.'

All conversations with royalty are the same, he thought. He had already told two lies.

The island continued to rotate. Through a gap between a camellia and a lilac he had seen two successive villas on the shore of the lake come into view and withdraw. He must say something. Should it be about the island? Should it be about the cats? There were a number of cats, large and white and massively furred, who wandered in and out, noiseless as cumulus clouds. He settled for the island.

'There is no other island like it,' she said. 'I owe it to a dear friend of mine. As you see, I love simplicity and retirement. The bustle of rule is hateful to me. To escape it, I came here whenever I could. But the cares of queenship came with me. I had to go from one side of my island to another, to see that all was well on the mainland—for it was an ordinary island then. One day I complained to this dear friend of mine. He, too, loved retirement: he was a Magian. "Child," he said to me—I was young then—"it can easily be arranged. Your island must go round and round. Then you can sit undisturbed in your pavilion, and yet have your kingdom under survey." That night, I heard the reeds rustle. I felt the island begin to rotate. It has rotated ever since—never a hitch. But my dear kind old friend was gone. Sometimes I fear he may have come to a bad end. Eblis is a strict master. I planted a cedar in his memory.'

'It is a beautiful story,' said Joost.

'I do not tell it to everyone.'

During the beautiful story, he had happened to catch sight of Farouq and the lady-in-waiting, who listened with downcast eyes and composed faces. She must tell it fairly often. If he did not believe it, he had no reason to think the worse of her. Suppose the island had been set rotating by that ingenious Magian; suppose she did not wish other island owners to boast of similar islands, and had made away with him? Other royal patrons had done much the same. But it would not do to fall out with her.

'Might I see the cedar?'

'We will visit it together. Come with me.'

She fluttered before him, hovering a few feet above the ground. He had never seen such a method of flight before. It transformed an ordinary natural faculty into something poetical. His curiosity was swept away by a dazzle of marvelling delight. It is like following a butterfly, he thought, as she led him on from the cedar, zigzagging from one blossoming tree to another.

'And this is the landing place.'

She came to earth, just sufficiently out of breath to set the diamond on her belly winking. He saw that the reeds were an embankment of the island they surrounded; as it dragged them with it, the lake water hissed and chuckled among their stems. The sky had clouded over. There was a crack of thunder. The lake paled; a sudden sharp wind whipped crests of foam from it. Turning to look in the direction of the storm, he saw a small rowing boat with two passengers approaching the island. A moment later, everything was lost in a sheeting hailstorm. It ended as suddenly as it began. The boat was still there; one of the passengers was bailing hailstones out of it, the other still rowing toward the landing place. 'Some petitioner or other,' she said. 'There's another storm coming. We must hurry back.' She set off, flying in earnest this time. In the pavilion a faggot of myrtle twigs had been kindled. The lady-in-waiting wrapped an ermine cloak round Pehlevi. After a moment's hesitation, she brought a lambskin jacket for Joost. It was too small. His wrists protruded, red with cold.

One of the things which struck Joost during his stay was that Peris were considerably smaller than European Elfins. This could not be attributed to a decay of their ancient race; they were strong, active, and remarkably hardy. Their way of life reminded him of Eusebius's theory that civilizations are shaped by climate. The Purveyor's mountain hospitality, when they huddled for warmth against a stinking camel, the scented oils of his bathroom at lake level, bore this out. Hardy and luxurious, and making no attempt to reconcile these extremes, it was the civilization of a climate of contradictions. There was the same abrupt contrast in the condition of the ruled and the rulers—except that the ruled fed more substantially. The mortal notion that fairies feed on dew and nectar must have preserved a recollection of the parent race; banquets in court circles which he attended with the Purveyor alternated small kickshaws with water ices; even the soups were sweet. He was now at home with the Peris' antiquated dialect, but there was no following their conversation; a peaceful tipsiness would flare into furious altercations, insults, and taunts. Much of this, though interesting, was disillusioning. But he had not come such a long journey, or employed so much mortal machinery, to be interested. He had come to justify a desire. The event had justified it. Going ashore from the Rosa Mundi he had met Farouq. Farouq, Purveyor and probably Pandar, too, had conveyed him to Pehlevi—Pehlevi floating like a butterfly from bush to flowering bush on her island. Her ideas were limited, her voice seesawing, her wish to please regally automatic. She kept an unreasonable quantity of cats. But, hovering, she was the poetry of motion and could do no wrong. Day after day, he flew across the lake on some new pretext—to know if the budding magnolia had come into bloom, to smell the honeysuckle at dusk. Day after day, she complied. Once, marvel of marvels, she hovered over the lake, catching dragonflies. For the rest of the time, he was indifferent to her. He had got what he wanted, for he had got certainty. She was a Peri, she existed. Lesser curiosities dissolved. He no longer wondered if she wore her hat all night—she had afforded him no opportunity to find out; if her oboe music was traditional or extemporized; if she had ever loved; what she thought of him. Sometimes he speculated in a mild way about the lady-in-waiting, whose long eyelashes were all he knew of her downcast eyes, who agreed and obeyed and was always there, who laid out the chessboard, and brewed the coffee, and combed the cats, who was a presence and never became a person. Was she the obligatory Dame de Compagnie? A poor relation? (There was no likeness between them, though.) The hidden intimate who only emerged when he wasn't there? Was she essential, was she habitual—something kept about because it might come in useful?

It had crossed his mind that he might be on the same footing. By now, he had outstayed his purpose. He had secured what he came for; it remained that he should civilly go away with it. It was a question of finding the right moment. Time went by, the island went round, the moment was almost there, was swept away. Pehlevi began to play her oboe; he could not speak of departure while she was playing her oboe, still less when she had just stopped playing. The chessboard had been put ready; he must give her an opportunity to avenge her defeats. The game was unfinished; he must come back tomorrow to play it out.

His Circe—strange to think that Pehlevi perpetuated a dynasty that could have heard Homer sing—was an exasperating opponent. Her play was slow and devious, her strategy baffled him by its irrationality: he would array his men for an assault, she would ignore the threat and safeguard a pawn. She could have been a good player if she had not missed chance after chance by her caution, and made the right move a move too late. She was not above a little cheating. From time to time, by her tardiness, her incalculable vacillations, she would place him in a position he could not get out of without giving his mind to it. At such moments she would begin to talk, drum with her fingers, call for coffee, sing under her breath, revenge herself on the scrupulous silence he observed when she was in difficulties. The cats were valuable reinforcements.

It was a wet afternoon. They had played two games; he had unavoidably won them both. Now they were midway into another. It was going like a demonstration of how to plan and how not to plan a sequence of moves when, by one of her unforeseeable bungles, she hamstrung his positioned knight and put his queen in check. The largest of the cats was on her knee. She began to talk to it, asking behind which ear it preferred to be tickled, condoling with it on the rain, asking how many birds it had caught that morning, smacking it for being a cruel cat. He moved his castle. She fell into the trap and withdrew her bishop. The cat sprang off her knee and climbed into the lady-in-waiting's lap. His queen went her long stride down the board and snapped up a pawn.

Raising his eyes, he saw a pulsing crimson flash out under Pehlevi's chin, flood down her neck, suffuse her bosom and shoulders. Only her face, masked by its coating of white lead, did not disclose this torrent of fury. She stared fixedly at the cat. When they went on with the game, she played like a deranged automaton, moving at random, snatching up his pieces instead of her own. He broke off play, excusing himself with a plea of sick headache. Flying over the lake, he found that he had indeed a splitting headache.

By the morning it was gone. The rain of the day before had fallen as snow on the mountaintops; they looked childishly pretty under the blue sky. He delayed his flight to the island in order to give Pehlevi time to rearrange the chessboard. She had done so on other occasions, but this would need to be a more extensive rearrangement; he must suppress his principles and manoeuvre her into winning the reward of so much loss of temper and taking of pains. He flew slowly, feeling the bland sun on his wings, and decided, for the pleasure of it, and because he had always meant to, to make a complete circuit of the island. It seemed to bask in the sun, and he wondered again why no swans nested among the reeds. Perhaps it went round too fast for their liking. As though thinking of swans had called up an answering whiteness, he saw a white hand drawn through the water, half submerged, and submitting to the current which hissed and chuckled through the reeds dragged on by the island's rotation. It was the lady-in-waiting. She had been thrown among the reeds, and their roots were so solidly knit together that they still supported her. She lay face upward. Her throat had been cut; the water sucking her long hair had pulled her head back, widening the gash. Her eyes were open, but he would never know what colour they were, for they were bleared. A snail was feeding on one of them.

A piece had been moved ... A cat had jumped ... The island twirled on; already the Magian's cedar was creeping up on him. *Sometimes I fear he may have come to a bad end.* Pehlevi's seesawing voice pursued him like a mosquito. As if it were a matter of course, he knew he had to reckon with a killer. He looked at the snow grinning on the mountain, and thought of his warm gloves, folded precisely palm to palm, at the Purveyor's. He must go without them, he must escape before anyone knew.

He was not pursued. Pehlevi slept late that morning. She woke in a good humour, entertained by a prospect of cares of state: a new lady-in-waiting to choose, a new Purveyor to appoint. Farouq was past his work, if the best he could produce was that European, certainly an adventurer and probably a spy. The adventurer, too, must be dealt with. 'By the way, Farouq,' she said at the close of their interview. 'One more thing you can do for me. That European of yours must be got rid of.' Farouq's best spy had already reported seeing Joost flying westward at a great height. He prostrated himself and replied, 'Her will is law'—the traditional form of words.

Soaring from the island, Joost had felt the exhilaration of terror; he was confident and gay. The snow on the mountain was a bright mark to aim at. As he flew nearer, it tarnished. He was into a freezing fog—not for long, but long enough to feel afraid. It gathered again, persisted, finally thinned enough to show him he was among crags, and that he saw them by starlight. The cold was so intense that he put on visibility (there had been no call for it among Elfins), with an idea that it might keep in what warmth he had, and soared into the blackness and brilliance of night. Setting his course by the North Star, he flew on above the fog, his shadow sailing under him. Another shadow appeared, and swooped towards his, and he watched himself evading an eagle. After a few passes it lost interest and went away eastward. For a minute or two he regretted his dangerous playfellow. But it was only a superficial regret, a childish fancy, in comparison with the substantial triumph of looking down on the fog and remembering how painfully, how laboriously, he had crossed the mountain at ground level. There was his shadow, flying so splendidly, flying so easily ... The fog stirred, broke into fragments, blown on the wind like tufts of thistledown; the dawn wind seized him, tossed him like a tuft of thistledown, forced him downward, snatched him back, dropped him. A muffled cliff-face rushed upward, he caught at it, slipped, fell to the ground. Clutching a sense of direction, he got to his feet and staggered on. Savage gusts of wind threw him against the rocks like a puppet; he was reduced to crawling on hands and knees. Half dead, and despairing of dying, he saw mortal legs round him, and heard mortal voices. He had been seen by a band of travelling assassins, followers of the Prophet Hasan ben Sabah. They poured brandy between his clenched teeth, they rubbed his nose with snow. When he was sufficiently recovered, they tied him on the back of a mule and continued their journey. Drowsy with brandy and gratitude, he fell asleep. Twice he woke in terror, and thrust himself back into the safety of sleep. The third time, he felt the mule picking her steps downhill. When he opened his eyes, he saw daylight, herbage, the unknown calm faces of his rescuers. It was so sweet to be dependent that he hoped they would keep him indefinitely. But a couple of days later, within sight of the coast, they told him they were bound on an errand and farewelled him.

When Joost signalled the Rosa Mundi from the water's edge, Tomkin would not have recognized him if it had not been for the imperious gesture. He was in rags, haggard and unshaven; he limped; he had an open sore on his nose. Too abashed to sympathize, too appalled to ask questions, Tomkin fell back on his piece of good news. Joost's venture had been completely successful: everything had been sold, and could have been sold twice over. Such was the demand that Master Jacob had to supplement from his own share of the cargo.

When they had stocked up with the firms who supplied the regular imports, the Rosa Mundi could return with credit. Joost wondered what sort of credit he would return with, how much of his story to tell, how much to suppress. On an impulse, he had gone to Persia. On an impulse, he had fled. A successful tradesman would cut the better figure.

His return went almost unnoticed. The only topic at Zuy was an attempted revolt at IJmuiden, known to historians as the Cheesemonger's Rising. He sank back with relief into his old role of cutting no figure at all.

Eusebius saw this inattention to his cousin as a slight on the family. Traffic with Persia became part of Zuy's economy, carpets were a valued import, the Queen's turquoises were no less admired than her pearls. Was Joost to be passed over, who had foreseen the profitability of the Persian trade, and pioneered it? Eusebius organized presentations and deputations, he made Joost go to a different tailor and subscribe to the Royal Society for Improving the Weather. Joost was established; he had a place in society. He was always a rather legendary figure, as pioneers become if they do not keep up with the times. As the years went on, he grew almost legendary to himself. When the rota of distinction propelled him to ambassadorial standing and he was appointed Envoy to Brocéliande, he felt there was a symmetry in this belated visit to the Court whose pretensions to ancestry had made Eusebius so satirical and himself so wild to see a Peri. Sedate as a ghost, he listened to exactly what he expected: the pink turban, the cultural heritage, the laws of the Medes and Persians, the Afrits, and the permanent Astrologer. The Astrologer was called in to be introduced. A fluffy white kitten pranced in after him, clawing at the tassels of his gown. Joost fainted.

12 The Climate of Exile

When the military architects of Hadrian's Wall sited Procolitia, the seventh station between the North Sea and the Solway Firth, they invaded the territory of an Elfin Kingdom, governed at that time by a Queen whose British name is lost under the latinised form of Coventina. A good water supply is essential to satisfactory fortification, and whether or no they knew of the kingdom they invaded, the northerly bulge of the Wall at Procolitia shows they knew about the never-failing spring which was one of the brightest jewels in Coventina's crown. Later on, feeling themselves unpopular, the invaders resorted, in their practical Roman way, to flattery. The spring was promoted to sanctity, Queen Coventina was venerated as its nymph or patron goddess, and a small temple was built to enclose the spring and honour the *genius loci*. All this Coventina accepted with calm, as a passing tribute. The Romans would go away; their Wall would tumble; in the meanwhile, she was a goddess, with an altar and all the rest of it. One day one of her court, of an exploring turn of mind, reported a rival cult at Borcovicus. She flew into a rage: if her Roman worshippers supposed that she, a British fairy, was to be put on a par with that foreign upstart Mithras, they were mistaken! She gathered her court around her, left all in a night and settled in an uncontaminated waste, well to the north of the Wall, though not so far but that she could keep an eye on it and watch its decay. The new kingdom was called Catmere.

She lived to see the Wall abandoned, its garrison replaced by foxes, badgers and cattle-drovers. Till the day of her death she talked of returning to the family Kingdom, and it was expected that her successor, Coventina ll, would carry out the intention. But the climate of Northumberland does not encourage removals. When you have lived for several centuries in a new abode, warmed it with custom and come to terms with its disadvantages, you stay. The Catmere Lough was inferior to the lost spring; it depended on rainfall, was warm in summer, froze in winter, was coloured and flavoured with peat. But it was free from associations and believed to be stomachic—the browner, the better.

Further centuries passed: wars, forays, cattle-raids and pilgrimages straggled over the waste; the tumbled Wall was an admonition against taking on more than you could chew. Coventina III followed Coventina II, tall women both of them, with red hands. It was during the reign of Coventina IV that the Coventine Kingdom admitted a small innovation: it accepted fairies who were under sentence of exile from their native Kingdoms—only a selected few, and after strict enquiries, and subject to exact stipulations, and with an assured subsidy, and as a grace to other Elfin Courts, so unfortunate as to contain subjects they had to get rid of. No one at Catmere had ever incurred sentence of exile.

One of the stipulations was that before departure, exiles should be put under strong opiates and arrive with no notion of where they had got to. The exile called Snipe was put to sleep in the Kingdom of Arden, and kept unconscious during a journey of fifteen days. Having deposited him, and received a signed acknowledgment that he had arrived in good condition, his conveyors returned to Arden with all the speed they could.

He came weakly to his senses in a small room with ungarnished stone walls. It was strikingly cold and clean. A whisk broom hung on a peg by the door. The narrow window showed a sky of hurrying clouds. He studied this for a while, and slept. When next he woke someone in a hooded grey cloak was sitting by the bed with a bowl in his hands, and the chill of the room was slightly mitigated by a smell of mutton-broth. 'Where am I?' asked Snipe. 'Here,' replied the attendant—not unkindly, but without imagination.

Not since his humble beginnings in the Elfin bourgeoisie of Arden had Snipe tasted mutton-broth. A few shreds of carrot floated in it. 'I've been exiled to a monastery,' he thought. This idea was dispelled when a robust girl came in, unhooked the broom and swept the floor. The broom was replaced, she and the attendant left the room. Fortified by the mutton-broth, Snipe exclaimed, 'This is unbearable,' and burst into tears.

By the morning, the unbearable was twelve hours advanced toward becoming the accustomed.

Monks, prisoners, conscripts, have the support of rule: they live as they are ordered to. The exile has nothing but himself to depend on. If he chooses to lie on the ground and yell, he may be a nuisance but he is not an offender. If he tries to be a model exile, he makes ropes of sand. His conformity is of no account, and is based on guesswork, anyway. Accident may tell him he has guessed wrong, experiment on experiment may lead him to guess right. But that, too, is by accident. He plays a kind of Hunt the Thimble without knowing what a thimble looks like.

In his first weeks of desolation, Snipe played at Hate in Idleness. The robust girl swept his room morning and evening, but telling himself that he lived in filthy conditions, he also swept it several times a day. On one notable day he swept up a dead bee. Uncertain what to do with it, he put it in his pocket and swept it up again the next day, and the next, till it disintegrated and the robust girl performed the last offices. There was no need for him to remain in his room but as no one invited him out of it he did so. Though food was no longer brought him, no one invited him to a meal; but when hunger drove him towards the smell of meat and the clatter of dishes he found a place laid for him at the bailiff's table. The others went briskly back to their work and he went back to his room to listen to the wind.

Because he didn't want to go mad he thought as little as possible about Arden. Waking one morning he realized with horror that he was forgetting it. A moment later, another pit of horror opened at his feet: he had gone deaf! Yet he heard himself groan, he heard a sheep baa. He was not deaf. It was because there was no sound of the wind.

Till now he had stayed within doors. No one had forbidden him to go out, but his hate assumed he was forbidden. Seeing the main door open, he stood defiantly on the threshold. No one glanced at him and he went out.

It was one of those days in late autumn in which summer seems to have been laid up like a ripening pear. The sky was profoundly blue. A deeper, metallic blue reflected it from the face of the lough. The rushes round the lough were motionless as if they were cast in bronze. Nothing stirred except the sheep wandering slowly over the waste. Nothing sounded except their baa-ings and the sudden cackle of a grouse.

The sky was so blue, the waste so wide, the sun's warmth so embracing … his spirits bellied out like a sail. A bumble-bee flew past, and he gave chase to it.

He ran, he scampered, water spurted from the squelchy ground as he ran. He took to his wings to survey the waste from above, saw more of it, saw no end to it. Barren and ugly and extended, it lay basking in the sun like some rough-pelted animal. He forgot he was a wretched exile. He was an explorer, and free.

He looked back. Catmere was already some way behind him, a very workaday palace, with a few strips of cultivation on the farther expanse of waste that rose to a hummocked skyline. He had come farther than he thought, and now he would go farther still. Walking or flying, he wandered, without an aim in life except to gather a mouthful of cloudberries or a few wizened blackberries; and having feasted like a king, he stretched himself royally out to bask in the sun.

When he woke, the sun was down, the blue sky was green, the ground had stiffened with frost; it was the onset of a winter night. 'I'm lost,' he proclaimed. 'If I fall into a bog or die of cold, it will be all one to them.' The hatred in his voice was perfunctory; he was more interested in his plight. 'I'll stay where I am, and with luck I'll be dead in the morning,' he concluded. For all that, he flew up to get his bearings, and recognized the hummocked skyline he had noticed when he glanced back that morning. Somewhere between himself and that skyline was Catmere.

If he did not want to be dead in the morning, there was nothing for it but to make his way back. Footsore and wing-sore, he alternated between the darkening cold underfoot and the clear cold overhead. He was on foot when he saw a darker blot which moved through the darkness, and came nearer with a sound of brisk trotting hoofs and was a donkey with a rider. He ran to meet it, and asked his way. 'Catmere?' said a woman's voice. 'You're far east of it. But follow me and I'll put you on your way.' The donkey trotted ahead, too fast for conversation. It stopped, he caught up with it; the woman said, 'Keep to this track. Your feet will tell you when you're off it. And give the Queen my kind regards. Queen Jocasta's regards, say.' Before he could thank her, she turned the donkey and rode away. He trudged on, thinking that Jocasta was a queer name to hear spoken on this desolate waste; yet the speaker's voice matched it—a commanding voice, low-pitched and majestically unconcerned. But soon all he could think of was how to keep to the track, and of the biting cold of the night, and his slavery to it. They kept early hours at Catmere. By now, they would all be asleep; instead of dying on the waste, he would die on the doorstep. He was hating them as heartily as ever when he saw a glimmer of lighted windows. In his astonishment, he walked onto the cat-ice of the lough, and fell through.

If his teeth had not chattered so, he would have asked what the commotion was about. Apparently the commotion was about him. Hot ale was poured down his throat, his clothes were stripped off, he was rubbed and thumped, wrapped in blankets, and put to bed. 'You don't want to catch your death,' the bailiff remarked. Except for those who died of old age, Catmere had never lost an exile; he was concerned for its reputation.

They very nearly lost Snipe. He had not been much of a poet, but poet enough for his love-sonnets and satires to weaken his lungs. For many days he lay in a fever, coughing and spitting blood, startled into consciousness by mustard plasters, sucked back into stupor and a recurrent fever dream. The bailiff's words, 'You don't want to catch your death,' set him on an incessant pursuit of a death he must run down, a death which was almost within reach, which started up from a pretence of being a sheep, and eluded him, flapping ahead like a curlew. One morning he felt himself being cleaned and combed and propped up on pillows, and Queen Coventina came to his bedside, her women following her, all of them dressed in the same grey tombstone attire of hooded cloaks reaching to the ground. Staring over his head she began to sing a dirge. It was a dirge of many strophes with a die-away howl at the close of each. He did not realize it had ended till he heard the swish of her cloak over the stone floor. A habit of polite behaviour roused him. 'Your Majesty,' he called. 'Queen Jocasta charged me to bring your Majesty her kind regards.' But when she turned back and questioned him his mouth was filling with blood and he could not answer.

Being given up for dead, he recovered to find that he had become popular, interesting, a credit to society. The irresistible talent for rising in the world which had led to his downfall at Arden had somehow been at work again. But his vanity had perished during his sickness, it was no longer a pleasure to please. When he learned that in future he would eat at the Queen's second table, he said to himself, 'Just when I had settled in with those dullards. Now I must begin all over again with duller dullards.'

During his convalescence a winter wardrobe had been got ready for him: a massive grey cloak, woollen trews, a heavy knitted jerkin double-knitted round the chest, an armoury of knitted underclothes, woollen gloves, stockings and mufflers, and a pair of clumping boots lined with lambskin. He looked at the outfit with loathing. Already he was mutton within: mutton broth, mutton pies, mutton chops you could fell an ox with. Mutton within, he must now be sheep without. And every inch, the sumpter assured him, good Catmere produce, carded and spun, woven and fulled and tailored on the estate, the natural oil left in the wool to keep it rainproof, the very buttons shaped out of rams' horns. But there was nothing for it: they had taken away his clothes. Saving 'Baa!' under his breath, he dressed and went to join society.

The wool had got to grips with him, he was tickling all over, when the Major-domo led him up to a stranger. 'Now you will have a fellow-exile to keep you company, Master Snipe. He is a new-comer. Master Snipe, let me introduce you to Sir Bodach, from the Kingdom of Elfwick.' 'Magister artis,' added the stranger. He was long-boned, his voice was so soft that it sounded arrogant. He too was dressed in wool, but must have had a less sensitive skin, for he did not writhe. They talked about Snipe's recovery, and the snow, and politely avoided staring at each other. 'So I am to be fettered to this bore,' thought Snipe. Sir Bodach showed no sign of being at the other end of a fetter. He seemed to be impartially at his ease with everyone, and impartially indifferent to what they might think of him—as though the same happy insensitivity to knitted woollen underclothes underlaid all his contacts. If it had not been for the Major-domo's introduction Snipe would have supposed him a visitor—some distant Scotch cousin of Coventina's; as an exile, he could only be at Catmere on a short sentence for some trifling misdemeanour. 'What are you in for?'—the jailbird's opening rose and rose again to Snipe's lips. He converted it to: 'Will you be here long?' 'That I can't answer categorically,' said Sir Bodach. 'But I am under a life-sentence.' Snipe's tact was short-lived as hoarfrost. 'What for?' 'Heresy.'

Snipe had heard about heresy at the court of Arden: a mortal absurdity which made Tom burn Dick, Dick burn Tom, Tom and Dick unite to burn Harry. Surely not the uncouthest court in furthest Scotland could take such an aberration seriously? 'Heresy … How—how interesting!' 'Heresy,' said Sir Bodach obligingly, 'is to believe in what other people don't believe in. It is an offence against society. But if you are interested, I must begin at the beginning.' At that moment he was called away to explain the Fair Isle knitting to the Mistress of the Robes. His tame cat popularity with the elder ladies made it difficult for Snipe to learn more about heresy. It was not till the long snow melted that Sir Bodach began at the beginning, inviting Snipe to walk on the terrace with him.

A west wind blew. Spring had come as impetuously as a catastrophe. The sallow patches of snow diminished from moment to moment, the waste glittered with little water-courses, there were birds everywhere, chattering as they flew low over the muddied grass.

'You were going to tell me—'

'How I became a heretic. First, you must know that I was born with the noise of the sea in my ears. Have you ever seen the sea?'

Snipe had only seen it on maps.

'The important thing about the sea is that there is no end to it.'

The maps had shown it ending very concisely where it met the land. Snipe did not say so.

'The Kingdom of Elfwick lies in Eastern Caithness— barren country, but an admirable sounding-board for the sea. There isn't a day when one doesn't hear it pounding at the foot of the cliffs, and with an easterly wind one hears nothing else. Wave after wave strikes the land, and says Now! After it comes another wave, and says Now! and another, and another.'

Snipe dredged up a comment and supposed there were a good many shipwrecks.

'You must also know that I have always been a great reader. Elfwick has an excellent library, rich in the classical authors, and with a cabinet of books classified as "Curious"—treatises by the patristic authors, Jerome, and Chrysostom and Origen. When I had read everything else, I read these too—always, mind you, with the sound of the sea in my ears. Since those writers seemed taken up with the notion of endlessness I hoped to find some mention of the sea in their writings; but I did not. I hope I am not boring you?'

'No, indeed.' A black speck had appeared on the waste.

'When I had exhausted our library I made several excursions—to Saint Andrew's, to Oxford, to the German Universities—and read over the shoulders of mortal students. It was sometimes very trying not being able to turn the pages for myself, since I was a quicker reader than they; but invisibility had its drawbacks. I also attended lectures. There was a certain Master Faustus, who lectured on the planets— an able man, though very unpunctual. Whenever I came home I shook these mortal stammerings out of my ears and let them fill with the noise of the sea."

'Do you write yourself?'

'I made some notes on Aristophanes. Of all the mortal writers, Aristophanes is nearest the Elfin mind.'

The black speck had come nearer and had a perceptibly bobbing motion.

'I never learned to swim,' continued Sir Bodach. 'But I was very fond of flying above the sea, watching the waves begin to gather themselves up and swell toward the base of the cliffs, seeing the clouds cast purple on the sea's green, and the long lazy snake of foam undulating along the coast—on calm days, that is. It was on such a calm day, a day in early July, and I was flying above the sea and thinking about it, especially of its vitality—for there is not a pint-pot's measure of ocean, Snipe, which does not partake of the vitality of the whole—when my wings fell off.'

Icarus, thought Snipe. The donkey was halted, a woman got off.

'I saw them falling below me. I was surprised that I did not fall too. But I remained airborne, and began to rise. Glancing at my legs, I saw two trailing shafts of light. I watched my body dissolving and replaced by a shape of light. I was borne upward in a gentle spiral, clothed in my immortality. I was an immortal soul.'

Nothing happens for months, thought Snipe, and then everything happens at once. Sir Bodach has become an immortal soul and an old gipsy woman has mounted the palace steps, calling out, 'Queen Jocasta greets Queen Coventina.'

'But what did it feel like?'

'The most natural thing in the world.'

Like another of these most natural things in the world, Queen Coventina appeared on the threshold and sat down on the doorstep beside the gipsy. They fell into an animated conversation. He longed to know what they were talking about, but they were out of hearing. He turned his enquiring mind to Sir Bodach's immortality.

'And what happened next?'

'I wandered through the air like a bright vapour for an hour or so. Then I floated gently downward and became my usual self about halfway down the cliff.'

'And your wings?'

'They rejoined me. That is how I became a heretic, Snipe. That is why I am in exile. Elfindom rejects any idea of the immortal soul. It is considered anti-social and subversive, and all mention of it is banned. Naturally, I mentioned mine. By the way, please don't refer to what I have told you. I am here on the strict understanding that I don't proselytize.'

He strolled off along the terrace and was introduced to Queen Jocasta.

It was the wings that stuck in Snipe's gullet. There had been such coherence and candour in Sir Bodach's story—which in its way was rather poetical—that he might even have believed it if it had not been for those wings which hung about like a shepherd's collies waiting to be whistled up. 'They rejoined me.' The words, so casual, so inartistic, ruined the effect of the narrative. But the picture of Sir Bodach floating about in disembodied radiance and supposing himself to be immortal was such an antidote to the rusticity of life at Catmere that he shifted his disapproval to the establishment at Elfwick— fairies so prudish and cantankerous that they could not allow one of their number a delusion which harmed nobody. Delusions break no bones. Why exile him?—and to Catmere, of all places, where no wind would ever bring the sound of a wave, and where there were no books except a few sour old chronicles and some works on husbandry.

It was when Sir Bodach was telling him about Emperor Hadrian's Wall which stretched from one sea to another that

Snipe had his idea. It was June, the days were long, the Court was absorbed with sheep-shearing, no one would notice their absence: why not make an early start, fly through the cool of the morning, and spend a day at the sea? He had long wished to see the sea, he added.

'You should, you should. It would be the making of you,' said Sir Bodach. 'And bring me back a shell I can hold to my ear.'

'I meant we should go together.'

'My vow forbids me to fly.'

'Your vow?'

'My vow of poverty, chastity and gravity.'

'Gravity? But you laugh, you tell funny stories.'

'Gravitational gravity. I do not leave the ground.'

Sir Bodach explained that after he knew himself immortal he re-read the authors classified as "curious" and found they had much to say about the soul, and recommended vows as an excellent means of keeping it in good condition. His vow had been slightly burdensome at first, but now he would not for the world be without it. Why didn't Snipe take a vow? This conversation took place amid a great baa-ing and belling of sheep, and when a shorn ewe stepped out of its fleece and looked modestly round, as if astonished to find itself so slender and so white, Sir Bodach said a well-tended soul would look just so after death had sheared it. The next beast out of the shearing-pen was a ram, bloodied and vengeful, and Snipe made it a reason for walking away. Apparently Sir Bodach did not regard the strict understanding not to proselytize as a vow; but it would not do for him to be overheard misunderstanding it.

As regularly as the first warm days brought Queen Coventina out to sit on the doorstep with Queen Jocasta (who being a gipsy would not go under a roof) and bargain about pots and pans which needed tinkering, the June sheep-shearing drew

Sir Bodach to look on and make indiscreet references to scab, and fleeces matted with worldliness and gluttony. Fortunately the herdsmen were too busy to attend, or supposed he was referring to sheep in Scotland; but Snipe was in cold sweats of anxiety as they loitered under the summer sun. By now Sir Bodach had grown attached to him. Though this had the advantage of keeping him supervisable, it had its dangers; for the elder ladies, seeing their tame cat making off to caress a nobody, would be quick to pounce on any pretext for a hue and cry. But one goes on from day to day, averting or evading, till one takes jeopardy as a matter of course, and even comes to enjoy it.

If no one else admired his dexterity, Snipe was sometimes in ecstasies at it; as when Sir Bodach at the supper-table, apropos of herbs in stuffing, opened out on the disputed question as to how original sin is dispensed, whether inherited or individually implanted at the moment of conception; at which Snipe broke into a libertine giggle and said that Origen, that master of classical comic drama, was irresistibly funny but sometimes went too far. Later that evening he got Sir Bodach to himself and reproached him. Why couldn't he keep to blameless subjects, like the sea? Sir Bodach listened so meekly that Snipe decided to do a little proselytizing himself, and began on his own experiences: how self-confidence had lured him into taking part in a Church of England christening, and how that fatal first dallying round a font had led to his downfall. Sir Bodach seemed impressed, and asked about the nature of the rite: was the child immersed? Snipe replied that one drop had been enough to cook its goose.

He began to hope his admonition might have cooked Sir Bodach's immortal soul. With the first ten years of his exile behind him, he felt that he had not come to Catmere in vain, for this year's sheep-shearing had passed without a single indiscretion from Sir Bodach. Sheep after sheep had come from the pen without reminding him of the immortality of the soul—even the new merinos which every one was so excited about. Sir Bodach had never been a more ample companion, talking about his studies, his travels, his childhood, trying to teach Snipe the Greek alphabet, describing the Roman burial customs and those prevailing in the Orkneys, and turning from these to ask Snipe about the Kingdom of Arden and to persuade him to recite one of his satires.

It was the halcyon calm before the storm.

They were standing by the lough, admiring the dragonflies among the rushes, when Sir Bodach gripped him by the shoulder. Before he knew what was happening, they were knee-deep in water and Sir Bodach, keeping a strong hold on him, was splashing him in the face. 'Don't be alarmed, Snipe,' he said. 'I'm just giving you a soul. You'll be much happier with a soul, I assure you. Don't kick, dear boy! You said one drop would do it, but it's best to be on the safe side.' Pinning Snipe's arms behind his back, he scooped up another handful of water and poured it over Snipe's head. 'You've been so kind to me, Snipe, you've listened so patiently, it's the least return I can make you. Did it go in your eye?'

It had gone in his eye, it was trickling down the back of his neck. Shoals of minnows darted from under their feet as they struggled. He wrenched his arms free and hit out. Sir Bodach was the larger and heavier fairy and at some time in his youth must have studied wrestling. Snipe was reduced to scratching his face. Sir Bodach got his head in chancery, drenched him into submission and assisted him out of the lough.

Two gipsies went by, studiously not looking at them, and went on toward the castle.

That evening the Queen called a Council. As exiles, Sir Bodach and Snipe were excluded from it. It seemed plain to them that the gipsies must have made some reference to their fight in the lough, but they did not speak of this. They were barely on speaking terms, and waited for adversity to reconcile them. Snipe thought of the attack on his principles and the scratches reddening on Sir Bodach's face. Sir Bodach talked about wildcats and how they can always be known by their bushy tails.

In the morning, they knew what everybody else knew. The gipsies had come to announce the death of Queen Jocasta and to convey her dying command that the obsequies should be held in front of the Castle of Catmere. Queen Coventina had ordered that her whole court should attend the ceremony. As a mark of respect, visibility would be worn.

It was because of the sheep that Snipe and Sir Bodach had been fighting visibly when the two gipsies went by. Sheep were animals of such imprecise perception that if they heard grasses brushed by invisible feet they scattered in all directions, entangled themselves in brambles, foundered in bogs. Though the gipsies did not appear to have reported the fight, it was bound to get out sooner or later—so Snipe thought, looking at Sir Bodach's scratches, beginning to reproach himself while at the same time thinking he had had no option, and finally casting the blame on the sheep. If it had not been for the sheep, Sir Bodach and he could have fought unperceived and the gipsies would have supposed the splashing in the lough was due to pike.

There was plenty of time for these reflections; it was not till past noon that the funeral procession neared. Jocasta's caravan was dragged by a team of male gipsies harnessed to the shafts. Behind it followed the women of the tribe, the older men and the children. They moved in a block of silence. The caravan was halted in front of the castle, hind-foremost. The tilt-curtains were drawn back, so that all could see the dead Queen of the Faas, sitting stiffened upright, with her brown hands on her knees, and her possessions massed round her: her shawls and ornaments, pots and pans and flagons, her napery and feather pillows. The women, their swinging gold earrings tarnished in sign of mourning, came forward with inflammables. Gunpowder and gorse-faggots were laid beneath the caravan, and faggots heaped round it, and a trail was laid. They all stood back as the spark burrowed along the trail. The caravan seemed to leap into the air as the gunpowder ignited. Then it settled down and burned steadily.

Snipe, remembering the vitality in the low-pitched indifferent voice telling him to keep to the track, sighed without knowing it. Sir Bodach patted him. 'I have not the least uneasiness about her. I talked to her once, and found her ideas of the soul very correct and enlightened. She said she would be well looked after by the Flying Daddas—some sort of blessed spirits, I take it. I assured her—'

Snipe felt a breathing on the back of his neck. He turned. The Mistress of the Robes was behind them, taut as a cat at a mousehole. They were standing a little apart, she could call no witness; it would be his word against hers. But already he felt despair.

When the scandal broke, she had plenty of witnesses. Half the court had been solicited by Sir Bodach or heard him canvassing for the soul. Youthful virgins testified that he had made suggestions to them, suggestions they could not make head or tail of but knew to be improper. At the Court of Enquiry Snipe and the bailiff maintained that he was mad. The bailiff put up a sturdy fight. His mother was an Orkney fairy, he felt a blood partisanship. Snipe's testimony counted for nothing. He was under suspicion himself, and anyhow it was a case of one exile sticking up for another. Sir Bodach was not called, and spent the day fishing. When he came back with a basketful of trout he was told the result of the Enquiry and asked what he had to say for himself. He replied, numbering it off on his fingertips, *(a)* that he was known to be a heretic; *(b)* that heretics are persons who believe what rightminded persons do not believe; what they believe in, therefore, must be a delusion; *(c)* that those under a delusion are, by common consent, counted as madmen; *(d)* that a madman could not be held answerable for what he might happen to say or what undertaking he might chance to ignore. His manner, as usual, was affable and scholarly, and several members of the Court of Enquiry were won round by it, and convinced by his chain of reasoning. Were they not all rightminded persons, and as such inaccessible to his proselytizing? So why not go on as before? His trout were served at supper, grilled, and did much to plead his cause. Pending the Queen's decision, he was put into protective custody.

Queen Coventina was in one of those quandaries which beset absolute monarchs. She had known for some time that Sir Bodach proselytized and that others also knew this. She had said nothing and assumed that they would loyally follow her example. Now his offence was in every mouth. She would gladly have skinned the Mistress of the Robes, but what good would that do? Her court was too small to support a schism and too poor to endanger a source of income. Exiles paid well. She was in treaty for another, young and very promising—a flaxen hoyden from a Dutch Kingdom who had played one practical joke too many. If it became known that Catmere was an Alsatia where exiles could play fast and loose with the regulations, above all, if it became known that Sir Bodach had been free to proclaim his immortal soul, farewell to reputation and revenue. She decided that this was a time when honesty was the best policy, and sent her confidential secretary to Elfwick to explain the situation and ask what should be done about it.

Elfwick replied that the procedure with stubborn heretics was to put them to death—either by stoning, which was traditional, or by burning at the stake, which was the current method.

The confidential secretary returned to Elfwick with an expression of the Queen's thanks and an enquiry when Sir Bodach should be sent off. He brought back word that as Sir Bodach was an exile, Elfwick had no further liability for him. Stoning or burning, the death sentence must be carried out at Catmere.

Catmere had never carried out death sentences except on sheep and backsliding collies. There was some reluctance to start doing it now, and a general resentment at being ordered about by Elfwick. The whole affair might have rested in abeyance, and Sir Bodach remained in his cell writing a Natural History of Sea Birds with increasingly blue fingers, if a messenger from Elfwick had not arrived with a letter from Queen Gruach to say that her deputy would attend the execution but could not manage it before the first week in January; she hoped this would not inconvenience Queen Coventina.

The confidential secretary was again sent on his travels, this time to the Kingdom of the Guadarramas, if possible to observe an auto-da-fé and in any case to get details of procedure. It wasn't the liturgical season for Acts of Faith, but he brought back details. They were simple: a stake, a platform, a sufficiency of ropes and fuel, an executioner. When the Court slaughterer had been disabused of the idea that he would have to cut Sir Bodach's throat he consented to be the executioner.

Sir Bodach was informed: asked if he had any last requests to make, he answered, 'More ink.' When Snipe heard this, he was pierced to the heart, for he had felt sure Sir Bodach would ask for a farewell interview.

It was the fifth day of January. The deputy from Elfwick had arrived—a lacklustre fairy with a cough; all was in readiness. Sir Bodach was brought out for his death. He looked uncommonly healthy, unsuitably so for the occasion, and walked with an easy gait as though he were strolling out on a spring morning instead of a very cold winter one. The spectators were aligned in order of precedence, the grandest in front. As he passed between their ranks he paused here and there for a word of greeting, a how d'y'do. When he bowed to the Mistress of the Robes, she cut him dead; at which the bailiff commented very audibly that he wished it could be the old bitch. Sir Bodach smiled demurely, looked round for a fellow-feeler, caught sight of Snipe and gave him a wave of the hand. When he mounted the platform there was a murmur of relief.

It was one of those occasions when everything goes wrong. The Queen had overslept. Several of the faggots had been mistakenly appropriated by the kitchen staff and were already heating the oven. The executioner tied a succession of granny knots. It had begun to rain. Sir Bodach stood quietly on the platform getting wetter and wetter. His glance rambled over the scene and once he put up his hand and smoothed back a lock of hair from his forehead—for during his captivity he had grown shaggy. After several tries the executioner struck a spark and kindled a tallow candle. Guarding the flame with his hand, he thrust it among the brushwood. There was a reassuring crackle, a puff of smoke. In a loud voice Sir Bodach said, 'I release myself from my vow,' spread his wings, glided out of the granny knots and soared upward. No one knew quite what to do. There was a confusion of voices giving advice. When the executioner's lads were sent in pursuit, Sir Bodach was already high above them, his wet garments glistening in a brief burst of sunlight. Heading north, he vanished into a cloud.

He came down in the Moray Firth, landing on a whaling vessel bound for Atlantic waters. A storm was raging, the faint glimmer of his person was taken for Saint Elmo's fire. For some days he remained invisible; he did not wish to find himself among mortals who might also wish to burn him for heresy. But hearing the seamen pledge themselves to eternal damnation if such and such a statement were not true he realized that they were sound—if a little off-hand—in respect of the soul and its immortality. By venturing into visibility at discreet intervals he established himself as a new hand who had come aboard at Peterhead or Lybster and stayed below till he got his sea-legs. From that day on he led a happy, secluded, sea-faring life, reached a great age and was buried at sea.

Snipe was not so fortunate. Thirty-nine years of exile stretched before him, years of long winters and reproachful summers. No positive offence could be laid to his charge, only the offence for which there is no acquittal: of being involved in a scandal. It was not merely the scandal of Sir Bodach's opinions, it was the scandal of his inadequate execution that Catmere wanted to hear no more of, least of all from his lackeying follower. So Snipe was avoided, at first from caution, and afterwards by habit. The bailiff continued friendly; but when they had finished praising Sir Bodach there was not much else to say, and as time went on, the hue of life ebbed from the praises, though there was no slackening in the bailiff's resentment against the Mistress of the Robes. From time to time Snipe nursed a precarious fancy—it never had the dimensions of a hope—that Sir Bodach would reappear; hailing him from a cloud, perhaps, his legs two trailing shafts of light, his wings waiting about for him; that he would float gently downward and become his usual self, and resume their conversation as though nothing had interrupted it; and that he, Snipe, would not feel the slightest surprise. But now he would be able to apologize for those scratches and for his pettish reaction to Sir Bodach's intention of giving him a soul. On clear days he used to stand beside the lough, looking at his solitary reflection. Nothing was left him but himself.

The companion, whom he had so anxiously tried to protect, who had so trustingly befriended him, was gone; he was bare on both sides. As the years of his sentence ran on, listening to the wind and the baa-ing sheep, being punctual at meals, he knew the final intimidation of exile: he was afraid to go home.

13 The Late Sir Glamie

When the recurrent appearances of the late Sir Glamie, respected Lord Chamberlain of the Elfin Court of Rings in Galloway, could no longer be ignored, the working fairies were triumphant: they had said so all along. Some had seen him semi-transparent and a livid shade of blue; others, gigantic and frowning portentously; others, again, holding his head under his arm; others, rosy and smiling. In every case he was unmistakably recognizable, and usually carried a large fish. The fish clinched it. During his lifetime Sir Glamie had been an ardent dry-fly fisher. Examples of his prowess, stuffed, varnished, and with their death histories engraved on brass plates, hung in glass cases in the North Saloon.

When Sir Glamie's ghost became an accepted feature of life at Rings Castle, the working fairies were forbidden to mention it. This did not prevent them from seeing it. A footman would stand suspended with a plate of soup trembling in his hand. Soufflés came to table sunken and supernaturally chilled by an encounter with Sir Glamie in an anteroom. Housemaids went about their work in pairs, ladies' maids stuck pins into their ladies; there was a marked reluctance to eat salmon. The infection spread among the Castle animals: lapdogs barked, peacocks tore out their plumes, quiet old cats put up their backs and hissed. A smell of fish provoked them to frenzy.

In a mortal court, apparitions are unobjectionable—even picturesque, and creditable. The occupiers of Grace and Favour apartments at Hampton Court are not disturbed when Queen Katherine Howard runs screaming down a corridor with her hands about her neck. An appearance of the White Lady was little more than a postman's knock at Herrenhausen. But Rings was an Elfin Court, where Sir Glamie was now, as the current Lord Chamberlain put it, *persona non grata*. For one thing, his reappearances proved that he had not been so well-bred as he should have been. Elfins have no souls: when they die, they are dead: it is as simple as that. Therefore, at some point or other of Sir Glamie's pedigree an Elfin lady must have yielded to a mortal lover, and immortality, like the pox, has run in the family ever since. This was painful enough. More painful was the thought of the scandal which would ensue if the facts became known. Most painful of all was the threat to the calm negation on which all Elfindom reposes. Once this was undermined by Sir Glamie's reappearances, libertine speculations and surmises would widen the breach, superstition, proselytizing, fear of an awaiting life after death, would rush in, and Elfins sink to the level of mortals.

The Queen displayed the professional calm of a monarch.

'If I may say so, I think all this is rather a fuss about nothing. Working fairies have to gossip about something or other. It keeps up their self-importance. They will soon tire of seeing Sir Glamie. If they don't they can be dismissed.'

It was humbly represented to Her Majesty that this would spread the scandal.

'Well, well. Maybe. In that case, they must be given a great deal more to do. I will order a spring-cleaning, to occupy their minds. The time of year is immaterial.'

Spring-cleanings have a peculiar fascination for those employed in them. A mysterious pair of spectacles is found in a sauceboat; a rusty strongbox in the muniment room is forced open and contains nutmegs; rolls of green baize and a painting of Vesuvius in Eruption are brought to light from the beer-cellar; when the brown bed-hangings from the Librarian's bed-chamber are hung on the line and the dust beaten out of them, they are discovered to be cloth-of-gold and fall to pieces. A pioneering spirit reigns. Unheard-of feats of cleaning are achieved; hinges are polished, statuary scoured into its remotest crevices, bookcases scaled like mountain peaks, folios waxed and camphor bags renewed on the topmost shelves. In this triumphing flood of industry the great Venetian-glass chandelier that hung from the height of the throne-room ceiling had somehow or other escaped attention till the house-keeper saw a page doing nothing, put a feather whisk in his hand, and told him to fly up and dust it. He hovered enthralled by the blue glass leaves and pink glass roses in their embowering crystal, and was only vaguely aware of a dark mass of cobwebs at its centre. Poking with his whisk, he dislodged Sir Glamie—and dropped to the floor in a dead faint.

The palace was much the better for its thorough cleaning. The chandelier was unharmed, the page was brought round with smelling-salts. When he opened his eyes, they were fixed in a squint of terror, which ruined his chances of preferment, and impaired Sir Glamie's popularity among the working fairies. Every broken plate, curdled sauce, grazed elbow, was now laid to his charge. There were mutterings about exorcism.

Feeling that no scandal could attach to a dwelling in such a high state of polish, the Queen decided to invite the Elfins of the neighbourhood to a New Year party. She was discussing the arrangements with Lady Moorit, Mistress of the Robes, who alone could be trusted to comb the Queen's hair. The mirror reflected the seated Queen, the standing assiduous lady, and everything was just as it should be and just as usual when another figure was interposed. Sir Glamie was looking over the Queen's shoulder. The comb dropped from Lady Moorit's hand. She stared at Sir Glamie's reflection as if she had never seen, never would see, anything else.

'Don't you think so?'

The Queen spoke as if nothing had happened in the mirror since her last remark about not seeming to put their best foot forward, which might look suspicious. But between the two speeches there had been a perceptible pause. And in that pause she had certainly recognized Sir Glamie. Her hands had not stirred, her features had not sharpened; but there had been a sudden blackening and dilation of the pupils of her eyes. Lady Moorit assented, and picked up the comb.

'And what happened then?' the Master of Ceremonies asked. He had been Lady Moorit's lover for many years. She trusted him as one trusts one's own pillow.

'What happened then, what did Glamie do?'

'He left off.'

'Vanished?'

'Left off—like a note of music.'

'I wonder what she will do.'

'Nothing—if I know her.'

Lady Moorit was right. The Queen did nothing. Nothing was done by anyone. But gradually the question of apparitions became a subject of private conversation among the graver fairies. A theoretical subject, of course: an aspect of mortal peculiarity, like their Standing Stones and their insistence on calling objects so obviously phallic, Maidens—a habit so ingrained that the spired churches of a later cult were more often than not dedicated to the Virgin Mary. One could not live on the same planet, and indeed cheek by jowl with mortals, without an occasional glance at the conventions and convictions which made them a race apart.

'A race apart. And a race akin,' said the Master of Ceremonies, who was talking with the Chancellor, the Chamberlain, and the Treasurer over their wine.

'I dispute it. I dispute it entirely,' cried the Chamberlain. 'They are not akin.'

'There are resemblances,' said the Treasurer. 'The same social structure. The same number of toes.'

'The same number of toes! So have monkeys. Does that make us akin to monkeys?'

The Chancellor suggested that the essential distinction was wings. The Master of Ceremonies said that a mortal might maintain the essential difference was the faculty to survive after death. 'An uncomfortable privilege,' he added.

They agreed. But the Treasurer, who had a habit of seeing both sides, remarked, that given the mortal condition, belief in survival was understandable. 'They lead such unsatisfactory lives. They are so short-lived, and so prolific. They see their children dying by the dozen and in the twinkling of an eye are dead themselves. So they avenge themselves on their limitations by thinking there's more to it than that.'

'They may think so,' said the chancellor, 'but a fallacy won't take them any further. Pass the wine.'

'As a hypothesis, purely as a hypothesis,' began the Treasurer; but the Chamberlain overtook him. 'Whether or no they believe in a life after death, they believe in death all right. Look at their feudings. When a mortal kills his enemy, he doesn't fancy he'll survive.'

'Not only their feudings,' said the Master of Ceremonies. 'Their loves. When I was studying deportment at Brocéliande, there was a mortal employed as a shepherd (it was the fashion to be pastoral just then, and feed lambs) whose wife was drowned. Day after day, he used to walk by the river, waiting to see her body come to the surface. He didn't want to see what had survived. It was her dead body he wanted to see again.'

'Crying over spilled milk,' commented the Chancellor.

'He was an honest man, at any rate. He didn't pretend he'd seen her ghost,' said the Chamberlain.

'What are these ghosts supposed to come back for?' This was the Treasurer.

'Revenge,' 'Nostalgia,' 'Nothing better to do,' answered the Chamberlain, the Master of Ceremonies, and the Chancellor respectively.

'This presupposes that they are free agents, possessing memory, will and reason—some degree of reason, anyhow,' said the Treasurer.

'Reason? If they had a grain of reason, they'd do no such thing,' said the Chancellor, and the Chamberlain added, 'If they had a grain of reason they'd know they can't exist.'

The Treasurer was about to go on, when there was a loud dissatisfied grunt. There sat Sir Glamie.

'You know nothing whatever about it.'

Before their eyes, he rose to his feet, picked up his fish, and wasn't there.

They agreed to keep this strictly private. In fact, they kept it so private that they only referred to it guardedly, and later, not at all. There was a feeling that Sir Glamie had somehow done something rather disgraceful and that the kindest thing would be to ignore it. It was as though he had taken the hint, for he was not seen again.

'And yet,' said the Master of Ceremonies, talking it over with Lady Moorit, on whose discretion he relied as he relied on his tailor, 'and yet, I still feel we behaved rather churlishly. We should have found something civil to say—wished him well, or hoped he'd come again.'

'We can't always do the right thing,' she said. 'Even you.'

Lady Moorit had a little dog; and when the Master of Ceremonies visited her after finishing his evening routine, he used to take it out for its final walk. There was an endearing domesticity about these errands and the small silver lantern she handed him. At the end of a long day indoors, among voices and trifling problems and the upkeep of formalities, it was agreeable to step into the freedom of the night, and feel himself surrounded by processes that needed no supervision or adjustments by him. The noise of the river told him what quarter the wind was in. To-night, it blew from the south-west, a slow gentle wind with a forecast of rain in it—an upstream wind, he thought—and charged with the moisture that draws out every scent and makes it explicit: the smell of violet leaves, of rabbit dung, of rotting wood, the red geranium smell of the red fox. The next moon would be the new moon of spring. But the wind was stirring bare boughs. His ear told him that, though he could not see them; they were blotted out by one of those brooding, nocturnal mists that gather in a mild interval before the equinoctial gales rip open the cloud-cover and send it flying.

The little dog had been snuffing and scuffling among the drifted leaves. If the night-smells were interesting to him, they must be intoxicating to her. It would not do to let her go out of sight—out of lantern-light, rather. He flipped open the lantern door, and played the beam of light this way and that. A hoary little world with no little dog in it. He whistled. All of a sudden, blown from nowhere like a dead leaf, she was rubbing against his legs. He put on her lead, to take her back to their mistress—who would not thank him for the state she was in, her stomach draggled, her feathered legs and ears bestuck with holly leaves. Where had she picked up holly leaves? He did not remember a holly in this stretch of the policies. He played his lantern in search of it, saw it lurking behind the bulk of a clipped yew, admired its glistening foliage, turned away. But as the beam of light slipped from the yew, he caught the glint of a pair of motionless, reflecting eyes. By night the eyes of the mildest dog reflect back a savage red. Cats' eyes shine topaz or amber. The eyes of a fox are a vivid breath-taking green. The eyes staring out of the darkness of the yew, the darkness of the night, were a steely blue.

'Good evening,' he said pleasantly. 'And good luck for to-morrow. The wind's upstream. It should be a good day for your fishing.'

He bowed and walked on. His mind was eased of its burden. He had redressed a discourtesy, saying the appropriate right thing. The little dog pattered along beside him. 'Good girl,' he said. For she had not barked; she, too, had behaved well.

14 Castor and Pollux

Beauty is in the eye of the beholder. In the eye of Elfins the qualities considered to constitute beauty are slenderness, narrow hands and feet, sharp-cut features (rather small eyes are admired), arched eyebrows, the fineness of detail one associates with moths and butterflies. These canons are conditioned by Elfin build and longevity: majestic contours are irreconcilable with flight, and a *jolie-laide* countenance is likelier to remain charming over centuries than a classically moulded one. Elfins are averse to any variation from the racial type. Few of them really enjoy Ovid's 'Metamorphoses'. Above all, miscegenation with mortals is reprobated because of its probable results—corpulence, coarse skin, broad smiles, dimples, premature decay, and flat fingernails.

But from time to time an Elfin may be born who transcends the typical *jolie-laide* of the race by an absolute beauty. Such a one was Tiphaine, of the Kingdom of Elfhame, in Scotland, and so was the legendary Morgan le Fay. Nel, of the Kingdom of Pomace, in Herefordshire, was another of these shining exceptions. Her parents, respectable members of the lesser aristocracy, looked at each other with amazement, unable to account for her. They expected her to vanish like a rainbow. But she throve, and took herself easily, and accepted admiration with no more fluster or false demur than one of the thousand daisies on a lawn accepts the dew. In the same modest, matter-of-course spirit she accepted an admiring husband. It was a resplendent match. Hamlet was faultlessly well-bred, wealthy, intelligent, handsome, an orphan. In his youth, despite these advantages, he was looked at askance by the staider Elfins of Pomace, who, enjoying a sheltered climate and a traditional calm, did not like excesses. Ordinary libertinism they would not have objected to:

Hamlet was a mental libertine. He founded the Pomacean Society for Unregulated Speculation, which, meeting at irregular intervals—in itself subversive—discussed such subjects as Sleeping Out-of-Doors, Compulsory Gymnastics for All Ages, the Badness of Good Taste. After lecturing on Mortals and Their Future, he put it to a vote: That Mortals Are More Interesting Than Elfins. When even his most committed disciples rejected this, he put another motion: That Elfins Are Not Interesting. After three hours of debate, the members of the Pomacean Society went home chanting the national anthem *sciolto e fortissimo*, and next day were officially required to consider themselves dissolved. Hamlet then founded the Pomacean Society for Promoting Dissolution, tired of it, dissolved it, and went to visit his Great-Aunt Angelica at La Recondita, her estate in the Apennines. Angelica was a lady of illustrious gallantries. She deplored Hamlet's rusticity—blaming it on his upbringing in Pomace, a provincial Kingdom in a clownish country—and, having nothing else on hand at the moment, set herself to comb it out of him. For six months he wrote a Petrarchan sonnet daily, alternately amorous or pastoral, practised the *manège* on a winged horse—a rare animal, out of the Astolfine stable—and learned the scandals of every Elfin family of distinction. After the one hundred and twenty-third sonnet she thought him adequately combed, gave him letters of introduction, and sent him off to make the Grand Tour.

In Foligno he was so entranced by a travelling puppet theatre that he followed it from city to city, disregarding cascades, Roman arches, vistas, Vesuvius, the Vatican Library, for the pleasure of seeing Orlando furiously raving with an unmoved white calico face.

He came home supposing that this kind of ludicrous high-flownness could be found only under Italian skies, and quite accidentally, on a wet day, discovered the theatre of his native land, performing at the top of its voice in an innyard of the county town. Forgetting that he had gone to watch the races, he stood entranced, listening to squeaking empresses and bellowing tyrants, spectres with hiccups, malignant Jews with a sturdy Midlands accent, and watching victims of the plot flump to the ground like a shower of acorns. And all of them mortals—stuffed with beating hearts and fiery livers and intricated guts instead of sheep's wool. Only mortals could be so majestically and endearingly absurd. Like him, they were there for the races, and moved on. Angelica had done such marvels for Hamlet that he had been appointed Regulator of Court Festivities; there was no need to follow as he had done in Italy. He became an anonymous patron of the drama by sending one of his pages nightly to disquiet the local lord mayor's slumbers with a gigantic badger, threatening disclosures and ruin unless The Spotted Cow was given a covered gallery and a covered stage with two trapdoors and a thunder machine. This done, Hamlet (excusing himself from Court on the ground of an intermittent fever caught in the Pontine Marshes) regularly attended performances at The Spotted Cow. They were frequent, thunder machines being rare in the provinces.

After his marriage, Nel went with him. The fact that she took the action seriously and only regretted that the actors were so badly dressed made her companionship even dearer, and as they sat invisibly in the gallery he would gather her to him when anything particularly ludicrous happened on the stage, and hug her loveliness and his low taste simultaneously. These escapades came to an end. There was an outbreak of plague, then of morality, and the theatres were closed by order.

When the order was rescinded and the travelling players came once more, Hamlet was in attendance on the Queen, indispensably regulating a *conversazione*. He bore his disappointment so gracefully that Nel said she would go to the opening performance alone, to give him an account of it. She had an answer to all his objections. She would plead her belly as an excuse for absence from the afternoon assembly. She was no more with child than she had ever been, and Elfin pregnancies are so infrequent that hers would have been in the Court Circular; but the excuse was a formality employed by every lady at Court. In case anything went wrong with her invisibility, she would wear a mask. If he insisted on a chaperon, she would take her lady's maid, vowed to secrecy. At the thought of a lady's maid vowed to secrecy over his cherished foible of low taste, Hamlet's self-respect revolted. Nel went alone.

It was a sultry afternoon. The birdless silence of July intimidated her; she would have been glad of the lady's maid. As she took her place in the gallery, what had seemed an adventure darkened into an ordeal. The coachman had got her there too early; nothing was going on except some thumpings. Her mask stifled her. The blood drummed in her ears; she would not be able to hear a word the players said. And without Hamlet's expression to guide her how was she to know where to be amused? The house was beginning to fill up, the smells of mortals rose from the pit, there were voices and repartees all around her, and a boy in a butcher's apron was being successfully impertinent to a fat jolly woman, declaring she was his idol and the queen of his heart. Nel gave herself a shake. She must fix her whole attention on the play and remember everything in order to give Hamlet an exact report when they were together again that evening. Perhaps looking through the eyeholes of the mask would clarify what was going on. The cornet player and the drummer finished their flourish. A red-haired young mortal in pink came forward and spoke a speech about Destiny. He was destined to unhappiness. So far, so good …

The play was over. The spectators were leaving. A boy with a tray of pots of beer came on to the stage. The actors, wiping the sweat and the greasepaint off their faces, gathered round him and drank. A cracked looking glass hung on a side screen, where the players, making their entrance, were in the habit of taking a quick glance at themselves, and the young man in pink was at this moment staring into it. Lovely as Adonis, he had tripped over a cat, missed two cues, sneezed in the peroration of a speech of defiance, got very little applause, and hurt his back in a death fall. A skirt rustled behind him. He turned and saw a lady taking off her mask. Her face was so beautiful that he almost forgot his own. In a low hurried voice she began to praise his courage under misfortune, to beg him not to despair. Ungloving her hand, she pulled off a ring and gave it to him, saying it was a keepsake. Not for nothing had he played Joseph in a religious drama, leaving a blue taffeta cloak in the clasp of Potiphar's wife and rebuking her in fleshings. Here was another of them—one of those grand ladies, shameless and glorious. He listened to her directions. He was to take seven turns to the left, jump the brook, and come in by a garden gate. Before he could answer, she was gone.

He looked disdainfully at the group of beer drinkers.

It was the garden gate of her parents' home and led into their kitchen garden—an unintimidating entrance, Nel judged. Even so, he opened it uneasily: he suspected she was not all she seemed—or was more. A carrot fell on him from above. It had slipped from the apron of a fairy flying briskly overhead. He had decided on a prudent departure when he saw her running toward him, shameless and glorious, with her finger on her lips. A little later, her uncle, who was eating gooseberries at the farther end of the garden, heard a sharp cry of delight, thought he recognized Nel's voice, looked round, and saw her heels in the air. Remembering the joys of his youth, he began to sing a villanelle. A gardener burst through a line of French beans, and attacked the young man with a hoe, shouting, 'Get out, you dirty marauding mortal, you!' The young man fled. But it was too late. Nel became pregnant.

Everyone pitied her. Attempts were made to procure an abortion with the renowned decoction from the bark and leaves of the savin tree—a species of juniper. Her burden could not be dislodged. She went her full term—growing unrecognizably hideous, her face peaked, her legs swollen, her existence reduced to an appurtenance of her enormous womb. The birth of the first child rent her in pieces; she was already dying when a second child was born. They were both boys, wingless, and plainly mortal. Washed and swaddled, they were carried to Hamlet to be named. 'Gog and Magog!' he exclaimed. Looking out of his misery, he saw the midwife was affronted. 'Call them Castor and Pollux,' he said, and signed for them to be taken away.

It had been hoped that they would be born dead—failing that, snuffed out by a little timely neglect. But nothing had been organized: it was as though the calamity so long foreseen had taken them by surprise. Nel's parents were stupid with grief, Hamlet in agonies of earache. It was left to the midwife to take command. Mercilessly professional, she gave them every care. She had never delivered a demi-mortal before, and these were demi-mortal twins; she was determined they should live to her glory. They were strong, healthy infants, matched like carriage horses. No Elfin will suckle a mortal child: it is believed to cause warts on the breast. Mortal wet nurses were found, and the midwife stayed on to supervise the nursery.

Nel's parents, Sir Bartle and Dame Petronel, found they must take on the duties of grandparents, for Hamlet was closing his establishment and going to Greece—where he had

KINGDOMS OF ELFIN

no relatives. The midwife resented having to quit Hamlet's mansion for Sir Bartle's modest residence, but kept up her self-respect by assuring her friends that it would be much wholesomer for Castor and Pollux to be reared in a humble home, and letting it be generally understood that she was prepared to put up with anything for the dear children's sake. The move was made, and society sighed with relief to know that everything was comfortably settled and that henceforth the unfortunate affair could be forgotten and life be happy and rational again. What's done is done; it is vulgar to dwell on the past.

Bartle and Petronel, dwelling in the present, found that the duties of grandparents consisted in having no duties permitted them, in asking no questions, making no demands, querying no expenses, never setting foot in the nursery except by invitation, and for the rest of the time being seen and not heard. Bartle took to breeding pigeons; their voices condoled with him without reference to his loss. In his private heart, he blamed everything on his son-in-law. Petronel blamed no one; she merely grieved, and then grieved on because with the passage of time her original grief had lost its intensity. On the day the midwife sent word that Castor and Pollux must be measured for their first boots, it reasserted its hold on her. Mortal children, already old enough for boots, they would grow up, grow old, die in their puny longevity of threescore. And the last remnant of Nel, the last possibility of seeing a glance like hers, would be gone! She leaped to her feet, ran to the nursery, and went in without so much as knocking on the door. 'Now that the children are old enough for boots, they won't need you any longer.' Interrupting an outcry about devotion and dependence, she said, 'You are dismissed,' and left the nursery with shaking knees and a calm expression. That evening, the midwife expressed her devotion to the children by attempting to murder them. Burges, the butler,

212

was bringing her usual nightcap of honeydew and hot milk to the nursery when he heard Castor scream with terror. The door was locked. He broke it open. Her hands were round Castor's throat and Pollux's teeth were set in the calf of her leg. She let go with one hand to smack with the other. Castor writhed out of her grasp and hid under a table; Pollux sank his teeth deeper into her leg and growled. Even when the butler had knocked her out, Pollux held on with a bulldog's grip. Not till the butler had picked up the fainting Castor and said, 'Come on, Master Pollux, we're going down to my pantry,' did Pollux relax his hold, lift a face streaming with the midwife's blood, and smile.

It was after this that the household began to remark on how much the brothers seemed to love each other.

The wonder spread to other households and rose by capillary attraction from kitchens to drawing rooms, where the bond of love between the twins provided a soothing new theme for conversation. Bartle, to his annoyance, Petronel, to her surprise, found themselves congratulated on their ownership of those interesting children. Visiting ladies brought toys—identical but distinguished by red or blue bows. When the twins were extricated from their private life and brought in to be grateful, their size proved disconcerting. It was plain they had outgrown toy lambs.

Till now, Castor and Pollux had not been aware they loved each other. Publicly assured of it, they felt constrained and began to quarrel. Without any distinct idea who the enemy was, each felt the other had gone over to the enemy. With the midwife, they knew where they were: she was food, clothing, a hand scrubbing their faces and yanking tangles out of their hair, a familiar scolding voice that grew maudlin at bedtime, a besetting providence. And in a flash she was gone, and they were pitchforked into a world of Elfin smells, Elfin voices, Elfin caresses that tickled; a world where they stuck out, large and lonely, and always knocking things over. If Castor had not screamed, if Pollux had not bitten, if Burges had not intervened, she might be with them now and all be usual and secure. Burges was no substitute; he was always busy. They moped and squabbled and were told they loved each other and would be much happier now she was gone. And, with nothing to cling to, they clung to each other in despair.

Their grandparents also were at a loss without the midwife. She had monopolized the children and tried to murder them, had allowed them to pick their noses and talk with their mouths full, stamp and shout; but under her rule at least they were heard and not seen. Neither child had the smallest resemblance to Nel; neither showed a trace of Elfin blood. The thought of their mortality afforded Bartle an illicit satisfaction. Even if they survived measles (they had won through all the other diseases of mortal childhood), their survival would not entail more than a few decades of endurance: they could be lived down. Something would have to be settled about their brief futures. Meanwhile, they grew.

They developed measles simultaneously and simultaneously recovered.

By law, they were Hamlet's children. Since Hamlet had gone to Greece, no word had come from him. 'I wonder if Lady Elissa could put her finger on him,' Bartle said to Petronel. 'She goes in for crystal gazing.'

Petronel replied that Elissa had given up her crystal ball. Staring into it had given her such eyestrain that she looked like a bloodhound. Why didn't he ask Master Caraway?

'Ask who?' Castor and Pollux, in all the vigour of convalescence, were playing table tennis overhead.

'Master Caraway. Hamlet left him in charge of his affairs, you remember.'

Bartle said it was an idea and he'd think about it.

The idea of applying to his son-in-law's rascally solicitor

was unpleasing, and he thought of it as little as possible. The twins grew; so did the cost of their upkeep. Petronel spoke of selling her pearls. Bartle swallowed his pride and visited Master Caraway's office, which was as orderly as a shark's teeth. Master Caraway assumed what Bartle called his abracadabra airs and pressed a button. A drawer sprang open and Master Caraway took out a letter from Hamlet. Hamlet had tired of Attica and was going to an island called Orplid. 'He may be there by now,' said Master Caraway, looking at his spotless fingernails.

'Where is this Orplid?'

'That I cannot say. Being an island, one presumes it is in the sea. But one can't be positive. If you feel any uneasiness, Sir Bartle, I can assure you Lord Hamlet's affairs are in a very satisfactory state. It is a pleasure to administer them.'

'Those two boys of his—they're growing up, you know.' Only his dislike of Master Caraway and the warming prospect of wrenching money out of him overcame Bartle's reluctance to ask for it.

'Two boys—' The solicitor appeared to scan a horizon of boys. 'Two boys. Exactly.' He pressed another button. Another drawer sprang open, and he took out a wad of receipts and handed it to Bartle. 'I think you will find them in order.' The midwife was still being paid her wages.

As Bartle reached home he heard an outburst of cheering. When Burges opened the door he was out of breath, and explained that he had been to see if the pigeons were all right. The young gentlemen were wrestling in the lime-tree court and the working fairies were watching them, cheering them on and betting on the upshot; with so much noise and fluttering of wings, he was afraid the sitting birds might be scared off their nests. There was another burst of cheering. Bartle hurried to the defence of his pigeons and instantly forgot them in the beauty of what he saw. Castor and Pollux were wrestling naked. From head to foot they were happiness. Their stature, their long identical limbs, their matched expressions of fierce, unwavering gaiety existed in a world of their own and a moment they were born for. As they clasped and eluded, locked and slid apart, forced one another down, pliable as willow wands, and pliable as willow wands sprang up again, it seemed as though they would wrestle forever, as a brook flows chiding in a rocky channel.

Elfins are incapable of repentance—a fortunate provision, in view of their longevity. Bartle's delight in the beauty of the wrestlers was untrammelled by recollecting he had thought of them, not an hour before, as the ungainly louts he carried as a disgrace and a burden and hoped to get rid of. The annoyance of his visit to Caraway's office was wiped out. Nothing mattered except what was going on before his eyes. He heard himself cheering, and Burges asking him if he had ever seen the like of it. 'How did they come by it?' Bartle asked. 'How did they learn?' Burges replied that he had given them a hint or two, but most of it came by nature.

Mysteriously consenting, the wrestlers let go and slipped to the ground, where they lay panting and sprawling, pulling each other's hair and pretending to quarrel. A groom hurried forward with towels and rubbed them down. It was suddenly evening. Shafts of light drifted through the lime trees; the smell of lime blossom filled the air. The pigeons flustered a little, and settled to sleep. Castor and Pollux walked toward the house with their arms round each other's necks. Deep in conversation, they noticed no one.

'I could have watched them forever,' said Petronel, who had seen it all from her window; and she described the match from its beginning, and how at one moment Castor had hooked his leg round Pollux's knees and almost thrown him. Bartle mentioned Burges's boast about having given a few hints. 'Oh, but that—' She stopped, and looked confused. 'Burges gives himself too much credit. The truth is, they went off without telling anyone, visited a fair, and saw two mountebanks wrestling. And when the mountebanks asked if anyone would like to have a try, Pollux jumped at it. He could scarcely move next morning, poor Pollux! But I believe they went back and had some sort of lessons. I thought I'd told you. By the way, what about Hamlet?'

Bartle said he would never go near the lawyer again. Petronel applauded the decision, and continued, 'So I've decided what to do with my pearls. I shall sell them, and buy two riding horses. They've far outgrown their ponies. Don't you agree?'

The riding horses were bought. Castor and Pollux mounted and rode away.

Nothing more was heard of them. Advertisements were posted on trees, rewards were offered, Lady Elissa strained her eyes; all was in vain. Finally, Queen Annot herself was invoked. In her heyday (she was a great age) she had been renowned for Divination and Art Magic, and made them fashionable at Court. Now she caused wormwood, tansy, and white lavender to be burned on a hot plate, and cast herself into a trance. After a day and a night, the ladies watching her heard her cry in the voice of one far distant, 'Cantuar! Ebor!' But the spirits she called on did not comply, for when she woke much later, blinking and smiling, and asked for a bowl of bread and milk, she brought nothing out of her sleep and did not know how the words came to be spoken.

Her loyal fellow-adepts explained that mortal grossness resists Art Magic: Castor and Pollux were insufficiently Elfin to be divined. It was a different matter with Hamlet. He came back at short notice, but preceded himself in several people's dreams. Elissa's bowerwoman, polishing the crystal ball, had seen him sailing up the Severn in a gondola drawn by two swans, but said nothing about it at the time, as she did not want to be thought a trespasser on her mistress's domain. Thanks to an admirable housekeeper, Hamlet's house was ready for him to walk into; all that needed to be done was to put the warming pan into his bed, and prepare a quick banquet.

By the time he lay down in it, his bed was cold. Midnight sounded before he could get rid of his welcoming guests—all of them disconcertingly unchanged. When they were gone, he strolled about the house, going from room to room and everywhere coming on presents which he had given Nel, which Nel had given him: presents of the moment, whether precious or trivial, for they had scorned to be sensible. All the disorder of her dying had been cleared away from the room she died in.

Never in his mind had she ceased to be dead, and she remained as dead as ever. He had seen his parents-in-law at the impromptu banquet—Bartle the same old stick, Petronel the same compound of the good, the silly, and the sly. There were notes in her voice, particularly when she wished to seem impressed and wasn't attending, which she had in common with Nel. As she was questioning him about Orplid and the strangeness of living on an island, he heard them again. He had said nothing about those monstrous infants, Gog and Magog. It was to be hoped they were dead.

No one referred to them. But in Pomace displeasing subjects were peaceably ignored, so this avoidance might just as well indicate that they were alive. After a while, he asked Master Caraway what had become of them, and was told that they had grown up typically mortal: noisy, and oversized. They were said to love each other. Some time ago, they had gone off. Nothing had been heard of them since.

That should have been good enough. They were nothing

to him; they existed only as an old rusty pain. Yet since his return he had been teased by an uneasy curiosity about them—as though there were some button left unfastened.

To set his mind at rest, he invited Petronel to see his roses. Between picking a musk rose and a damask he said, 'Forgive me if the subject is painful. But what became of those children? Are they alive?' She dropped the roses and wrung her hands.

'I don't know, I don't know! It was all my stupidity. They looked so handsome that I gave each of them a horse. And we never saw them again.'

'Were they good riders?'

'They rode as if they were gods.'

So they were back again, disguised as the riders he had admired on the Parthenon, aloof in a naked sang-froid above the jostling Turks below. It was to rid his mind of the Turks that he had gone to Orplid. Its inhabitants had an interesting belief that they were deities. Their placid energies were devoted to agriculture; they talked of vines and olives, flocks and herds, of when they should irrigate the meadows. They were remarkably weatherwise. It struck him that they were survivors from a prehistoric Elfin society, Elfins who had yet to develop wings, intellect, invisibility, and property—for they held everything in common. Hamlet had never lived in the country. At first he was charmed by this substantiation of pastoral poetry—rising at daybreak to walk barefoot through dewy grass, doing a little weeding, eating goat's-milk cheese. He did not discover how bored he was growing till he met Hecate, who sat on a headland looking out to sea with her distaff idle beside her. She was a deity, too, but had seen something of the world and had more conversation. She taught him several spells. When her spindle had its full load of yarn, she said, he must go. When next he visited her, the spindle was full.

'Farewell, Goddess.'

'Farewell, Elfin.'

Her low-pitched, rasping voice hung in his mind, and the spells stayed on with it. Perhaps it was for the last spell she taught him that he had travelled and returned. It was a Summoning Spell and would bring him anyone he wished to see, whether from this world or the world beneath. He had neglected to ask her for a Dismissing Spell. If Castor and Pollux came to appease his curiosity, from the face of the earth or beneath a mound of it, it might be awkward if they could not be got rid of. Two gigantic footmen, dogging his heels ... a stink of corruption choking him ... But his curiosity had grown so overmastering that he recited the spell. What leisure time he had during the next two days he spent memorizing it backward. He was word perfect and calling himself a fool when his major-domo asked leave to tell him that two mortals were sitting on the steps of the entrance of honour: that they refused to go away, and children were throwing stones at them, which might crack the marble.

The spell had worked.

'Show them in.'

He heard their footsteps approaching. They were wearing cheap boots that squeaked.

They entered and bowed deep, identical bows. When they straightened up, they towered over him. They were middle-aged and the worse for it; their red hair was grizzled. The resemblance between them was like a cruel joke. At some distant time they might have had a sort of florid beauty.

'Pray sit down.'

'We must introduce ourselves. I am Brother Castor. He is Brother Pollux. We are here because we have a call—a call to the Ministry.'

'But we start with a shocking handicap. We've no money,' said Brother Pollux.

'We were not brought up in a Christian home—'

'And there was something odd about us.'

The usual blackmailers, thought Hamlet.

'We will not dwell on the past, Pollux. We must not take up the gentleman's time. It is enough to say that we left home and took to loose company and evil courses. Drinking, gambling, Sabbath-breaking—'

'Horse-coping—'

'Prizefighting, thimble-rigging, and fornication. Led by above, we joined a travelling circus. Those who go to circuses see the wonders of the Lord. We saw our weakness and utter depravity.'

'The tiger did it. We'd never seen a tiger.'

'The tiger was instrumental. But let us not despise the performing fleas. One of them got loose, and we sought it all over the place. The manager, a God-fearing man, told us it was worth a great deal of money. How much more so, he said, is the soul.'

'We got it in the end,' said Pollux.

'How did you know it was the right flea?' They were Hamlet's first words.

Brother Castor swept on. 'In that same hour, we heard our call—both of us. It was a call to join the Ministry and search for lost souls.'

Hamlet could not believe his luck. They were more innocent than the puppets, more wholeheartedly ludicrous than the players. Whatever the cost, he must keep them.

'It's a call from God. But we've got to be worthy of it,' said Pollux. 'That's why we wouldn't move off your steps. Anyone at the top of these steps, I said to Castor, is bound to be rich. And we've got to raise money for our schooling before we can obey the call. There's Hebrew and Greek, and the missionary journeys of Saint Paul, and the Athanasian Creed, and the Augsburg Confession, and the Sundays after Trinity, and the

Four Last Things, and the Thirty-nine Articles; we must have
them at our fingers' ends before we can go into the Ministry.'

'I'll see to all that,' Hamlet said.

'You'll be our teacher? Castor, did you hear that? He must
be in the Ministry himself.' They were so grateful that he had
to send them away, promising that if they came back ten days
later they would find everything arranged.

For it had darted upon him that as he had formerly been an
anonymous patron of the drama, he would now anonymously
foster a theological college. Or possibly he might buy one
ready-made: Master Caraway had bought a bank—which
would prove useful as a source of mortal specie when fairy
gold was not negotiable. Master Caraway was plucked from
his office by four of Hamlet's corps of winged messengers,
strong-flying fairies who could carry any weight and subdue
any resistance. When he had recovered his breath he said
that a theological college would not be a sound investment;
Christians are notoriously fickle and the slaves of fashion
in matters of dogma. If Lord Hamlet wanted a theological
college, it would be better to rent one, with protective clauses
about structural and interior repairs. Lord Hamlet said
suavely he thought not. Master Caraway could not imagine
what had happened to his client, till now so tractable. His
hold on the discussion was weakened by distracting surmises
as to why Lord Hamlet wanted a theological college; if it was
to shelter an amour, why not consider a quiet castle? He was
handed over to the four winged messengers and charged not
to return from an aerial survey till he had found something
suitable.

Late that evening, he returned with a theological college in
North Wales, a spa at Wenlock, and a condemned seminary
in the neighbourhood. That, except for a drain on his bank,
was all he knew of it till a letter told him the renovated
seminary would be called Caraway College and dedicated to

Saint Caraway, Virgin and Martyr.

During the interval required for its renovation, Hamlet divided himself between the Sacred and Profane. He sat up all night reading polemical divines of the Church of England and spent the day equipping the seminary with everything a theological college should have, from a laundry to a teaching staff. In the course of his reading he developed a passion for Christian niceties, and was exquisite in his selection of the staff, detecting an Anabaptist at a glance.

With so many teachers hovering over them like vultures, Castor and Pollux made steady progress. When further pupils were enrolled in Caraway College, the twins naturally fell back a little. But they always did well in examinations. Castor whisked through his papers and then replaced Pollux and did his. Neck and neck, they finished the course and were ordained deacons on the same happy day. All this time, they never gave Hamlet a moment's uneasiness. They were unfailingly serious and unfailingly absurd. Visibly or invisible, he was a regular visitor to the college, where he gave lectures on Gothic architecture and instituted the custom of Disputations. Neck and neck, Castor and Pollux climbed the Establishment. Only one incident jarred their smooth ascent. In their gaiters and aprons (by then they were deans) they visited the God-fearing circus manager to thank him for his part in directing them to the religious life. He called them backsliders, hirelings, and truckling Erastians: he was a Nonconformist. As time went on they became bishops—Castor admired for his eloquence and known as The Saintly Bishop, Pollux venerated as an administrator and known as The Manly Bishop. Hamlet designed their mitres, hung on their antics, and read their Pastorals with squeals of delight. At the death of the Archbishop of York he was in agonies of indecision as to which of his two Bishops to back, but was speedily released by the death of the Archbishop of

Canterbury. He tweaked a few last strings. He had filled two Archbishoprics; Caraway College was flourishing; he would now look round for a new source of entertainment. He enjoyed Castor and Pollux longer than he expected; they had inherited a certain amount of Elfin longevity and lived on to the ripe old age of a hundred or so.

15 The Occupation

It is widely known that a group of dissident fairies seceded from the court of Elfhame in order to have more time for self-improvement. The Elfhame Dissidents had sickened of the frivolity of court life: pleasure was a burden to them; so was politeness. Beset with banquetings, love affairs, sonnets, whist drives, masquerades, and lotteries, they had no time to take themselves seriously. Their dissatisfaction gathered to a head and they planned a departure. Imprimis, their flight must be unequivocal. Defying the etiquette that Elfins of good breeding do not fly, they would leave by air, rising in a body without a word of explanation. As none of them had flown since childhood, the departure, if to be properly demonstrative, called for rehearsal. The surveillance which riddles court life, where everyone is on the lookout for something to talk about, made rehearsal difficult; they would have to practise in secret, or on the plea of needing violent exercise. Secondly, they must secure their peace of mind. However austerely they lived, they would need a few servants. At first they thought of requisitioning half a dozen changelings, to carry luggage, collect fuel and foodstuffs, prepare simple meals, and ward off intruders. Changelings seemed the answer till it was remembered that changelings are permanently visible, cannot fly, and have large appetites. An influx of visible pedestrian marauders would inevitably excite comment, and thus defeat their intention of living retired from the world. Changelings being out of the question, they were forced back on working fairies. In many ways, working fairies would be preferable: they knew their jobs, they were trained in obedience, they were cleanly. Unfortunately, the working fairies of Elfhame were passionately loyal to their Queen and content with their living conditions; but inquiries unearthed a few Dissidents in their lower ranks. It was arranged that on the day of departure these should rise early and hover round with the baggage till the main party led them to their destination. As for the destination, that need not be exactly decided on. The world is full of suitable solitudes, and if a solitude proved unsuitable they could move to another. For the first flight, they would not go very far.

The ascent took place on a fine September morning. Summoned by Lady Beline, the Court Harpist, with some rousing arpeggios, the Dissidents gathered on the terrace. So did the rest of the Court, to see what Lady Beline was up to. With a final glissando, she took to the air; the Dissidents rose more or less in a body and without a word of explanation. The working Dissidents joined them; some bundles, a cold ham, and a toasting fork fell among the onlookers. The Elfhame secession was achieved.

Lady Beline, flying and harping like Apollo, led them in a north-easterly direction, till she fell into an air pocket and damaged a wing. Sir Maugre and Sir Hune supported her to the ground. Forgetting that one of the conventions they had renounced was politeness, they sympathized with her and said nothing of the interrupted journey. They were on a bare grassy hillside, and the grass was wet, for the day had turned to rain. Looking about for shelter, they saw a ruined castle on the hill-top (at that date the Scottish Border was peppered with ruined castles). The working fairies were sent up to investigate. Some sheep bolted out. When the working fairies came back they reported that much of the castle was still standing, though the roof was gone. The Dissidents climbed the hillside, exclaiming at the view and the thistles. When they reached the castle they were pleased to find that an ash tree, the patron tree of fairies, had grown up inside it, and that they would look down on a river's twisting course through a hilly landscape, hill after hill interlocking like the fingers of clasped hands. Any little discomforts, said Lady Ellin, would be negligible in such surroundings. Sir Hune added that mountain air would ennoble appetite to an essential part of being. The ham had been lost but the working fairies were told to fly off and collect any rustic fare they could lay hands on.

They were absent for some time. Gibbie, the most enterprising of them, returned with a ewe's-milk cheese and an armful of barley bannocks. Others brought watercress. Sir Maugre spoke of the Artotyrites, a Phrygian sect, who offered barley-bread and cheese to their god. This roused up a conversation about offerings: the flesh offerings of the heathen, the blameless figs and apples and radishes of classical Greece, the sacramental wine of the Christians, in whose Jesus a lingering strain of Dionysus is clearly perceptible. They conversed, and chewed. Eventually, Sir Maugre laid aside the remainder of his cheese and bannock, saying it defeated him, so he would offer it to God.

In the morning, it had gone (Gibbie had eaten it). But this was scarcely remarked on. There had been a frost during the night and they all woke up with colds in their heads. Their sneezes mingled with the baa-ing of sheep and the lilting of larks. Fairies are invisible, but they cannot always manage to be inaudible. Jamie Hogg the shepherd, making his morning round, was perplexed. He was accustomed to his sheep coughing, but he had never known them to sneeze. They were not sleeping in their usual place, either. Something must be wrong with them, as there was with the rest of a fallen universe.

A west wind blew away the frost but brought more rain. Yellow leaves fell from the ash tree, mist retrenched the landscape. The Dissidents would have lost heart if it not been for hot meals. The working fairies, foraging for themselves, caught enough trout and moorfowl to feed the party, roasting them in the ashes of a heather fire. Jamie Hogg, connecting the sneezes and the smell of scorched grouse, said to himself, 'Damned tinkers,' and was comforted. The valley was full of supernatural nuisances—the red-eyed dog who blasted good grazing land by dragging a coffin over it, the kelpie in the deep pool by Cossar Hill, the Brownie of Bodsbeck. Tinkers could be damned and left at that.

Invisibility has many advantages, but it does not immunize its wearers against cold and wet. Gibbie and his fellows were enjoying their respite from Elfhame; he did not wish to see the Dissidents worsted by bad weather. Local mortals wrapped themselves in plaids, but plaids were not easy to come by. A working fairy named Neep happened to see a travelling webster peddling his wares—splendid plaids with the grease still heavy in them. Neep flew level with him, waiting for him to reach the head of the pass, where he would certainly sit down out of the wind to rest. He did so, easing the pack from his shoulders. It was much too heavy for so old a man, thought Neep, flying off with it.

There were nine plaids, one for each Dissident, and one over. They were accepted, like the hot meals, as a matter of course—though with complaints about the smell. Beline said romantically that it was a step toward self-knowledge to learn what you could put up with. Beline was visionary and rather smug. Of all the party she was the most bent on self-approval. Her career as Court Harpist had given her exacting ideals of putting herself in tune, here tightening, here loosening, till all her strings were in accord with her intentions. Considered as strings, the rest of the party were apt to slip. Sir Maugre's erudition was so wide that whatever anyone said reminded him of something that had no bearing on it—as when a reference to the music of the spheres set him off on the conjectural compass of the Roman trumpet. The

Roman trumpet reminded Sir Hune of an ancestral anecdote about Queen Boudicca, Sir Moray trumped Queen Boudicca with a family ghost. This outraged a Dissident called Titmuss—a flaxen-haired fairy with a mild manner, and the most embattled Dissident of them all. There could be no such thing as an Elfin ghost. Ghosts were a mortal appurtenance. If Moray's pedigree embraced a family ghost, it was a blot on the scutcheon, and nothing to boast about. Beline seized her harp to restore harmony. Moray protested it was the ghost of a hare. The sun went down on their wrath.

The sun continued to go down earlier and earlier, but it was still some time before the shortest day. Conversation persisted, since in the main they talked about themselves, but was repetitive. Already Malise and Barco had taken to meditating with their eyes shut. Ellin wished she had brought her fancy-work. Ellin had joined the Dissidents because she was tired of being told she was always so serene. Titmuss continued to assure her of this, and now that she could no longer dispose of him in a satin-stitch rosebud she took to going for long walks and frightening any children she met by planting spiders on them. During one of these rambles she saw a family of mortals come out of a cottage, lock the door behind them, and walk up the valley. Their gait was resolute, as though overcoming unwillingness. Presently other families joined them, and were greeted with curt grunts of acknowledgment. They went forward with an air of being banded together to commit some crime they were not wholehearted about. If a dog or a child (their dogs and children accompanied them) dallied or strayed, it was shouted back. Such a gathering of mortals in a landscape where as a rule mortals were scanty was physically oppressive, but Ellin's curiosity was stronger than her fastidiousness; she determined to follow them to their appointed crime. The small noise of a bell came on the air. She remembered the massacre of St Bartholomew (Maugre had cited it as an example of mortal *trop de zèle*), and guessed that something of the same sort was impending. The bell was perched on top of a lean stone building. The conspirators filed in and sat down in silence, the men holding their hats on their knees, the women their babies. Ellin was perplexed. Was it to be a massacre in reverse? If they were there to be slaughtered it would account for that air of unwillingness. Presently a man wearing a black gown came in, walked up the aisle without looking to right or left, and opened with prayer.

No one was slaughtered. At intervals, everyone sang. Finally, they paid to go away.

When Ellin recounted what she had seen, there was a volley of explanations. It was a means of livelihood, it was a mass migration, it was a fertility rite, it was a religious observance, it was an endurance test, it was a way of keeping warm. All agreed in regretting that Ellin had not stayed to see what happened next. It might have been a massacre after all.

Next day she led the Dissidents (except for Malise and Barco, who preferred to meditate) to the scene of whatever it was. The lean stone building was locked and empty. A few sheep were feeding in the enclosure round it, a few old discoloured bones lay in one corner, but there was no trace of a mass grave. A path led through a plantation of fir trees to a dwelling-house with damp-stained walls. It too was locked and seemed lifeless, but a thread of smoke rose from the chimney and a smell of mutton hung on the air—boiled mutton; but after grouse for so many weeks boiled mutton was a thing to languish for. They languished for some time with chilling feet, standing markedly apart from Ellin, who had brought them all this way with her talk of massacres to nothing better than a smell of boiled mutton in a lifeless house. Back in the castle, they felt even more aggrieved. Malise and Barco had been questioning Gibbie, who told them that the belled building was Cotho Kirk. Six days a week it was locked, and on the seventh day the local mortals went there to hear a sermon. This was known as observing the Sabbath.

No more was said of the morning's excursion till Saturday, when Malise and Barco said they would like to observe a Sabbath; would Ellin guide them to Cotho? That night there was a snowfall. It did not dissuade the other Dissidents from coming too.

Till three o'clock that morning, Gideon Baxter, Minister of Cotho, had sat up revising his sermon. The house was full of the silence of snow. The least sound was portentous. The wall clock ticked as though the fate of mankind hung on its leaden weights. When he put down his pen it fell on the desk like a hammer blow. Jael took a hammer and drove a nail into the head of Sisera. In eight hours' time, under God's will, he must hammer his sermon into the heads of his congregation. It was the last sermon in Advent, the last chance to hammer in the reality of a Day of Judgment, the wrath of an offended God, the untiring pains of Hell. For on the heels of Advent came Christmas, that backsliding season of riot and drunkenness, of going from house to house singing and shouting like revellers, of kissing under the heathen mistletoe, of neighbour toppling neighbour into damnation in the name of mirth and good fellowship. And on the heels of Christmas came Hogmanay, puffing Christmas embers into a flaring godless defiance of the cold and scarcity the New Year would bring. How many would remember his words then, how fast would his nails hold?

When the Dissidents arrived the building was already full of mortals, looking as if they had never stirred out of it. A smell of wet dogs reinforced the smell of fusty clothes. The fairies perched on a couple of windowsills. The door closed behind the Minister. Seeing him from above, Ellin noticed that he was going bald, and that scurf lay in the puckers of his gown. Because she had seen him before, she felt an embarrassed ownership. It was needless. The others had come for a spectacle, and were making the most of it. They commented in whispers, as though they were at Court, admiring, speculating, exclaiming—in Sir Maugre's case, explaining. Beline and Hune took part in the singing, vocalizing drawn-out fa-las. A dog started up and gave a long tremulous howl. Other dogs joined in. A man charged down the aisle and beat them to silence. Maugre was already so at home with the Church of Scotland that when the gowned man climbed into the pulpit he whispered commandingly, 'Quiet, all of you! This is the sermon.'

'This may be the last time some of you will hear me,' the preacher began. He looked sickly—but not so sickly that he would die within the week, thought Ellin. It appeared that it was the death of others he was expecting.

From the opening of his sermon, Gideon Baxter was conscious of something unusual—an indefinable, unmistakable awareness, such as a change in the wind might bring to a man in a closed house. He was being listened to with attention. He was so flooded with gratitude that he scarcely dared to go on. He lost his place, repeated himself, missed half a sentence, stammered like a lover. The manuscript dazzled before his eyes; he turned over two pages at once and had switched from avarice to carnality before he noticed it. His hearers did not seem unsettled. They listened as though they had never before been told of the uncertainty of human life, the certainty of what would follow it. Their listening infused his words with such freshness and fervour that he was as much preaching to himself as to them, and in the first elation of a conversion. He broke away from his text to enlarge on the joy—only one degree lower than that of angels—of the man who is so fully assured of the terribleness of God that he can love him with the whole energy of a purged heart. Here and there a child whimpered, now and then a voice threatened a dog; there was the customary shuffle of feet. Today it was no more to him than a crying of curlews.

'And finally...' 'Finally' was the warning, the nail driven in at the close of every last sermon in Advent, to be knocked out by merry Christmas. It was the warning against relying on the efficacy of a deathbed repentance. The Christmas before, he reminded them, two of their number while going from one merrymaking to another had lost their way in the dark and fallen into the river. They had been heard shouting for help before the strength of the river had thrust them under and drowned them. They had shouted for help, and found none. If they had cried for mercy, would they have found it? Leaning over the pulpit's edge as though he would have embraced his hearers, he adjured, he implored them to bear in mind the words of Master Thomas Boston, Minister of Ettrick. 'Let not the profligate think he can leap from the harlot's lap to Abraham's bosom.'

The fairies broke into animated discussion. Who was Abraham? Maugre knew but could not at the moment remember. Why was his bosom preferable to a harlot's lap—Surely it would be bony and less reposeful? Maugre remembered that some races swore by the beard of Abraham. Beline exclaimed that she detested beards; nothing would induce her to such a leap. Let sleeping dogs lie, added Hune. They were still debating when the last member of the congregation had paid and gone; then, seeing the door about to close on the preacher, they hurried after him in a buzz of conversation like bees swarming. He went home saddened. The hope had occurred to him that one, at least, of those attentive hearers might have a word of commendation. Instead, a little girl wished him a merry Christmas.

The nail did not hold. On Christmas Eve a party of drunken shepherds came to his door, stuck a holly sprig in the keyhole, and stood in a row singing a ballad about John Barleycorn and inviting him to come for a drink. The invitation was not lost on Moray and Titmuss, who leaped from an upper window and followed the shepherds.

By now, the Dissidents were living in the manse. It had its drawbacks: there was no view, the rooms were dark, it was dirty and malodorous, its few ornaments were in the worst of taste. But it had a sound roof and the kitchen was warm. Except for a bannock and the occasional egg, they did not have to depend on Mistress Baxter's providing; the working fairies had come with them and the supply of grouse was kept up. The kitchen was warm because a continual peat fire smouldered on the hearth, to be puffed into a blaze when needed. It was not often needed. The working fairies were censorious about the parsimony prevailing in the manse kitchen: the mouldy turnips that went into the pot along with the sound ones, the salt herring boiled with a dish of kale to give it a whet, and withdrawn to help out another meal. A smell of singed wool drew them one and all to the kitchen, where it was an ever-fresh delight and marvel to see that frail woman, great with child, split a sheep's head with one blow of a hatchet. Before the two halves were bound together with a tape, as the jaws of a dead man are bound, the tongue and the brains were taken out to be a regale for Mr. Baxter and the boy—the eyes being left in to add richness to the broth which would feed herself and her daughter. She was a woman whose work was never done. Cooking, scouring, laundering, sweeping, fetching peats, carrying water, putting patch on patch, she ran from one labour to another, tripping over her skirts. When Gibbie's notions of cleanliness drove him to sweep a floor or rub the stair rail, she was too tired to notice the difference. He felt an appalled admiration for the woman, and when the other working fairies moved to better quarters in a cow byre he stayed on.

While admitting the drawbacks of life at the manse, the Dissidents made light of them—perhaps because they had chosen to go there: members of the ruling class are unwilling to admit themselves mistaken. As Beline said, Inward contentment is at home anywhere. Maugre and Titmuss made themselves at home in Gideon Baxter's study. Titmuss studied cobwebs, Maugre proceeded along the bookshelves, learning with pleasure about heresies in the Dark Ages. Ellin played with the children.

Ellin had a knack with children. By listening attentively, she could hear their thoughts, and put new thoughts and and fancies into their little minds. At Elfhame children resisted, some rushed from her, screaming, but she was popular with parents and nurses relied on her.

There were always some children at the manse, though their number fluctuated with mortalities. At this time, there were two, Ezekiel and Margaret. Ezekiel was undersized and rickety, but thought to be promising: at the age of five, he had mastered three alphabets—European, Greek, and Hebrew. Ellin had practised on changelings, so mortal children came easy. She soon discarded Margaret, whose thoughts dwelt on food and arithmetic. Ezekiel, the younger of the two, was more rewarding. By listening to his thoughts, and clearing away what his father had taught him, she discovered that he lived in a world of words—turning them over in his mind, repeating them to himself, fitting them with new meanings or deepening the meanings he knew. Ellin put new words into his mind, choosing them carefully and observing what he did with them. She got some of her best results with simple technical terms which he could not relate to anything in his experience. "Hemming and felling" absorbed him for days. In the end, they became a ceremonial leaping from pew to pew. In the course of listening to his thoughts she picked up several words unknown to her, such as Urim and Thummim, which according to Ezekiel were blue lamb's-wool mittens; but she was content to leave them a mystery.

Whenever the ground was free of snow, the children were sent out to collect fir cones for kindling. The fir plantation neighboured the graveyard; there were always cones to be found there, and entertainment—especially for Margaret, who added up dates of births and deaths, divided the sum total by 666 (the Number of the Beast), or the seven lean kine, or the Ten Commandments, or whatever she fancied at the moment, and calculated the average age of demise for living parishioners by the statistics of the dead. She was hampered by the insufficiency of her material. Many of the inscriptions were blunted by time and lichen: it might be a 5, it might be an 8. Others had gone underground with their swallowed headstones. One word was so deeply cut that it was inescapable. It was incised on a large slab which was embedded in the ground above a family grave: the word was 'LAIR'. Ellin had noticed that Ezekiel avoided this slab, leaving its fir cones for Margaret to gather. She drew his attention to it. She heard a turmoil of thoughts, words snatched up at random to smother the thought beneath. She imposed a word. A tiger striped with blood leaped out of the lair, and the boy ran screaming, just as the changelings had done when she experimented with wolves. His screams were heard. His mother ran from the house, bundled his head in her apron, and told him to be quiet, for his father was writing the sermon.

When Gideon Baxter sat down to compose his last sermon for the year, he disciplined himself with admissions of delusion and vainglory. He would not expect it to be received with such attention as its precursor had been—or seemed to be. Preaching was his duty; in his unquestioning acceptance of it as a pleasure he had accepted a temptation, and sinned. The temptation recurred. He had not spoken his first sentence before the feeling of being attended to sang in his ears. This time, he had known it for what it was—a permitted assault, Satan's licensed try at him, which he must both resist and submit to. By the end of January he had resisted so efficaciously that though the attention persisted he got no pleasure from it.

The permitted assault moved to a different field; instead of being listened to, he was watched. To mortify his vanity, the watching was fitful, directed on him from here, from there. It sported with him as if he were a toy to be taken up, then tossed aside. It surprised him when he prayed, when he defecated, while he was hearing Ezekiel conjugate *fero, ferre, tuli, latum*. In sleep he would become aware of a scrutiny that observed his dreams.

As for what Ellin saw there, she kept it to herself. It amused her to be better informed about the Minister of Cotho than were the other Dissidents, whose surmises were often wide of the mark. Moray attributed Mr Baxter's melancholy to the traditional liability of mortal husbands to suffer the discomforts of a pregnant wife. Seeing him clutch his head in his hands, Moray said knowingly, 'You see? He's got toothache now.' At which Maugre remarked that Genghis Khan was born with teeth.

The days lengthened, the cold strengthened, the house grew dirtier and dirtier. Gibbie was in despair. On the first of March, Mistress Baxter fell in labour. The midwife knew what to expect and brought a stiff broom. Gibbie saw the bedchamber cleaned and set to rights, the kitchen table scrubbed, the dirty linen washed and hung out to sweeten in the frost. He was not the only person to be grateful to this admirable woman. Gideon Baxter's window was open when a crony came to the door to ask how things were going.

'Well, she's just taking her time. But it's an awful house for mislaying things. There's three eggs I can't put my hand on, and the sugar I beat small for making the caudle, half of it has clean vanished.'

'Mice, likely,' said the crony.

'And what would mice be doing with eggs? No, no, there's more than mice about this house. It's themselves, Ailie, it's the Good Folk. They're always pilferers.'

The Good Folk ... The little People ... Fairies. As if the wind entering by the open window had blown him, Gideon Baxter went to the bookcase, where, on the top shelf, there was a manuscript his uncle had given him, commenting that if it weren't idle nonsense it would be a case for the Kirk Session. But the manuscript was written in a scholarly hand, and from respect for scholarship he had kept it. Now, when he wanted it, he could not find it. He searched on, and found it on a lower shelf, where it stood the wrong way up.

THE SECRET COMMONWEALTH

(A Treatise displayeing the Chiefe Curiosities as they are in
Use among diverse of the People of Scotland to this Day;
SINGULARITIES for the most Part peculiar to that Nation
... By Mr Robert Kirk, Minister at Aberfoill. 1691.)

'These *Siths*, or FAIRIES, they call *Sleagh Maith*, or the Good People, it would seem, to prevent the Dint of their ill Attempts, (for the Irish use to bless all they fear Harme of); and are said to be of a midle Nature betwixt Man and Angel, as were Daemons thought to be of old; of intelligent studious spirits, and light changable Bodies, (lyke those called Astral,) somewhat of the Nature of a condensed Cloud, and best seen in Twilight. Thes Bodies be so plyable thorough the Subtility of the Spirits that agitate them, that they can make them appear or disappear at Pleasure. Some have Bodies or Vehicles so spungious, thin, and desecat, they are fed by only sucking into some fine spirituous Liquors'—'Those eggs,' Gideon Baxter said; and read on—'... for they are empowred to catch as much Prey everywhere as they please.' In which case they were no pilferers, and further more possessed Free Will. He stared round at his empty room, smiling as if to welcome these guests: intelligent, studious spirits, a companionship he had longed for ever since coming to Cotho. Undoubtedly it was they who listened to his pre-Christmas sermon, listened as his congregation had never done. 'They are clearly seen by these Men of the SECOND SIGHT to eat at Funeralls and Banquets ... So they are seen to carry the Beer or Coffin with the Corps among the midle-earth Men to the Grave.' And he had slighted these friendly courteous beings in all his sermons since, shutting his ears to their attention, refusing to take pleasure from it. Dolt! Ingrate! But he would make amends. Watching him as they did (and he had even felt irked by it), they would recognize his change of heart and make allowance for the slow-wittedness of a middle-earth man. He looked at the clock and calculated how many hours of the extended daylight must pass before the twilight when they would be best seen.

He never saw a fairy, but from time to time he heard snatches of harp music and a lulling voice. At all times he lived in hope and happiness—a state so strange to him that had it not been for the warrant of Robert Kirk's treatise, he would have supposed himself out of his mind. His household battered on; Sabbaths recurred; his child had been born, a boy, and hastily baptized Benjamin, for there was doubt whether it would live. It lived: he had three children, a wife, a stipend, a God, and the companionship of fairies. It was to the fairies he preached, disregarding Lent to dwell on the wonders of Creation. It was the fairies his mind conversed with, consulting them which text he should draw from the folio Bible that lay always on his desk, which reading of a vexed passage he should follow; and relieved by their assurances that its meaning was quite otherwise and perfectly simple, as he himself had privately thought. They far excelled him in speculation, in subtlety of reasoning, but had their bounds and limits, like mortals. 'They live much longer than wee; yet die at last, or at least vanish from that State. 'Tis ane of their Tenets, that nothing perisheth, but (as the Sun and Year) every Thing goes in a Circle, lesser or greater, and is renewed and refreshed in its Revolutions.' It was this passage that his uncle had particularly censured, declaring that Robert Kirk was no better than an apologist for Hindoos; but Gideon had used the substance of it in a sermon, as an illustration of God's property of mercy, which even in Heaven refreshes the souls of the elect—at regular intervals, too, as the stars move in their courses. And he had looked toward his invisible congregation, hoping the allusion would please them. He was anxious to show his gratitude—except that he was no longer anxious about anything. So, for seven weeks, he lived in bliss.

When Mistress Baxter was back on her feet, she was so weakened by her lying-in that she could not cleave a head or carry a bucket. Sarah Lowes, the daughter of an elder, was hired as a daily help. She was young and strong and willing, and Gibbie rejoiced in her arrival. Housecleaning was getting beyond him; he had his work cut out to feed the Dissidents in this lean time of year, when trout sulked under the stones, and kites and foxes were quicker after the grouse than he. At midnight he would blow the peats under the girdle-plate and make barley bannocks—fortunately, there was still a fair supply of meal in the meal chest. The noise of the baby's wailing drifted through the house. It was a fretful little creature, always grizzling and lamenting its lot. Beline, and unexpectedly Titmuss, felt kindly toward it: Beline harped to it, Titmuss rocked the cradle. It only wailed the more. Malise and Barco complained that it was impossible to meditate through such caterwauling. They waited for a moment when the child was left alone, took it from its cradle, hurried to the kitchen, and shut it in the meal chest. They had barely resumed their meditations before a new uproar broke out. Mistress Baxter had found the cradle empty. She rushed up and down, calling and exclaiming, opening doors and banging them shut, slapping Margaret and Ezekiel out of her way. Sarah Lowes rushed beside her, declaring that the fairies must have taken the child. Gideon had not heard such a commotion since the day the hen flew up the kitchen chimney. He roused himself and went downstairs. His wife cast herself on his neck, crying out, 'Minister, Minister, the fairies have stolen my baby!' She paused to draw breath. He heard a faint wailing, like an echo of her screams. 'Hush,' he said. 'You can't have looked properly. I can hear it.' 'Aye, we can hear it well enough,' said Sarah. 'It's crying overhead. It's loath to go with them, poor innocent!' Ellin, who had enough of the fun, gave Gideon a shove toward the meal chest. He lifted the lid. The child was half-buried in meal, sneezing and choking, but still with enough strength to bewail. He picked it up and looked at it. They were too late! The wizened, sharp-faced creature in his arms was a changeling, substituted for his own child.

He felt the weeping resentment of a man betrayed. He felt the fury of a man made a fool of. And reason stood up and told him that both resentment and fury were unjustified. He had only his own simpleton self to blame.

Maugre, who had ignored the uproar and gone on reading, was taken aback by the man who re-entered the study, and thought he must have been murdering his wife: nothing else could account for such looks of calm and finality. Maugre too had read 'The Secret Commonwealth', and thought it passable, though somewhat old-fashioned, and too full of mortal violence. He had particularly disliked the Second-Sighted person who boasted he had 'cut the Bodie of one of those People in two with his Iron Weapon'. This was going too far, even for a legend. No one fancies the thought of being cut in two like a wasp in the marmalade.

The Minister sat down at his desk, as usual. The pages he had been writing so impetuously not ten minutes since lay before him. He took them up and with great composure tore them in half. When the wall clock uttered the rasping grunt with which it prefaced striking the hour, he seized the heavy Bible which lay on the desk and hurled it at the clock with his whole force. It smashed the glass over the clockface and fell on the floor, where it lay gaping, its back broken, while bits of broken glass dropped more slowly after it. The clock struck. Deranged by the blow, the clock went on striking—the next hour, the hour following, the hours after that.

Margaret stood outside, counting the strokes. Midnight past and Wednesday begun: sixty-three. Wednesday noon: one hundred and forty-one. Wednesday midnight: two hundred and nineteen. Thursday midnight: three hundred and seventy-five. Friday midnight: five hundred and thirty-one. By Saturday morning the strokes began to lag. She had fastened her ambition on eleven o'clock of Saturday night, which would exceed the Number of the Beast by nine. At six hundred and fifty-eight it paused, but began again. Six hundred and sixty-two. It paused, choked, and struck. Six hundred and sixty-three. A much longer pause. Then, like the last drops of blood wrenched from a wound, there were two strokes, and no more. The Beast had won by a single stroke.

She felt lonely, and on an impulse she knocked on the door. There was no answer. She opened it, but did not cross the threshold. Her father was sitting at his desk. In a tranquil voice he said, 'Go away, Margaret. I might kill you.'

Obediently, she went away. As she closed the door, Maugre slipped out. That night the Dissidents agreed that the noise, disorder, and dirt of the manse had exhausted their patience, and that they would leave on the next tolerably fine morning.

As Gideon Baxter refused to set foot in the kirk, alleging that he was damned, the Cotho elders felt obliged to report him to the Overseers. Students were sent on Sundays to take his duties, and as no one could be induced to settle at Cotho he was allowed to live on in the manse with the hope he might recover his reason. He was harmless, except for his conviction that Benjamin was a changeling and, as such, should be exposed in some silent place where the fairies would find him and carry him away. He wished the boy no harm, he said, only that he should be happy among his own people. He showed astonishing pertinacity and cunning in getting hold of the child, and a degree of reason in choosing where to abandon it—if on the open hillside, with a heather windbreak; if in the valley, on the soft grass that grows beneath elder trees. In the end, there was nothing for it but to have him declared a madman and taken to the County Bridewell, where he lived to a great age. Mistress Baxter went with the children to live with her sister above a grocery shop in Glasgow, where she was much happier, just as dirty, and insisted on her standing as a Minister's wife.

16 Foxcastle

He could not imagine in what way he had offended them.
Ever since he could remember, they had fascinated him. His
nurse sang him to sleep with ballads about them; he pursued
the hinds and shepherds on his father's estate for stories of
how they danced round the Cranach Loch, of the pebbles
aimed by invisible hands that skipped over its surface in games
of duck-and-drake, of how, on a sudden, they would leave
all together, whirring their wings and whistling; how they
stole butter from Mungo's mother's churn, hated sluttishness,
danced rings into the grass; how, wearing mourning scarves,
they were seen following the crazy Minister's bier to the grave;
how it was impossible for them to weep, how they must never
be mentioned on a Good Friday, how wary one must be not to
offend them by pulling as much as a dead bough for fuel from
a thorn tree. When he was sent to the University of Aberdeen
and could get at books, he read everything he could find on
their subject: that they were the scattered remnants of Satan's
host, were a superstition, were the old Picts; and reading the
English poets—a fanciful lot—that they slept in cast snake-
skins, drank from acorn-cup goblets, sat on mushrooms,
drove teams of mice. Grounded on ballads and folklore, he
discounted most of this, except as evidence substantiating
their existence—since to be dismissed as a superstition
proves a preliminary belief. Time went on, he took his degree
as MA, and was appointed to the Lectureship in Rhetoric.
The learned life suited James Sutherland so well that he was
careful not to jeopardize his hold on it by mentioning his
private opinions. Yet sometimes they broke from him, as
when in a Disputation with the Professor of History, a fanatic
for the Picts, he found himself being an Apologist for the

Kingdom of Elfin—and thereafter was spoken of behind his back as Fairy Sutherland.

During the summer vacation, when many of the scholars went home to help get in the harvest, the Professor of History travelled about in search of Pictish remains—the likeliest sites for them being the so-called Fairy Knowes, which proved conclusively that fairies were imperfectly remembered Picts. The Lecturer in Rhetoric also travelled about for his own purposes, and was not above examining Pictish remains, in case they afforded a small footprint or a strain of harp music. If, as sometimes happened, the two men met, they conversed on blameless subjects, such as the prevalence of horse-flies or the clear atmosphere which presages rain; and parted. But in his forty-ninth summer James Sutherland had Foxcastle to himself. One might say it came to him as a reward of faith. A visiting Lecturer in Jurisprudence had remarked that, whether or no fairies existed, they influenced leaseholds: the legendary teind to hell which bound fairies to offer a living sacrifice every seven years making many tenants unwilling to begin a seven-year lease, or a lease of multiple sevens. On the offchance of finding a fairy legally recorded, James Sutherland used to buy bundles of old law papers off the scrivener's stall in the market. Nothing came of it till the day he saw the name Foxcastle in a disputed ownership of a sheep walk in Peeblesshire. Foxcastle. Folks Castle. The meaning jumped to the eye. It was a long journey to make on foot, but if it had been as far as the Indies he would have made it.

Foxcastle was a hill among other hills, steep-sided, flattened at the top. If it had been a sheep walk that must be long since, for the heather had taken over, covering the summit and lapping down the sides. It was heather of long-established growth, standing over knee-high on thickened stems. As he was forcing his way through it he thought that the Professor of History would be hard put to it to trace any Pictish remains. He was still relishing the thought when he fell into a pit. He had got into a formation of peat hags, which started up from the heather like foes from an ambush. The stagnant water streaking between them reflected the sky with a savage blue. He scrambled out, none the worse except for wet feet and a twisted ankle, and with a sharpened appreciation of the nature of moorland peat: dry as a bone above, wet as corruption below. Walking more cautiously, he skirted the peat hags, and sat down on the western slope to shake the water out of his shoes and rub his ankle. He had never felt so imperially alone. In all the wide expanse around him there was no sign of man. Nothing moved except a few sheep on the opposite hillside and the burn flickering and rattling down the valley between. He watched a hawk flying in wide surveying circles overhead, saw it gather its flight into a poise and strike down on its kill. It was as though this imposed an edict of silence; not a small bird uttered. After a while he saw it lift nonchalantly away.

It was its own hawk. But manned hawks must often rise over Foxcastle. Fairies were known to go hawking, using merlins, he supposed, to bring down larks: a merlin would be proportionate. Angus the shepherd, who had seen a fairy, said it was a head taller than the tallest thistle, portly, and holding itself very stately and erect. So much for sleeping in a snake's cast weed! But poets always spin nonsense out of reality, piling Pelion on Ossa for a giant, whitening a lady's hand to new-fallen snow. There was considerable variance about the Elfin complexion, authentic reports ranging from pallor to gipsy swarthiness. The fairies who came out of a hill in Suffolk were green. Other authorities held that they are invisible to mortal eyes, or only to be seen at dusk, when colours would be muted. Angus had seen his thistle fairy at dusk.

James Sutherland rubbed the ache from his ankle. His shoes were dry. He put them on, but did not get up. There was still a good stretch of the long summer afternoon to run; the sheep on the opposite hillside had not begun to move upward to their sleeping place. With every moment the rich drowsy scent of the heather intensified. He would stay a while longer.

When he woke, it was night. Clouds had gathered, blotting out moon and stars. It was cold, the heather had lost its scent. He lay unmoving, to husband his warmth. Later, he woke again. It was still mirk night, and so silent that he could hear, as though it were close at hand, the burn in the valley. Lulled by its unresting voice, he fell profoundly asleep.

A fingernail pricked him awake. The heather was gone, the clouded sky was a shadowy stone vault; he lay on a stone floor, and was bound hand and foot in swathings of cobweb, so elastic that when he moved they yielded, so tough that they would not let go. The fingernail explored the convolutions of his ear, left it, traced the lines on his cheek. Other hands were fingering him, lightly, delicately, adroitly. His shoes were taken off, his toes parted, the soles of his feet prodded. His coat was unbuttoned, his shirt opened. Fingers tweaked the hair in his armpits. The watch was pulled from his fob pocket. He knew they would not stop at that. The cobweb bonds yielded as he writhed and struggled, and each time he thought he had snapped them they tightened again. The explorers waited till he lay exhausted, replaced the watch, and proceeded methodically to his genitals.

Not once had they inflicted the slightest pain, except to his feelings. He did not even know when they left him, only that they were gone. He lay in his cobweb bonds and wept. For these were fairies, these silent invisible tormentors.

Throughout his life they had been his dearest preoccupation. He had believed in them, venerated them, championed them. How had he offended them? Why were they so ungrateful?

A bowl of milk and some sponge fingers appeared beside him.

'Wash your hands first.'

The speaker was invisible. The voice was unmistakably that of a servant of position. He was propelled toward a jet of water which cascaded from a hole in the wall, brimmed a rocky basin, and vanished with a gurgle. He implored the speaker to appear, asked why he was made captive, thanked for the milk. He was speaking to the empty air. The jet of water splashed, gurgled, and went its way. While his back was turned a truss of dry fern had been spread out beside the milk. It smelled of sun and the outer world. The milk, too, was restorative, the sponge fingers so exquisitely light that they melted in his mouth. A sense of purpose returned to him: he must wind his watch. He pulled it out. It had stopped. Till that moment, he had been perplexed, or angry, or cut to the heart; but he had not felt intimidated: it had been too storylike for that. Now he fell into the blankness of despair. He was lost, lost! His watch, sole ally of his rational man, had stopped. He sat with its accustomed weight in his hand and looked at its dead face. An expedient of fear, disguised as common sense, sneaked into his mind. It would be possible to set it going again, its hands adjusted to a conjectural position. The conjecture need not be far out, and in any case he would be sure of a measure of time. With an odd scruple of honour, he buried the dead watch in his pocket.

Presently they came back again—or were back again. He was stripped of his clothes, his wig was pulled off, he was again propelled to the jet of water and washed. The water cascaded over his head and shoulders; soapsuds exploded in his ears and stung his eyes. There must have been half a dozen of them at work on him, hissing as though they were grooming a horse and tut-tutting at the dirt ingrained on his knees and elbows. When they had washed and dried him they cut his nails, cleaned his teeth, and handed him his clothes. The clothes smelled rancid; he was averse to putting them on, but did so because he was chilled. He was also very hungry. No food appeared. Instead, there came a new relay of fingerers, who stripped him once more and began to measure him; he felt the tape slipped round him, laid along him. The hope that he was being measured for new clothes was unfounded. He was being measured from motives of biological curiosity: the length of his nose, the span of his nostrils, the girth of each toe, the exact position in relation to spine and thighbone of the mole on his buttock, the dimensions of the callus on his pen finger. They also took his pulse and counted his teeth.

After this, he thought, they will cut me open and anatomize me. But when they had finished their measurements and repeated some in order to be sure of them, they were gone—silently as they had come, silent as they had been throughout their leisurely, meticulous investigation.

Then came a bowl of soup, bread, cheese, and bullace plums. After that—how long after he had no watch to tell him—came nightfall. In the darkness he was woken by the sound of a desperate voice: a shout of despair which had broken from him in a dream, re-echoing from the vault overhead. He recognized it, and heard it die away.

He had renounced chronometry. It was not so easy to renounce habit. From habit, he continued to pull out his watch and consult its dead face. Each time, he said to himself, 'I won't do that again,' but he went on doing it; for how long he could not have said, but certainly for several months, for the fern they brought him for his bedding had lost any smell of the warm summered earth. He judged by the hollowness of the wind and the lessening of the mysterious daylight, which came and went in the windowless gallery where he lay like the flow and ebb of a tide, that it must be well past Martinmas. By now his absence from the Faculty would have been remarked on, one or another of his pupils accounting for it by saying he had been stolen by the fairies; the hypothesis would have come to the ears of the Professor of History, who would have poured reason on it. Legend supplants reason: in days to come there would be a tradition that a Lecturer in Rhetoric at the University of Aberdeen had been stolen by the fairies—as, indeed, he had been. It was easier to speculate on what was going on in the outer world than on his own circumstances. He saw his food appear (there was never enough of it), he heard the wind blowing, he heard the water splash into the rocky basin with an unchanging voice; he felt himself washed, and saw every fragment of litter, every crumb and cobweb, removed by invisible hands and *de facto* becoming invisible: his attendants (he had come to think of them as such) had a Presbyterian zealotry for cleanliness. His beard was cultivated daily. He had never thought to have a beard, only beggars and peasants were bearded; he supposed it was let grow as a badge of captivity. It was combed and trimmed, and anointed with oils like Aaron's. In a moment of curiosity, he pulled out a hair. He was swarthy, but the hair was bright red. He grew attached to his beard; it replaced the mouse or the spiders which ameliorate the lot of ordinary prisoners. But it was reaped off, and after that they kept him clean-shaven.

At lengthening intervals he was measured, but now a little perfunctorily. Before long they would lose interest, and there would be no more visits. Whatever they had had in mind— entertainment, the pursuit of knowledge, the pleasure of being busied about something—they had intended him no harm, no good. It was impersonal, the traffic of water flowing over a stone. And one day, when they were finished with him, he felt a pat on his shoulder. It intended him no harm, no good—and it almost destroyed him. It was as if he were falling apart with happiness. For the first time, a fairy hand had rested on him with the wastefulness of a caress.

He froze, he burned; he was immortally awake, he was overwhelmingly sleepy; he experienced all the vicissitudes of love simultaneously. Even when he had dwindled down to his ordinary self, his mind had been jolted to a different tilt, and took a different retrospect. If he had offended them and so put himself in their power, they had shown a most moderate resentment, imposing nothing worse than solitude—which he had always preferred to company—and cobweb fetters. They had washed him, fed him, bedded him in a comfortable thickness of fern; their hands had always been gentle. Where was the farm animal who could say that of a mortal master? Why had he wasted all these months in being unappreciative?

He detached his fetters, coiled them up, laid them in a corner, and walked easily to the door. As he expected, it was locked. Remembering his mortal weight he put his shoulder to the door and forced it open. Behind rose a winding stairway, its steps very shallow. He mounted it, rising into gradual warmth and light, hearing the splash and gurgle of water sounding on in its solitude. The stair ended in an anteroom where two fairies were playing beggar-my-neighbour, as intently as though crowns and kingdoms depended on it. He stood for a while, watching the fall of the cards; they were the same as any other cards, but smaller and more brightly painted. These were the first fairies he had ever seen. He saw them without surprise or particular elation. The fortune of the game wound and unwound, governed by the chance of a card. The fortune of his game had brought him fairies—but he had always known fairies were in the pack. He walked into the adjoining room. It was a large room, lit and scented with bayberry candles, and an assembly of fairies moved about in it, moving with such small gliding steps that they seemed to melt rather than move. Angus was not far from the mark: taller than a tall thistle, he had said. Well-grown thistles on the family estate must have reached a good four foot; he could remember them overtopping him when he was a child, and how majestically they fell when his father slashed them. He stationed himself in a recess, to be out of the way, and undisturbed by being noticed.

One is always disconcerted by the ease with which foreigners talk their native tongue. The speech he heard resembled no civilized mortal language; slurred and full of hushed hisses, it was more like some dialect of Gaelic; but though he listened, hoping to catch a word which would put him on the track of what they were talking about, all he knew was that some proposal had been made and accepted. They gathered into a circle, sat down on the floor, and began to sing, softly clapping their hands to mark the measure. It was a wandering melody, a melody of no enterprise, but it must have had some charm for them, and the words, perhaps, some rustic association, for why else should these well-dressed persons sit in a ring on the floor, like peasants in a hayfield? Or were they rehearsing a masque? He had got the tune by heart and learned nothing of the words when there was a brisk tooting of trumpets. All rose to their feet. In came the trumpeters—two children, bright as parakeets in their gold—laced uniforms. The Queen followed. She was small—not taller than her trumpeters—cat-faced, and carried a knitting bag on her arm. She acknowledged her court by a ceremonious inattentive curtsy, and beckoned to a fairy who was obviously a person of importance. He hurried forward, bowing deeply, and knelt before her, holding out his hands. She looped a skein of wool over them, wound it into a ball, dropped another curtsy, more of a bob this time, and withdrew, followed by her trumpeters, whose gold-laced demeanour contrasted with her air of modest simplicity.

He was still smiling over the trumpeters when another music began—a sort of Turkish march, played by two fiddlers and a drummer. By degrees, everyone was dancing: here a minuet, there a reel, there a prancing hornpipe. It seemed they danced as the fancy took them, with little regard to the music, till with a rap on the drum it quickened and commanded them into a circle that gathered and dispersed, gathered and dispersed, faster and faster, whirling by like swallows. He watched till he could watch no more. In the anteroom the match of beggar-my-neighbour was still going on. Burrowing into his fern bed he told himself he must remember all this.

He awoke hearing an airy scuffle overhead. His attendants were flying up and down the gallery, contesting for a pair of stockings. It was gratifying to see them at last, though embarrassing to know he had been in the charge of these flippant young persons. He coughed. They descended looking as grave as tombstone cherubim. When he glanced round for his clothes, they held out new ones. The measuring had certainly not been for these. Everything was too large; the shirt pouted, the sad-green suit would have fitted a Hercules; as for the stockings, they were so inordinately long that they had to be rolled half a dozen times before they could be gartered. He was not a vain man, or luxurious, but he esteemed his legs, and wore silk stockings. These were woollen, and the word that came to his mind was 'Pictish.' It struck him that just as the English poets underestimated the size of fairies, fairies over-estimated the size of mortals. The reflection was philosophic, and soothed him; but not entirely. The theory of pockets had defeated the Foxcastle tailor, so he had to hang his watch on a ribbon round his neck and tuck it into the bosom of his shirt, like a loyal Jacobite locket.

From an outer-worldly point of view his attendants' good will was a trifle hail-fellow. But he was grateful for it. They were fairies, visible and well disposed, who might be useful as teachers of their native tongue; and they had the merit of being reliably available. When he went upstairs into good society it was disconcerting to find himself alone, as he often did.

Accustomed to a methodical social order where time is respected and persons occupy the portion of space where you expect to find them, he reconciled himself to the vagaries of Foxcastle by seeing it as an exemplification of the *Fay ce que vouldras* of Thélème. What would next be wished and when, and for how long, and by how many was unforeseeable. They were fickle in their loves and hates, fickle and passionate in their pursuits. Some devoted themselves to astronomy. Others practised the French horn. Others educated squirrels. Some, he presumed, made measurements. Only one thing was certain: they never quarrelled. Even in their fickle hates, they hated without malice. Whisking from one pursuit to the next, they never collided. The best comparison he could draw from the outer world was the swarm of mayflies, indivisibly borne aloft, lowering, shifting, veering, like a shaken impermeable gauze veil over the face of a stream.

Somewhere beneath her court the Queen of Foxcastle sat in her private apartments and knitted. *Fay ce que vouldras.* She was devoted to knitting and never tired of it. When his attendants told him this, and that if she had no more wool at hand she unravelled her work and knitted it up again, he exclaimed 'Penelope!' But of course they had never heard of Penelope.

Though by now he had learned enough Elfin to be able to converse in it, and was considering a treatise of Elfin Grammar, he found it difficult to acclimatize himself to a society which had not a vestige of mortal scholarship—except in mathematics: the stargazers astonished him by the dexterity of their calculations, looking at him blankly the while if he spoke of Orion or Cygnus. His previous researches into fairies had not prepared him for this divergence between their values and his. They had a practical knowledge of the world; they also knew it was round; but that was the extent of their knowledge; they knew nothing of its ancient history and celebrated characters and did not care to. They had no more than a loose hearsay acquaintance with their own history, and were satisfied to be without any written record of it, since they attached no importance to what might be learned from a book and were amused by the mortal dependence on pen and paper. It was this that blighted his project of the Elfin Grammar. They were not unfriendly to it, and when he explained the laboriousness of inscribing it on tables of stone (another allusion lost on them) a party of working fairies was dispatched to steal a load of paper, while others compounded ink and collected goose quills. But the Grammar was never written, because the load of paper was stolen from a cooked-meats shop, and consisted of a manuscript cantata soaked in grease.

It was also disconcerting when a fairy he was talking to became invisible.

But the overruling disconcertingness was to find himself unconcerned. It was as if some mysterious oil had been introduced into the workings of his mind. If a thought irked him, he thought of something else. If a project miscarried, a flooding serenity swept him beyond it. He lived a tranquil truant, dissociated from himself as though by a slight agreeable fever—such a fever as one might catch by smelling a flower. This happy state had begun when he stood watching the game of beggar-my-neighbour, and became aware that the players didn't notice him, that his large obtrusive mortality made him in some way invisible to them—invisible in that they did not connect with him, felt no obligation to do so. In his former life, he lived in a balancing act between obligations. He had an obligation to do such-and-such, he had no obligation to do the other. He performed the obligation; and the best he was likely to get out of it was the thought that it was done with, for the time being. He omitted the non-obligation; and was lucky to get off without a kick from his conscience. He had never conceived of the total release of not being an obligation himself. Day after day, month after month, went by and not once did he see a fairy's face clouded with a look of obligation. Whether they conversed with him, praised his pronunciation, said how much better he looked without his wig (it had eventually fallen to pieces); whether they vanished leaving him halfway through a sentence, their motives were pure as the heavens. They had done as they wished.

But why, feeling no obligation toward him, had they plucked him from the heather and added him to their establishment? And why, if he were to be added, did they hide from him, and keep him a prisoner—to make him desolate, then change his desolation to happiness? Such a motive, stern and sentimental, might obtain in Aberdeen, but not under Foxcastle. To be useful? But he was useless. To be informative? At the least breath of information they melted into air. To be a trophy? Of all his speculations, this was the only one he paused at. A despot of the Renaissance, his court swarming with poets and philosophers, experts on Plotinus, sumptuous harlots, bishops, boys, artists and artificers, inventors, assassins, dancers on the tightrope, had fixed his ambitions on owning a giraffe. He had forgotten which despot. The learning he had brought from the outer world was mouldering from disuse; only legends and trivia like the giraffe remained. What happened to his wig might well be happening to the compartmented order inside his skull. In his blessed condition of being nobody's obligation he could spend his intellect as he pleased, sometimes thinking, sometimes observing, coming to conclusions and unripping them for the pleasure of knitting a new one from the same material, as the Queen did. It was as though he had always lived at Foxcastle, accepting his good fortune without surprise as the fairies accepted him, and endlessly fascinated by their unaccountableness. The more he studied them the more baffled he became. It was not that they were mysterious: they were as straightforward as the scent of a rose, as a wasp sting. It was impossible to love them: they were too inconsistent to be loved. It was unavoidable not to be drawn to them. And they defied conjecture by taking themselves for granted. Theologically identified as the scattered remnants of Satan's host, rationally dismissed as superstition, they were a race of pragmatists. Just as they were content to know next to nothing of their own history because they were living in the present, they took Foxcastle for granted because it was their dwelling place. Yet how was it that living inside a solid, sizable hill he could hear the wind blowing and recognize from what quarter it blew? How could he know day from darkness, with all that bulk of earth between him and the sun? When he questioned his attendants they looked blankly at him, blankly at each other, and said the bayberry candles were regularly lit at sundown. When he asked the leading fiddler, who enjoyed conversation and had never made himself invisible, he was told 'Rabbit holes.' And by degrees he gave up the problem, and was grateful for the light that drifted in like a mist and need not be accounted for.

Whenever the fairies trooped off on a raiding excursion into the outer world, he wandered about the halls and corridors of Foxcastle, almost and never quite familiarizing himself with its layout. For instance, he never discovered how the fairies quitted it. Quit it they certainly did, since they came back with spoils. Perhaps they used some watery stair; the hill was veined with springs; some were trapped for the water supply, others only existed as murmuring voices at a distance. When he was left alone, he could hear them quite plainly. But this was only possible when he was alone. The raiders came back, the silence was painted by their gay glittering voices, they were extremely hungry, they had tricked all the mortals they had met. Fingering his watch, that old harmless acquaintance, he sat listening to their brag, and admired the faithful traditionalism with which they recounted exploits well known to him before ever he met a fairy: Mungo's mother gaping into her churn, the elf bolt spanged off an invisible thumb that knocked the peddler senseless as he made off with his load of thorn-tree wood, the girl laid on her back in the greenwood. 'Burd Janet' was one of the ballads he had fallen asleep to. But Janet's babe had been fathered by Tam Lin, who was a stolen mortal like himself, and so uneasy lest at the end of his seven years in fairyland he should be picked as the teind to hell that he invoked the girl to lie in wait and snatch him out of the Queen's retinue. He himself was safe from such a rescue, since no one in the outer world had loved him enough to snatch him back to it.

Falling into dreamless sleep in his bed of fern, waking to the splash and gurgle of the running water, opening his eyes to the brooding dusk of the stone roof it was inconceivable that he had lain there unreconciled and heard his shout of despair re-echoing from the vault overhead. A fuss about nothing, a midge-bite madness, a fit of the tantrums. For by the simple act of discarding his fetters and walking up a winding stair he had attained the wish of his heart. Watching these happy beings for whom weeping was impossible, he had become incapable of grief; watching their inconsistencies, he had become incapable of knowing right from wrong; disregarded by them he had become incapable of disappointment. Alone or in their company, listening to music or to silence, he lived in a perpetual present—like the Queen with her knitting, each stitch the stitch of the moment.

It was her custom to appear every evening and knit publicly, as she had done the first time he saw her. He had then supposed that the business of the skein of wool wound off the supporting hands of a kneeling courtier was a formality of etiquette, like his approaching bows and the tooting trumpeters. Afterward he learned that it was a signal mark of favour, and rarely bestowed. Like all etiquettes, it was thought slightly funny and viewed with great respect. On the evening when she beckoned to him he was so far from expecting it that he had to be nudged by a stander-by before he realized what was happening. Remembering to bow and feeling painfully aware of his disproportionate size, he made the long journey toward her and crouched at her feet, holding out his hands like a suppliant. Out of her knitting bag she drew a ball of wool and two needles. 'Attend,' she said. 'This concerns you. I cast on seven stitches. Two plain, two purl, two plain, one purl. And reverse. One plain, two purl, two plain, two purl. And reverse. Two plain, two purl, two plain…'

She knitted slowly and firmly. Already he saw the rib emerging. 'And one purl. And break off.'

She bit through the thread. A squadron of flying fairies swooped down, seized hold of him, bore him up and away. He was shoved and squeezed through a twisting crevice into the outer world.

A couple of sheep took fright and galloped off, their hoofs drumming on the shallow turf. The hill had been fired, nothing remained of the heather except a few charred stumps. He would not have known where he was except for the peat hags and the hurrying burn in the valley. He watched the blood congeal on his leg, and his consciousness wandered over his body from one ache to another. The aches were specific; they corresponded with the bruises, the scratches, the punctures of being forced through an exit much too narrow for him. But there was a further ache, an underlying discomfort which corresponded with nothing and existed totally: an ache of weariness, of bodily mistrust.

'*Castellum* ... a fortified enclosure.'

It was a mortal voice, the voice of a person of culture! He sprang up—and almost fell over. His legs were tottering, he had lost his sense of balance. He had become an old man.

The speaker was quite close. He was dressed in black, he wore a voluminous white neckcloth, he carried a most peculiar hat in a gloved hand. He had spoken to a group of ladies, who were even more oddly dressed than he, wearing white shifts down to the ground. Their waists were under their arms, the shifts fluttered in the wind and showed the shape of their legs. A couple of young men made up the party; they, too, had waists under their arms, and a general resemblance to clothes pegs. But all these were mortals.

He staggered toward them, making noises. He had lived so long with the fairies he had forgotten his native speech; he could only gibber and stammer. When they turned to look at him, he realized that he was in rags and half-naked. The ladies started back. The young men stepped forward defensively.

'Do not be alarmed, do not be alarmed! He is merely one of our half-wits, too common in these days—poor unfortunate creatures, allowed to stray about for their living. But harmless. Our country people call them Innocents. Leave me to deal with him.'

He turned to James Sutherland.

'Go away, my poor fellow! Here is a guinea, to buy yourself better clothing before the winter finds you out.'

The ladies were making a little collection amongst themselves. Now one came forward with it, her eyes averted.

He stared at her. Words were coming back to him.

'Take it, take it,' said the gentleman. 'Go away, and be grateful.'

Notes

BY KATE MACDONALD

1 The One and the Other

nonpareil: from the French, 'without equal', a term of praise used in elite western societies in the eighteenth and early nineteenth centuries. Its use in this peasant context indicates the social class of the narrative voice.

Icarus: the son of the classical Greek inventor Daedalus, who made him a pair of mechanical feathered wings. Icarus flew too high to the sun, the wax holding his feathers melted, and he fell to his death in the sea. The story is a common metaphor for pride coming before a fall, which in Tiffany's case may also be considered as a warning from the court to be properly and cautiously humble.

bower: the private rooms of a lady where men are not admitted except by invitation.

lozenge panes: the panes of glass in the church windows set diagonally rather than square.

First Corinthians: verse 15, in which St Paul discusses man's relation to death.

fleam: instrument used for drawing blood.

phlebotomy: the practice of making an incision in a vein.

Brownie: spirit of the home, who can choose to be useful in helping with the housework.

Lars: lares, lesser gods, as in *lares penates*, the gods of the Roman home and hearth.

Kelpie: Scottish water spirit, said to assume the appearance of a horse.

bolster: a long pillow lying along the width of a bed, used for back support.

anatomists: surgeons of the eighteenth and nineteenth centuries who bought fresh human bodies to dissect when giving instruction in surgery and medicine.

2 The Five Black Swans

croup: viral respiratory infection that frequently killed children until vaccination against diphtheria came in. Dipping a child with croup in freezing water was as likely to cure by shock and the subsequent expulsion of phlegm from the body, as to kill through pneumonia.

wainscotted: panelling around the walls to keep out draughts and improve insulation, usually in finely carved wood.

bouts-rimés: French name for a poetical game devised in the seventeenth century, in which a sequence of end-rhymes for each line is given to a player from which to compose an acceptable, even a skilful poem.

hum of bees: the sound of bees is a traditional indicator that fairies live in the vicinity.

lèse-majesté: French, causing offence to the monarch.

Salic law: the French legal tradition that held that a woman could never inherit the throne.

ordeal: an ironic reference to the inherent and un-human cruelty of Elfindom.

Morel and Amanita: both are names of poisonous mushrooms, which appear out of nowhere overnight.

Thomas of Ercildoune: True Thomas, Thomas the Rhymer, thirteenth-century Scottish laird from Berwickshire, reputed to have the gift of prophecy as well as poetry. He was famous for having been the lover of the Queen of Elfhame.

hawthorn brake: a stand of hawthorn trees, which produce white blossom after their green leaves have emerged.

composing draught: a drink to compose or soothe her disordered emotions, that is, a sedative.

3 Elphenor and Weasel

IJmuiden: seaport in the northern Netherlands. 'IJ' is considered to be a single letter in Dutch, so both elements are capitalised in proper nouns.

quack: a medical practitioner with no skill or qualifications except persuasiveness.

mandora: an eighteenth-century form of lute.

alembic: two glass vessels connected by a tube, used for distilling cordials and other concentrated liquids.

henbane: also called stinking nightshade, a poisonous plant that produced hallucinations, among other properties.

clarify: to make into a clear liquid by removing suspended particles of fat by boiling and skimming, a hot and dirty process.

Mustela: the weasel's Latin name for its genus is *Mustela*.

Golconda: area of southern India famous for its diamond mines.

4 The Blameless Triangle

board wages: reduced pay for live-in servants to compensate for their having a much reduced workload.

sans: French for 'without', used in elite speech to dignify terms of social etiquette.

Almanach: *Almanach de Gotha*, a directory of European royalty and nobility, and an arbiter of court usage.

portmanteau: Victorian suitcase consisting of two halves of equal capacity.

infra dig: from Latin *infra dignitatem*, beneath one's dignity.

Wanderjahr: German, the tradition of a year of travel after one's studies.

ding an sich: German, 'thing in itself', a philosophical concept discussed by Kant.

partisan: following a single particular cause or ideal.

Abendmusik: German term for an evening concert, normally held in a church.

specie: coins.

paunched: gutted, removing the offal for cooking and discarding the undesirable parts of the animal.

soutane: long black robe worn by a Catholic priest.

Aesculapius: Greek god of medicine, whose attribute was a snake coiled around a staff, thus snakes were sacred to him. Tinkel has had a Classical education.

tillage: ploughed agricultural land.

prisoner on the tower: the mullah is making the call for prayer from the tower of a mosque, which they have never seen before.

Walpurgisnacht: feast of St Walpurga, synonymous with a celebration of witchcraft, since her feast-day is 1 May, the pagan festival called Beltane in Scotland.

gimlet: a slender tool used to drill a hole in wood by turning.

inversion: Warner makes a pun on the English term from her youth used to describe homosexuality, and the relationship that Banian is to be asked to enter into.

Sclavonian: one of the languages of Croatia.

tutorially: they expect Banian to perform as they have taught him.

au-delà: French, the beyond, the hereafter.

5 The Revolt at Brocéliande

Brocéliande: Wace was the first whom we know of to write about Brocéliande, now considered to be the Forest of Paimpont in Brittany. The quotation is from the *Roman de Rou*, Wace's twelfth-century verse chronicle of the dukes of Normandy written for Henry II of England. Warner quotes lines 6415–20, which read in English: 'I went thither [to the forest] on purpose to see these wonders / I saw the forest and the land / I sought for the wonders, but I found none / I came back a fool, [as] I had gone like a fool / I went like a fool, and so came back / I sought after folly, and hold myself a fool for my pains.' Adapted from Edgar Taylor's 1837 translation *Master Wace, his chronicle of the Norman conquest from the Roman de Rou.*

table-turning: holding séances around a table, hoping to communicate with spirits or the dead who will answer by rapping on the table, or moving it.

vestigial: once functional, then, when the design alters, remains in place but is useless.

three-handed: for three players.

mandragora: a toxic plant, can also produce hallucinations and unconsciousness, so it is not clear whether the Favourite intended to kill himself out of despair, to cause a dramatic scene to draw attention to himself, or merely to sedate himself to avoid taking sides in the revolt.

formalist: a mode of thinking that ignores context, suggesting that the Ambassador would be unpleasantly rational.

6 The Mortal Milk

una corda: Italian, the soft pedal on a piano.

whipper-in: from fox-hunting, an assistant to the huntsman who keeps control of the hounds, or, in this case, werewolves.

murrain: archaic and nonspecific term for an animal or crop disease.

chawbacon: American English term for a bumpkin, a clod.

Antecessor: this scene of a witches' dance recalls Warner's first novel, *Lolly Willowes* (1926).

tail: followers, attendants.

shagreen: a raw hide, so in this case from an animal with white skin, which suggests the unpleasant possibility that this is human shagreen from the Brocéliande estate.

baisemain: French, literally 'kissing of hands', a formal courtesy visit to a monarch.

quid pro quo: Latin, 'something for something', a formal exchange that begins when the first item is offered.

congé: French, the formal dismissal, or taking of leave.

7 Beliard

Vivien: Merlin's grave is said to be in the Forest of Brocéliande, placed there by the sorceress Vivien.

coeval: of the same age as.

Carnac: the celebrated Neolithic standing stones in Brittany.

Pomponius Mela: held to be the earliest Roman geographer, active in the first century CE.

flageolet: a small (and thus more portable) woodwind instrument, played like an oboe.

doing the polite: early twentieth-century slang for performing a social duty.

8 Visitors to a Castle

Mynnydd Prescelly: strictly speaking this is a range of hills in west Wales, the Preseli Hills.

Giraldus Cambrensis: twelfth-century cleric and historian of Wales. The *Itinerarium Cambriae* is an account of a journey through Wales in 1188.

torque: torc, solid neck ornament made and worn by Bronze and Iron Age peoples.

Plynlimon: the highest point of the Cambrian Mountains, in mid Wales.

scrofulous: infection of the lymph nodes, associated with tuberculosis, and manifesting in blueish growths around the neck.

Morgan le Fay: queen and witch of the Arthurian legends, and King Arthur's sister.

Taliesin: Welsh poet of the seventh century, associated in myths with King Arthur.

Thomas Tomkins: Welsh keyboard composer of the seventeenth century.

Three Choirs Festival: the world's oldest music festival, dating from the early eighteenth century, held in rotation at Worcester, Gloucester and Hereford cathedrals. Handel's *Messiah* was first performed in the 1740s.

Nottingum: the District Nurse is from Nottingham.

lockjaw: tetanus, caused by infection from an open wound contaminated with soil or manure. The District Nurse is applying iodine as a disinfectant, which stings vigorously, and has a distinctively strong smell.

Zeitgeist: German, spirit of the age, or of the times.

9 The Power of Cookery

Dreiviertelstein: German, three-quarter stone.

Styria: formerly a Duchy in what is now south-east Austria, bordering modern Slovenia.

oriel: an upper bay window that projects out from the wall.

Cisalpine: on the Italian side of the Alps, that is, further south and east than Dreiviertelstein, and considerably nearer sea level.

Michaelmas: the quarter of the year between autumn and winter, and the feast of St Michael on 29 September.

Ural Mountains: the range of mountains running north-south between western Russia and Kazakhstan, part of the traditional boundary between Europe and Asia.

white lead: a naturally occurring lead carbonate, used as a cosmetic for centuries, though it can cause lead poisoning.

Four Thieves vinegar: traditional vinegar blend used to ward off the plague.

skyey: a reference to Shelley's poem 'The Cloud', and to Count Luxus' earlier metaphor.

arrière-pensée: French, an ulterior motive, a concealed intention.

cicisbeo: Italian, a lady's acknowledged gallant or lover.

bon-aller: French, a send-off, a farewell salute.

10 Winged Creatures

Bourrasque: French, a squall.

Grive: French, a thrush

Bouvreuil: French, a bullfinch

bar sinister: heraldic term, denoting an illegitimate birth.

bilboquet: cup and ball, a game of catching a ball attached by a string into a cup.

salacity: salaciousness, lecherous, lustful.

wicket: wicket gate, a small servant's entrance.

Martinmas: St Martin's Day, 11 November.

Turdus philomelos: the song thrush.

spatchcocked: cooked with its backbone removed to allow more of the flesh to roast.

11 The Search for an Ancestress

Mazulipatans: fine woven fabrics from Machilipatnam, Andra Pradesh, India.

marrons glacés: candied chestnuts.

fowling pieces: early shotguns for shooting geese and game birds.

orgeat: an almond syrup, flavoured with orange or rosewater.

kickshaw: miniature portions of appetising food.

Prophet Hasan ben Sabah: Hassan-e Sabbāh, twelfth-century Persian, founder of the Islamic sect called the Assassins.

12 The Climate of Exile

Procolitia: an auxiliary fort, now called Carrawburgh. Its walls have inscriptions of a dedication to Coventina, a water goddess, and also contain a Mithraeum.

genius loci: the local god(dess) or spirit.

Borcovicus: an auxiliary fort, now called Housesteads.

Magister artis: Latin, Master of Arts. Sir Bodach is making sure, politely, that Snipe knows of his educational status.

Origen: Snipe has either got the wrong Origen, or is being wittily sardonic about this early Christian philosopher and theologian.

in chancery: a wrestling term, locked under Sir Bodach's arm.

Alsatia: an area outside the reach of the law, from the area of that name in London designated as a sanctuary from the fifteenth century.

auto-da-fé: a ritual of public penance and then punishment as decreed by the Inquisitions of the Catholic Church.

cut him dead: refused to acknowledge his presence, as a sign of her extreme displeasure.

Saint Elmo's fire: the natural phenomenon of a glow around a sharp object caused by electrical discharge.

Peterhead or Lybster: fishing ports on the north-east coast of Scotland.

13 The Late Sir Glamie

Grace and Favour apartments: an apartment in a castle or palace, loaned, often rent-free, to former servants of its well-dowered owner. Hampton Court Palace is well known for them.

Herrenhausen: former royal summer palace in Hanover, birthplace of George II of Great Britain, destroyed by Allied bombing during the war, rebuilt in 2008 after Warner's death.

persona non grata: Latin, a prohibited person.

muniment room: the room housing an estate's archives and documentation.

camphor bags: bags of camphor chips used to repel moths from laying their eggs in clothing and other textiles.

monkeys: the Chamberlain was evidently pre-Darwinian in his beliefs.

policies: eighteenth-century term for the grounds of an estate.

14 Castor and Pollux

jolie-laide: French, 'pretty-ugly', beautiful in an unusual way.

Metamorphoses: the 'Book of Transformations' by the Latin poet Ovid, containing many classical myths of alteration and changing state, and the results of the inter-racial coupling of gods and humans.

sciolto e fortissimo: Italian, 'loose and strong', making a considerable noise.

Petrarchan sonnet: typically devoted to expressions of love.

manège: French, horsemanship.

Astolfo: character from fourteenth-century French courtly poetry and later in Renaissance epics, who owns a magical horse called Rabicano which is made of hurricane and flame and feeds on air.

Orlando furiously raving: possibly a reference to a puppet performance of Ariosto's *Orlando Furioso*.

conversazione: Italian, an evening of formal conversation on subjects from art, literature or science.

villanelle: a poem with a fixed arrangement of stanzas, most often on pastoral themes, appropriate for Nel's behaviour in frolicking in the kitchen garden with a lover.

Gog and Magog: mythical British giants named after the persons from the Book of Ezekiel, represented by wooden statues in London's Guildhall from before the seventeenth century.

Castor and Pollux: twin boys born to Leda after her rape by Zeus. They became demigods, later the constellation Gemini; their half-sisters were Helen of Troy (extreme beauty) and Clytemnestra (murdered by her son). They were patrons of horsemanship, boxing, wrestling and other athletic pursuits.

capillary attraction: water in a tube rises upwards against gravity by capillary action.

Orplid: a fantasy fairyland invented by the German Romantic poet Eduard Mörike in his poem 'Song Weylas' in 1831.

Cantuar! Ebor!: the formal abbreviations of the archbishoprics of Canterbury and York.

Anabaptist: a nonconformist Christian who rejects baptism of infants, and requires the baptism of adult professors of Christian faith. Along with Unitarians they are the sects most often rejected by the Established Church of England.

Erastians: a Protestant sect that asserts the superiority of the state over the Church.

15 The Occupation

webster: Scots for weaver.

scutcheon: heraldric shield, metaphor for the family reputation.

massacre of St Bartholomew: a notorious slaughter of Protestants on St Bartholomew's Day in 1572, during the French Wars of Religion.

the untiring pains of hell: Gideon Baxter is a Presbyterian minister with a strongly Calvinist approach to salvation.

Abraham's bosom: Protestant metaphor for heaven.

whet: some flavour.

hemming and felling: needlework terms, evidently unknown in the Baxters' unhandy household.

Urim and Thummim: objects mentioned in the Hebrew Bible, used by the High Priest for divination.

caudle: a sweetened alcoholic egg drink, reputed to be health-giving.

16 Foxcastle

teind: Scots, a tithe, support in kind for the clergyman of the parish.

scrivener: the old profession of a fair copyist and scribe for those who could not write, which mutated into a supplier of writing materials. The backs of the law papers would have been worth something as blank parchment.

sheep walk: land where sheep were pastured.

peat hags: high formations of peat in moorland country, broken into miniature but still formidable gullies by watercourses.

It was its own hawk: an echo of T H White's *The Goshawk* (1951), Warner wrote an acclaimed biography of White, published in 1967.

snake's cast weed: a snakeskin.

piling Pelion on Ossa: from the Greek myth of Otus and Ephialtes, who desired to storm Mount Olympus and gain Artemis and Hera as their brides, so they stacked Mount Pelion on top of Mount Ossa.

his wig was pulled off: this sets this story in the eighteenth century.

their waists were under their arms: this places Mr Sutherland's emergence into the world again in the early years of the nineteenth century.

Sylvia Townsend Warner

Of Cats and Elfins

Short Tales and Fantasies

Of Cats and Elfins

by Sylvia Townsend Warner

'Sylvia Townsend Warner was one of our finest writers. I'm thrilled that Handheld Press are bringing some of her uncollected fantasy stories back into print to delight and amaze a new generation.' - Neil Gaiman

Warner's remaining four Elfin stories are gathered together with her essay on Elfins, a strange story about a dryad, and the remarkable forgotten tales of The Cat's Cradle Book (1940), eighty years after its first publication. This is a new selection of Warner's remaining fantasy short stories, collected for a new generation of fantasy enthusiasts and Warner fans.

The Cat's Cradle Book reflects Warner's preoccupation with the dark forces at large in Europe in the later 1930s. It opens with a story about the talking cats that die of a murrain in a manor based on Warner's own Norfolk home with Valentine Ackland. 'Bluebeard's Daughter' narrates the adventures of Bluebeard's daughter by his third wife, and her propensity for locked doors. Warner mixes fables and myths with storytelling traditions old and new to express her unease with modern society, and its cruelties and injustices.